WHAT PEOPLE ARE

BREAKING THE MOT

The author is to be congratulated for giving us this brilliant and utterly absorbing work of detection, which traces in great detail how ancient beliefs and practises related to the Great Mother and Great Goddess of pre-patriarchal societies were incorporated into fairy-tales, folk-lore and even nursery rhymes. A wonderful, informative book opening the door onto the hidden meaning concealed in many of these treasures that have fortunately survived to our time.

Anne Baring, Jungian analyst, lecturer, and author of several books including *The Dream of the Cosmos: A Quest for the Soul*. Co-author, with Jules Cashford, of *The Myth of the Goddess: Evolution of an Image*

Studebaker is on fire as she cleverly and humorously retells Goddess history that has been hidden for thousands of years.

Karen Tate, author, radio show hostess, and film maker; author of *Sacred Places of Goddess: 108 Destinations* and *Walking An Ancient Path*; www.karentate.com

Praise for *Switching to Goddess*

This is a revolutionary book. The writer is fearless... I got myself so fired up reading this book that I just jumped up and yelled, "I must call up this woman. I must tell her how much I loved this work. She is one of us! Yeah!"

Z. Budapest, author, activist, and one of the founders of the American feminist-spirituality movement

Switching to Goddess is a feisty, upbeat exploration of the place of Goddess in the ancient and modern worlds....
Kathy Jones, author, organizer of UK's Glastonbury Goddess Conference and a co-founder of the Glastonbury Goddess Temple

The author makes a strong case for switching to Goddess as a viable option for restoring a balance in our social lives, a balance that once existed in the Neolithic oecumene or commonwealth, a model of society based on the principle of socioeconomic egalitarianism...
Dr. Harald Haarmann, culture historian, internationally-known linguist, Vice-President of the Institute of Archaeomythology, Sebastopol, CA, and author of over 40 books, including *Interacting with Figurines*

A hard-hitting get-up-and-go book that challenges the reader with its racy style and punchy arguments. Backed up by scholarship, it is a clarion call for our times.
Claire Hamilton, author of *Maiden, Mother, Crone,* and *Tales of the Celtic Bards*

I am normally a silent reader, not one who leaps into the air, fist clenched, shouting "YES!" every now and again. My unusual cheerleading behaviour was entirely due to the fact that I was so happy to read a book about goddess that actually proposes some real, radical solutions to the mess our world is in right now... The greatest thing about the book is – quite apart from the fact that it might help to save the planet and us all – is its readability and the feeling of breathless adventure I got from it...
Geraldine Charles, editor, Goddess Pages, http://www.goddess-pages.co.uk

Switching to Goddess is almost certain to provoke lively, animated discussion.
Dr. Elinor Gadon, culture historian, Brandeis University, and author of *The Once and Future Goddess*

Breaking the Mother Goose Code

How a Fairy-Tale Character Fooled the World for 300 Years

Breaking the Mother Goose Code

How a Fairy-Tale Character Fooled the World for 300 Years

Jeri Studebaker

MOON BOOKS

Winchester, UK
Washington, USA

First published by Moon Books, 2015
Moon Books is an imprint of John Hunt Publishing Ltd., Laurel House, Station Approach,
Alresford, Hants, SO24 9JH, UK
office1@jhpbooks.net
www.johnhuntpublishing.com
www.moon-books.net

For distributor details and how to order please visit the 'Ordering' section on our website.

ISBN: 978 1 78279 022 8

A CIP catalogue record for this book is available from the British Library.

Design: Lee Nash

Printed and bound by CPI Group (UK) Ltd, Croydon, CR0 4YY

We operate a distinctive and ethical publishing philosophy in all areas of our business, from our global network of authors to production and worldwide distribution.

CONTENTS

Acknowledgements

I am deeply grateful to Joann Sica, Gina Hoffses and Dr Deborah Fleming for reading the manuscript and offering their suggestions, feedback and advice.

Illustrations

Since this book is being published in ebook as well as hard-copy format, it includes no illustrations. However, the following sources contain pictures of Mother Goose that you might find both fun and useful:

Books

Kissinger, Barbara Hallman. 2008. *Mother Goose of Yesteryear*. Gretna, Louisiana: Pelican Publishing Co.

Websites

Pinterest: A picture collection site; includes illustrations of Mother Goose on book covers, advertising items, and ceramic figurines.
http://www.pinterest.com/search/pins/?q=Mother%20Goose
eBay.com: One of the best sources of late 19th-century and early 20th-century illustrations of Mother Goose. Enter "antique Mother Goose" into eBay's search box and you should get 50 to 60 pictures of old nursery rhyme books. A few of these will show Mother Goose in her witchy outfit riding a goose to the moon.
http://www.ebay.com
Wikimedia: This has pictures of Mother Goose as she was shown in various editions of Charles Perrault's *Tales of Mother Goose.*
http://commons.wikimedia.org/wiki/Category:Mother_Goose
Mother Goose: A Scholarly Exploration includes several pictures of Mother Goose on the covers of old children's books.
http://eclipse.rutgers.edu/goose/
The Mother Goose Society includes a few pictures of Mother Goose. This site is owned by Gloria T. Delamar, author of *Mother Goose from Nursery to Literature*. Jefferson, NC, and London: McFarland and Company.
http://www.delamar.org/mgs-illus.html.

Introduction

There is great controversy over the Mother Goose designation: From a fable about a goose instructing her brood? From a goose-footed statue (Queen Pedauque) in old churches? From fairies who left goose tracks? Merely a phrase for "impossible events"?
Appelbaum, 2002: viii, *The Complete Fairy Tales of Charles Perrault*

For many Western adults, one of their earliest and most delicious memories is the warm old woman in the tall, pointed hat riding a goose to the moon while clutching an old-fashioned broomstick in one hand. Wherever you found her, she brought magic. In North America, she brought the magic of your mother's lap, your body snuggled into hers as you listened to her sing-song voice repeat rhymes so seductive they lulled you into a sleep swimming with dreams of hot cross buns, lost sheep, kittens with mittens, silver bells and cockle shells, and cows jumping over the moon. In Europe, Mother Goose brought the magic of fairy tales:

emerald-green enchanted forests, frogs morphing into princes, golden geese, magic mirrors, cats in boots, and wicked witches.

Many of us have wondered who this lovely old memory was, exactly. Where did she come from? Who was she? How old was she? How did she get connected to children's rhymes and fairy stories? How and why did she ride on the back of a goose in flight? The answer to all these questions is, we don't know for certain. Mother Goose is an enigma lost in the mists of time. But she did leave a few telltale clues to her identity, and it is those clues that this author attempted to follow in a concerted effort to see where they might lead.

Although we don't know precisely how old Mother Goose is, we do know that the oldest reference to her in print comes from the year 1626 (Houlihan 2012). Because most works published or printed in the early 17th century have been lost or destroyed, we can assume that Mother Goose was mentioned in print even earlier than 1626. In 1650, a Frenchman named Loret also mentioned Mother Goose. In his *La Muse Historique* he wrote,

> *Mais le cher motif de leur joye,*
> *Comme un conte de la Mere Oye,*
> *Se trouvant fabuleux et faux,*
> *Ils deviendront tous bien penauts*
> (Whitmore 1969: 2)

In English, this rhyming verse would go something like this: "Since the reason for their happiness is as fabulous and false as a Mother Goose tale, they will eventually be very disappointed." Loret doesn't bother to explain who Mother Goose is, so it seems obvious that in mid-17th century France most people already knew.

Another quixotic reference to Mother Goose comes in 1656, from a Madame de Sevigne, a Frenchwoman known for her witty letter writing. Like Loret, de Sevigne too refers to Mother Goose casually – as if Mother needed no introduction: "And if, Mademoiselle, you must know, this is not a tale of Mother Goose, but of the drake of Montfort, there are strong resemblances between them" (Harries 1996). A drake is a male duck, of course – and in fairy tales, ducks are interchangeable with geese and swans (all three belong to the family *Anatidae* – and are the only three birds in the family).

Who was Mother Goose exactly, and where did she come from? The usual list of suspects includes the Queen of Sheba; Clotilde, wife of Clovis, King of the Franks; and two different Berthas from medieval continental Europe. One Bertha was the wife of King Robert II of France (c 970 to 1031 AD), and the other the mother of the great Emperor Charlemagne (742 to 814 AD). This second Bertha supposedly sported a goosefoot, did a lot of spinning, and loved to tell stories to children.

Some think, however, that Mother Goose might have originated in connection with a set of mysterious statues found in certain old French churches (Appelbaum 2002: viii). Called "Queen Pedauque" (or *Reine Pedauque* in France), all of these puzzling statues have one human foot, but a second foot that is webbed – like the foot of a goose. In 1912, *The Catholic Encyclopedia* opined that the statues represented Saint Clotilde (Goyau 1912). Saint Clotilde, however, was really Queen Clotilde (470-545 AD), wife of King Clovis of the Franks (Hendry and Uglow 2005), who ruled the Franks around the time the Roman Empire was crumbling.

Then there was the grandmotherly Elizabeth Foster Goose of Boston, Massachusetts. Ms. Goose spent much time singing nursery rhymes to her grandchildren gathered at her knees and, although no one has ever uncovered a copy of it, Elizabeth's son-in-law, in 1719, supposedly published either a book or a broadside titled *Songs for the Nursery, or Mother Goose's Melodies*. The problem with Elizabeth Goose is she died in 1756-57, so unless she was over 130 years old at her death, she wasn't born yet when the name "Mother Goose" was first mentioned in early 1600s France.

The explanations above were never very convincing or satisfying to me, and years ago I began to form my own ideas about who Mother Goose was and where she came from. In the chapters that follow, I'll tell you what these ideas were, how I came to them, and what I finally decided about the real identity of the legendary "Mother Goose".

Part I

Chapter 1

Beginning My Search for Mother Goose

It was years ago – as far back as the early 1990s – that I first began to suspect that Mother Goose might be a goddess in disguise. My theory was this: Mother Goose and her fairy tales form a secret code cobbled together by our pre-Christian ancestors during "the burning times" – a period several centuries long during which the Church murdered tens of thousands of so-called "witches", people who'd supposedly made pacts with the Devil. I knew that academics were beginning to suspect that far from being just ordinary bystanders unfortunate enough to have been caught up in the Inquisition's deadly net, "witches" were actually some of Europe's last magico-religious practitioners, many of whom probably still believed in strong, powerful and beneficent female deities (later academics have increasingly added to the evidence for this; see Klaniczay 1990, Behringer 1998, Wilby 2005 and

Bever 2008, among others).

Throughout the 16th and 17th centuries especially, the Church worked hard and fast to destroy the last vestiges of non-Christian religion in Europe. According to my theory, the few non-Christians left standing were desperate to find a way to hide their ancient Mother Goddess until it was safe for her to appear in the open again. What they came up with was ingenious: they hid their beautiful deity in the guise of an ugly old crone, a grizzled grandmother who spun innocent "fairy" tales around the kitchen fire. These tales, however, were far from innocent. They carried within them the secrets of the Old Religion. What better way to safeguard a great and ancient faith than to tuck it away in "harmless" stories for children?

I probably got the idea of the Mother Goose/Mother Goddess connection from the goddess scholar Buffie Johnson. In *Lady of the Beasts,* Johnson includes a glossy, full-colour picture of Mother Goose looking exactly like a Halloween witch: straddling a broomstick, Mother shoots to the moon in a dark night sky, her blood-red cape flapping in the wind; under the cape she wears an ankle-length black dress, and snake-like strands of her white hair escape from under her tall black hat. Behind her stands a white goose, its webbed feet clutching her broomstick with a vengeance (Johnson 1988).

Buffie stuck the same picture, in black and white this time, in a section of her book in which she says certain goddesses were strongly connected to geese. She also notes that for years a small group of scholars suggested that European fairy tales originated in pre-Christian mythology and religion. I knew also that the Church believed that the women they were burning at the stake for being witches were still holding on to pre-Christian beliefs and practices. So, just like the old European goddesses, Mother Goose too was mixed up with witches and geese.

Around the same time, I read a fascinating take on the fairy tale Cinderella. According to this explanation of the tale, the

Western version of the Cinderella story is secret code for the fact that Westerners will eventually return to their ancient Mother Goddesses. Cinder-Ella is the ancient Great Mother Goddess Ella (or Hella, Hel, Holda, Holla, along with several other names, depending on which part of Europe you're in during which time period), whose regenerative powers have burnt out and become cinders rather than the full-blown fire the Goddess needs to keep the earth and its inhabitants strong and healthy. The bad people in the story – the wicked stepmother and her two obnoxious blood daughters – represent the Church, the landed nobility, and the Church hierarchy (bishops and so forth), in that order (Walker 1996).

Waltzing these ideas a bit further down the road, it seemed clear to me that Cinderella, her fairy godmother, and her birth mother form a holy trinity. Just like the Father-Son-and-Holy-Ghost trinity, many ancient European goddesses too were organised into trinities, typically labelled Virgin-Mother-Crone (or, Daughter-Mother-Grandmother) – Persephone-Demeter-Hecate, for example, or Persephone-Artemis-Hecate (Leeming 2005: 268). In the Cinderella story, Cinder-Ella would be the Virgin, her birth mother the Mother, and her fairy godmother the Crone. Disguised as a fairy godmother, the Crone aspect of the goddess uses her powers to remove Cinderella's ugly cinder disguise, so that humanity (played by the prince) can once again become cognisant of Ella's monumental beauty, and accept her as their principle deity.

This view of the Cinderella story as prophecy roused me into rooting around for more information on the tale. Where had it come from and when? Early on I discovered that one of the first Westerners to publish Cinderella was one Charles Perrault, a Frenchman who included it in 1697 in a book of eight fairy tales, *Tales and Stories from Times Past, or Tales of Mother Goose.* Here again loomed another nagging, shadowy suggestion that Mother Goose might connect somehow with ancient European Mother Goddesses.

Of the eight stories in Perrault's *Tales of Mother Goose,* five have become almost universally popular: in addition to Cinderella these include Little Red Riding Hood, Sleeping Beauty, Puss in Boots and Blue Beard. The other three – The Fairy, Riquet with the Tuft, and Little Thumb – are less well known (see Appendix D for a synopsis of each). After thinking about these stories for a while, I couldn't really see the Mother Goddess hiding incognito in any of them except Cinderella. One possible exception, however, was Sleeping Beauty. Like Cinderella, Perrault's Sleeping Beauty has fairy godmothers in it — but eight to Cinderella's one.

Seven of these "God Mothers" gave good gifts to baby Sleeping Beauty. The eighth, however, an old fairy, gave a deadly gift; when Beauty grew up, the young woman would "pierce her hand with a spindle and die..." To me, this didn't seem very goddess-like. On the other hand, I mused, this elder fairy could represent the death-cycle aspect of the old triple goddess – that part in charge of making certain all living creatures eventually move on to make room for new life on a finite planet. In this case, the Virgin-Mother-Crone trinity would play out like this: Beauty is the Virgin, the good godmothers are the Mother, and the elder godmother is the Crone.

Still, unlike the Cinderella tale, Sleeping Beauty didn't seem to have anyone playing the parts of the bad guys, the bullies who shunted the Great Mother Goddess underground in the first place (I'd learn later that Perrault had dropped the part of the tale with the bully in it). These would be the patriarchal religions. Beginning with the ones ushered in during the fourth millennium BC by the first invading wave of Indo-Europeans, and ending in the 300s AD with the Christians, the patriarchal religions had been a thorn in the side of the European Mother Goddess for quite some time. Overall, the connection between Perrault's tales and Mother Goose seemed tenuous at best, and for a few years I put aside my interest in Mother Goose to concentrate on other writing projects.

Recently, however, I began again to get serious about exploring the mysteries and secrets surrounding Mother Goose. Could she really, as Buffie Johnson suggested to me years ago, be secret code for the Mother Goddess? A way to keep female deities from disappearing during times when Europe's power elites shifted into overdrive to cripple and crush them? Near the beginning of this new phase of my research, I began to wonder: if Mother Goose is secretly a goddess in disguise, exactly which goddess is she? Although in the past much of Europe apparently worshipped goddesses, the separate European culture groups were by no means all married to the same local deities. The goddesses of the Germanic tribes, for instance, differed from those of the Romans, and from those of the Celts, Slavs and other regional European groups.

Remembering that years ago I'd seen pictures in Buffie Johnson's *Lady of the Beasts* of goddesses riding geese, I picked the creamy, linen-covered book off my bookshelf and leafed through the index until I got to the word "goose". Buffie had only a few references to geese, but they all pointed to one and the same goddess: Aphrodite, the Greek goddess of love and beauty. Or at least that's the way most people think of Aphrodite. Actually, modern scholars say she was much more than a pampered beauty queen (see, for example, Bernard and Moon's *Goddesses Who Rule*). Although this is the one-dimensional deity the Greeks and Romans turned her into, in other times and places Aphrodite was a powerful and complex goddess of fertility and new life – in addition to sensuality and romantic love.

In *Lady of the Beasts* I found two ancient images of Aphrodite flying through the air on a goose. In the first, the goddess perches side-saddle on the bird, and in the second she stands regally and bolt upright on its back. Actually, in the second image the bird is a swan, but as Johnson points out, in ancient Classical imagery swans, geese and ducks are used interchangeably. A main trait all three birds share is their ability to travel on air, water and land alike. Not many of earth's creatures possess this special set of abilities, and scientists would eventually place all three birds into the family *Anatidae,* alone, with no other birds sharing their separate little corner of the biological classification system.

It's easy to see why these three birds might have been considered sacred to ancient peoples – so sacred, in fact, that among the Celts it was forbidden to eat them (Green 1986: 114). Of course geese are far from sacred today – think "silly goose", "to cook someone's goose" and Christmas goose for dinner, and you can see how far geese have fallen from grace. Interestingly, they fell at exactly the same time "witches" were being burned at the stake.

Even though I'd found my goose goddess (or so I thought), I admit I was a tad disappointed. Aphrodite didn't exactly fit my idea of who I thought Mother Goose should be. She wasn't ancient enough, for one thing, and she seemed to originate among people I had little respect for: the warlike, patriarchal Indo-Europeans. But, oh well, there it was. Aphrodite was the goddess who rode geese, so I was stuck with her – or so I thought.

Around this time I invested in a copy of Marguerite De Angeli's *Book of Nursery and Mother Goose Rhymes*. In it I found the only nursery rhyme known to mention Mother Goose: Old Mother Goose When She Wanted to Wander ("…flew through the air on a very fine gander."). This rhyme contains several symbols directly connected to goddesses: an owl (Athena's bird), an other-worldly woman who flew in the sky on the back of a goose (Aphrodite), a woman with a magic wand she used to morph her son Jack into "the famed Harlequin", and the moon – that celestial entity almost always associated with goddesses, probably because it shares its 28-day cycle with the menses, women's magical ability to shed blood without bleeding to death. Later I would learn that this rhyme was first published in 1815 in a chapbook by T. Batchelar, who titled it Old Mother

Goose, or, The Golden Egg (chapbooks were small, inexpensive booklets sold by peddlers from the 15th century through the 18th century) (Delamar 1987: 252).

Harlequin, however, was a puzzle. What connection did he have, if any, to Aphrodite, or any other European goddess? Harlequin had long been a character in European stage entertainments, a jester of sorts, good for a chuckle or two and sometimes even a belly laugh. Not very goddess-like. But neither, of course, were pictures of Mother Goose as the prototypical, homely Halloween witch. This homeliness did, however, fit with my idea that Mother Goose was the goddess in disguise. Like Cinderella and not a few other fairy-tale females, was she hiding her exquisite beauty behind a mask of extreme bad looks? And could Harlequin too be hiding behind his dunderhead disguise?

As is the case with Mother Goose, Harlequin's origins are shrouded in mystery. Digging around a little I found a confusing stew of possibilities. One that snagged my attention was this: Harlequin was really Hellequin, or the ancient northern European goddess Helle (aka Holda, Holde, Hel, Ella, etc.) (Lecouteux 2011: 179-80). Shades of Cinder-Ella! Mother Goose being code for the ancient pre-Indo-European, pre-patriarchal goddess Helle was a fascinating possibility. All the evidence pointed to Helle being one of the last Great Goddesses of Europe before the patriarchy hit, the goddess who probably stood for peace, nonviolence, and social and gender equality (Studebaker 2008). Of course back then Helle went by different names in different parts of Europe, but "Helle" she was in northern Germanic areas (Gimbutas 2001: 190-95).

There was only one problem: Helle didn't ride a goose. It was Aphrodite who rode the goose. It looked like Helle and Harlequin were dead ends in my search. The only other goddess Buffie Johnson mentions riding geese is the East Indian goddess Devi. Europeans are distant cousins of East Indians – through their common Indo-European language and heritage.

For a while, I laid the whole goose issue aside and turned back again to Perrault's *Tales of Mother Goose.* Did these tales have anything in common, anything at all that might connect them to the Mother Goddess? After reading all eight tales again, carefully this time, one thing hit me immediately: in a full half of them, fairy "godmothers" (God Mothers? Mother God-esses?) rushed in to rescue the main characters in their times of need.

These magical god(ess)mothers rescued Cinderella, Sleeping Beauty, the good daughter in The Fairy, and both Riquet and the princess in Riquet with the Tuft. Years before, I'd been struck by the similarity between the terms "godmother" and "God the mother". Add the word "fairy" into the mix, with its connotations of supernatural powers, and it seemed fairly obvious to me that "fairy godmother" could well be code for "God the mother", aka "the Mother Goddess".

After weeks of mulling over Perrault's tales, the only thing I found in common among most of them (seven out of eight) was this: all but one includes a mother and her daughter(s). Cinderella and Sleeping Beauty had good mothers who died young, and Red Riding Hood, the princess in Riquet, the daughters in Blue Beard, and the little ogre daughters in Little Thumb all had good mothers who were nevertheless powerless to rescue them from the trouble they tumbled into. The only story missing a mother-daughter dyad was Puss in Boots; in it Perrault includes a daughter character, but mentions only her father, not her mother.

At this point I became curious about Perrault himself, the first person on record ever to use Mother Goose in a book title. Who was he exactly? What I read at first was intriguing: Perrault hadn't signed his own name to the first edition of *Tales of Mother Goose,* but had instead signed his son's name (Appelbaum 2002: ix). Not only that, he used a form of his son Pierre's name so vague and obscure that it seemed almost intentionally designed to hide even his son's identity: "P. d'Armancour" ("Armancour" was the name of a piece of land Perrault had given Pierre) (Philip 1993: 125-27). Even more telling was the fact that on later copies of *Mother Goose,* Perrault didn't use even his son's name, but left his readers guessing who the author of the book was. To me this sounded like a man who'd written revolutionary material and didn't want his name anywhere near it.

But the more I read about Perrault, the more uncertain I became that he might have been purposely promoting a pre-Christian agenda with his *Tales of Mother Goose.* Perrault dedicated the book to the niece of Louis XIV, and at least one writer has suggested that he did this to introduce Pierre into high society (Perrault himself, who worked for one of Louis XIV's influential ministers, was quite prominent in French society). If you're dedicating a book to the king's niece, what better motivation for making your tales about young girls and princesses? What's more, Perrault had monkeyed around quite a bit with his Mother Goose stories, changing each from the folk versions into "literary folk tales" that some scholars suggest were more palatable to his wealthy, upper-class friends. Of course, such monkeying might also make for a better disguise for Mother Goose, and that's what I was looking for…

At any rate, at this point I lost a bit of enthusiasm for Perrault. I even began wondering if it was pointless to suggest Mother Goose was a mother goddess, or that she was code for anything. Wasn't it a bit unrealistic to think that any trace of goddess worship would have survived after centuries of abuse, beginning in the 300s AD with the Roman Emperor Constantine, and ending with the extremely efficient Inquisition that was finally closing up shop around the time Perrault wrote *Tales of Mother Goose*? This was 14 centuries of terror and brutality – could any religion have survived such a thrashing?

Soon, however, I picked myself up, dusted myself off, and hiked out of Charles Perrault's France and into the Germany of the Brothers Grimm. Maybe some of the Grimm tales would offer better evidence of an underground, secret pre-patriarchal code. Although they didn't attach the term "Mother Goose" to any of their tales, a few were in fact about females closely connected with geese. Jacob and Wilhelm Grimm uncovered one tale in particular that to me seemed a dead giveaway: Mother Holla. Mother Holla was a dead ringer for the ancient Mother Goddess Holda (aka Holla, Holde, Helle, Ella, Hell, Hel, etc.), bringing me full circle around again to the same goddess hinted at in Cinderella and the nursery rhyme Old Mother Goose When She Wanted to Wander. According to the Lithuanian-American archaeologist Marija Gimbutas, Holda was a continuation of the Great Mother Goddess of "Old Europe", a peaceful, non-hierarchal and sophisticated pre-civilization that prospered from around 5000 BC to 3500 BC in what is now large parts of south-eastern Europe (Wilford 2009).

The story line of Mother Holla is very similar to Perrault's in The Fairy: a mother has a good daughter and a bad daughter, and after the good daughter helps a magic woman connected to a well, the woman rewards her. But when the disagreeable daughter shuffles on stage, she treats the woman poorly, and in return the woman treats her to an obnoxious "reward". However similar their story lines, the particulars of the two tales differ markedly. For starters, Mother Holla includes several symbols directly connected to the goddess Holda/Ella/Hella: not only the well, but also apples, baking bread, a weaving shuttle, snow, and "snow white" feathers. Also, Mother Holla's gifts differ from the gifts of the magic woman in Perrault's The Fairy. While the magic woman's gifts were flowers and reptiles, Mother Holla's are golden rain and pitch.

The two tales differ in further respects. In The Fairy the girls bump into the magic woman outside the well, but in Mother Holla they are forced to fall down into and move through the well water to reach the goddess. As Jacob Grimm noted in 1835 in *Teutonic Mythology*, the way humans made direct contact with the goddess Holda was by passing through a well – to me strongly suggestive of the birth passage from the womb of a Great Mother Goddess (See Appendix C for the text of Mother Holla).

But once again, where was the goose? How could a goddess with no connections to geese possibly be Mother Goose? On the other hand, I mused to myself, the feathers Holla shook in the story might be goose feathers. In the story, Holla instructs both daughters to shake out her bedding daily, and when they did, feathers flew far and wide. Jacob Grimm says Holla is always connected with feathers, and that a falling snow meant the goddess was shaking out her feather bed.

According to Jacob Grimm, Holda was the ancient Mother Goddess of what today is northern Germany. But Holda had a sister goddess, Perchta, who served as her counterpart in the south of Germany and in Austria and Switzerland. Vaguely I remembered reading somewhere about Perchta – something about her being a forerunner of Santa Claus; during the Yule season children would leave out milk and cakes for her, and in exchange she would leave them gifts. In other words, like Mother Goose, Perchta too seemed strongly connected to children.

But was this just one more tantalising thread taking me nowhere, leading me on "a wild goose chase"? At times my journey became so frustrating that I paced through the house, trying to shut down my thinking brain and set my instinctual brain free to tackle the mass of tangled, multi-coloured threads of information. Sometimes the clues came so thick and fast, and tugged at me from so many directions, that I became overwhelmed. At other times I would rush to my bookshelves to find, say, a specific bit of information on Aphrodite, and in the process stumble across seven tantalising threads leading to Charles Perrault, Cinderella, Sleeping Beauty, godmothers, geese, or the goddess Hel.

Sometimes I managed to pop blinders on and concentrate on

what I'd come for, but at other times I went with the flow. My eyes would brush across various books I felt compelled to open, like *Roles of the Northern Goddess*, in which Hilda Davidson says godmothers were common in Perrault's time, and totally accepted by the Church. Not the fairy kind of godmother, obviously, but ordinary women who took a deep interest in a child, came to the child's christening, etc. Okay. Tuck that bit of data onto a notecard and file it later under – what? Something. In the future it might fill in an important gap.

At some point I turned back to Jacob Grimm's *Teutonic Mythology* to check out his views on the goddess Perchta. Grimm said one reason he knew Perchta was a mother goddess is that she rode in a wagon through the sky, "like Mother Earth". She spent inordinate amounts of time spinning, shuttle and distaff moving constantly through her hands. And then, as I read, a lightning bolt split across my mental landscape: In English-speaking countries, said Grimm, Perchta was known as Bertha – and Perchta/Bertha had a goosefoot! (Grimm 1835b).

As noted earlier, several of my sources suggested that one possible origin for Mother Goose was "Goosefooted Bertha", the mother of Charlemagne. But none of these sources had remotely hinted that Goosefooted Bertha might have been a goddess. Here, however, was Jacob Grimm, of the-brothers-Grimm fame, assuring me that Goosefooted Bertha was indeed a female deity. All of which suggested that the goddess Mother Goose was meant to portray might indeed be the old pre-patriarchal Germanic goddess Holda, also known as Perchta/Bertha.

It made sense: Holda, Perchta and Mother Goose; all three were associated with children and with spinning. On the frontispiece of Perrault's late 17th century *Tales of Mother Goose*, Mother Goose is busily spinning with a spindle and distaff in her hands, while two children listen at her knees to her tales. As for the goose, the feathers from the bed Holda shakes could very well be goose feathers, and even if not, her other half, Perchta, possessed the foot of a goose. Finally, Holda, Perchta and Mother Goose all flew through the air: albeit Holda and Perchta in a wagon, and Mother Goose directly on the back of a bird.

But here again I was bogged down in the same tired, old problem I'd been stuck with almost from the beginning: more than anything, what makes Mother Goose, Mother Goose, is that she sits on the back of a goose and flies through the skies. The one nursery rhyme mentioning Mother Goose, Old Mother Goose When She Wanted to Wander ("...would fly through the air on a very find gander.") makes this abundantly clear. As far as I could tell, neither Holda nor Perchta ever sat on the back of a goose to fly. From what I knew at this point, the only European goddess who did that was Aphrodite.

But that very same day I was to stumble across two more extremely critical pieces to the puzzle. On the same day I found Perchta/Bertha and her goosefoot, I suddenly felt an urge to look at old pictures of Mother Goose. Around 2004, I'd begun collecting 19th century and early 20th century Mother Goose children's books – mostly ones with Mother Goose on the front cover decked out like a Halloween witch. After a few years, I possessed a collection of roughly ten vintage books with witchy-looking Mothers Goose on the covers: an old woman riding side-saddle on a goose heading straight for a bright, silvery moon. The woman wears a floor-length dress and a tall conical hat, often but not always black, and her white hair creeps out from under it and flies helter-skelter in the wind. Often the old woman brandishes a broom, a cane or a weaving spindle.

If I'd been willing to pay more than $10 for these old books (which I wasn't), I'd have had dozens of them. They're not uncommon. Unfortunately, I lost my collection of Mother Goose books in a 2012 cross-country move. Since I no longer had witchy pictures of Mother Goose in my library, I turned to the Internet, opened eBay, did a search for "vintage Mother Goose books", and found a few. All were priced over $10, however.

I did though purchase the front cover of an old Mother Goose book (the back cover, insides and spine were missing). On it, Mother Goose sits side-saddle on a snow-white goose, its wings outspread. At a 45-degree upward trajectory, Mother and goose rise toward a blood-red moon, Mother in a black floor-length gown, a black conical hat, a white cape, a snow-white Elizabethan ruff, and white accordion wrist ruffs. Mother clutches a brown and yellow broom ("symbol of the sacred hearth" [Seligmann 1971: 177]). Judging from the print style, the art style, and the age-signs, this book was published in the late 1800s.

Next I turned to my internet search engine and entered the search words "vintage", "Mother Goose" and "pictures". Adding the term "vintage" to the mix would, I hoped, eliminate recent pictures from 1950 on up. It worked. Most of the images appearing on my screen dated from before 1950. Scrolling through the pictures, I came to a very small one that looked odd: it didn't seem to include an old woman, a group of children, or a goose either. I clicked on and enlarged the image.

What I saw was a photo of an older woman holding up in front of the camera a vintage child's puzzle – or rather the box the puzzle came in. The title under the picture indicated that this puzzle had at one time been for sale in a Halloween shop somewhere in the States. In red and black letters emblazoned across the top of the box were the words "Mother Goose Puzzle Box". But what startled me was the picture on the puzzle. It did indeed show Mother Goose, and it did show geese – two of them, in fact. But Mother wasn't riding on either goose, she was riding instead in a wagon being pulled by the two geese. She, her geese, and her wagon flew not far from, but well above, the ground.

Although Jacob Grimm noted that both Holda and Perchta flew in wagons, he'd mentioned nothing about what – if anything – had pulled the wagons. But here right in front of my eyes was a vintage colour picture of Mother Goose riding in a wooden wagon pulled by two geese! In all my years of collecting

Mother Goose books, I'd never seen anything like this. I'd never seen her in a wagon – let alone in a wagon pulled by geese. I was astounded. One more bit of evidence that Mother Goose might indeed be the ancient Germanic wagon-flying goddess Holda-Perchta.

Hmm, I thought. Maybe I needed to look for Mother Goose on items other than books. So turning back to eBay, I entered the words "vintage", "Mother" and "Goose", opening the search to eBay items in general instead of books specifically. The result: several hundred items sporting Mother Goose pictures on everything from old tin cups and a bottle of Mother Goose Furniture Polish, to Mother Goose Jack-in-the-boxes and Mother Goose drinking straws. Scrolling through the items, I noticed some of these Mothers Goose were the witchy variety. And then I stopped, inhaling sharply. Sitting on my screen was a copy of the very puzzle I'd seen when I'd done my search a few minutes earlier! Only this was the actual puzzle, not just the box it came in – and it was for sale. This one I could buy.

Now I'm not a wealthy woman, but I knew no matter what the cost I had to have this puzzle. Fortunately the price was reasonable. Several interlocking puzzle-piece nubs were missing, as was the box the puzzle came in, and this undoubtedly brought the price down. Also, fortunately for me, the seller was selling the item not in auction format (in which case I might have lost it to another bidder) but outright. I clicked the "buy" button immediately, and in the next instant was the owner of a rare picture of Mother Goose flying through the sky in a wagon – just like Holda-Perchta, the ancient Mother Goddess I was beginning to think Mother Goose undoubtedly symbolised.

It's worth noting that none of the other items on eBay showed Mother Goose riding in a wagon pulled by geese, and that in all my years of collecting Mother Goose books I'd never seen this kind of image of her. I put an eBay "saved search" on vintage Mother Goose puzzles that same day, so that eBay would send me a notice whenever such puzzles came for sale. Although at least once a week for well over a year eBay sent me pictures of Mother-Goose puzzles up for sale, not in all that time did they ever send me another picture of this particular puzzle – or anything like it.

But I'm still not done describing the surprises that hit me on that same day late in September of 2012. On this same day, a vague memory popped into my mind of a picture I'd seen years ago, of a goddess riding in a wagon being pulled by birds of some kind. After thinking a few minutes, I thought I remembered seeing the picture in Johnson's *Lady of the Beasts*. Retrieving the Johnson once again, I rooted around in the book and finally found it: a picture of a goddess flying through the air in a low-sided wooden wagon pulled by six swans. As noted earlier, in ancient iconography swans, ducks and geese are interchangeable. This picture was an old illustration painted in the 14th century for a French manuscript about the Roman orator Seneca. The goddess was Venus, the Roman goddess of love – and the equivalent of Aphrodite the Greek goose rider.

So Aphrodite-Venus rode not only on the backs of geese, but also through the air in wagons pulled by geese. And Holda-Perchta rode through the air in wagons. But wagons pulled by geese? I didn't know. I couldn't rule it out, but neither had I found any evidence of it.

So the same old nagging problem remained: the old riding-the-goose problem. Mother Goose did it, but I'd seen no pictures of Holda-Perchta doing it. Of all European goddesses, I'd seen only Aphrodite ride "goose back". And then, for some reason, my eyes dropped down to the print on the page opposite the picture of Venus and her swan wagon. The words on the page read, "After the Gothic conquest of Rome, Hel and Venus were united in Bertha..." (Johnson 1988: 85).

My jaw dropped. Slowly I leaned back in my chair. Never before had I read this in Buffie Johnson – if I had, it certainly hadn't registered as important. So this was the answer. Mother Goose was *both* Holda-Perchta *and* Aphrodite/Venus. She was both because as the Roman Empire crumbled, both goddesses had merged into one and the same deity.

This was indeed a day of discovery. It was the first time I'd ever seen a picture of Mother Goose riding the sky in a wagon – just the way the goddess Holda-Perchta rode the skies. And then stumbling across the same rare Mother-Goose image for sale on eBay, and being lucky enough to grab it before another buyer did. And best of all – still on the same day – my fortuitous discovery that the two goddesses who'd been teasing me for weeks with their separate claims on Mother Goose, had merged, near the end of the Roman Empire, into one and the same deity. I shook my head. What were the odds of all of the above happening on one and the same day?

Well, one thing seemed certain: behind her disguise, Mother Goose was none other than the deity born as a result of a merger of the goddess Holda-Perchta and the goddess Aphrodite-Venus. As the Germanic Goths toppled and then mixed with the Romans, one consequence was that a Germanic deity and a Roman deity had united into one. Maybe, I mused, the Goths thought their Holda-Perchta needed a beauty makeover?

* * *

Although I now felt reasonably satisfied that Mother Goose served as a stand-in for the Germanic Holda/Helle and the Mediterranean Aphrodite/Venus, I knew my journey had only just begun, and that many questions remained. How was the knowledge of this connection lost? Was it simply the result of a loss of interest through time? Was the creation of Mother Goose an intentional plot to disguise and thus preserve this goddess during a time when it was dangerous – and frequently lethal – even to mention her name?

Did Mother Goose fairy tales carry coded messages left for us by our pre-Christian ancestors during a time when non-Christians were routinely rounded up, roped to stakes, and roasted alive? If so, what exactly were our ancestors trying to tell us? If we'd "break the code", what would we learn? The questions just kept coming: if Mother Goose was code, what was the point of dressing her as a witch? To European Inquisitors, witches were like cream rising to the top of the pail; the more witches they caught and turned to ashes, the richer they became. To the Inquisition, wouldn't a witchy garb raise a bright, red flag? Once again, I felt my head spinning; it looked like I had my work cut out for me.

Chapter 2

Old Mother Goose When She Wanted to Wander: The One and Only Nursery Rhyme about Her

One – and only one – nursery rhyme mentions Mother Goose by name: Old Mother Goose When She Wanted to Wander. First appearing in print in 1815 as Old Mother Goose, or, The Golden Egg (Delamar 1987: 252), this is a disjointed rhyme, with very few transitions weaving one event into the next, and with important information seemingly missing between verses. Although things happen in this rhyme that need explaining, they aren't explained. In a nutshell here's the gist of the poem: a woman named Mother Goose lives in the woods, in a house guarded by an owl. For a good time she flies around on the back of a male goose. Her son Jack buys her a female goose, which, after mating with Mother Goose's gander, produces a golden egg.

Jack then sells this egg to a sleaze ball, who cheats him, forking out only half the egg's worth.

Does Jack try to retrieve the egg? No, instead of becoming bitter over being cheated, confronting the sleaze ball, or doing anything else about the egg, Jack begins to date a woman instead. We don't know the woman's name or anything else about her except that she's "fair as a lily, And sweet as the May." We learn nothing about this budding relationship before being catapulted into the next critical event: the important man in town ("the squire") and the sleaze ball join forces and rough Jack up in a dark alley. Why? Did Jack irritate them in some way? We haven't a clue.

And then – with no advance warning or reason given for it – Mother Goose turns Jack into Harlequin, the famous European stage character. Next, someone pitches Jack's golden egg into the ocean – the sleaze ball? The squire? The rhyme doesn't say. It does, however, tell us that Jack jumps in and rescues the egg. Finally a cause-and-effect relationship! This doesn't last long, however; instead of sticking around to celebrate her son's good fortune (as one might expect), Mother Goose leaps astride her gander and strikes off for the moon without even so much as a faretheewell.

Later I would discover why this nursery rhyme is so mysterious and disjointed. For now, however, here is the actual rhyme:

Old Mother Goose
When she wanted to wander,
Would ride through the air
On a very fine gander.

Mother Goose had a house,
'Twas built in a wood,
An owl at the door
For a porter stood.

She had a son Jack,
A plain-looking lad,
He was not very good,
Nor yet very bad.

She sent him to market,
A live goose he bought;
"Here! Mother," says he,
"It will not go for naught."

Jack's goose and her gander
Grew very fond;
They'd both eat together,
Or swim in one pond.

Jack found one morning,
As I have been told,
His goose had laid him
An egg of pure gold.

Jack rode to his mother,
The news for to tell.
She called him a good boy,
And said it was well.

Jack sold his gold egg
To a rascally knave.
Not half of its value
To poor Jack he gave.

Then Jack went courting
A lady so gay,
As fair as a lily,
And sweet as the May.

The knave and the squire
Came up at his back,
And began to belabour
The sides of poor Jack.

But Old Mother Goose
That instant came in,
And turned her son Jack
Into famed Harlequin

She then with her wand
Touched the lady so fine,
And turned her at once
Into sweet Columbine.

The gold egg in the sea
Was thrown away then—
When Jack he jumped in
And got it again.

And Old Mother Goose
The goose saddled soon,
And, mounting his back,
Flew up to the moon.
(d'Angeli 1954: 158-59)

After its disjointedness, what I noticed first about this rhyme is that it fairly screams "Mother Goddess". For starters, you have to admit that this old Mother Goose is not your ordinary, run-of-the-mill mother or grandmother. She flies to the moon on the back of a bird, for goodness sake. Using a wand, she turns her son into a famous stage character. Unlike Old Mother Hubbard, the Old Woman Who Lived Under the Hill, and the Old Woman Who Lived in a Shoe, none of whom are capable of performing any magical tricks whatsoever, Old Mother Goose possesses powerful magic.

But back to the disjointedness: Rather than one story, this rhyme seems to be a string of them. What prompted Jack to sell his exquisite magic egg? We don't know. Why turn Jack into a stage character? And what ignoramus dropped a solid gold egg into the ocean, and why? Jack dates a woman, and then wham! He's suddenly beaten up, for no reason, by the town ruffian, who's backed up by the town hierarchy. Why would the ruffian want to hurt Jack? He already got a solid gold egg out of the boy – at half price, no less. And why would the Big Man in Town want to hurt Jack? We don't know.

Jack, whose mother turned him into Harlequin presumably to save his life, rescues his egg from watery oblivion. And then his mother – who knows why – wings off to the moon. And we are left dangling. Not only are we left in the dark about why Mother flies to the moon, we haven't the foggiest notion what happens to Jack, Jack's sweetheart Columbine, or the golden egg.

If this rhyme is code for something, what is it code for exactly? If we'd break the code and read the message, what would it say? One possible way to tackle this problem is to look at some of the objects and concepts in the rhyme and determine what they meant to our medieval and early-modern (16th-18th centuries) European ancestors. In the next chapter we'll examine the following rhyme elements to see what they might reveal: the goose, the owl, the dove, the moon, golden and goose eggs, the sea, and the forest. Since they're so meaty and important to the rhyme we'll deal with Harlequin and his partner Columbine in a separate, later chapter.

Chapter 3

Geese, Golden Eggs, and the Silvery, Silvery Moon: Symbols in Old Mother Goose When She Wanted to Wander

[By 1697] Mother Goose already had a reputation among French peasants and even in the court as a sort of mythical fairy birdmother who told marvellous yarns to children.
Maria Leach 1950: 751

In the one nursery rhyme specifically mentioning Mother Goose we find a number of natural phenomena not only highly symbolic, but among the most highly-charged symbols in Western history. For many of our ancestors, geese, owls, doves, the moon, eggs, the sea and the forest were symbols so electrifying that some of them, in certain places and times, even managed to reach divine, sacred status. We'll look at each of these phenomena in turn, beginning in ancient Egypt with the goose.

In pre-patriarchal Egypt it seems that the sun was created by a goddess who managed the feat by turning herself into a goose that laid "the golden sun egg". The renowned psychologist Erich Neumann (1991), in his book *The Great Mother*, talks about "...the birth of the sun from the cosmic egg laid by the Nile goose, which is worshiped as the 'great chatterer,' the creator of the world... [It is] evident that the layer of the cosmic egg ... must originally have been a female." But which female deity was it who created the sun? The goddess scholar Barbara Walker suggests it might have been Hathor, the ancient Egyptian goddess who in predynastic times was "the high god" of Egypt, the source of all life, the creator goddess (Baring and Cashford 1991: 252; Walker 1988: 402). Interestingly, the Greeks identified Hathor with their goddess Aphrodite – the goddess who flew gooseback (Budge 1969: 435; Witt 1997: 123). Hathor was identified not only with the sun but – like Mother Goose – also with the moon. According to one Egyptian myth she was the "mother of light", her eyes being the sun and the moon. Witt tells us that Hathor "often wore the crescent moon..." (Witt 1997: 123).

The goose has an ancient and hefty connection not only with Egyptian goddesses but with ancient European goddesses as well. Several centuries before Christ, in Neolithic south-eastern Europe, goddesses in the form of geese watched over birth and destiny: "The Bird Goddess presided over the realm of birth and fate in the form of ducks, swans, storks, and other waterfowl [and geese, of course, are one of the major species of waterfowl]" (Everson 1989). Later, around 600 BC, images of goddesses holding rabbits or geese were "widespread" in Greece, France and southern Germany (Gimbutas 2001: p. 178). Moving forward in time to the first century BC, Caesar wrote that the ancient Celts were forbidden to eat the goose due to its sacred connection to "the Sun-Egg" (Green, 1986: 114).

And, of course, in ancient Greece and Rome Aphrodite and

her counterpart Venus rode through the air on the back of a goose. About this the archaeological evidence is clear. For example, on the side of an ancient cup from Athens, the Greek "Pixtoxenos Painter" depicted Aphrodite sailing through the sky on the back of a white goose (Benard and Moon 2000: 17). A terracotta figurine from Tarentum, Italy, dated to around 380 BC and now in the British Museum, also shows her riding on the back of a goose or swan, this time with her son Eros. Other examples come in the form of a statue of Aphrodite – "a fragmentary goose lies beneath the figure of the goddess" (Dexter 2011: 189, Figure 7) – and a drawing on a Celtic tile from Roussas, in Drome, France, showing her "winging along on a giant bridled goose" (Johnson 1988: 77 and fig. 89).

In other parts of Europe too goddesses were connected to geese. As we've seen previously, the Germanic goddess Perchta had the foot of a goose. Also, during the Middle Ages geese were supposedly ridden by witches (Jameson 1950: 460). According to Jewish folk religion from medieval Germany, Northern France, England, Austria and Poland, anyone who killed a goose between mid-December and mid-February already had one foot at death's door (Trachtenberg 2004: 258).

What happened next to the goose has happened to more than one powerful pre-Christian symbol: it was battered and crushed into something as non-sacred as pocket lint. By the time Dickens wrote *A Christmas Carol*, the goose was not only *not* too sacred to eat, it was the main course for that most sacred of Christian holidays. From being a goddess so powerful she birthed the sun, the goose had morphed into "silly goose", responsible for the "goose egg" – no longer the celestial sun, but a large and painful lump on the top of one's head. In short, from its lofty perch as one of the most divine creatures in the non-human world, the goose has taken an incredible nose-dive, ending up as one of the most ditzy, dim-witted birds on the planet.

But never forget "the lady who doth protest too much".

Could it be that the goose became silly only because it was so intrinsically and numinously powerful? One way to drain the power out of intensely transcendent symbols is to wage smear campaigns against them. For example, one way the Church turned people against pre-Christian deities was by erecting statues of them in town squares and paying people to hurl rocks at the statues, and it seems obvious that if Europeans had not been vigorously insistent upon worshiping these deities it's unlikely the Church would have gone to this kind of trouble.

In addition to the goose, two other birds appear in Old Mother Goose When She Wanted to Wander: the owl, and the dove ("Columbina" means "little dove" in Italy, the country in which the rhyme's character Columbine seems to have originated). Now, why geese, owls and doves? Why not pheasants, partridges or pelicans? Crows, cuckoos or cranes? Possibly because for millennia geese, owls and doves have basked in sacred association with European goddesses while pheasants, partridges, pelicans, crows, cuckoos and cranes have not.

Although geese, owls and doves are not the only birds sacred to ancient European goddesses, they are three of the most powerful and pervasive of the birds honoured by these female deities. Most everyone knows the Greek goddess Athena and her Roman equivalent Minerva, for example, were associated with owls. However, this night bird is also associated with other goddesses too, including the Welsh Blodeuwedd and the Basque Mari. The dove too is heavily associated with goddesses. Because it was so connected to European goddess worship that the Church couldn't get people to stop going giddy when they saw the bird, the Church co-opted it. Ergo the Holy Ghost – a dove. Long before the Church came up with its Holy Ghost, however, the dove was the close companion of Aphrodite, and her "most persistent symbol" (Johnson 1988: 74).

In addition to birds, the moon is a prominent symbol in the Old Mother Goose When She Wanted to Wander rhyme. At the end of the rhyme, Mother mounts her goose and flies to the moon. Not to the treetops, clouds, stars or the sun mind you, but the moon. Interestingly, the moon is intimately connected to geese – both are spot-on reminders of the grand and mystical cycles of nature, of natural change and metamorphosis. Whereas geese fly south every winter and north in the summer, the moon travels through its four phases every 28 days: waxing, full, waning and "lost" (the three days of darkness before the moon begins to expand again).

All the world over, it's goddesses, not gods, who are linked to the moon (Leeming 2005: 268). It's easy to see why: as if by magic, women shed blood in time with the moon's cycles – and still live to tell the tale. This link between goddesses and the moon seems to be an old one, with moon goddesses apparently going back to the Palaeolithic. Just one example is the Venus of Laussel, a 20,000-year-old goddess figurine holding a crescent moon in her right hand (Leeming 2005: 268).

In more than one ancient European culture the triple goddess was considered to be one and the same with the moon: the Virgin aspect of the goddess was embodied in the waxing moon, the Mother in the full moon, and the Crone in the waning moon (Gottner-Abendroth 1995: 185). The moon "…was experienced as the Mother Goddess, so that … the crescent moon was the young girl, the maiden; the full moon was the pregnant woman, the mother; the darkening moon was the wise old woman, whose light was within" (Baring and Cashford 1991: 18). Personally, more than anything ever had, this analogy between the triple goddess and the moon drove home to me the concept of a deity being one and yet at the same time three. Although we experience the waxing, waning and full moons as three separate entities, we also know they're three different visual aspects of the same celestial body. To those who worshipped her, the moon/goddess might also have represented the course of human life, its disappearance representing death, the three days of darkness time spent in the Great Mother's womb, and the first sliver of the waxing moon one's reincarnation into a new earthly body and lifetime: "With death they would have felt that they were taken back into the dark womb of the Mother and believed that they would be reborn like the moon." (Baring and Cashford 1991: 19)

A third key symbol in Old Mother Goose When She Wanted to Wander is the egg. Originally the title of this nursery rhyme was Mother Goose, or, The Golden Egg – a hint that the egg must be of greater-than-average importance to the meaning of the narrative. In the rhyme, Mother Goose's goose lays a golden egg and, as we learned previously, an Egyptian goddess created the sun by becoming a goose and laying the golden sun-egg. We also learned that it was most likely Hathor who did this honour – Hathor, the goddess directly connected to Aphrodite, the Greek goddess who rode geese. Are we seeing a pattern here yet?

As a mythological symbol, the egg is linked to several elements in the Old Mother Goose rhyme, including bird goddesses, other goddesses, and water. First, as one might expect, the egg is connected to bird goddesses. But eggs are also associated with other goddesses – Sirona, for example, a Celtic goddess of abundance. And by eating the eggs of the goddess Clidna, one could acquire shapeshifting ability. Third, the egg is linked to water, "the primordial element in which life gestates ... the foetus-egg first comes alive in the waters of the womb." (Monaghan 2008: 90, 146)

In addition to geese, owls, doves, the moon and eggs, yet another symbol in the Old Mother Goose rhyme holds important clues to the rhyme's hidden meaning: the sea. Someone in the rhyme pitched Mother's golden egg into the sea (in a later chapter we'll discover who). In general, the sea symbolises things like the womb, birth and regeneration. For instance, in mythology the source of life is often the sea or other kinds of bodies of water (Neumann 1991: 17). Interestingly, our Mother-

Goose goddess Aphrodite is deeply connected to the sea. For starters, she was born from sea foam (the Greek word *aphros* means "foam"). Also, probably because the sea was the source of her birth, Aphrodite possessed the ability to protect ocean-going sailors (Benard and Moon 2000: 17-18).

The final critical symbol in Old Mother Goose, the forest, was where Mother Goose's house was located. To ancient Europeans the forest was a numinous, mystical land of the spirit, a place where their deities resided. For example, the south Germanic goddess Perchta, who along with her northern equivalent Holda prefigured Mother Goose, lived primarily in forests (Motz 1984: 155-56). Forests were part of nature, and it was nature that ancient Europeans found holy. Both our Celtic and our Germanic ancestors "worshipped their gods in nature, paid cult to trees … placed sacrificial offerings in bogs and lakes, [and] had mother goddesses…" (Filotas 2005: 36).

At this point in my research, I imagined that the secret message in the rhyme Old Mother Goose When She Wanted to Wander might be this: the egg is code for the old pre-patriarchal religions. The powerful guys (the squire) and the bad guys (the knave) team up to try to destroy these old religions, symbolised by the egg. But Mother, Jack and Columbine save the egg. Later I would change my opinion, here – but that's a story for another chapter. For now we need to take a closer look at the goddesses Mother Goose probably represents: Holda-Perchta, and Aphrodite-Venus.

Chapter 4

Goddesses Who Loved Geese: Goddesses Mother Goose Resembles

> *[Aphrodite] is the only goddess who … kept life and reality. Artemis becomes unreal from sheer inhumanity; Athene … becomes a cold abstraction; Demeter … is but a lovely metaphor… Only the mystery of life, and love that begets life, remained.*
> Harrison 1955: 314

When trying to get a handle on any particular ancient deity, it's important to keep in mind that most gods and goddesses were viewed differently in different places and in different time periods. From time to time and place to place, people didn't always agree on who Aphrodite was, for example, or where she came from, or even what she stood for and, since authors usually forget to mention this little fact, reading about ancient deities can be frustrating. When you read on page one, for example, that Eros was the son of Aphrodite, but on page 101 that his mother was Tartaros, you can sometimes want to tear your hair out, or pound a pillow. The fact of the matter is, it was Hesiod, in the 7th century BC, who said Eros' mother was Tartaros. Later Greeks said no, it was Aphrodite. And in another ancient Greek tradition, the "Orphic", Eros was born out of the World Egg, with wings like a bird, the "first articulate god, source and creator of all." (Harrison 1955: 626)

Although I didn't know it when I began my research for this book, some writers think Aphrodite began as a powerful goddess who was gradually besmirched by the Greeks and Romans when they adopted her into their pantheons. The general picture the Greeks painted of Aphrodite is not a pretty one. And yet it's all most of us have ever heard about her. First and foremost, we've been told Aphrodite was a somewhat empty-headed physical knockout. Also though, according to the Greeks, she was a vamp. Her vampiness might have been the result of Zeus forcing her to marry the god Hephaistos, who was lame, misshapen and mean (Zeus felt he had no other choice – Aphrodite's spellbinding beauty constantly riled up all the gods). Since she had nothing in common with Hephaistos, and also didn't take kindly to being forced to marry anyone, Aphrodite began going out with other guys (for starters, Ares, Adonis and Anchises, father of the Trojan hero Aeneas).

It's generally agreed that Aphrodite was born from the sea. According to the 7th century BC Greek poet Hesiod, the universe began when the following four entities appeared spontaneously, out of nowhere, and in this order: Chaos, Gaia (Mother Earth), Tartaros (Sorrow), and Eros (Desire). At some point, Gaia gave birth to Ouranos, the Heavens, and when Ouranos grew up, he mated with Gaia to produce several children, including the god Kronos. But Ouranos hated all his kids so much he hid them in a dark hole. So Gaia gave her son Kronos a big sickle, with which he could (and did) sacrifice his father's genitals. After liberating them, Kronos pitched Ouranos' reproductive organs "from land into the turbulent sea" – and they supposedly morphed into Aphrodite (Caldwell 1987: 35-39). Therefore (say Baring and Cashford, 1991), Aphrodite brought life to earth, and time, and the beginning really of almost everything.

Get this picture in your head: according to the early Greeks, before Aphrodite was born, there was no light – anywhere. You had Gaia the Earth, who was covered all around with Ouranos, the Heavens, and until Heaven and Earth were separated, light had no room to exist:

> Light, or the space between Heaven and Earth, is here, as in Egyptian myth, the image of consciousness that sets in motion the changing forms of time... Aphrodite is then the daughter of Heaven and Sea – the original mother goddess in many traditions – and the first fruit of the separation of Heaven and Earth... Aphrodite is no longer the one Great Mother Goddess who is the origin of all things, but, as daughter of the sea, she is the child of the beginning. (Baring and Cashford 1991: 352-53)

Here is Aphrodite herself, speaking to us through the mouth of the Greek playwright Aeschylus:

> *The great and amorous sky curved over the earth, and lay upon her as a pure lover.*
> *The rain, the humid flux descending from heaven*
> *For both human and animal, for both thick and strong,*
> *Germinated the wheat, swelled the furrows with fecund mud*
> *And brought forth the buds in the orchards.*
> *And it is I who empowered these moist espousals,*
> *I, the great Aphrodite...*
> (Baring and Cashford 1991: 353; from the play *Danaides*)

Like Mother Goose and Holda, Aphrodite could never quite settle down with one man. Although the Greeks forcibly married her off to the crusty old fire god Hephaistos, she nevertheless spent considerable amounts of intimate time with several other gods. Classics scholar Jane Harrison thinks that before the Greeks demoted her into a sex goddess, Aphrodite was a goddess who just never married, a parthenogenetic deity who could create life without mating with the opposite sex (1955: 307-08) – which of course suggests that originally she was a Great Goddess, the uncreated source that created everything other than herself, including all the other deities.

Several scholars believe that before the Greeks had a go at her, Aphrodite was a gorgeous goddess both inside and out:

> Erich Neumann … states the divinity of Aphrodite has been sacrificed to the patriarchal sexualization of the feminine, causing us to forget who she really is. Aphrodite is a zest for love and sex without fear or shame. She is the sweet smelling gardenia wrapped in wisdom. She makes things beautiful and life worth living. She showers humankind with her golden laughter. According to … Sappho, she prevents life from being overtaken by cares and weariness. (Tate 2006: 37, quoting from Baring and Cashford 1991)

The German culture historian Heide Gottner-Abendroth presents a fascinating description of Aphrodite – one eerily reminiscent of Mother Goose in Old Mother Goose When She Wanted to Wander. Before the Greeks roughed her up, says Gottner-Abendroth, Aphrodite gave birth to the universe and everything in it by morphing into a bird, flying up into the heavens, and laying the world egg, i.e., the moon. Since she was the only animate being in the universe, she had to birth it without help from males, which explains why she's always called a Virgin Goddess. What's more, according to some traditions she birthed a son, Eros, and this son helped her bring the universe to life. Later, Aphrodite did mate with men, but afterwards she'd bathed in water to magically restore her virginity:

> The Pre-Olympian Aphrodite Urania was the primordial Creatress-Goddess. As the Great Goddess of the Mediterranean she reigned over land and sea… Transforming herself into a dove she soared above the chaos and laid the world egg, the full moon, from which all things sprang when it cracked open… This was the parthenogenetic act of creation and it explains why Aphrodite is attributed with virginity. Furthermore, after each erotic union, she immersed herself in water, thus restoring her virginity… Her child, Eros, androgynous and gold-winged, was the creative principle … who brought forth and supported the entire cosmos. Eros was not degenerated into a foolish, fickle cherub until patriarchal times. (Heide Gottner-Abendroth 1995: 21)

If we substituted "Mother Goose" for "Aphrodite" in this paragraph, and "goose" for "dove", we'd have a story in many ways identical to Old Mother Goose When She Wanted to Wander:

> [Mother Goose] was the primordial Creatress-Goddess. As the Great Goddess … she reigned over land and sea… Transforming herself into a [goose] she soared above the chaos and laid the world egg, the full moon, from which all things sprang when it cracked open… This was the parthenogenetic act of creation and it explains why [Mother Goose] is attributed with virginity. Furthermore, after each erotic union [symbolised by the Jack/Columbine and the goose/gander unions], she [as the golden egg] immersed herself in water, thus restoring her virginity… Her child, Eros [the deity Jack/Harlequin/Hellequin/Holda], androgynous and gold-winged, was the creative principle … who brought forth and supported the

entire cosmos [it was Jack/Hellequin/Holda who rescued the golden egg from the ocean].

The number of close parallels between Gottner-Abendroth's Aphrodite and Mother Goose in Old Mother Goose When She Wanted to Wander is astonishing. First, while Mother Goose kept a goose and flew it to the heavens, Aphrodite turned herself into a goose and flew herself to the heavens. Second, while Aphrodite laid a gold egg that turned into the moon, Mother Goose's goose laid a gold egg, and later flew to the moon. Third, while Aphrodite immersed herself in water, Mother Goose's gold egg was immersed in water. Fourth, both Aphrodite and Mother Goose gave birth to sons, and, fifth, both gave birth parthenogenetically (although no father is ever mentioned in Old Mother Goose, Mother nevertheless gave birth to Jack). Sixth, both sons are androgynous (Mother magically turned Jack into Harlequin, the well known male stage character, but, as we'll see later, Harlequin originally was a female deity – Holda). Finally, both sons sustain and protect their mothers' valuables (while for Eros it's his mother's creation, the cosmos, for Jack it's his mother's gold egg – likely a symbol for the cosmos, the Great Goddess "Mother Goose", or both).

To find clearer proof than this that Mother Goose is a secret symbol for the goddess Aphrodite would be difficult. Of course Mother Goose is generally pictured as an elderly woman deeply connected to children – but this is where Holda-Perchta comes in: like Mother Goose, Holda-Perchta is deeply associated with children (as well as with childbirth, human fertility, and coming-of-age initiation ceremonies), and she does typically appear as an old woman (actually, she can shapeshift into anything she wants). Also, like Charles Perrault's original Mother Goose, Holda-Perchta is connected to spinning and, of course, geese. Although Holda-Perchta typically took on the guise of an older woman, mortals did sometimes spy her in her beautiful, young-woman form, which she usually donned in spring – when life on earth is young. According to German folklore "at noon [Holda] can often be seen, a beautiful white lady, bathing in the lake, [but] as she is observed she disappears under the water" (Leach 1950: 500).

Like Mother Goose, Holda-Perchta is decidedly fond of children. She might even have been the original Santa Claus – just one indication of how much children must have loved her back: "Holle brought presents for children in her wagon on New Year's Eve, attended by a troop of children." (Hammer 2005: 75) Holda-Perchta also presided over girls and their spinning and weaving, rewarding those who worked hard, and either punishing (in some Germanic communities) or simply failing to reward (in other communities) girls who shirked their duties. According to Jane Hammer, "Holle is the *Erd-Mutter* (Earth Mother) from whom all children must separate in order to become people, though they still need her strength in order to grow." (Hammer 2005: 79)

And yet despite her deep connection to children, Holda-Perchta is not a mother, a fact that sets her apart from Aphrodite and Mother Goose: "Few instances show [Holda-Perchta] as wife or partner in a love relation"; instead, she is "seen as a foster-mother, nurse or teacher to the growing." (Motz 1984: 155, 156) Even though she wasn't a mother, Holda-Perchta was nevertheless heavily involved with children's souls. Whereas the Church condemned babies who died before being baptised, Perchta gathered the souls of these infants back into her loving care (Motz 1984: 155), and in many Germanic communities Holda led the Wild Hunt, a procession that sometimes included the souls of babies who tagged along with the crowd (Cohn 1977: 213) (more later on the Wild Hunt). Also, when children's souls needed bodies to be born into, Holda-Perchta was there again, working to help women conceive (often, women who failed to become pregnant sought out Holda, believing that bathing in her ponds or springs would stir up a pregnancy for them) (Motz 1984: 155; Hammer 2005: 79).

In the minds of her people, Holda also helped them through various romantic-love issues: "Perles quotes spells involving Frau Holle or Frau Venus as a protector or a bringer of love. One example is the protective spell found in the thirteenth-century writings of Baruch Ahrweiler: '*Ver Holda git mich urloup, dass ich ga in iuren hof un breche ein blat, das mich si guot*' ('Lady Holda, allow me to go into your garden and break a leaf, so that it will be good for me')." (Hammer 2005)

Likewise, in Old Mother Goose When She Wanted to Wander, Mother Goose too is depicted as a protector of love: when Jack and Columbine were threatened by the Squire and Knave, it was Mother Goose who used her magic to protect them.

Childbirth too was Holda's territory. Babies came straight from her wells, ponds or trees (Cohn 1977: 213). Her wells were "simply where the child is before it is born. In this mythic context, Holle is ... the symbol of the earth – or of the mother's womb – giving forth life from her mysterious depths." (Hammer 2005: 79) According to an old German folk ditty, babies emerged from Holla's well with the help of a "cat with boots on" (Shades of Perrault's Puss and Boots!). In this ditty, the cat asks the questions:

Hop, hop hazel-tree man [or man from Hesse, or possibly rabbit man]!
Our cat has boots on.
Runs with them to Holla's well.
Finds a child in the sun.
"What shall it be called?"
Kid or little goat.
"Who shall lift it?"
The drinker with his wine.
"Who shall wash the diapers?"
The woman with the dim [or empty] pocket.
(Hammer 2005: 78)

Also within Holda-Perchta's purview were ancient initiation rituals for girls, for which the goddess whisked girls off to her home in the Otherworld. Similarly, in indigenous societies too young initiates are often snatched from their parents' homes by supernatural beings who then subject them to trials, tests and lessons designed to swing them from child to adult status. The fairy tale Mother Holla, discussed in an earlier chapter, might describe an initiation ritual over which Holda presides. In the tale Gold Marie is carted off to Holda's subterranean home to learn the arts of agriculture (symbolised by her removal of the bread from the oven), horticulture (her shaking the apples off the tree), and animal husbandry (in some versions of the tale Marie milks a cow) (Motz 1984). (See Appendix C for the text of Mother Holla.)

Like Perrault's Mother Goose, Holda too was into spinning. Actually, she was into both spinning and weaving, and would "push gifts through the windows" of girls who excelled at these two vital Medieval tasks (Cohn 1977: 213). Keep in mind that in the Middle Ages people considered spinning an awesome, almost magical art: out of a shapeless lump of animal hair or scruffy plant matter, a spinner could coax an almost endless length of clean thread, and from it create everything from clothing, hats, socks, undergarments, coats, shawls, capes and coats, to blankets, bags, towels, bed sheets, curtains, table cloths, napkins and scores of other items necessary for living a decent life. Today, for a dollar or two any American can sashay into a thrift store and pick out a serviceable machine-produced blouse or shirt and a pair of slacks. This of course was not always the case. In the Middle Ages and early-modern era (16th-18th centuries), a simple shirt or pair of slacks would have taken dozens of hours to create, given that they often began as hair on the back of a sheep, an animal hand-fed for years, then hand-sheared, the wool hand-cleaned, hand-carded and hand-spun into thread, the thread hand-woven into cloth, and the cloth hand-dyed, hand-cut, and hand-sewn into the final finished product.

> It seems that in archaic thought the labour of producing thread from a shapeless mass of wool or flax created the same awe as the forming of a tool from stone or iron, so that spinning, like smith craft, was imbued with magical properties... The place where girls and women gather to spin may become the site of the enactment of the female mysteries, as the smithy may become the meeting place of men's secret societies. (Motz 1984: 161)

If the details I've provided so far about Holda-Perchta seem skimpy, it's because very little information has sifted down to us about her – for two good reasons: First, unlike Aphrodite's Greeks, Holda's people possessed no written language at the time the Church pummelled them into giving up their goddesses. The Germanic peoples, "left no written account of their own to throw light on their [religious] beliefs" as they existed before the Church grabbed hold of Europe (Filotas 2005: 36). What's more, once Holda's people did learn a written form of German, any works written about goddesses were, if found by the authorities, burned or otherwise destroyed. Second, during the entire span of the Middle Ages goddesses in general were routinely sliced, diced and pummelled into the ground, so that by the end of the medieval period they were, as far as we know, rarely if ever mentioned in public – at least not as goddesses per se. In short, we should not imagine that what information has sifted down to us about Holda-Perchta comes anywhere near to painting a complete picture of her as she once existed in the minds of Germanic Europeans.

Although we don't know much about Holda-Perchta, we do know this: Holda and Perchta are actually one and the same goddess. And Holda is not only Perchta, but also Hel/Ella/Hella. In fact the German word for the Christian Hell is *Holle*: "It is somewhat ironic that Holla, initially the goddess of the hearth fire of each home, was later [as Hel] associated with the burning fires of Hell…" (Stone 1979: 354) This Holda/Hella connection no doubt reaches far back into history. And as we'll see later, it leads us directly back to Old Mother Goose When She Wanted to Wander, in which Mother Goose waves her magic wand and changes her son Jack into "Harlequin", who is directly related to the goddess "Hellequin", who is in turn related to the goddess Hella.

If you are now totally confused, I wouldn't blame you. Just remember that the same ancient goddess often had different names in different locations and time periods. So the goddess I've chosen to call "Holda" throughout this book (just to make things easier for you, dear reader), had different names depending on when and where you found her. And then there's also the matter of spelling, which became standardised only in the past few centuries. The results:

- Holda is also Holla, Hol, Holl, Holde, Hulde, Hulda, Huldra, Hulle, Hella, Hel, Helle, Hellequin, Ella, etc.
- Perchta is also Percht, Perahta, Berchta, Berchte, Behrta, Bertha, Hertha, etc.

Although Holda, Perchta and Hella are actually one and the same goddess, the merger that occurred between them and the goddess Aphrodite/Venus was a comparatively recent one. You might remember from the beginning of the book that this merger occurred after the Goths conquered Rome. Evidence of it shuffles through the Middle Ages and the early-modern era as well. Early in the 17th century, for example, as a result of visiting Holda in the mountain called "Venusberg", a German man claimed a new skill: he could now predict the future: "…in Calvinist Isenburg-Budinger … Diel Breull said that he 'visited Frau Holle in her mountain castle and was therefore able to foresee the future.' The conflation of Holda, Venus and the Fairy Queen was not unusual." (Bever 2008: 189, 191)

Before she suffered a savage smear campaign at the hands of

Church and State alike, much evidence indicates that Holda-Perchta was a magnificent goddess, simultaneously both powerful and loving. Above all she was powerful. One of her most vital tasks was keeping the earth fertile enough for crops and plants to grow and flourish, a task she accomplished by travelling the earth (presumably in her flying wagon) every year for the 12 days between Christmas and Epiphany (Cohn 1977: 213). As mentioned earlier, she seems to have been the original Santa Claus, showering children the earth over with gifts at the winter solstice.

Holda was powerful enough to control the weather. She also created the physical environment – mountains for example. "As a theological image, Holle needs neither a male partner nor a female 'shadow'; she is strong and beautiful, housewifely and wild, fierce and gentle." (Hammer 2005: 81) Through her name itself Holda is associated with healing and all good things: "The name Holla ... is cognate with holy, heal, hallow, hello, whole, all, halo and holly..." (Stone 1979, AM: 355) According to Bever, Holda was known for "binding up the lame and maimed." (Bever 2008: 191)

But both Perchta and Holda were "degraded" by European authorities determined to stop Europeans from worshiping these breathtaking twin deities. For reasons unknown, Perchta fared worse than Holda: "In the stories of dame Berchta the bad meaning predominates, as the good one does in those of dame Holda; that is to say, the popular Christian view had degraded Berchta lower than Holda." (Grimm 1835a: 1) Holda, however, didn't escape damage either, as Jacob Grimm points out: "The next step is that Holda, instead of her divine shape, assumes the appearance of an ugly old woman, long-nosed, big-toothed, with bristling and thick-matted hair. 'He's had a jaunt with Holle,' they say of a man whose hair sticks up in tangled disorder..." (Grimm, 1835a)

Nevertheless, Holda never seems to go to the extremes Perchta does. In the folklore of certain (but not all) German-language areas of Europe, when children misbehave Perchta sometimes reacts with astonishing violence. One particularly draconian example: she opens their stomachs and fills them with straw, mud or debris. Was the pre-patriarchal Perchta this bad, or was this a story attached to Perchta by the Church to help destroy her? Evidence that this was indeed the work of the Church flows from places like the village of Lautenthal, Germany, where Perchta's response to misbehaving children is similar to Holda's, that of the Celtic goddess Macha, and of the Basque goddess Mari: after whisking them off to her own domain Perchta non-violently teaches them correct behaviour (Motz 1984: 155). On the other hand, Motz points to certain modern indigenous societies in which puberty initiations involve symbolic violence as a way of helping tear a child away from the relative ease and innocence of childhood and into the more difficult realm of the adult. Is it possible then, asks Motz, that Perchta's violence is an echo of ancient initiation ceremonies?

As we've seen previously, the Brothers Grimm collected a fairy tale about the goddess Holda-Perchta – Mother Holla – in which a mother forces her industrious daughter down a well to retrieve a weaving shuttle the girl accidentally dropped there. After falling into the well, the girl passes out, but when she comes to, she's in a magnificent magic meadow. As she strolls along, loaves of bread call to her to remove them from their oven, and she does. Then apples beg her to shake them from their tree, and she does, stacking them neatly around the tree's base.

Eventually the girl stumbles upon Mother Holla:

> At last she came to a little house, out of which an old woman peeped; but she had such large teeth that the girl was frightened, and was about to run away. But the old woman called out to her, "What are you afraid of, dear child? Stay with me; if you will do all the work in the house properly, you shall be the better for it."

For an untold length of time the girl works for the goddess, with one of her more important tasks being to shake out the goddess's feather bed every morning, a process that causes the snow to fly. Before the girl returns home Mother Holla rewards her with golden rain that sticks to her clothing, and upon seeing her sister covered in gold, the lazy daughter is eager to visit Mother Holla herself. But when the bread and apples beg for her help, the lazy daughter turns up her nose at them. And she refuses to work for Holla. She's consequently sent home covered not in gold but in pitch (See Appendix C for the entire story).

What does this story reveal about the goddess Holda-Perchta? First it shows she was a powerful goddess who controlled the weather. If and when the snow fell was her choice and hers alone. Second, it underscores Holda's role as a teacher of young girls, reinforcing the notion that she played a role in the initiation of young Germanic women. And since it was by dropping their weaving shuttles down the well that each girl wended her way to the goddess, it also reinforces Holda's connection to spinning and weaving. Tangentially the story links Holda to geese: although he doesn't come right out and say it, Jacob Grimm implies that Holda's bed is stuffed with goose feathers, and that it is these that cause the snow to fall: "Dame Holle shakes her bed… They say in Scotland, when the first flakes fell: 'The men o' the East are pyking their geese, and sending their feathers here awa'." (Grimm 1835a)

One interesting aspect of the Mother Holle story is the animation of inanimate objects: bread and apples talk and have feelings. This undoubtedly links back to ancient times when Holda's followers were animists, people who believed everything has soul and spirit – not only humans, but animals, bread and apples as well. The indigenous Ainu of Japan were animists, so we can look at them and get an idea of what European animists might have been like. Traditionally, the Ainu believed that even clothing, tools and tents had souls, that these and all other items were controlled by male or female supernatural forces lodged within them, and that when people use clothing, tools, tents or other inanimate things they must treat these objects kindly so that their spirits would treat their human users kindly (Levinson 1998: 7). In Mother Holla, because the good daughter honoured the animist version of reality, she was rewarded.

According to Heide Gottner-Abendroth, Mother Holla is a disguised religious myth about the Great Goddess Holda and the initiation of one of her priestesses who for clarity's sake Gottner-Abendroth calls "Gold Marie" (her washout of a sister is "Pitch Marie"). The plunge into, through, and out of the well is code for Gold Marie's death and resurrection: "She patiently suffers torture and death (the dive into the well) and experiences, therefore, her own Return. It is the most ancient form of matriarchal initiation." As mentioned earlier, while living in the enchanted realm with the goddess, Gold Marie masters the old matriarchal arts of agriculture (the bread), horticulture (the apples), and the domestication of animals (the cow). But by learning to shake Holla's bed to create weather, she also masters the art of magic.

And the stepmother and Pitch Marie? They represent a "...duplicate, but negative transparency superimposed on" the holy relationship between the goddess and her priestess. What's more, says Gottner-Abendroth, in this fairy tale gold is not money, but code for "the wealth deep in the womb of the Earth: fertility, in every sense the richness of life." (Heide Gottner-Abendroth 1995: 138-139)

How old is Holda-Perchta, and where did she originate? Motz thinks belief in this goddess began not among outsiders, but among the Germanic peoples themselves, and when they were nomadic hunter-gatherers. Mythologically, both Holda and Perchta are found almost exclusively in wilderness areas, regions uncultivated by humans – the kind of places wandering hunter-gatherers called home. Both Holda and Perchta can shapeshift into animal forms, and both are closely associated with animals in general, especially dogs – a fact that ties in with the ancient Germanic connection to wolves.

> [S]ince dogs are closely related to wolves we might understand the alliance of the Lady with her pack as a vestige of her more archaic form as Wolfshirt ("shepherd of wolves"), a figure of Germanic and non-Germanic tradition. (Motz 1984: 158-59)

Unlike Motz, archaeologist Marija Gimbutas thinks Holda is a Germanic descendant of the ancient goddesses found in south-eastern Europe from around 5000 BC to 4000 BC. Although the Neolithic Old Europeans were settled agriculturalists, they could of course have carried Holda forward from their own hunter-gatherer ancestors. Gimbutas says both Hella and Holla are the Germanic version of the Old European goddess of death and rebirth – in other words the all-powerful Great Mother who births all living creatures, then escorts us through a death phase, and then on into another new life (Gimbutas 2001: 195).

Interestingly, the first recorded reference to Holda is linked to Emperor Charlemagne (742-814 AD), whose mother, remember, was "Goosefooted Bertha", named by some as the original Mother Goose. According to Jacob Grimm, "The very earliest mention of Holda is in Walafrid Strabo's eulogy of Judith, wife of Louis the Pious," son of Charlemagne. The eulogy begins like this: "'*Organa dulcisono percussit pectine Judith; O si Sappho loquax vel nos inviseret Holda,*' etc." (Grimm 1966c: 1367) Loosely translated, this becomes, "Sweet instrument, strike heartily to stroke Judith, if you wish to visit loquacious Sappho, or even Holda." Is Strabo comparing Judith to the goddess Holda? Was Charlemagne's mother presented to certain of his subjects as the embodiment of the old bird goddess of ancient Europe, known in southern Germany as "Perchta" and in Britain as "Bertha"?

Where Holda-Perchta made her home depended on who you

talked to and which area of Europe you're in. Although in many parts of Europe she lived below and above the earth both, Cohn says she usually "lives in the upper air, and circles the earth" (Cohn 1977: 213). While Perchta inhabited large, general wilderness areas – the forest mostly – Holda lived in more specific locales; Kyffhauser and Horselberg mountains, for example, or in specific stones, trees, and lakes. Neither goddess, however, ever lived near human settlements (Motz 1984: 155-56).

Even after being reviled and maligned by religious and civil authorities for century after century, Holda remained popular.

> To read [Jacob] Grimm's and [Lotte] Motz's sources on the extensive winter celebrations of Holle, one must imagine that everyone in the Germanic lands knew of Holle or Holda ... [She represented] the idea that a divine feminine force, embodied in nature, was the ground of life. (Hammer 2005: 80)

One fascinating indication of Holda's former glory is the number of landscape features, celebrations, and calendar bits and pieces that even now carry her name, prompting Motz to proclaim that Holda's name, "has entered German speech." The following is a small sampling of how and where:

- *Perchtennacht* – Styria – the night before Epiphany
- *Frauhollenabend* – Rhongebirge – the name for Saturday
- *Hollenabend* – Westerwald – the Thursday before Christmas
- *Frau Hullibaum* – Central Germany, mountains – the name of certain trees
- *Frau Holles Badeplatz* – Central Germany, mountains – a pond
- *Frau Hullistein* – Central Germany, mountains – a rock Holda sits on
- *Perchtenjagd* – Salzburg and Tyrol – a masked performance
- *Streggelejagen* – Switzerland – an Easter performance
- *Posterlijagen* – Switzerland – a winter performance

- *Bechtelen* – Switzerland and Alsatia – masked procession or feast (Motz 1984: 152, 153).

Remarkably, even today in some parts of Europe Perchten rituals still thrive. In 1950, for example, Gertrude Prokosch Kurath described a ceremony held in Salzburg, Austria, by followers of Perchta. Called "Perchten", these followers "retain the pagan connotations…" In this ceremony "Schonperchten" (good Perchten) fight in hand-to-hand combat with "Schiechenperchten" (bad Perchten) and in the end defeat them. While the good guys are dressed in "high, ornate headdresses with chains, ribbons [and] flowers," the bad Perchten are a "motley, tattered and rowdy crew." (Kurath 1950: 856) Three decades later, in 1984, Lotte Motz wrote that in some areas of Europe Perchten ceremonies still "dominate the seasonal traditions… [W]e may understand that in such areas she was the most important of the supernatural powers in whose hands, it was believed, would lie the prosperity of the population." (Motz 1984: 152)

Motz describes a typical ritual ceremony still being carried out in the 1980s in German, Austrian and Swiss Alpine regions, one that swept along in two phases: first, boys decked out as wild animals in fur cloaks, fur hats (usually black), and horned "masks of terrifying aspect" tore through village streets. "Their race proceeds from house to house, or even from village to village, through the valleys, amidst the deafening clamour of their bells, their whips, their shouts of joy." This first phase seems to echo an ancient sacred part of the ceremony in which boys shed their human persona, become wild animals – possibly animal deities – and revel in symbolising the ferocity of such animals. In the second, or "handsome" Perchta phase of the ceremony, the boys wore normal folk costumes, apparently symbolising their new "civilised" adult status (Motz 1984: 153, 160-61).

Even now, in the second decade of the 21st century, simply punching "Perchten festivals Austria" or "Perchten ceremonies" into your favourite internet search engine will pull up scores of websites describing festivals dedicated to the goddess Perchta, festivals still alive and well today. Some of these websites are sprinkled with photos of 21st century Perchten in their elaborate and colourful ancient masks and costumes. In other words, despite gargantuan efforts and an intense desire to do so, the Church has failed to erase all memory of one of Mother Goose's major prototypes, the magnificent Germanic goddess Holda-Perchta.

* * *

Although of all European goddesses, Holda and Aphrodite most closely resemble Mother Goose, other European goddesses share certain of Mother's characteristics and connections. For example the Etruscan goddess of love Turan is related to Aphrodite, the swan and the dove, and even has wings of her own (Jordan 1993: 269). The North Germanic goddess Frigga too might lay a claim to Mother Goose's ancestral line; Guerber says Holda and Perchta "had attributes exactly like" Frigga (1993: 383). Also resembling Mother Goose to some extent is the ancient Russian goddess Mokosh, who was linked to the "archaic hunting moon goddess through spinning, childbirth, patronage of animals, and rain..." Mokosh, one of the last goddesses to fall to the Church, was – amazingly – still included in the official Russian pantheon as late as 980 AD (Hubbs 1988: 16-17 & 53).

In addition to Turan, Frigga, and Mokosh, the ancient Basque goddess Mari also possesses several Mother Goose traits. For example, Mari is often mentioned in the same breath with ducks, owls, birds generally, the moon, gold and spinning. Living in the mountains on the border between France and Spain, the Basques are some of the few Europeans still speaking a language other than Indo-European, and although they are very secretive about her, they also still worship a goddess – one who might very well be older than the Indo-European invasion of Europe. This goddess goes by many names, one of the most common being "Mari". Mari is "a goddess who displays characteristics both non-Christian and non-Indo-European, and who has much in common with the Neolithic European goddess as reconstructed from the archaeological and mythological record." (Everson 1989)

Like Mother Goose, Mari is a bird goddess, and in a part of Basqueland known as Baragarza, Mari, a shapeshifter, sometimes appears as a woman with the feet of a bird. What's more, her supernatural "servants" the *laminak* appear as humans with the feet of chickens, ducks or goats. Mari is a Great Goddess associated with birth and life but also with death and regeneration, and it is in relation to the latter two phenomena that she is connected to birds of prey like vultures, eagles and ravens – and Mother Goose's bird the owl (Everson 1989).

Mari is also linked to Mother Goose through the moon. In the Basque region of Azcoita she has been seen as a woman whose head is encircled by the full moon, and in Escoriaza she's been seen in the figure of the full moon emitting flames. Also like Mother Goose, Mari is connected to gold and spinning:

> It is generally believed that Mari's habitations are richly adorned with gold and precious stones... A legend of Cenaruzza tells that Mari gave to one of her captives a piece of coal, which, later, when taken from the cave, was transformed into purist gold.

And in Zuazo de Bamboa the Basques say Mari spins thread out of gleaming gold, winding it around the horns of a ram in her cave called Anboto, while in Zarauz and Amezqueta she has been seen spinning thread with a golden spindle (Everson 1989).

In short, Holda-Perchta and Aphrodite-Venus aren't the only goddesses who share traits with Mother Goose. On the other hand, just because a goddess shares one or two things in common with Mother Goose doesn't make her a contender for one of Mother Goose's prototypes. For example, although Athena is heavily identified with the owl (one of the birds in Old Mother Goose When She Wanted to Wander), she is not known for flying. Nor is she associated with the goose, the moon, spinning, wells, human fertility, love or childbirth. Likewise, the Roman goddess Diana is heavily linked to the moon and the woods, but not to flying, spinning, children, the sea, hearth or home, wells or springs. And the goddess Demeter has a son, yes (like Mother Goose's Jack and Aphrodite's Eros), but that's just about all that ties her to Mother Goose.

Other than Aphrodite, Holda, and maybe Frigga and Mari, the only other goddess who might have a shot at claiming the title "The Real Mother Goose" is the Celtic goddess Brigit. Even though Brigit doesn't fly on a goose, she's associated with the goose's sister, the swan, and in addition also shares the following traits with Mother Goose, Holda, and Aphrodite:

- She is associated with the moon
- She is associated with spinning
- She is associated with human fertility
- She is associated with wells and springs
- She has a son (actually three sons) (Tate 2006: 67, 68; Condren 1989: 57, 60, 65, 66; Leeming 2005: 55).

Brigit is clearly associated with the *Anatidae* (geese, ducks, swans), through the swan:

> Yet above all it was "the fairy swan of Bride" that would prove to be the most enigmatic of [Brigit's] avian forms. Aside from Scottish poetry that alludes to her connection with this beautiful creature, a large number of "Bride," "Bree," "Brid," "Bright," and "Brig" place-names are found in England and Wales, some with clear swan associations... (Collins 2006: 97-98)

There's even archaeological evidence suggesting Brigit's link to swans. Recently, in the town of Saveock Water, Cornwall, Britain, several cryptic "swan pits" radiocarbon dated to the 1640s, were excavated by archaeologist Jacqueline Wood. Containing swan skins, swan feathers, and bird eggs these pits are almost certain proof that as late as the mid 17th century pre-Christian magico-religious rituals were still being performed in southwest England – and Wood believes the rituals were associated with Brigit. As of 2012, 35 small feather-lined pits dug into a clay platform had been excavated with "the tops of many more appearing". And although most of the pits were empty, they nevertheless showed signs of having been filled – bits of feathers and other paraphernalia remained as telltale signs (Wood 2012).

After the swans were killed their skins were removed whole and tucked into the pits feather-side up, so that the 15"x10" pits were feather-lined. Although the shells of the eggs had deteriorated, the pits' moist environment had allowed their membranes to survive, and in one pit excavators discovered seven fully-formed chicks that, over 350 years ago, had been ready to peck their way out of their shells. Also tucked into the pits were talons from several species of birds, and stones from "Swan Pool" 15 miles downriver from Saveock Water.

But the pits weren't the only exciting find at this site. Nearby Wood also uncovered the remains of two spring-fed pools, one carefully lined with white quartz and filled with 350-year-old scraps of cloth, "six medieval straight pins, shoe parts, heather branches (associated with luck), fingernail clippings, human hair, and – it doesn't get more witch-like – part of a cauldron." (Ravillious 2008) If Wood is right in thinking these pools were used for at least 6,000 years, this places their initial use well before the Indo-Europeans arrived in Britain with their dominance hierarchies and warrior culture. According to the *Archaeology* magazine reporter who interviewed Wood, "Looking at the textile fragments stored in little plastic boxes in Wood's barn, it is hard to believe they are 350 years old – the vivid blues, golden yellows, and vibrant greens were preserved by the moist environment." (Ravillious 2008)

Eventually the pools were destroyed by the British government: "[I]n the late 17th century … the crown paid locals to fill in the pools (along with other 'holy' wells in Cornwall) to prevent pagan rituals." (Ravillious 2008) The purpose of the pits? Wood believes they were part of magic spells designed to help women conceive. And since the goddess Brigit was associated with swans, children and childbirth, Wood thinks the pits were linked to her. She offers a possible set of ritual instructions for the spell that might have accompanied the pits:

> Take a swan and wring its neck * Skin the bird and, under a full moon, lay its skin in a shallow hole with the feathers face-up * Add eggs – five for every child you want to bear * Atop each egg, place the talon of a blackbird and a black stone * Circle the hole three times, clockwise, then close it with a clod of earth *As soon as you are with child, empty the hole, or terrible things will come to pass. (Ravillious 2008)

I would add: "Offer a prayer to the Great Goddess Brigit: 'Dear Mother, I present to you these offerings from your sacred bird, and beseech you to seed a child in my womb before Yuletide…'"

Wood has failed to find other archaeologists familiar with anything like her swan pits – in all likelihood because they were part of a very dangerous "game" to play. Because they were playing with fire, Wood believes the practitioners who performed the rituals over the swan pits very likely carried them out in absolute secrecy. This falls in line with the probable felt need of early-modern Europeans to create a figure like Mother Goose to serve as a smokescreen for the old Mother-Goddess philosophy and worldview. Later we'll see that Wood's discovery fits in remarkably well with a particular genre of fairy tale – the so-called swan-maiden tales.

Wood's archaeological find underscores the deep significance to early modern Europeans of both magic and the *Anatidae* alike. In 1640s England people were at risk of being executed if even a hint existed that they were associated with magic – in any way. Yet practising magic was so important to Saveock Water residents that they were willing to risk their lives to do it. And it seems that at least some of their magic was possible only with the help of the swan, a member of the family *Anatidae*.

Was it just accident that one of the few late-pre-Christian rituals archaeologists have uncovered in Europe involved the feathers and eggs of a bird so closely connected to Mother Goose? Or was religious reverence for the Anatadae (and the goddesses they represented) more common in the early-modern era than we've previously thought? It might be worth noting that even today in Britain it's a punishable crime to kill a swan (Ravillious 2008).

In the next chapter, we return to one specific part in the one rhyme in which Mother Goose is named specifically, Old Mother Goose When She Wanted to Wander. In this rhyme, Mother's son Jack gets in serious trouble with two malicious men who want to do him harm. In response, Mother Goose waves her wand over Jack, instantly turning him into "Harlequin" – one of the most enchanting, captivating and yet mysterious of all literary characters ever to come out of early modern Europe. Which brings us to a perplexing question: why would Mother Goose do that? What was the point?

Chapter 5

The Harlequin-Hellequin-Helle-Holda Connection: Mother Goose, Folklore and the Theatre

Among other mysteries tucked away in Old Mother Goose When She Wanted to Wander is the sudden, unexplained appearance in the rhyme of "the famed Harlequin". You'll remember that immediately after Mother Goose's son Jack begins to court a "fair lady" in the rhyme, the squire and the knave get Jack into a dark alley and try to chew him up a bit, whereupon Mother Goose materialises, uses her magic wand, and turns Jack into the famous stage character Harlequin. Next she turns to Jack's "fair lady" and changes her into Harlequin's stage lover, Columbine:

Then Jack went courting
A lady so gay,
As fair as a lily,
And sweet as the May.

The knave and the squire
Came up at his back,
And began to belabour
The sides of poor Jack.

But Old Mother Goose
That instant came in,
And turned her son Jack
Into famed Harlequin

She then with her wand
Touched the lady so fine,
And turned her at once
Into sweet Columbine…

In early-modern European theatrical productions, Harlequin cut a striking figure, sweeping onto the stage in a brightly coloured half-mask and form-fitting, multicoloured, diamond-patterned tights. He carried a slapstick, or a sword, both of which were actually magic wands. What's more, he was the kind of guy you might like to go have a beer with: happy go lucky, full of fun, street smart; the guy who breaks all the rules – but without hurting anyone. Often he got himself "into difficulties from which he managed to extricate himself by cleverness and irrepressible high spirits. He was amoral without being vicious, and, unlike his fellow commedia servants, he did not hold a grudge or seek revenge against those who tricked or cheated him." (Harlequin 2012)

But why would Mother Goose want to turn her son into a

stage character, and why this one in particular? After lots of digging, I finally found what almost certainly has to be the answer; over time Harlequin evolved from a mythical being called "Hellequin", and Hellequin in turn evolved from the goddess Helle/Holda (Holle, Holla, etc.). In other words, Mother Goose turned her child into a deity – a perfectly logical and natural way to protect him against bad-mannered mortals. Interestingly, however, she turned him into part of her own godhood, making him part of her own divinity.

The easiest way to explain Harlequin's evolution is to trace it backwards in time, starting with Harlequin, and then back to Hellequin, and from there back to Helle/Holda. Although as a stage character popular in Europe from the mid 1500s through the early 1900s Harlequin's personality changed through time and from place to place, for most of his "life" he was a captivating jester-like character who could perform magic. His lady friend was Columbine, and often much of the "Harlequinade" involved Columbine's father or guardian sweating bullets to break the two lovers apart.

Hellequin on the other hand, was one of the putative leaders of The Wild Hunt, a supernatural troop of mostly dead people that roamed the medieval countryside in the dead of night. Although belief in the Wild Hunt has been traced back to 1091 AD in France, we know about it almost exclusively from reports of hostile churchmen (in fact the 1091 report came from the monk Orderic Vitalis of the St. Evroult Abbey in the Lisieux diocese of France [Lecouteux 2011: 99]). Like Holda-Perchta and Aphrodite-Venus, Hellequin too was known by slightly different names in different parts of Europe: Hellekin, Helkin, Herlaquin, Harlekin, Herlechin, etc.

But originally Hellequin seems to have been the goddess Helle, and by now you know that "Helle" is simply another version of the goddess Holda-Perchta, one often found a bit further north than Holda and Perchta. In Teutonic mythology

"Hel" was the daughter of the deities Loki and Angur-boda of the Vanir. Banished to the Underworld by the god Odin (of the Aesir), Helle was said to rule there over those who died of disease or old age while warriors who died in battle got to go to a better place than Helle's Underworld – Valhalla. Helle in other words was simply one in a long line of goddesses subjected to a patriarchal smear campaign; like Holda and Perchta, she was to a great extent revamped, rewritten and reprogrammed.

So what's the proof that Hellequin, leader of The Wild Hunt, was actually Helle/Holda, ancient Germanic goddess of life, death and regeneration?

1. First of all, of course, there's the similarity of the names: "Helle," "Helle-quin." But there's more – much more.
2. Recently, a former professor of medieval literature at the Sorbonne, Claude Lecouteux, intensively studied the tangled mass of information that's trickled down to us about the mysterious Wild Hunt. According to Lecouteux there were actually two kinds of Wild Hunt: one led by Hellequin, and the other by Holda. Holda led "The Good Women" type, Hellequin the "Wandering Dead" type (Lecouteux 2011). The Wandering Dead could be dangerous or not, but were always very noisy (shouting, instruments playing, moaning, horses braying – anything to make noise). Often they seemed to have no purpose beyond wandering around making a racket.

   "The Good Women" on the other hand, were quiet. Also, they had a specific purpose: to leave gifts and blessings at each house where they stopped (as long as the inhabitants left food and drink out for them on the kitchen table). The leader of the Good Women was the goddess Holda, or, depending on what region in Europe we're talking about, one of her namesake twins – Abundia, Fortune, Bensozia, Satia, and so forth (Lecouteux 2011: 8-23).

3. Also according to Lecouteux, Perchta sometimes took Hellequin's place as leader of the Wandering Dead. Often, however, the troops she led consisted of babies and young children instead of adults (2011: 15, 73). And if you've read through the present book from the beginning, you know by now that Perchta is essentially the same goddess as Holda, with Holda inhabiting the north of Germany and Perchta the south.
4. At some point, says Lecouteux, Holda's troop of Good Women merged in people's minds with Hellequin's troop of Wandering Dead: "It is important for us to recognise the close relationship that links Fortune and Hellequin... Fortune is only one of the shapes adopted by the Good Woman called Abundia, Satia, Bensozia, or Percht [or Holda]. We therefore find in France the exact same shift of the legend: these hosts of women and the Mesnie Hellequin are brought together and made one." (Lecouteux 2011: 174)

So Hellequin, leader of the Wild Hunt, eventually merged in people's minds with Holda. But how do we get from the goddess Hellequin-Helle-Holda to Harlequin, acrobatic jester of Europe's medieval and early-modern stage? For starters, in their book on word origins, Stephen Potter and philologist Laurens Sargent just come right out and say that "Harlequin" of the stage got his name directly from the Old High German phrase "Hella cunni", or kindred of Hel, and that it's a designation going back to the medieval legend of the Wild Hunt (Potter and Sargent 1974: 73).

Lecouteux too, though, writes about Hellequin/Helle becoming Harlequin, contending that the shift happened by way of "Carnival", the annual pre-Lenten festival celebrated in many Catholic countries still today, its roots sunk deeply into pre-Christian religion:

> ... Hellequin ... has been subjected to transformation into a figure of Carnival, as testified by the *Jeu de la feuillee* [*The Play of Greenwood*] and *Fauvel*. This is the same process that turned Hellequin into the Arlecchino [Italian for "Harlequin"] of Italian theatre... This is why Arlecchino's coat designated the curtain that masked the entrance to hell or represented it on the medieval stage. (Lecouteux 2011: 179-80)

In sum, when Mother Goose waved her magic wand and turned her son Jack into "the famed Harlequin", it seems she was really changing him into one aspect of herself, the goddess of birth, death and regeneration, Helle/Holda. If so, it appears that, like Aphrodite's son Eros, Mother Goose's son too was androgynous: "[Aphrodite's] child, Eros, androgynous and gold-winged, was the creative principle ... who brought forth and supported the entire cosmos." (Gottner-Abendroth 1995: 21) And is Jack, also like Eros, the grand creative principle? When he jumped into the sea and pulled out the golden (world) egg, could this action have been secret code for "birthing the universe"?

Chapter 6

Witch, Peasant Nurse, or Saintly Grandmother? Mother Goose and the Graphic Arts

To say artists' portrayals of Mother Goose are confusing is a gross understatement. While in 1697 Charles Perrault showed Mother as a young, harmless-looking peasant nursemaid, a hundred odd years later some 19th century artists were picturing her as severely-aged, evil-looking and witch-like. And then, from around the 1940s on, artists began favouring two additional ways to represent Mother Goose: as a kindly old grandmother, or as a cheerful, matronly white bird outfitted in old-style clothing and bonnet. So which was she? Who was "right"? It could be they all are.

When Charles Perrault's *Tales of Mother Goose* first appeared in print in 1697 it included a frontispiece showing two children aged about six and 11, along with an older boy, all three of whom are facing a perhaps 30-something young woman. The woman is seated. While she sits spinning thread, she simultaneously "spins yarns" to her young audience. To her left is a door hung with a sign: *"contes de ma mere loye"* ("tales of my mother the goose") (Darton 1982, figure 15a). While a hearty fireplace fire and the children's hats and robes suggest it's winter, a lit candle on the mantle and the black shadows cutting across the floor-boards from the young man's chair imply it's night-time.

Many assume this young woman is Mother Goose herself (see, for example, Tatar 2002: 4), and I've encountered no writer arguing that she's not. However, it is possible that in his own mind Perrault was picturing not Mother Goose but an ordinary woman telling Mother-Goose tales to her charges. As we'll see below, in later editions of Perrault's books his young woman becomes increasingly older. Although this fits in with non-Perrault-related depictions of Mother Goose as an older woman, in the present book I will consider Perrault's initial 1697 spinning storyteller a depiction of Mother Goose herself.

While Perrault dressed his Mother Goose in peasant clothing, the home she sits in is not a peasant home. For starters, running above, around and inside the fireplace is complex wooden molding, and on the fireplace mantle sits a burning candle in a tall, elaborate candle holder. Next, the children's gowns appear to be silk, and are brightly coloured and lined with fur cuffs and fur bordering the collar down to their waists. They also wear elaborate hats. The young man too is dressed in clothing outside the reach of the typical 17th century French peasant: a bright blue coat with five-inch-tall gold-coloured cuffs, orange tights extending up over his knees, and white lace at his wrists and throat. Perched on his head is a grey tri-cornered hat.

In contrast, Mother Goose wears a coarse white blouse under a simple, loose-fitting orange vest. She also wears a plain white apron, and underneath the apron a plain blue skirt. Her hair is completely hidden under a New-England-Pilgrim-type bonnet with a wide U-shaped strip of cloth in front extending over the top front of her head, then dropping to her shoulders. In short, the children in the picture "appear to be of a higher social class than this Mother Goose" (Tatar 2002).

But after 1697, and through successive editions of Perrault's *Tales*, Mother Goose changed in appearance. Forty years after its debut in 1697, for example, an English translation of *Tales of Mother Goose* (published by R. Montagu and J. Pote) still included Perrault's 1697 frontispiece. But there were minute differences. Mother Goose's nose is slightly sharper, for instance, and the girl has a narrower mouth and a higher neckline on her dressing gown (see Darton 1982: figure 15b). And then in 1764, an edition published in London "for J. Melvil, Bookseller" and titled *Tales of Passed* [sic] *Times by Mother Goose* also shows much the same frontis as Perrault's original – but this time with several heftier changes – one of them absolutely stunning.

In this 1764 edition, instead of standing, the children are now sitting on the floor gazing raptly up at Mother Goose, their hands resting not at their sides but on her lap. Also, instead of lounging off to the side in a chair as he does in Perrault's 1697 frontis, the young man now stands behind the children, his hands on their shoulders. And instead of elaborate fur-lined robes the children are now clothed in peasant dress. But the most shocking change of all is this: Mother Goose has aged, and sharply. She's now stoop-shouldered, and her mouth is sunken, a suggestion that she's lost all her teeth. In short, this Mother Goose is no longer a young nursemaid; she's become an old peasant woman spinning yarns to the village children, or perhaps to her own grandchildren.

In a third frontispiece, from an undated French edition of Perrault's *Tales*, Mother Goose is depicted as older still – almost grotesquely so. In this image she's an extremely stoop-shouldered old woman with a decidedly sunken mouth. Her oddly tilted head suggests an arthritic neck or spine. Otherwise, this frontispiece is identical to the 1764 English frontis described above, as if one artist literally traced 95 percent of the other's work. Both drawings show the same clothing, body postures and facial expressions for the three children, identical detail in the mantelpiece, and even the same patterns in the smoke rising from the fireplace. The only real difference is that in the French image Mother Goose has morphed into an extremely old crone.

In conclusion, these early images of Mother Goose only bolster the conjecture that Mother Goose was the goddess Holda-Perchta. Although the description of Holda-Perchta shifted from place to place and through time, she shared everywhere certain characteristics in common: she was a winter goddess associated with children, spinning, home and hearth, a solitary deity "seen as a foster-mother, nurse or teacher to the growing" (Motz 1984: 155, 156). She could shapeshift – from young woman to old crone, for example, depending on her whim and fancy, and the four frontispieces described above show Mother Goose shifting among three aspects: young nursemaid, young mother or grandmother, and crone. Furthermore, Holda was a goddess of the night, a spiritual time to Germanics (Motz 1984: 162, 163), and judging from the candle on the mantelpiece, the children's gowns, and hats, and the long black shadows in the room, these four Mother Goose frontispieces are indeed night-time scenes.

* * *

American artistic portrayals of Mother Goose have run the gamut from grandmotherly, to frightening old hag and anthropomorphic goose, and back again to grandmotherly figure. In her first portrait by an American artist, Mother Goose is simply a pleasant-looking grandmother (Vandergrift 2012), and over time many American artists have continued to show her as such.

Through time, however, others have depicted her as an anthropomorphic goose or as a frightening witch-like woman. But in the post-WWII era, American artists began to drop the Mother Goose-as-witch pictures, and instead have mostly shown Mother as a plump, smiling grandmother surrounded by children, as a young and attractive 40-something grandmother, or as a goose with or without human characteristics. Occasionally Mother appears as a young woman or child in Mother Goose's witchy cone hat and other accoutrements – usually in pale pastel colours, however, rather than the blacks, candy-apple reds, and other richer, denser colours used for elderly Mother Gooses.

In America Mother Goose made her pictorial debut in 1822 in the book *Mother Goose's Quarto*, appearing on the title page as a slim and smiling grandmother with two adoring young children in tow. But a decade later, when *Mother Goose's Quarto* was reissued, Alexander Anderson (1775-1870) illustrated the rhyme There Was an Old Woman Tossed Up in a Blanket with a figure of a...

> ...cronish, witchy sort of figure possessed of a long, pointed nose and chin, clutching a broomstick. She sits comfortably on nothing, on air, as she sails through the night, slicing effortlessly through a strong wind. Her bent figure mimics the curve of the crescent moon below her, its shape reiterated in the curve of her cupped hand, lifted, in a gesture of attentiveness, to her ear... With his orchestration of crescent shapes, Anderson tells us that, on the level of poetic metaphor, the old woman is the waning moon. Her sharp features suggest the horns of its crescent shape. (Vandergrift nd)

What follows is the earliest recorded version of There Was an Old Woman Tossed Up in a Blanket (from *Mother Goose's Melody*, approx. 1765):

There was an old woman toss'd in a blanket,
Seventeen times as high as the moon;
But where she was going no mortal could tell,
For under her arm she carried a broom.
Old woman, old woman, old woman, said I!
Whither, ah whither, ah wither so high?
To sweep the cobwebs from the sky,
And I'll be with you by and by.
(Baring-Gould and Baring-Gould 1962: 50)

In the third line, the phrase "no mortal could tell" certainly suggests the Old Woman was not mortal. Otherwise why not just say "where she was going *no one* could tell," or, "no person could tell," or "no man could tell"?

Like Mother Goose, this old woman flies to the moon. With her she carries a broom – just as Mother Goose does in certain 19th century images. According to Opie and Opie (1997: 521) the rhyme Old Woman Tossed Up in a Blanket might have been a dance tune belonging to Morris Dance, an ancient pre-Christian ritual related to similar pan-European rituals, including the Austrian Perchten ceremonies we've discussed in earlier chapters, named after the goddess Perchta. Morris dances are performed by men in costumes, bells, and traditionally either face masks or face paint designed to disguise their identities (Morris Dance 2013).

It was in the second half of the 19th century that American artists began producing significant numbers of witchy Mother Gooses. The years 1865 to 1890 saw the heyday of McLoughlin Brothers, one of America's most prolific publishers of Mother Goose books, and during this time artists depicting Mother Goose "continued to reproduce the grandmother types ... as well as the typical barnyard goose, and the anthropomorphic goose. [However, they] also included wizened crones, or Halloween hags (sometimes on crutches, or with a walking stick; sometimes air-borne on a broom or a goose)." (Vandergrift nd)

Although I stumbled across more than one writer discussing witchy American Mother Gooses (see Warner 1995 and Vandergrift, for example), none included copies in their publications of these fascinating pictures of Mother. And since I wanted to see for myself to what degree these illustrations resembled the American Halloween witch, I decided to carry out a bit of my own research. As a result, over a period of time I collected and studied 18 different images of Mother Goose, all wearing the witch's conical hat, and all dating from the late 1800s through the early 1900s.

My 18 images came from a variety of sources. Thirteen were from Barbara Kissinger's *Mother Goose of Yesteryear* (2008) and five were from the covers of books being sold by Internet antique book dealers. Kissinger's images were found in or on books published by McLoughlin, "Sam'l Gabriel Sons", Graham & Matlock, John C. Winston, Harper's Weekly, Harper's Young People, and Lothrop, while the five antique dealers' books were published by McLoughlin, Holiday, Century Co. and Rand McNally. These 18 images were published in 1880, 1885, 1887, 1888, 1890, 1893, 1898 (2), 1906, 1909, 1913, 1915 (2), 1916 (2), and 1917. Although two images were undated, they nevertheless fall within the date range of the other 16, since they were published by companies that began and folded during this time period.

After gathering my 18 witchy Mother Gooses, I examined each to determine which resembled Halloween-style witches. I was looking for long, warty noses and chins, "evil looks" in the eyes, and/or other characteristics typically found on images of the American Halloween witch. On the basis of the above criteria, I decided that eight of the 18 images qualified as witch-like Mother-Goose figures; these dated from 1880 to 1916.

Actually, almost all of my 18 images give Mother Goose at least some of the characteristics of the Halloween witch. For example, as noted above, all 18 show Mother Goose in the wizard's pointed cone hat (although in two images the point is sliced off). What's more, almost all give Mother Goose a larger than normal nose and chin. However, the noses and chins of some of the witchy eight shoot off into the outer limits, giving Mother a grotesquely and even preternaturally large nose and chin – well outside the range of normal human physiognomy. With many of these eight figures, the nose and chin are not just grotesquely large, but also sharply pointed, making Mother Goose look even less human.

Mother Goose's sometimes large nose could be another indication of a connection between Mother Goose and Holda-Perchta. In some medieval descriptions of her, Holda-Perchta becomes an older woman sporting an extra-large, beak-like nose. According to Motz this might have signified a bird's beak – leftover from a time when the goddess was an actual bird. The long or "iron" nose of Perchta and Holda, says Motz, appears to be the vestige of a bird form of the goddess, and the *Schnabelpercht* – an image of Perchta used in Austrian midwinter processions – does in fact sport a bird's beak (Motz 1984: 163, 156).

The major characteristic shuffling my eight witchy Mother Gooses apart from the others, however, is not the size of their noses and chins, but rather their facial expressions. The "witchy eight" march onto the artist's canvas with facial expressions rendering them far more frightening than friendly. One way artists create malevolent looking characters is by striking an imbalance between emotions playing in the eyes compared to those on the mouth. Several artists have accomplished this with Mother Goose; at the same time they give her angry or vacant eyes, they also show her grinning – sometimes widely – so that one experiences the grin as almost predatory. These Mother Gooses shake out as dangerous, possibly even evil.

One of the best examples of a predatory Mother Goose was created in 1916 by the famous book illustrator Arthur Rackham, who created her for the children's book *Mother Goose: The Old Nursery Rhymes*. (Entering the following in a search engine will probably pull up a copy of this illustration: "*Mother Goose: The Old Nursery Rhymes* Rackham pictures.") Flying on her goose slightly above the heads of four unsmiling children, from under her pointed hat Mother Goose sports a preternaturally large nose and chin. From tip to base her nose is a whopping four inches long. And while her hands are the size of normal human hands, they're attached to wrists no bigger around than a broomstick. She hunches over her goose so far that her chest almost touches her knees, and her face is the greenish hue of moss that rarely sees sunlight. But what renders this Mother Goose truly frightening are her small, vacant, unsmiling eyes set above her unnaturally wide grin.

Another good example, from the 19th and early 20th century American magazine *Harper's Weekly*, is a Mother Goose drawn by Thomas Nast. Cartoonishly tall and thin, Nast's Mother Goose is dancing a jig with a short, chubby Santa Claus (Kissinger 2008: 18). Titled "A Merry Christmas from Harper's Weekly", this drawing dates from January 3, 1880. In it, Mother Goose wears a six-inch-deep neck ruffle with a large white bow-tie tucked under her chin. Over white sausage curls sits a cone hat with the top lopped off a quarter of the way up. Although her nose is long and thin, it's not grossly so, and her chin, while abnormally long, is not pointed.

So far not very scary, right? But the bad is yet to come. Although a strange, crooked grin turns up the corners of Mother's mouth, her brows are angled sharply over her eyes, toward her nose, making her look not only extremely angry but also malevolent. Through half-closed lids she's also looking stealthily out of the far corners of her eyes. In short, Nast has made Mother Goose look mean, shifty and evil. Her eyes, deeply set in black shadow, have bags under them. All in all she looks like she wouldn't mind eating a child or two for lunch.

Eighteen years later, in *Gems from Mother Goose Rhymes, Chimes and Jingles* (1898, McLoughlin), an unknown artist constructed a picture of an old woman riding on a broom with a black cat sitting on the back end of the broom. Although this woman looks identical to many Mother Goose images of the time, she was created as the woman in the rhyme There Was an Old Woman Who Rode on a Broom:

There was an old woman who rode on a broom,
With a heigh, gee-ho, gee-humble.
And she took her old cat behind for a groom,
With a bumble, bumble, bumble.
(Kissinger 2008: 61)

Deep creases creep across this woman's forehead and around her mouth and eyes. Although she's grinning, her brows are tilted angrily down over her eyes and toward her nose, and so, like Rackham's and Nast's Mothers Goose, she has an evil air about her.

From the cover image of an old book called *Mother Goose Old Style* published by McLoughlin Brothers comes a final example of a scary-witchy Mother Goose. Although the book is not dated, McLoughlin closed its doors in the early 1900s, placing both book and image in the date range of our sample. This cartoonish Mother Goose would have no trouble qualifying as a Halloween witch. Seated securely on the back of her goose in a plain and unadorned red gown and cape, she flies high above the clouds, pulling vigorously on a set of short reins fitted into her goose's mouth so that the goose's head is pulled half way backwards. The goose's iris is completely surrounded by its white sclera, making it appear wide-eyed with fright. Not only are this Mother Goose's nose and chin grotesquely large, both end in points as sharp as the point on a pencil. To finish the picture, Mother's mouth is turned down at the corners, and her brows slant angrily over unsmiling eyes.

If we lay these frightening Mother Goose images alongside those showing Mother as benign and rosy-cheeked, the intensity of the fearsomeness of the former is ratcheted up a notch or two. In our sample are three benign Mother Gooses, all dating from the end of our 55-year sample, i.e., from 1915, 1916, and 1917. In the first, published in 1915 by Graham & Matlock, Mother Goose rides high in the sky in a flying chariot pulled by seven white geese (Kissinger 2008: 36). This Mother is full of colour, her gown grass-green, her cape and pointed cap ruby-red, and her Elizabethan neck ruff, wrist ruffs and head covering all snow-white. With her left hand she waves a broom in the air, as if urging her geese onward and upward. Two smiling young girls, ages five to seven, sit facing her. Mother Goose has a gentle, quiet smile on her unlined face, and her brows are lifted high, making her seem full of knowledge, good humour and self-esteem. She's a beautiful grandmother made to look 40-something.

In 1916, Rand McNally published the highly successful and still popular *The Real Mother Goose*, with a colourful, cartoonish and lovable old Mother Goose painted on the front cover by the book illustrator Blanche Fisher Wright. Like Graham & Matlock's Mother Goose, Fisher's too wears a green dress, red cape, a pointed wizard's hat, and an Elizabethan ruff around her neck and wrists. Although her nose and chin are alarmingly long, she has a twinkle in her eye, and her smile is broad and beneficent. As she sails high in the sky on her goose she carries a wicker basket cradling an infant in white swaddling clothes. Mother Goose looks back lovingly at the baby, who with a delighted smile on its face raises its chubby arms toward the sky.

The third beneficent Mother Goose in my sample of 18 images was published in 1917 by John C. Winston Co., on the cover of their book *Mother Goose Nursery Rhymes*. In this image, Mother and her goose are just lifting off the ground, and young children are close to scuffling with each other in order to lay claim to one of the few remaining empty seats on the goose's back. Tucked in Mother Goose's lap, a two-year-old clutches the reins controlling the goose, and behind Mother a three-year-old, head resting against Mother's back, wraps his arms tightly around Mother Goose's waist. Off the back end of the goose dangles a small girl just barely holding on to the rear ends of the goose reins, and three little tykes almost on top of one another clamber up onto the goose's right wing. A tiny boy clutches the goose's right leg, and is in the process of being lifted off the grassy hill from which the ensemble is taking flight. Three other disappointed children raise their arms to climb on board, but have "missed the boat", so to speak.

The large, satisfied smile on the face of this Mother Goose matches the smile in her eyes. A spring, not a winter goddess, she wears a tall daffodil-yellow wizard's hat with a wide, willowy grass-green brim. Waving out of its hatband is a three-foot-long grass-green feather that ends in a tight curl. Although her hair is arranged in short, snow-white ringlets, her face is unlined; like Graham & Matlock's Mother Goose, this one too is a young 40-something.

In conclusion, while these 18 images certainly don't constitute a representative sample of all the Mother Goose images available from their time period, they do show that at least some Mother Goose images from late 19th and early 20th century North America shared several characteristics with the Halloween witch. Most importantly these include body postures, facial features, and facial expressions that make them appear grotesque, frightening and malevolent. That Mother Goose would ever appear frightening is at odds with the fact that in America at least, she is the grand dame of light verse for infants and small children. So why would the patron saint of American toddlers ever be shown as a malevolent, almost predatory creature? From 1697, when Perrault showed her as an ordinary young peasant nursemaid, through the early 1800s, artists seemingly failed to depict Mother Goose as a witch. Why, in the early 1800s, did this change? For quite some time these questions nagged at the back of my mind. And then I managed to snag a publication I'd been having trouble getting my hands on: Ryoji Tsurumi's 1990 article "The Development of Mother Goose in Britain in the Nineteenth Century", published in the journal *Folklore*.

After I read Tsurumi's article, it became clearer to me why Mother Goose eventually became witch-like. Tsurumi says it was after an 1806 production in London of a play starring Mother Goose as a witch, that book and magazine illustrators also began depicting her as a witch. Written by Thomas Dibdin and produced in Drury Lane at the Theatre Royal, the play was *Harlequin and Mother Goose* (Tsurumi 1990), part of the "Harlequinade", a type of theatrical performance that came into vogue in Britain in the early 1700s. The Harlequinade was characterised by stock characters and a standard plot. Characters always included the young lovers Harlequin and Columbine, along with an older man, Pantaloon, and Pantaloon's male sidekick. The plot was simple: Pantaloon and his sidekick tried to break the two lovers apart, an endeavour that always involved chase scenes and constant action including acrobatics and magic tricks performed by Harlequin as he and Columbine are chased from one locale to another by the two older men.

Of course this meant I had to get my hands on a copy of Dibdin's play, which turned out easier said than done. At this point, my free and easy flow of library materials from all over the state of Maine became dry as a canyon gulch. Nowhere in Maine did anyone have a copy of this 200-year-old document. The closest place it could be found was Harvard, and according to my research librarian, Harvard librarians weren't letting it out of their hands. The thought of making the two-hour trip to Boston and then getting to Harvard, its library, and finding my way around it was not a happy one. Then it occurred to me: maybe

Harvard would sell me a photocopy of the script.

I emailed Jenny at the library: "Could you ask if I could buy a photocopy?"

"I don't know how that's done," she said, "but I'll see what I can do."

Miracle of miracles: the next day Jenny emailed me with a photocopy of the 1806 play attached to her email. "I think I've done it! See if you can open this," she wrote. I could. And in old early 19th century typeface, there it was: Thomas Dibdin's *Harlequin and Mother Goose; or, the Golden Egg!: A Comic Pantomime.* 1806. London: Thomas Hailes Lacy.

Although I didn't know it at the time, I was about to be introduced to an utterly fabulous old Mother Goose.

Dibdin's play was an eye-opener. For starters, it explains much of the mystery in the one nursery rhyme we have about Mother Goose, Old Mother Goose When She Wanted to Wander. What's more, it decidedly strengthens the hypothesis that Mother Goose is a goddess in disguise. In Scene One, in the middle of a storm she has raised, Mother Goose opens the play by descending from the skies on the back of her gander and landing in a village churchyard. Immediately the storm clears, a rainbow appears, and Mother Goose vanishes. In the churchyard, villagers are assembled for the wedding of young Collinette to the village's wealthy Squire. Unfortunately, Collinette doesn't love the Squire, she loves Colin. But because the Squire's paid Collinette's guardian (Avaro) more handsomely than Colin could ever hope to, Collinette is stuck with the older man. (Spoiler alert: Later in the play Collinette morphs into Columbine, and Colin into Harlequin.)

After a chorus sings a wedding song for Colinette and the Squire, the Beadle and a "countryman" enter with Mother Goose in tow. She's wanted for witchcraft, the two men tell the Squire. Even though Mother Goose denies she's a witch, the Squire nevertheless orders her to the ducking stool (if she's ducked in the pond and drowns, she's innocent; if she survives, she's a witch – and dies anyway).

Before Mother Goose can drown or re-emerge from the pond's depths, however, Colin jumps in and saves her, and Mother Goose speeds off through the air on her gander. Before disappearing totally, however, she raises the ghost of the Squire's first wife, Xantippe, from her grave in the church cemetery, and Xantippe "shakes her hands at" her ex so that he "runs off terrified".

Scene two takes place at Mother Goose's house in the forest, with an owl and the moon both serving as props: "The front [is] … thick wood, on one side an entrance, on the other thick foliage, etc.; an owl, seated on branch, very prominent in the perspective; a clear blue sky with moon and stars, etc." In this scene Mother Goose sings a song. In stanza one, she sings about the world of nature but in two other stanzas, she orders her supernatural helpers to collect spells she can use to unite Colinette with her rightful lover, Colin:

Then haste from dog rose, briar and bell,
From dingle, brake, or daisied dell,
Collect each potent fairy spell.
Our magic can produce.
To plague yon squire, and to aid
Young Colin to obtain the maid;
And when my orders are obeyed
You'll laugh with Mother Goose.

At this, Mother Goose "waves her stick" (magic wand), and four sprites appear – presumably the helpers who will collect her spells – and dance around her. Next, to repay Colin for saving her from the ducking-stool, she presents him with a goose that lays a golden egg a day – wealth he can use to win Collinette from the Squire. But when Colin offers the first egg to Collinette's guardian Avaro, the greedy man isn't satisfied. Pulling his knife out, he tries to kill the goose to get his hands on all the golden eggs at once. At first Colin stops Avaro. But when the Squire marches onto the stage, the young man becomes fearful he'll lose Collinette, and so shuffles aside to let Avaro plunge his knife into the goose. Before Avaro can kill the bird, however, Mother Goose materialises, prevents the sacrifice, and blasts both Avaro and Colin for their self-centred greediness:

Thou avaricious, selfish, ingrate elf,
Like other fools too cunning for thyself;
Thy ward shall still perplex you by her flight –
Lo! Thus I change the lovers.

And with this, Mother Goose magically transforms all the play's characters into the Harlequinade cast: Colin becomes Harlequin, Collinette turns into Columbine, Avaro becomes Pantaloon, and the Squire morphs into a fourth stock character, the Clown. And then, after pitching the golden egg into the sea, Mother Goose informs Colin and Collinette that until they rescue it they will never be happy. Since Mother Goose has a big heart, however, she also gives Colin/Harlequin a magic wand – but warns him to protect it better than he did her last gift, the goose: "This gift receive, amend what's past, And guard it better than the last…"

At this point, the script instructions read "…the comic business begins here – they [the Squire and Avaro] endeavour to secure Harlequin, who eludes their grasp, and leaps through the face of the clock…" From here on out, most of the rest of the performance is a dizzying Three-Stooges-type chase scene, with characters morphing into acrobats and magicians. Scene five through 17 are chase scenes that quickstep the audience from a country inn, a market town, a "pavilion by moonlight" and a flower garden, to St. Dunstan's church, "the orchestra in Vauxhall Gardens", "a grocer's shop and post office" and a farmyard. Using his magic wand, Colin causes his pursuers to fall off chairs, causes their chairs and tables to rise "six or seven feet" off the stage floor, changes their hats into bells, makes a live duck fly out of a pie, and so forth.

After the chase ends, the threads of the Mother-Goose narrative are taken up again. In "Scene Eighteenth – The Mermaid's Cave", Mother Goose tells her four fairies she's over being angry, and it's time to stop the nonsense:

Your task concludes, your mistress' rage is o'er,
These wandering mortals, I'll perplex no more,
Go wake the favourite of my sprites, who sleep
Within the briny bosom of the deep;
The spell-bound egg, from bondage to redeem,
Reward true love, and end our magic dream.

Notice that Mother Goose refers to Colin/Harlequin and the others as "mortals", clearly implying that she herself is something more (a goddess, perhaps?).

Mother Goose's "favourite sprite" is Oddfish, who "rises out of the sea ... comes forward smacking the serpents that twine around his legs, and takes up two shells and devours the fish..." After Oddfish and his serpents drive the Squire away from Colin and Collinette, Colin pours wine into Oddfish's mouth from his sword and orders the sprite to dive into the sea and retrieve the golden egg. When Colin delivers the egg to Mother Goose she "reconciles all parties". To Colin and Collinette she bequeaths a magical submarine palace, the sides of which are made of dolphins.

In the play's finale, Mother Goose, the Squire, and the Chorus leave the audience with a few thoughts. Among other things Mother Goose mentions laughter: "Accept our wish to pleasure you, And laugh with Mother Goose." For emphasis, the Chorus adds, "And laugh with Mother Goose." This is important because, as we'll see in a later chapter, laughter was actually a very integral and sacred part of pre-Christian theology. Mother ends the entire production with a plea to avoid cracking her golden egg:

Who humbly begs,
On bended legs,
That you, good lack,
Her cause will back,
And scorn to crack,
Her golden egg.

In this play Mother Goose possesses exceptionally powerful magic. Not only can she raise the dead, but with a flick of her "stick" she's able to transform characters into entirely different ones. Furthermore, she gives Colin/Harlequin a magic wand with which he can do anything, limited only by his own imagination. But Dibdin's Mother Goose is clearly more than just a piddling low-level supernatural being or magic practitioner. Far from being a mere priestess, witch, or wood sprite, Mother rises here to the level of deity; she talks about others in the play being "mortals" – indicating that she herself is not one. Mother is immortal – like the gods.

And not only is she a deity, she also seems closely to resemble the deities Holda-Perchta and Aphrodite-Venus. Like Holda, she controls the weather. Also like Holda, she rewards mortals for good behaviour; for saving her from the ducking stool she gives Colin the magic goose, and for retrieving the golden egg she gives Colin and Collinette the right to wed and a submarine palace – the kind of gift Aphrodite, born from the sea, might bequeath them. And of course also like Aphrodite, Dibdin's Mother Goose flies through the air on a goose.

To re-enforce the notion that we are in the realm of the gods, Dibdin refers to three deities from classical mythology: Aurora the Roman goddess of the dawn, Bacchus the Roman god of wine, and Pan, the Greek woodland and shepherd god: on page

10 of the script Mother Goose says, "Now softly see Aurora's blush, Bide cease your revels – hush, hush, hush!" The second classical reference, to Bacchus, comes from the script directions: "Harlequin leaps from the window, smacks his sword, and the rum puncheon descends from the sign post, which he transforms into a fruit barrow, and a painted puncheon, with a Bacchus astride, ascends in its place..." Finally, the show includes a Pandean Minstrel, a reference to the Pan pipes played by the god Pan.

According to Tsurumi it is in this 1806 play *Harlequin and Mother Goose* that Mother Goose is first associated with flying on a goose, with owls, with witches, and with magical powers. Before this play, says Tsurumi, almost all we knew of Mother Goose came from Perrault's *Tales of Mother Goose*, which shows Mother as an ordinary child's nurse, or as a grandmother (who in Britain and France at least gets progressively older as the book is republished). And then seemingly out of the blue comes the Dibdin script. In it, Mother Goose, if not a deity, is at the very least an extremely powerful supernatural, immortal being of some sort. The question is, did this new characterisation of Mother Goose come directly out of Dibdin's imagination? Or was the playwright drawing on already existing folk images of Mother Goose?

According to historian and mythographer Marina Warner portrayals of Mother Goose as witch began in Britain in the late 1700s – before Dibdin's play was produced or published (Warner 1995: 156). Even Tsurumi admits that Mother Goose's ability to fly on the back of a gander may predate Dibdin's 1806 theatre production.

> The appearance of the gander that can fly with Mother Goose on its shoulder in the lore of Mother Goose may belong to an older tradition. Already in the pantomime Mother Goose enters by "descending from the skies mounted on a gander" during the storm which she has raised. (Tsurumi 1990: 32)

As we'll see in a minute I eventually found a bit of circumstantial evidence at least that Dibdin's witchy Mother Goose came not wholesale from his imagination, but from an image of her already set in the minds of British country folk of his time period.

First, however, let's look at the physical appearance of Dibdin's Mother Goose. Fortunately, we have pictures of the actor who played her, Samuel Simmons, dressed in his Mother-Goose stage costume (Mayer 1969: 25). Interestingly, all that sets the costumed Simmons apart from any other early-modern peasant woman is his mask, which has preternaturally large facial features. The mask's chin and nose are extremely long and pointed, with the chin looking almost exactly like someone glued two-thirds of a large sausage onto the end of a human chin. The eyes are opened wider than humanly possible, with irises and pupils unnaturally large. If you were expecting her hat to be black, tall and pointed, you'll be disappointed; here Mother Goose's hat looks more like those worn by American Marines – like a snow-white muffin with its rounded top flattened and slanting backwards.

Dibdin's Mother Goose seemed fond of the "layered look". Over two blouses she's wearing a horizontally-striped vest covered by a shawl – and with a scarf covering the shawl. Also over the vest are two white straps crossing over Mother's breast, forming an "X". At the bottom of her ankle-length white skirt is a black strip, along which six-inch-tall white ducks waddle in a line close behind one another. She's in buckled shoes with two-inch-high clunky heels, and covering her hands and arms are long, black gloves with cut-out fingers. Mother's hair is thin, white, wispy, and a little shorter than shoulder length.

In her left hand she holds a large golden egg, and in her right she's pointing left with her magic wand, which is a little longer than a cane and gradually comes to a point, its handle a carved white goose twice as wide as Mother Goose's hand. What appears to be a live goose stands on Mother Goose's left, its head turned in her direction, its body facing the audience.

So where did Dibdin's Mother Goose come from? Solely out of his own fertile imagination? Or did he draw to any extent on images of her already extant in the minds of British country folk? I found no answer to this question. I did, however, uncover a bit of information about Dibdin – information that might shed some light on the question.

Thomas Dibdin was born in 1771 to songwriter Charles Dibdin and actress Harriet Pitt. As a youth Dibdin was apprenticed in London to one William Rawlins, later to become "sheriff of London". After Dibdin took Rawlins to court for mistreating him but lost his case, he "ran away to join a company of country players. From 1789 to 1795 he played in all sorts of parts..." (Dibdin, Thomas John. 1911) Being a part of a troupe of country actors for six years, one that presumably toured the British countryside producing all kinds of small theatre productions for country folk, would have been the ideal place for Dibdin to learn folk conceptions of Mother Goose. Although only circumstantial evidence, this is tantalising evidence nevertheless.

One thing is fairly certain: unless an older and now-lost "parent" source led to each of them independently, Harlequin and Mother Goose was the original source of the one and only nursery rhyme we have about Mother Goose, Old Mother Goose When She Wanted to Wander, a rhyme still appearing in nursery rhyme books even today (Tsurumi 1990). Dibdin's play fills in many of the missing pieces of the nursery rhyme. For example, we now know who threw the golden egg into the sea and why, and it's now clear why the Squire and the Knave beat Jack up in a dark alley.

It's clearer too what the meaning of the rhyme might be. Although readers in the past might have seen multiple meanings in the narrative, at least one comes through loud and clear – one related to the never-ending cosmic-drama cycle of creation, death and regeneration, all presided over by female deity. At the play's opening, for example, Mother Goose foreshadows the death-and-resurrection theme by raising a woman from the dead. And then, peppering the play throughout are numerous pre-Christian symbols connected to creation, to birth, or to death-and-regeneration. First, the goose, the egg, Mother Goose, the moon, and the sea are all symbols of either birth and creation, or death and rebirth. And second, the egg pitched into the sea and then rescued is powerfully symbolic of death followed by regeneration.

Another part of the rhyme's meaning obviously has to do with the importance of female deity. Everything in the play smacks of female deity. Mother Goose/Goddess controls the weather and raises the dead. All over the world the moon is many times more often connected to female than male deity. I believe the same could be said of the egg. And as we've seen previously, even Colin/Harlequin was originally female, originating from the goddess Helle through the mythic Hellequin.

Chapter 7

Miscellaneous Evidence that Mother Goose Was a Goddess

> *The "great accomplishment" of Christianity was its transformation of goddesses, sorceresses, and fairies into demonic and malevolent figures, whether real or fictitious.*
> Jack Zipes 2013: 77

So far in this book I have tried to show that Mother Goose is actually a goddess in disguise. To do this I've used two streams of evidence. First, similarity: in many ways Mother Goose shows a striking similarity to some of Europe's old goddesses. Not only Mother Goose but her companions and accoutrements too show a heavy resemblance to certain pre-Christian European goddesses and *their* companions and accoutrements. Second, timing: Mother Goose seems to pop up out of nowhere at exactly the same time

European pre-Christians were being dealt their final deadly blow (the Inquisition and mass witch burnings). Instead of abandoning their goddesses, it seems just as likely that some would have attempted to hide them – by dressing them up in disguises.

But is there further evidence to show a Mother Goose-goddess connection? I believe there is. For starters there's the fact that her titles "Mother" and "Old Mother" referred in the past to those humans able to mediate between other humans and the supernatural. What's more, there's the fact that both Mother Goose and the goddess Holda-Perchta have been referred to as "Frau Gode" – which at least one researcher translates as "Mrs. God". And finally there's the fact that the word "goose" is a partial anagram of the word "goddess".

Back in the 1500s – and possibly before – the titles "Mother" and "Old Mother" were conferred upon women known to be deeply in touch with the supernatural: "In the popular literary culture the term 'Old Mother' almost always had some connotation of an intermediary between the everyday world and the world of the supernatural..." "Mother" was also "a term of address for an elderly woman of the lower classes... This use of 'Mother' goes back at least to the 15th century." Later, however, after the great witch persecutions, the same titles became prickly and pejorative (Tsurumi 1990: 30-31).

An example of another "Mother" is Mother Shipton, a legendary British prophetess who, it is claimed, accurately predicted several events during the reign of Henry VIII and beyond, including the great fire of London in 1666; she may have been Ursula Shipton (1488–1561) of Knaresborough, Yorkshire (Shipton, Mother 2013). Thirteen years before Mother Goose starred as a witch with Harlequin at the Theatre Royal, Drury Lane, Mother Shipton starred with him too – also as a witch – in *Harlequin's Museum; or Mother Shipton Triumphant,* which played at Covent Garden in 1793 (Tsurumi 1990: 31).

Yet another bit of proof that Mother Goose is a goddess has to do with the German phrase "Frau Gode". In her *Mother Goose from Nursery to Literature*, Gloria Delamar notes that certain "commentators" refer to Mother Goose as Frau Gode. Delamar says she can't figure out why, since in German the word for goose is "gans", not "gode" (Delamar 1987). In 2005, however, Jane Hammer cleared up the mystery here. Hammer notes that in German literature the goddess Holda too is called Frau Gode, and that the title translates into English as "Mrs. God" (2005: 72). In the past, therefore, both Mother Goose and the goddess Holda were labelled "Mrs. God", giving us a direct verbal conflation of Mother Goose with the ancient Germanic goddess Holda-Perchta.

Finally, the word "goose" is a partial anagram, or word scramble, for the word "goddess". As we'll soon see, in at least one historical instance anagrams and partial anagrams were used to disguise information until it was safe to unveil it. Could someone have anagrammatised "Mother Goddess" into "Mother Goose" as a way of disguising her until it was safe for her to come out of hiding? Here are a few examples of anagrams: "debit card" scrambles into "bad credit". "Conversation" can become "voices rant on", and "election results" can be anagrammatised into "lies – let's recount".

In the anagrams above, every letter in the first word (or set of words) is used in the resulting anagrammatised word (or set of words). Complete anagrams for the phrase "mother goddess" aren't all that classy: some of the best I can scare up (even with an online anagram generator) are "Heeds Dog Storm", "Moth Dogs Deer" and "Ms. Hedged Roots". Complete anagrams for "goddess" are even thinner; they include only two: "Ed's dogs" and "Ed's gods." Because of this scarcity of good anagram possibilities in the phrase "mother goddess", anyone wanting to disguise the identity of the Mother Goddess in a memorable, useful English anagram would be forced to resort to a partial anagram.

And "Mother Goose" is indeed a partial anagram for "Mother

Goddess". In the past, since spelling was not standardised it's entirely possible that someone at one point or another spelled Mother Goose "Mother Gose", and Mother Goddess "Mother Godes". And to get from "Mother Gose" to "Mother Godes" is simple: just add a "d" to "Gose" and shift the "s" to the end of the word. Interestingly, there's a "d" in the word "gander". Coincidence? Maybe. But maybe not.

Dropping the Mother Goddess underground during the early-modern period by hiding her in an anagram would not be the first time Europeans of this era had used anagrams to hide information. In the early 1600s, Galileo sent anagrams to his friend Johannes Kepler that capsulised some of Galileo's most important scientific discoveries. Kepler failed to unscramble the anagrams, but in case anyone else duplicated Galileo's discovery the anagrams would have served as proof that Galileo had snagged the discovery first: "…he's sending the message in code so that at some later date he can always unscramble the code and say, see, as of this date, I had made this discovery." (Glass 2012)

Unscrambled, one anagram revealed Galileo's discovery that the planet Venus, like the moon, has phases. But in the original message were two letters that Galileo couldn't fit into his anagram, an "o" and a "y" – so he just tacked them onto the end of his new anagrammatised word, and they just kind of hang there (Glass 2012). So this wasn't a perfect anagram – just as "goose" isn't a perfect anagram of "goddess". At any rate, the point is, Galileo was using partial anagrams to disguise and hide information in the 17th century – the same century in which Mother Goose pops onto the scene for the first time in history.

One weak link exists in this chain of reasoning, however: the earliest surviving use of the term "Mother Goose" comes from mid 17th century France, and in France she is not "Mother Goose", but "Mere L'Oye". On the other hand, the majority of print matter from the 15th, 16th and 17th centuries has not survived. Much of it consisted of cheap broadsides and chapbooks that were read and then used for wrapping food, for example, or even as lavatory paper (Spufford 1982: 48-50). And chapbooks and broadsides were exactly the kind of print matter a folk figure like Mother Goose would have appeared in. Given that her prototype is a Germanic goddess, Mother Goose could have originated in Germanic lands as Frau Gode, Frau Godes, Mutter Godes or Mutter Gose. Transported to France she would have become Mere L'Oye, and to Britain as Mother Gose/Goose.

However, all of the above begs the question: why exactly did "Goose" become part of Mother Goose's name in the first place – because Mother Goose's prototypes Holda-Perchta and Aphrodite were so closely related to geese? Or because the word "goose" is a partial anagram for the word "goddess"? Alternatively, if one of the prehistoric European goddesses appeared to ancient people primarily in the form of a goose, then the word for the bird we now call "goose" might originally have been the same as the word for "female deity" – or even deity in general.

But whether Mother Goose got her name from Aphrodite's goose, from an anagrammist, or from both, the evidence now seems fairly good that she was indeed a goddess. What kind of goddess, however? One that originated in Europe's pre-patriarchal past? Or one dragged into Europe by immigrant patriarchals? This topic will be the focus of the next chapter.

Chapter 8

Was She Around Before the Patriarchy Crashed into Europe? (Is Mother Goose a Pre-Patriarchal Goddess?)

How old is the goddess disguised as Mother Goose? Could she have survived from a time before patriarchals swarmed over Europe – a time, that is, in which many scholars now believe life was kinder and gentler? Before we dig any deeper into this thorny mystery, it might be good to define "patriarchy" and "pre-patriarchy". Also, we should talk a bit about the relationship between the two. In a nutshell, a patriarchal social system is one ruled by a small, powerful, elite group of mostly males. It includes a complicated and snooty social hierarchy in which everyone is considered "lower" than those one rung above them on the social ladder (Birnbaum 2005: 335; Clark 2005: 394). Typically what holds patriarchal systems together is violence – or the threat of it.

Archaeological and other evidence strongly suggest that patriarchal social systems are relatively new in human history. Although we homo sapiens have been stomping around planet earth for at least 150,000 years, it's only been during the last 0.04 percent of that time – i.e., the past 6,000 years – that we've been plagued by patriarchy:

> [P]atriarchy was an unknown political condition throughout earlier human existence when small, egalitarian, highly dialogic communities prevailed. Even today, small remnants of such societies still exist in corners of the planet that have escaped ... Western colonisation [and I would add "Eastern colonisation" as well]. (Clark 2005: 394)

So pre-patriarchal peoples would be the opposite of patriarchal peoples, right? Not necessarily. After studying the modern pre-patriarchal system of the East-Indian Minangkabau, anthropologist Peggy Reeves Sanday came to the surprising conclusion that pre-patriarchal is not just the reverse of patriarchal. While patriarchal systems are about a small group of elite males hogging all the power and authority, pre-patriarchal systems are not about power at all, says Sanday, but about "maternal symbolism" guiding everything in and about a community – guiding the thinking, behaviour, beliefs, institutions and so forth.

> I began to think of matriarchy not as female rule but rather in terms of the dominant maternal symbolism that defines and guides Minangkabau thought, ceremony, and practice, which the Minangkabau refer to as *adat matriarchaat* (matriarchal customs). (Sanday 2005: 95)

Before the Indo-Europeans began parading into Europe (in the fourth millennium BC), large parts of Europe seem to have been pre-patriarchal. German culture historian Heide Gottner-Abendroth says, "All of Europe ... presumably went through a matriarchal phase of not insignificant duration in the pre-Indo-European period. This is reflected in the European mythology..." (1995: 95) Those in south-eastern Europe ("Old Europe") were agriculturalists who made sophisticated art and probably had a written language. And since they possessed few implements that could be called weapons, and no fortified settlements, they were probably peaceful. The evidence points to them being equalitarian. And they seem to have centred their lives around female deity (Dexter 2005: 143).

When it peaked around 4500 BC, says archaeologist David W. Anthony, "Old Europe was among the most sophisticated and technologically advanced places in the world" and was developing "many of the political, technological and ideological signs of civilization." In the north of Old Europe a few towns of the Cucuteni people, a later and apparently robust culture, grew to more than 800 acres, which archaeologists consider larger than any other known human settlement of the time (Wilford, 2009). A distinguishing feature of these communities was a superabundance of female clay figurines, many of them otherworldly. And then the Indo-Europeans hit town – and that was the end of peaceful, egalitarian Old Europe.

So who were the Indo-Europeans? In many ways they seem the polar opposite of the people they supplanted. They were probably patrilineal, patrilocal and patriarchal. They were warlike, worshipped male gods (the main one being the forerunner of the god Zeus), and were fond of arranging people into categories of "good", "better", and "best". They were not settled agriculturalists but semi-nomadic animal herders. And by about 3500 BC, they had swamped out the peaceful, sophisticated, settled, goddess-centred "Old Europeans" of south-eastern Europe – possibly the most advanced people on the planet at that time (Dexter 2005: 144-46).

Evidence suggests that what sets patriarchals apart and also goes far in explaining why they're so nasty, is their deep-seated fear of not having enough – food, clothing, heat, shelter – it doesn't matter what, they just have a generalised, subconscious fear that the stuff they need is going to run out. This in turn leads them to focus on taking-behaviour (war, violence, theft) and hierarchy (getting "to the top", which means that if things get scarce, those at the top will be the last to suffer) (Studebaker 2008: 192-206). Since patriarchals have honed violent taking-behaviour to a fine art, they long ago mowed down most of the world's pre-patriarchal goddess-centred peoples. Few non-patriarchal societies remain, and those that do are non-patriarchal in certain respects only. Some of these include the Hopi of the American Southwest, the Moso (or Mosuo) of Western China, and the Basques of France and Spain (Studebaker 2008: 46-69).

Although patriarchal systems might not be the exact opposite of pre-patriarchal ones, the two systems nevertheless don't have a whole lot in common. First, while patriarchals teach blind obedience to a small group of elite males at the top of a social hierarchy, the evidence suggests that many pre-patriarchals teach that all individuals are relatively equal, and that very few deserve blind obedience. Second, whereas patriarchal societies more often than not consider pain sacred, pre-patriarchals see pleasure as sacred. Third, while patriarchals focus on fear, pre-pats seem to focus more on risk-taking and adventure. Fourth, most patriarchal societies seem to celebrate warfare, violence and the individual, whereas pre-pats celebrate nonviolence and community. Fifth, while pats focus on "serious" matters like war and human competition, pre-pats are more interested in communal fun, festivities and laughter. Sixth, hoarding money and material possessions is more likely to be found in patriarchal societies, giving things away and sharing resources is found in pre-pat societies (Studebaker 2008: 46-69).

Much evidence too suggests that pre-patriarchal societies

often tended to revolve around a Great Goddess Creatrix who gave birth to the universe and everything in it, including all other deities. Baring and Cashford suggest these societies believed in animism: the idea that everything is powered with the same kind of energy and spirit – even rocks, trees and water:

> In the beginning the Great Mother Goddess alone gives birth to the world out of herself, so that all creatures, including the gods, are her children, part of her divine substance. Everything is living, animated – with soul – and sacred. (1991: 660)

Of course the ancient European pre-patriarchal goddesses differed from place to place and time to time. Interestingly however – from the point of view of this book especially – one pre-patriarchal goddess enjoying popularity over thousands of years was a Neolithic bird goddess (Gimbutas 1991: 231). As we saw previously, Mother Goose herself was viewed as a "bird mother". Even before Perrault published his *Tales of Mother Goose* in 1697, Mother Goose was considered by the French a "sort of mythical fairy birdmother" (Leach, Maria 1950: 751). So it's only logical: if Mother Goose was a bird goddess, and bird goddesses were widespread across pre-patriarchal Europe, then the odds go up that Mother Goose did indeed originate in pre-patriarchal times.

At this point it might be worth our while to zoom in and take a closer look at Europe's Neolithic bird goddess. Often this goddess appeared with the body of a woman but the head of a bird. Although she possessed a woman's trunk, arms and legs, above the shoulders she was almost completely avian. Instead of facing forward, her eyes faced sideways – as birds' eyes do, and where a human's nose should be was a long, curved bird's beak. Often the bird goddess lacked a mouth, her neck was enormously long – like a bird's neck, and she possessed wings or "winglike projections". Although the bird goddess's body possessed all the requisite human parts, it sometimes "bent forward like that of a bird". Her characteristic markings were "chevrons, meanders, parallel or zigzag lines, and the number three". Like the goddess Mari of the Basques, the Neolithic bird goddess was most likely both a giver and taker of life. And like Mari, as taker-of-life she probably morphed into a bird of prey – the vulture, for example, or Mother Goose's guardian the owl (Gimbutas 1991: 230-31).

Modern European folklore too includes women with birdlike characteristics. One example is the "amazingly archaic Baltic" water nymph, the *laume,* who often magically finished a woman's spinning or weaving for her. Although *laumes* looked human, they had the feet of a bird – and if their clothing happened to fall open, you'd see the body of a "hen, a goose or a duck." (Gimbutas 1991: 234) Interestingly, hundreds of miles south of the Baltic Sea, in the Basque area of Baragarza, the goddess Mari too sometimes appears as a woman with the feet of a bird, and her supernatural "servants", the *laminak,* "are beings with human form but the feet of a chicken, duck or goat." (Everson 1989)

UCLA/Harvard archaeologist Marija Gimbutas, who studied them both, does not suggest there's any direct continuity between the Neolithic bird goddess and the modern *laume*. Neither does Rutgers professor Kay Vandergrift suggest any continuity between the Neolithic bird goddess and Mother Goose. Vandergrift does admit, however, that the two are definite look-alikes:

> Certainly no solution of continuity [exists] between Mother Goose and the Bird Goddess of Old Europe... One must acknowledge, however, that the figural characteristics of Mother Goose certainly remember the rich heritage of figuration that precedes it... A child in nineteenth century New York, holding a crisp, new copy of *Mother Goose's Melodies* on her lap, could not possibly have any conception of

> the airborne Aphrodite of Boeotia, or the Bird Goddess of the Sesklo culture, or care about their shared physical attributes. But, just the same, they're there. (Vandergrift nd)

While Gimbutas sees no continuity between the Neolithic bird goddess and the Baltic *laume*, she does see it between Mother Goose's prototype Holda, and the Old European, pre-patriarchal goddess:

> The oral tradition of Germany preserves the ancient goddess of death and regeneration in many forms: in the figure of Hel/Holle, Holla (best known as Frau Holla from Grimms' fairy tales) and as Holda, Berchta, and Perchta… Holla is … a regeneratrix. She brings out the sun, and as a frog, she retrieves the red apple, symbol of life, from the well into which it falls at harvest… The images of Freyja, Valkyrie, and Holla witness the continuity of the Old European goddess as life giver, death wielder, and regeneratrix. She can be young, beautiful, and strong, or old, ugly, and powerful, representing a full cycle from birth to death to rebirth. (2001: 195)

Gimbutas thinks Brigit, another Mother-Goose-like goddess, is also pre-patriarchal:

> Brigid was descended from the Old European great-goddess… It is remarkable that, in spite of both Indo-European and Christian influence, the Irish and Welsh oral tradition and historic records preserved the primary Old European goddesses – especially the life giver and death wielder – with little change since Neolithic times… These goddesses, whose attributes sometimes overlap, are known as Brigid, Ana (or Anu or Danu), the Morrigan, Macha, and Badb. (Gimbutas 2001: 187, 184)

In conclusion, Mother Goose might indeed go back to pre-patriarchal times. She was a bird goddess, and the bird goddess was among the most popular of ancient European goddesses. Also, the evidence that Mother Goose is a veiled version of the Germanic goddess Holda is overwhelming, and if Marija Gimbutas is right that Holda goes back to pre-patriarchal times, then Mother Goose does as well. If so, Mother belongs to the kinder, gentler world that existed before the war-torn Indo-Europeans entered Europe to crush it. Please keep Mother Goose's probable pre-war-and-violence origin in mind while reading the next chapter, which reveals some of the secrets certain Europeans a few centuries ago wanted to make sure made it through dangerous times to reach us today.

Chapter 9

Mother Goose's Secrets Hidden in Nursery Rhymes

> *The history of fairy tales and nursery rhymes ... is a record of strong self-preservation under neglect and deliberate persecution... They were not "respectable"... They were the imbecilities of the peasantry.*
> Darton 1982: 85

At the "end of the beginning" of my research on Mother Goose (see Chapter 1), several questions were nagging me. For instance, did Mother-Goose nursery rhymes and fairy tales carry coded messages generated by our pre-Christian ancestors during a time when pre-Christians were routinely rounded up, roped to stakes, and roasted alive? If so, what exactly were our ancestors trying to tell us? If we'd "break the code", what would we learn?

During the course of my research I eventually came to believe that many nursery rhymes and fairy tales do indeed carry messages left to us by those who came before us. I also now believe that many of the secrets Mother Goose tries to whisper in our third ear concern the easier, happier kind of life she presided over as an ancient Great Goddess. Her view of life is virtually the opposite of that found in, say, the textbook used in most 18th century American schools, the patriarchal *New England Primer*. Remember: what sets patriarchals apart is their deep-seated (yet not fully conscious) fear of never having enough – enough food, shelter, heat, water, protection. Because of their semi-conscious or subconscious fears, patriarchals engage in – and even glorify – taking-behaviours: war, violence, rape, theft and so on. For the same reason, they're also addicted to social hierarchy, a system in which some rise to the top and from there can command things at the drop of a hat (Studebaker 2008).

I believe certain of our forebears lacked this core fear, and so lacked the need for war, interpersonal violence, or social hierarchy. In their minds it was okay if everyone was equal, because there's enough for all and always will be, especially if we all work together and – when it makes sense – pool our resources. For them it was fine as frogs' hair to be zany. Without the need to worry about war, violence and social hierarchy, people had more free time to let loose a little. As a matter of fact, I wonder if behaviour now reserved only for children used to be kosher for adults as well:

> Mother Goose will show newcomers to this world how astonishing, beautiful, capricious, dancy, eccentric, funny, goluptious, haphazard, intertwingled, joyous, kindly, living, melodious, naughty, outrageous, pomsidillious, querimonious, romantic, silly, tremendous, unexpected, vertiginous, wonderful, e-citing, yo-heave-ho-ish, and zany it is. And when we come to be grandmothers, it is just as well to be reminded of these twenty-six attributes. (Opie and Wells 1996: Introduction)

Not all Mother Goose nursery rhymes are pre-patriarchally wonderful. Those that are, however, clash noticeably with the patriarchal view of children. Whereas medieval and early-modern church teachings about children stressed working hard, conforming to standard behaviour, staying "pure", suffering punishment for bad behaviour, and above all obeying adults (children's superiors in the social hierarchy), many Mother Goose rhymes are about just the opposite: having fun, making merry, taking risks, being zany, letting loose, laughing, enjoying one's physical senses, social equality, flouting the rules, and showing kindness to humans and animals alike.

In general, you can tell if a rhyme or fairy tale has been tampered with by comparing it to the following chart, which compares the patriarchal and pre-patriarchal worldviews. While the first column describes the behaviours and values important to patriarchal peoples, the second describes the corresponding (and almost always opposite) behaviours and values important to pre-patriarchals:

Important to Patriarchals	***Important to Pre-Patriarchals***
War	Peace
Obedience	Questioning authority
Social hierarchy	Social equality
Pain	Pleasure, beauty
Fear	Adventure, risk-taking
Self control	Sensuality
Focus, concentration	Creativity, curiosity
Violence	Nonviolence
Seriousness	Laughter, lightness of heart
The individual	The community

Imagine a Viking stomping off to *war* and you will be imagining everything on the patriarchal side of this chart. Of utmost importance is the man's *obedience* to his warrior-band leader, who is higher in the *social hierarchy* than he is. As a Viking this man belongs to a society bursting with *social hierarchy*, including a slave class. His ability to withstand *pain* without flinching is glorified. *Fear* is central to his way of life; as a warrior he must learn above all to *control* it. As a warrior he must also train his mind to *focus and concentrate*, and not wander off in "idle speculation" or flights of zany fancy. *Violence* too is central to this warrior's way of life: the Viking economic system was based on raiding – *violently* taking what others produce instead of producing anything themselves. Although he's no stranger to laughter, war is *serious* business, so this Viking warrior is often *serious*. When he dies, he will be interred in an individual, not a communal, grave, something archaeologists agree means his society places less emphasis on the community than on *the individual*.

Many of the behaviours and values in the second column above seem related to the ability to avoid warfare. For example, since they do war rarely if at all, pre-patriarchal societies have more time and opportunity to be creative, adventurous and nonviolent. Also, with no warriors to train there's no need to glorify pain. Instead, people are actively taught to treasure beauty, music, dancing and the other gifts that come through the five senses – gifts they have more time to develop since time is not wasted warring and then mopping up after each war. As mentioned previously, examples of pre-patriarchal societies include the Hopi of the American southwest, the Moso/Mosuo of the Tibetan-Chinese borderland, the Old Europeans, the peoples of the ancient Indus Valley Civilization, and the ancient Minoans (Studebaker 2008).

It's time now to take a look at some of Mother Goose's nursery rhymes to see what hidden messages they might contain – not just for children, but for adults as well. One of my favourite Mother Goose rhymes is Hey, Diddle, Diddle, the Cat and the Fiddle. Although the oldest version dates from around 1765, a reference to the first line of this rhyme appears almost 200 years earlier – in a 1569 document called *A lamentable tragedy mixed ful* [sic] *of pleasant mirth, conteyning the life of Cambises King of Percia,* by Thomas Preston. The reference reads as follows: "They be at hand Sir with stick and fiddle; They can play a new dance called hey-didle-didle." (Opie and Opie 1997: 240)

Hey Diddle Diddle,
The cat and the fiddle
The cow jumped over the moon.
The little dog laughed
To see such a sport,
And the dish ran away with the spoon.
(Opie & Opie 1997: 240)

Can you even begin to imagine seeing anything like this rhyme in the 17th century *New England Primer*? It's all light-hearted silliness, laughter, rule-breaking, and wild magic (cows can't jump over the moon! Unless, of course, they're magic cows). It's about risk-taking and adventure (the dish ran away with the spoon!). It's about animals and people being equal – a cat plays an instrument we thought only humans smart enough to master.

Interestingly, in 1791 this verse appeared in *Mother Goose's Melodies* with the word "craft" in place of "sport" – which makes for much better rhyming:

The Little dog laugh'd
To see such craft…
(Prideaux 1904; from *Mother Goose's Melody, 1791*)

So why was the wording changed? Could it be because the word "craft" holds connotations of magic and therefore pre-Christian religion? As a matter of fact, an old, obsolete meaning of the word "craft" is indeed "magic or a magical device; a spell" (Webster 1944: 616).

At any rate, at the same time children were reading about a cow jumping over the moon and a little dog laughing at this "craft", *The New England Primer* would be feeding them thrilling stories about dogs dutifully herding cows, cats dutifully catching mice, and Mother dutifully dishing up Father's porridge. As a matter of fact, here's a sampling of a few of the rhyming couplets used by the *Primer* to teach the alphabet; I give you letters "A" through "F":

A In Adam's Fall
We sinned all.

B Thy Life to mend,
God's Book attend.

C The Cat doth play,
And after slay.

D A Dog will bite
A Thief at Night.

E The Eagle's Flight
Is out of Sight.

F The idle Fool
Is whipt at School…

Another memorable Mother Goose rhyme is Diddle Diddle Dumpling, My Son John:

Diddle diddle dumpling, my son John,
Went to bed with his trousers on,
One shoe off, and one shoe on,
Diddle diddle dumpling, my son John.
(Opie and Opie 1997: 288)

Here's a boy following his soul. So what if other boys change into night clothes before crawling between the sheets? Doesn't mean John needs to! John is a nonconformist – something the Puritans would have frowned upon. And then there's the issue of John's dad. Does he reprimand the child for his nonconformist ways? Not. He's "my son John" at the beginning of the rhyme, and "my son John" at the end – even after his eyebrow-raising, nonconformist refusal to change into pyjamas at bedtime. Meanwhile the Puritan texts are preaching that sparing the rod spoils the child.

Another fine goddess-oriented ditty is Jack Sprat Could Eat No Fat, first put down in print (as far as we know) by John Ray in 1670 (Opie and Opie 1997: 280):

Jack Sprat could eat no fat;
His wife could eat no lean;
So 'twixt them both they cleared the cloth,
And lick'd the platter clean.
(Hale 1905: 80; from *The Only True Mother Goose's Melodies,* 1833)

Or,

Jack Sprat could eat no fat,
His wife could eat no lean;
And so between them both, you see,
They licked the platter clean.
(Opie and Opie 1997: 279-80).

In *The New England Primer,* and even in the later McGuffey Readers, Mother is still serving Father's porridge. Not so in the land of the Sprats, where Mother and Father work together as a team, each equal to the other, each equally valuable. There's no fighting between Jack and his wife, only a clean platter – the result of both getting their needs met. The ending of the rhyme is a fun surprise: although this husband and wife both have limitations, by working together their limitations no longer matter. In this small, 24-word rhyme we get creativity, light heartedness, humour, and respect for human differences all rolled into one.

In the 16th and 17th centuries "Jack Sprat" was a name for dwarfs (Opie and Opie 1997: 280). It should be noted that in her fairy tales and rhymes both, Mother Goose often mentions people who fall outside the physical norm. It's obvious she considers them as valuable as anyone else – just as any mentally healthy mother would love her children whether they were four feet tall or eight.

Ride a cock horse to Charing-Cross,
To see a young woman
Jump on a white horse,
With rings on her fingers
And bells on her toes,
And she shall have music
Wherever she goes.
(Hale 1905: 40; from *The Only True Mother Goose's Melodies,* 1833)

Why is this one pre-patriarchal? Because it's about our senses, our capacity to revel in our abilities to hear, feel, smell, taste and see. "She shall have music wherever she goes" suggests the author considers music and the enjoyment of it good things, not "acts of the Devil" or a waste of time that could be spent working, praying or raking the churchyard. What it's not about is passive women sitting at home mending clothes. This young woman not only rides horses, she "jumps" on her horse and gallops off out into the world looking for adventure.

In earlier versions of this rhyme, the woman is old: "The above wording is that commonly known today but early versions do not agree in their descriptions of the lady. She is 'an old woman' (1784), and has later (c. 1790) 'a ring on her finger, A bonnet of straw, The strangest old woman that ever you saw'." She's also old in Mother Goose's Quarto (c. 1825). Sound a bit like a magical Mother Goose to you?

According to De Angeli (1954) the next rhyme "is thought to be one of the most ancient, going back hundreds and hundreds of years...":

One misty, moisty morning,
When cloudy was the weather,
I chanced to meet an old man
Clothed all in leather;
Clothed all in leather,
With a strap beneath his chin.
How do you do, and how do you do,
And how do you do again?
(de Angeli 1954: 17).

Actually this rhyme is the first stanza in an old ballad, The Wiltshire Wedding. Although first published around 1680 as a broadside (Opie and Opie 1997: 370), the ballad could of course be far older. Why is this rhyme pre-patriarchal? First, because nature opens it, with "mist", "clouds" and the weather taking up the first two lines. Second, it's about positive human relationship, with an emphasis on politeness, civility and subtle light-hearted humour. This is fun to read aloud. When you do, make the word "clothed" into two syllables: "clothe-" and "ed" (rhyming with "said").

Before Christianity swept through Europe, religion was nature-oriented. Concerned as it is with winter, cold, snow, wind, and the way animals interact with nature, handle its vagaries, and shelter themselves, the following nursery rhyme seems pre-Christian. Also seemingly pre-Christian is its sensitivity to, and ability to empathise with, animals:

The north wind doth blow, And we shall have snow,
And what will poor robin do then? Poor thing!
He'll sit in the barn
And keep himself warm,
And hide his head under his wing,
Poor thing!
(Hale 1905: 31; from *The Only True Mother Goose's Melodies,* 1833)

In Little Boy Blue, instead of being violent, discipline is a gentle rebuke:

Little boy blue, come blow your horn,
The sheep's in the meadow, the cow's in the corn,
What! Is this the way you mind your sheep,
Under the haycock fast asleep?
(Hale 1905: 11; from *The Only True Mother Goose's Melodies,* 1833)

In Milk-man, Milk-man, mistakes and accidents aren't considered deserving of punishment, but are instead to be laughed at. To be able to laugh at yourself says the main character, is a good thing. At the end of the rhyme, an unexpected and zany thing happens:

Milk-man, milk-man, where have you been?
In Buttermilk Channel up to my chin,
I spilt my milk, and I spoilt my clothes,
And got a long icicle hung to my nose.
(Hale 1905: 96; from *The Only True Mother Goose's Melodies,* 1833)

Unlike *The New England Primer,* which emphasises a life for children full of drudgery, duty and dullness, Jack Be Nimble is all about movement for the fun of it, testing one's physical prowess, and perfecting one's athletic ability.

Jack be nimble,
Jack be quick.
Jack jump over
The candlestick.
(Opie and Opie 1997: 267)

It's just plain fun to move and jump! On the other hand, the rhyme might also be about magic: "Candle-leaping both as a sport and as a form of fortune-telling was practiced in England for some centuries, and possibly engendered this rhyme." (Opie and Opie 1997: 267-68) If you could jump over the candle without killing the flame, you would have good luck for the entire year (Baring Goulds 1962: 194 n. 53).

Since it's referred to in print in a 1701 anonymous poem called The Heaven-Drivers, we know that the rhyme Handy-Spandy, Jacky Dandy is well over 300 years old.

Handy-spandy, Jacky dandy,
Loves plum-cake and sugar candy.
He bought some at a grocer's shop,
And pleased away went hop, hop, hop.
(Hale 1905: 82; from *The Only True Mother Goose's Melodies,* 1833)

There Was an Old Woman lived Under a Hill is a "self-evident proposition" – a philosophical form much more popular in the 17th and 18th centuries than it is today (Opie and Opie 1997: 519):

There was an old woman
Liv'd under a hill,
And if she isn't gone
She lives there still.
(Prideaux 1904; from *Mother Goose's Melody, 1791*)

For our purposes, what's interesting about this rhyme is that its old woman might have supernatural powers akin to Mother Goose's. First, in the past, the power to enter hills was considered a supernatural, magic ability. In early-modern Britain, for example, "cunning folk and witches could enter into fairyland by going into a hill or beneath a lake…" (Wilby 2005: 147)

At the end of his article "Tenacity in Religion, Myth, and Folklore: The Neolithic Goddess of Old Europe Preserved in a Non-Indo-European Setting", Michael Everson suggests that in the nursery rhyme There Was an Old Woman Liv'd Under a Hill an ancient European Great Goddess has been remembered:

> There is one final word which may serve to remind us of the importance of the Goddess in prehistory as a legacy and heritage in our own mythology. It is a word which is fitting in the most literal sense: for it could fit easily into the folklore of any European culture of the present day, be it Basque, Greek, Celtic, Germanic, or Slavic. Fittingly too, it is the word of a woman, the word of our own Mother Goose: *There was an old woman Lived under a hill, And if she's not gone She lives there still.* (Everson 1989)

In the next rhyme, the child Mary is contrary but no one is punishing her for it! Definitely a pre-patriarchal piece:

> *Mistress Mary, quite contrary,*
> *How does your garden grow?*
> *With silver bells and cockle shells,*
> *And pretty maids all in a row.*
> (de Angeli 1954: 78)

As mentioned earlier, not all Mother Goose rhymes are pre-patriarchal. Since patriarchals have been mingling with Europeans since the arrival of the Indo-Europeans, they've left their footprint on several Mother-Goose rhymes. It's time to see how. Look out, because here comes a heaping plateful of fear, violence and social hierarchy.

I have no doubt that a large part of the reason the Woman Who Live in a Shoe was so mean to her offspring was because she was forced to bear too many. Violent physical punishment puts us bang into the belly of patriarchal society, as does women forced to bear children until they drop from physical or mental exhaustion. That it appears undeserved makes the violent physical punishment in this rhyme all the worse:

There was an old woman who lived in a shoe,
She had so many children she didn't know what to do;
She gave them some broth without any bread;
She whipped them all soundly and put them to bed.
(Opie and Opie 1997: 522)

This rhyme goes back at least to the late 18th century, a version of it appearing in a 1797 publication called *Infants Institutes*. In this 1797 version, the overwrought mother actually tries to murder her children and then goes out hunting for coffins:

There was a little old woman, and she liv'd in a shoe.
She had so many children, she didn't know what to do.
She crumm'd 'em some porridge without any bread;
And she borrow'd a beetle, and she knocked 'em all o' the head.
Then out went th' old woman to bespeak 'em a coffin,
And when she came back, she found 'em all a-loffeing.
(Opie and Opie 1997: 522)

Likewise, the rhyme Goosey, Goosey Gander has also been painted over with violence:

Goosey, goosey gander,
Whither shall I wander?
Upstairs and downstairs
And in my lady's chamber.
There I met an old man
Who would not say his prayers.
I took him by the left leg
And threw him down the stairs.
(Emerson 1988: 48)

In 1833, *The Only True Mother Goose Melodies* offered a variant of this, with "left leg" replaced by the phrase "hind legs":

Goosey, goosey, gander, where does thou wander?
Up stairs and down stairs, and in my lady's chamber;
There I met an old man that would not say his prayers,
I took him by his hind legs and threw him down stairs.
(Hale 1905: 77)

The Baring Goulds suggest that the second half of this rhyme was a later add-on, and refers to "cruel" children pulling the legs off "the insect we know as daddy-longlegs, harvestman, or crane-fly..." This add-on, they believe, was lifted from the following rhyme:

Old father Long-Legs
Can't say his prayers:
Take him by the left leg
And throw him down the stairs.
And when he's at the bottom,
Before he long has lain,
Take him by the right leg,
And throw him up again.
(Baring-Gould and Baring-Gould 1962: 70)

Tellingly, in the earliest recorded (1784) version of this rhyme, there was no violence whatsoever:

Goose-a, goose-a, gander,
Whither shall I wander?
Up stairs, down stairs,
In my lady's chamber;
There you'll find a cup of sack
And a race of ginger.
(Opie and Opie 1997: 224)

Everyone knows this one:

Bah, bah, black sheep,
Have you any wool?
Yes, marry have I,
Three bags full;
One for my master,
One for my dame,
But none for the little boy
Who cries in the lane.
(Prideaux 1904: 58; from *Mother Goose's Melody, 1791*)

In this rhyme, the sheep is part of a social hierarchy that makes some "masters", and others inferior to masters. Also, "bad" behaviour and punishment are emphasised. No matter what the reason, it's unmanly for boys to cry. In more recent books this rhyme is often less harsh, ending with lines like, "And one for the little boy who lives in the lane" – an ending far more in keeping with pre-patriarchal values.

Here's another rhyme switching suddenly from light heartedness to the darkness of patriarchy:

I will sing you a song,
The days are long,
The woodcock and the sparrow;
The little dog has burnt his tail,
And he must be hanged tomorrow.
(Opie and Opie 1997: 469-70)

Although in 17th and 18th century England it was considered "normal" to kill unwanted dogs by hanging them (Opie and Opie 1997: 470), I'd be willing to bet that this rhyme is the work of an angry, fearful child who replaced the last lines of the original verse with two of his own. The first part of this verse is markedly pre-patriarchal. The senses are evoked with pleasant noises, feelings and sights: the singing of songs, the aromas, warmth and bright colours of long summer days, the sight of wild birds flying or perched on limbs. There's not even a hint of violence.

And then, totally incongruously, the poem lunges into gratuitous violence. And not just any kind of violence, but an inexplicably cruel one: a dog accidentally burns its tail – bad enough – but then it gets punished for it? Or so it seems. Also, in the second part of the rhyme we move out of the natural world and into the arena of domesticated animals – the dog.

The next one's chock full of physical violence, mental violence, and implied inequality between the sexes:

Once in my life I married a wife,
And where do you think I found her?
On Gretna Green, in velvet sheen,
And I took up a stick to pound her.
She jumped over a barberry-bush,
And I jumped over a timber,
showed her a gay gold ring,
And she showed me her finger.
(Hale 1905: 39; from *The Only True Mother Goose's Melodies,* 1833)

Physical violence ("I took up a stick to pound her") and mental violence ("I showed her a ring, and she showed me her finger" i.e., the use of material possessions to direct someone's behaviour and shape her future) dominate this rhyme. About love, caring, cooperation, or any other positive emotion or behaviour we hear nothing.

I give the next one a mixed review:

Lavender blue, and rosemary green, When I am king, you shall be queen;
Call up my maids at four o'clock,
Some to the wheel, and some to the rock;
Some to make hay, and some to shear corn,
And you and I will keep the bed warm.
(Baring-Gould and Baring-Gould 1962: 113)

Although it's about the enjoyment of the senses (luxuriating in bed in the morning instead of working "at the wheel" or "on the rock"), it's also about social hierarchy; in a patriarchal system, people are shaken out into piles – those who are "good" enough only for hard labour shake out into one pile, and those who are "better" shake into another.

The next verse is a shortened version of an old ballad first appearing in print between 1672 and 1685 and called Diddle Diddle, or, The Kind Country Lovers (Baring-Gould and Baring-Gould 1962: 114 n. 7):

Cock a doodle doo!
My dame has lost her shoe,
My master's lost his fiddlestick,
And knows not what to do.
(Opie and Opie 1997: 149)

Not only does Cock a Doodle Doo embrace a great way of pummelling people (social hierarchy – "my master"), it's also a complete downer. In it there's no magic, adventure, daring, wilderness, sensuality, humour or awesomeness. It's about trouble and trouble only – with no solution given. A healthy rhyme would have provided a creative solution, or a solution that involved perseverance, wit, or some other kind of non-violent intelligence. On the other hand, de Angeli adds a second verse, which shapes things up a bit by adding a creative solution and some fun (dancing):

Cock-a-doodle-doo!
What is my dame to do?
Till master finds his fiddlestick,
She'll dance without her shoe.
(1954: 78).

Jacky in See-saw, Margery Daw needs to join a labour union:

See-saw, Margery Daw,
Jacky shall have a new master;
Jacky must have but a penny a day,
Because he can't work any faster.
(Opie and Opie 1997: 350)

If he dawdles out of spite or indifference, yes, it might be fair to dock Jacky's wages – but the rhyme suggests his slowness comes from illness or disability. Where's the fairness in punishing the disabled? And why does Jackie or anyone else for that matter need a "master"?

One of the most famous Mother-Goose rhymes of all is actually a lullaby: Hush-a-by Baby. When I asked a friend – who probably hasn't heard it for decades – to recite this lullaby, she cranked it out with barely a thought. She was totally amazed at herself. After completing the feat she sat motionless on my living room couch with her jaw dropped for several seconds. According to the Opies, this is the best known lullaby in either England or America, "regularly crooned in hundreds of thousands of homes at nightfall."

Hush-a-by baby
On the tree top,
When the wind blows
The cradle will rock.
When the bough breaks,
The cradle will fall,
Down tumbles baby
Cradle and all.
(Prideaux 1904; from *Mother Goose's Melody, 1791*)

What are we to make of the violence in this song? A baby hangs from a tree in a cradle, and we're told that at some point cradle, tree limb and baby all three will crash to the ground. At best the poor child will experience sheer terror as it falls, and at worst the fall will hurt, cripple, or even kill it. Is it a patriarchal tale? It might seem so – especially when you compare it to beautiful lullabies like, Bye Baby Bunting:

Bye, Baby Bunting,
Father's gone a hunting,
Mother's gone a milking,
Sister's gone a silking,
And Brother's gone to buy a skin,
To wrap the Baby Bunting in.
(Hale 1905: 20; from *The Only True Mother Goose's Melodies,* 1833)

In Baby Bunting, peace, love, and caring abound. To gather what baby needs – milk, corn and meat for food, a fur blanket for warmth – the entire family goes out hunting, milking, silking and buying. There's human interaction here, a coordinated family meeting family needs. Unlike the Hush-a-by Baby, this one is cradled in deep love.

In all likelihood Baby Bunting is a very old rhyme. Among the evidence for its great age is its structure, which uses much alliteration – a major characteristic of Old English poetry. Every line but one in this rhyme alliterates: Mother milks, Sister silks, Brother buys, and baby is "Baby Bunting". "Bunting" apparently is an old word of endearment for babies. It means "short and thick … as a plump child" (Baring-Gould and Baring-Gould 1962: 226 n. 6). In addition, the family in the rhyme is wrapping its infants not in cloth but in animal skins, and it's getting its meat from hunting. Since a silking machine is one used for removing the silk from corn (Webster 1944: 147), my guess is that "silking" here has nothing to do with the cloth, but with removing the stringy fibbers that grow between ears of corn and their husks.

Getting back to Hush-a-by Baby though – is it patriarchal or not? On the face of it, it might seem so, and yet historian and mythographer Marina Warner says no. According to Warner, English lullabies like Rock-a-bye Baby include serious violence in order to prevent the violence from actually happening.

> Many lullabies, like the most famous English example of all, "Hush-a-bye Baby," tell a tale that is characteristically set in the future… The end foreshadowed can be benign, the "golden slumbers" from *The Beggars' Opera* … or much more commonly, fatal, the "Down will come baby, cradle and all." Such nightmare possibilities are uttered to prevent them happening, either in the impending dream world or in reality – a manoeuvre akin to a blessing in the form of a curse, the "Break a leg" variety. (Warner 1998)

From Italy here's another example of a "break a leg" kind of lullaby:

> *Fai la nanna, che tu crepi, che ti vengano a piglia' I preti! Ninna, oh! nanna, oh! Questa bimba a chi la do? ... La daro all' Omo nero che la tenga un giorno intero.* (Go to sleep, may you die in your sleep, That the priest comes to take you to keep. Ninna oh ninna, oh! To whom shall I give this little girl? ... To the bogeyman I'll give her. So that he'll keep her a whole day long.) (Warner 1998)

According to historian Joanna Hubbs, Russian peasant lullabies were magic spells – sung to children to make them strong and healthy:

> As the child grew, the mother cast her spells upon it with lullabies: the word "*baiat*" (to sing these songs) also means "to charm". She raised it with incantations in the same manner as she invoked the fertility of the earth, with songs and rituals intended to make plants flourish. (Hubbs 1988: p. 59)

Along these same lines, the original purpose of baby rattles was not to entertain babies or to develop their hearing, but to frighten away any evil spirits lurking around the cradle (Warner 1998). Of course a rattle isn't going to scare anyone or anything unless it has some kind of magic associated with it – perhaps from an incantation sung over it, or an herbal concoction rubbed into it.

In sum, although the collections of nursery rhymes attributed to Mother Goose include violent, hierarchical ones, they include gentler, lighter ones as well. Is it possible that the source of the gentler ones is a strain of pre-patriarchal culture that has survived in pockets of Europe for hundreds and even thousands of years? If so, these gentler verses might open a window or two into the possible worldview of at least some of our ancient European ancestors, and into the kinds of lives they might have led. Whereas the violent, hierarchical verses tell youngsters to know their place, work hard, and solve problems through violence, the gentler democratic ones teach them to play, have fun, respect everyone equally (One Misty, Moisty Morning), and solve problems not with violence but through cooperation (Jack Sprat Could Eat No Fat). And, while the patriarchy tells children disobeying their parents is the gravest of sins, Mother Goose says grown-ups make mistakes, too, and can be fairly silly at times (Milk-man, Milk-man).

In the next section, we'll look at messages Mother Goose sends us through her fairy tales. Most agree that originally fairy tales were meant less for children than for adults (although children in the past were considered adults far earlier than they are today). Mother Goose's fairy tales seem to open even more windows into the world of the gentler past – and sometimes even a door or two.

Part II

In the fairy tale, the ancient faith survived.
Kurt Seligmann 1971: 177

Chapter 10

Mother Goose's Fairy Tales

> *Magical beliefs were passed on by word of mouth; behind ploughs, at spindles, on river banks and by hearths; magical rituals were performed in kitchens, in bedrooms, by roadsides and on hillsides under cover of darkness.*
> Wilby 2005: 255 (speaking about 16th, 17th and 18th century Britain)

We've already seen that the fairy tale Mother Holla is deeply connected to Mother Goose, but at least one other fairy tale too connects intimately with Mother: The Goose Girl at the Well. In this Brothers Grimm tale, Mother Goose herself makes an appearance. The basic plot of the story is this: a young count passes several tests set for him by a wise old woman who keeps geese, thereby winning the right to marry a princess. At the beginning of the tale, the old woman asks the count to lug her load of goose feed up a mountain to her hut. Although the load is heavy, the route arduous, and the man suffers, the woman will not let him off the hook: he must carry out his task to the end. Upon arriving at the old woman's hut the count meets her ugly daughter (the Goose Girl), after which the old woman sends him on his way with a gift: a book fashioned out of an emerald.

Next the count stumbles upon a castle, and when he opens his emerald book in front of the queen, a pearl falls out – the same kind of pearls that fell from her daughter's eyes whenever the girl cried. After this daughter said she "loved him like salt" (without which food is tasteless) the king had disowned her. When the king, queen and count journey back to the home of the old woman to recover the princess, the count gets lost and spies the Goose Girl at a well, under moonlight. She's morphed into a beautiful woman, and he falls in love. They marry and live happily ever after.

Many of the same motifs appear in this tale as in the only rhyme we have in which Mother Goose is named specifically: Old Mother Goose When She Wanted to Wander. Like Mother Goose in the rhyme, the old woman in this fairy tale too knows deep magic, keeps geese, and lives in the forest unmarried. Like Mother Goose, she too has the power to make people shapeshift. Instead of mothering a son, however, in this tale Mother Goose mothers a daughter. As in Old Mother Goose When She Wanted to Wander, the powerful people in this fairy tale also try to hurt Mother Goose's child. Finally, like Mother Goose in the rhyme, this woman too associates with an owl and the moon:

> The daughter sat down beside her, took her spinning-wheel, and twisted the threads as nimbly as a young girl... At last something rustled at the window, and two fiery eyes peered in. It was an old night-owl, which cried, "Uhu!" three times. The old woman looked up just a little, then she said, "Now, my

> little daughter, it is time for thee to go out and do thy work." She rose and went out… At last she came to a well, with three old oak-trees standing beside it; meanwhile the moon had risen large and round over the mountain, and it was so light that one could have found a needle. (Grimm et al 1972: 730-31)

Like Mother Goose in Charles Perrault's picture of her, this old woman also spins by the hearth:

> The old woman was standing on the threshold, and the girl was about to relate what had befallen her, but the old woman laughed kindly, and said, "I already know all." She led her into the room and lighted a new log. She did not, however, sit down to her spinning again, but fetched a broom and began to sweep and scour. "All must be clean and sweet," she said to the girl.

The Goose Girl at the Well seems to be a pre-patriarchal tale, including not only a powerful older woman, but also a highly respected man who deeply reveres elderly women (i.e., female deity) and is handsomely rewarded for it. Could Thomas Dibdin have heard this tale and used it (along with others long lost) to create his Mother Goose? Although The Goose Girl at the Well is a German fairy tale collected by the Brothers Grimm, there's no reason it or a similar tale could not have travelled to the English countryside.

Before we go any further with fairy tales, we need to pin them down. How are they different from other kinds of literature? Although fairy tales are usually classed as folklore, they stand out markedly from other kinds of folklore. For example, although they often begin and end in the family sphere they take place mostly in a "world of enchantment" in which time, place and characters are only vaguely identified ("Long, long ago, in a land far away, there lived a princess…"), and in which powerful helpers usually assist the main character in passing certain tests.

For example, in Charles Perrault's version of Cinderella the story opens with Cinderella living in the family sphere with her father, stepmother and stepsisters. She probably enters the world of enchantment when a powerful helper – a fairy godmother – waves her wand and turns a pumpkin into a carriage, mice into horses, and lizards into lackeys so Cinderella can attend the ball (although some might say she entered the enchanted world as soon as her father married her stepmother). Cinderella is tested: she must return from the ball each night before the stroke of midnight and she must wait patiently while the prince tries her shoe on almost every other woman in the kingdom. By passing these tests she earns the right to marry the prince, and thus returns to the family sphere at the story's end (by marrying the prince and creating her own family).

Another fairy tale that illustrates our definition of the genre is The Golden Goose, a story collected by Jacob and Wilhelm Grimm. At the beginning of this tale, Simpleton is living at home with his birth family. But when he is kind to an old man in the forest, the man presents the boy with a magic goose, moving Simpleton out of his birth family and into the land of enchantment. As soon as they touch it, people stick fast to the goose, and so Simpleton soon finds himself at the head of a long line of people stuck fast together. With his entourage, Simpleton travels through an unnamed land ruled by an unnamed king who is worried sick about his daughter, because she never laughs. The king has offered to marry his daughter to the first man who can nudge her into laughter. Merely seeing Simpleton's entourage sends the princess into a fit of laughter, and so Simpleton marries the princess – returning him to the family sphere.

Another example is Vasilisa the Fair, a Russian fairy tale collected by Aleksandr Afanas'ev. Before Vasilisa's mother dies, she gives her daughter a magic doll. Later Vasilisa is forced to work for Baba Yaga, a frightening woman in the woods who subjects the young girl to several difficult tests. With the doll's help Vasilisa manages to pass each, however, after which she leaves Baba to wander the countryside. Soon an old woman gives Vasilisa work as a spinner and weaver, and after spinning and weaving a shirt for the king, he marries her – thus returning Vasilisa to the family sphere.

How old are fairy tales? Although no one knows for certain, the overwhelming consensus is they didn't appear until the Middle Ages. Derek Brewer thinks they began in the late Middle Ages (1300s-1400s), while Jack Zipes thinks they began in the early Middle Ages (400s-900s). Zipes, however, says few (if any) were written down before it was safe to do so – i.e., during the late Middle Ages. According to Zipes, although many fairy tale motifs appear in "pre-Christian epics, poems, myths, fables, histories, and religious narratives," the fairy tale itself, as we know and love it today, didn't begin to take shape until somewhere between 400 AD and 900 AD – with 400 AD, remember, being roughly the time Christianity began marching into Europe (Zipes 2001b: 846-47).

In contrast, Derek Brewer suggests fairy tales began in the late Middle Ages. "Perhaps the fairy tale as we know it took on something like its present form in the late Middle Ages, though the elements go back into antiquity." (2003:16) Evidence for this late date for fairy tale beginnings: before the mid 1400s no one had recorded any fairy tale – at least we know of none recorded before this time. In other words, even though hundreds if not thousands of European scribes had been copying books and other written materials long before the mid 1400s, there's no record of them ever recording a fairy tale.

To recap, most think fairy tales didn't begin until Christianity waltzed into Europe. However, at least one scholar – Derek Brewer – thinks they didn't begin until the 1300s or 1400s AD. This was about 50 years after European Inquisitors acquired the right to torture pre-Christians (in 1252 AD) (Thurston 2001: 37), and during the time the *Malleus Maleficarum*, the "Hammer of the

Witches" first appeared. To say the least, for non-Christians this was a difficult time indeed.

If fairy tales were at one time subversive revolutionary communiqués, how exactly would they have been passed on from one person to the next? Especially after the witch persecutions began to heat up in the early-modern era (16th-18th centuries), it would have been exquisitely dangerous to be caught passing along any religious beliefs but the Christian kind. Even when the tales were told in secret code the transmission would have needed to take place in extreme secrecy. Davidson and Chaudhri note that with the invention of the cheap "chapbook" in the 1500s, many fairy tales, and especially perhaps the literary ones, travelled rapidly around Europe, carried by itinerant peddlers from town to town and village to village (2003: 1-2).

Marie-Louise von Franz describes a fascinating example of one way oral fairy tales were disseminated by itinerant peddlers. In 1926, one Father Bramberger, an Austrian Catholic priest, published a book of fairy tales called *Marchen aus den Donaulande*. Approximately one fourth of the tales in the book were collected from "Old Dog Girl", an elderly itinerant peddler and storyteller. Travelling the countryside, Old Dog Girl sold "shoe laces and the like" and also took children aside to tell them her tales in exchange for which the children's parents would serve her a good hot meal. Adults were not allowed into Old Dog Girl's storytelling sessions, and "Father Bramberger himself had to pay her with many sausages before he was allowed into the presence of the children to write down those stories." (von Franz 1997: 15)

Two facts stand out here. First, as an itinerant, if Old Dog Girl got into trouble, she would be practised at quickly and quietly moving on – with no one knowing exactly which direction she might have taken. Second, she told her tales to children, and children only. Since no adults were allowed into the story sessions, no adults could be quizzed by authorities about what this woman was telling their children. And if any authority insisted upon sitting in on a session, Old Dog Girl could easily "tidy up" her tales.

In other words, one way pre-Christians could have passed on their religion would have been through itinerant storytellers. If necessary, such transients could vanish in a hurry, leaving settled villagers safe from accusations they were teaching their children non-Christian ideas. Although the children might not understand the code in the tales they heard, at least the ideas would be transmitted from one generation to the next, and people must have hoped that at some point in the future it would be safe to de-code the stories and resume practising their spirituality openly.

If you think fairy tales were created specifically for children, however, you'd be wrong. Even the Brothers Grimm admitted fairy tales were not created just for children. They did, however, admit to tinkering with their tales to make them "suitable" for middle-class children. According to 19th century German standards, this required toning down the sex and ramping up the violence. The Grimms swept their tales clean of references to sexuality. A good example is Rapunzel. Did you know Rapunzel and the prince tumbled into a bit of lovemaking in the tower that led to a pregnancy for the girl? Probably not. The Grimms didn't consider the fact suitable for children and so removed it from the tale (Tatar 2012: xlviii).

The Grimms also padded the endings of their tales with violence, presumably to help German children see that the consequences for misbehaviour are severe. At the end of the original Rumpelstiltskin tale, for example, Rumpelstiltskin gets furious, yes – someone's guessed his impossible name! – but he doesn't stomp so hard he splits himself in two as the Grimms would have us believe. On the contrary, he only flies out of the window on a wooden spoon (personal communication with Michael Bachem, former chair of the Dept. of German, Russian and East Asian Languages, Miami University in Ohio). The Brothers Grimm also amped up the sexism in their tales, adding, for example, several chores to the list Snow White did for the Seven Dwarfs in exchange for their protection from her stepmother. And after collecting their tales from several different German women, which sometimes gave them multiple versions of the same tale, the Grimms willy-nilly combined these versions into "so-called contaminations, so that two, three, even four versions of one story came to represent a Grimm fairy tale for posterity." (Paradiz 2005: 63)

In pre-patriarchal tales we find little if any casual violence, a lack of shyness about sexuality, and active, intelligent and mobile women. In some fairy tales the heroines are still their strong, smart pre-patriarchal selves. We know less about such tales because they aren't ones Walt Disney and other Western power-people have held up for public scrutiny. At any rate, in all of the following fairy tales the heroines shine with intelligence, courage and assertiveness:

- **The Twelve Huntsmen:** To win the prince she loves, a princess disguises herself and 11 other women as huntsmen, and hires the group out to her beloved. After watching her display her intelligence, creativity and courage, the prince falls for and marries her (the Brothers Grimm).
- **Kate Crackernuts:** A not-so-pretty princess rescues her beautiful sister from an evil enchantment and a prince from a wasting sickness caused by his nightly dancing with fairies (Scottish; published by Andrew Lang).
- **Donkeyskin:** Using her wits, a princess prevents her father the king from incesting her. The king is persistent, however, and the girl has the courage to run away from home, and the intelligence to whip together a plan to get a prince to marry her (Charles Perrault).
- **The Nettle Spinner:** When an evil (and married) count tries repeatedly to molest the heroine, she begins to weave his shroud – and he begins to die. After his wife convinces the spinner to stop the shroud, the count recovers. Later,

however, he becomes so ill he longs to die, but can't. He begs the spinner to complete the shroud, she does, and he dies (Flemish and French; published by Andrew Lang).

- **The White Dove:** Using her magic powers, a princess saves both herself and a prince from an evil witch (from Lang's *The Pink Fairy Book*).
- **The Spindle, the Shuttle and the Needle:** A girl uses a magic spindle, shuttle and needle left to her by her godmother to win a prince (Grimms; also in Lang's *Green Fairy Book*).
- **The Iron Stove:** To win the prince of her dreams, a girl faces and conquers several challenges, including climbing a glass mountain (Brothers Grimm).
- **The Master Maid:** Through skilful use of the magic arts, the Master Maid saves a prince not once, but several times (Swedish; collected by Peter Christen Asbjornsen and Jorgen Moe).
- **Molly Whuppie:** A girl outwits a giant three times, and consequently wins a prince for herself (and one for each of her two sisters) (Scottish).
- **Vasilisa the Fair:** Vasilisa must not only work for the frightening supernatural woman Baba Yaga, but must also pass several of Baba Yaga's tests. After successfully completing Baba Yaga's initiation programme, she spins, weaves and sews a shirt for the king, who consequently falls in love with and marries her (Russian).
- **Snow-White-Fire-Red:** A girl devises a plan to tell the prince what has happened to break them apart. The plan involves sending doves to the palace to relay the message. The plan works, the two are united again – and live happily ever after (from *Italian Popular Tales*, by Thomas Frederick Crane).
- **The Old Woman in the Woods:** After a dove helps a girl lost in the forest, he asks her to retrieve a ring for him from

a witch. The girls tries, but as she rummages through the witch's rings the witch tries to sneak away with the dove, who has the ring in its beak. After the girl wrests the caged bird away from the witch, it turns into a prince. The witch had cast a spell on him. The girl marries the prince.

Fairy tales are different from all other kinds of literature. The following is a list of 12 characteristics that, taken together, set fairy tales apart from other fiction:

1. **The World of Enchantment is the Setting:** The action in fairy tales always takes place in a world of enchantment. The ordinary laws of physics do not apply here; anything can happen: loaves of bread talk, cats walk upright, pumpkins turn into carriages and frogs into handsome princes.
2. **The Supernatural is Taken for Granted:** Supernatural events are totally taken for granted by fairy tale characters. When animals suddenly morph into handsome princes, or pumpkins into full-sized carriages, no one bats an eye.
3. **Family Sphere at the Beginning and End:** Often, fairy tales begin and end in the family sphere: protagonists leave their parents to enter the enchanted realm, and at the end of the tale return to their birth family, or to one they've married into. Jack leaves his impoverished mother to climb the magic beanstalk, and returns home to her with great riches. Hansel and Gretel too leave home, enter and grapple with the enchanted world, and then return home with riches. Often characters leave their birth families and end up in families they marry into – Cinderella, Snow White and Sleeping Beauty are famous examples.
4. **Helpers for Protagonists:** Often the main character gets help solving the plot problem, and from the supernatural

or enchanted realm. Cinderella and Sleeping Beauty have fairy godmothers; the young man in Puss in Boots gets help from his magic cat; and Simpleton's helper in The Golden Goose is a little old man in the woods who gives him the magic goose.

5. **No "Earthy Realism":** Although earthy realism is present in other kinds of folktales, it is missing in fairy tales, where bodily processes are rarely given the time of day.
6. **Nature is the Setting:** Fairy tales almost always take place outside cities or even villages; often they take place in forests. Simpleton meets the man with the golden goose in the forest, Snow White meets the seven dwarfs in the forest, and Hansel and Gretel too meet their witch in a forest.
7. **Tests for Protagonists:** Often fairy tale protagonists must pass tests set by other characters in the tale: the heroine in Rumpelstiltskin for example must guess Rumpelstiltskin's name; Cinderella must tear herself away from the ball before midnight; and in The Golden Goose, Simpleton's test is this: will he or won't he share his food with the little old magic man?
8. **Geographical and Temporal Settings Vague:** Fairy tales are set in times and places invariably ill-defined, shadowy, and unnamed: "Once upon a time in a kingdom far away…"
9. **Characters' Identities Vague:** Characters' identities are also ill-defined and shadowy. They're referred to not by real names but by their function, status or personal attributes: "the king", "a poor man", "a princess", "Sleeping Beauty", "The Frog Prince".
10. **Helpers are Female:** Helpers are more often female than male. Fairy tales have no fairy godfathers or fathers helping their children from the grave, and magical "wise old women" seem to outnumber "wise old men". In the

Grimms' tales, for example, magical old women aid the protagonists in eight different tales: The Goose Girl at the Well, The Six Swans, The Nix of the Mill Pond, Sweetheart Roland, Donkey Cabbages, The Lambkin and the Little Fish, Mother Holla, and One Eye, Two Eyes and Three Eyes. In contrast, I could find only four tales in which magical old men helped characters: The Golden Goose, The Water of life, The Little Folks' Presents, and St. Joseph in the Forest. (Although dwarfs aid characters in The Blue Light, The Three Little Men in the Wood and, of course, Snow White).

11. **Antagonists are Female**: The fairy tale bad guys too are more often female than male: female witches, Baba Yagas, evil stepmothers — even dragons are sometimes female (in The Flower Queen's Daughter, for example). In contrast, although they contain several evil male dwarfs, fairy tales contain few if any wizards, warlocks or evil stepfathers. A search for "old woman" in the 200 Grimm tales brings up 216 matches, while a similar search for "old man" produces only 74 (Grimm and Grimm, 2006).
12. **The Old are Contrasted with the Young:** Often in fairy tales youth is contrasted with age. Little Red Riding Hood is very young, her grandmother very old. Hansel and Gretel are young and their witch is "a very, very old woman, who supported herself on crutches, [as she] came creeping out." And the 290 mentions of old people referred to above are mostly about oldsters helping young protagonists like Simpleton in The Golden Goose. (All but numbers 10 and 11 above were taken from Davidson and Chaudhri 2003b.)

Over the years, many have tried to explain the nature and purpose of fairy tales. Although Freudians believe "a great deal of folklore is preoccupied with sexuality in its many forms," more than one writer through the years has criticised this approach (Davidson & Chaudhri: 2003: 9-10). Psychological theorists in general see fairy tales as stories consisting of sets of symbols revealing aspects of human psychology; a king, for example, might symbolise "father" and magical gifts might symbolise those of a heroine's talents allowing her to succeed (Davidson & Chaudhri: 2003: 10).

Jungians on the other hand believe that fairy tales embody archetypal images affecting us on deep levels. Jung believed the "wise old woman/man" in fairy tales represented a person's "active intelligence" – that part of us that creates our dreams and "...in the most strange arrangements of fate, in synchronicities and in all those experiences where one has an uncanny feeling that one is being manipulated by a higher intelligence." But the wise old people only come to us, say Jungians, when we really need them – and only after we've worked hard first to help ourselves (von Franz 1997: 28). For Jungian Marie-Louise von Franz, a fairy-tale spindle symbolises both the phallus and a woman's animus (the masculine part of her personality), and one meaning behind Sleeping Beauty is this: sometimes only time can heal our wounds (von Franz 1974: 42, 43, 47).

According to the German culture historian Heide Gottner-Abendroth many fairy tales are about the "sacred marriage" between the ancient pre-patriarchal goddess and her *heros*, her mortal lover. The *heros* must pass several tests before becoming the goddess's lover, after which he dies, and is then reborn to begin the cycle all over again (a sequence thought to ensure the earth's fertility). A fairy tale example is The Four Ingenious Brothers, in which four brothers must pass tests set by a princess (symbol of the goddess) so she can determine which of the four will become her marriage partner (symbol of the sacred marriage). Since all four pass her first round of tests, she must subject them to a second round, in which the four men must fight a dragon.

Although the youngest brother kills the dragon, he's knocked out in the fight, and another brother absconds with the dragon's head, which he uses to trick the princess into thinking he's the winner. The princess agrees to marry this false hero, but when the youngest brother wakes and brings her the dragon's tongue, she marries him instead. Thus the full cycle of initiation, death/return, and sacred marriage is completed (Gottner-Abendroth 1995: 161ff). According to Gottner-Abendroth, over the years many fairy tales have been tampered with and are therefore missing parts of this schema – often the final two parts involving the *heros'* death and return.

For Gottner-Abendroth the spindle is a symbol of fate. For both Sleeping Beauty, and Gold Marie in Mother Holla, it was spindles that initiated their Otherworld journeys. And for Gottner-Abendroth the core meaning of Sleeping Beauty is not that time heals all wounds, but that in winter the goddess slips down into the underworld (Sleeping Beauty's long sleep), and re-emerges in spring to revive earth's plant life (1995: 146).

According to Gottner-Abendroth, an object in a fairy tale can mean one thing if the tale is still fairly pre-patriarchal, but another if it has been patriarchally altered. For example, in pre-patriarchal tales dragons are code for the death aspect of the goddess. In patriarchalised tales, however, they are code for the goddess herself — who at all costs must be conquered. Likewise, in a pre-patriarchal tale slaying a dragon is code for conquering one's fear of death or of the death goddess, while conquering a dragon in a patriarchalised tale means the feminine principal itself has been conquered (1995: 163). See Appendix E for more fairy tale code words identified by Gottner-Abendroth.

Vladimir Propp, one of the world's premier folklore scholars, says European fairy tales are not about symbols, archetypes or sexuality either. On the contrary, says Propp, they are records of actual historical events: our ancestors' ancient shamanic, initiation and death rituals. According to Propp many fairy tales are what ancient European shamans saw and experienced when they went into trance to journey into the Otherworld, the world of enchantment:

> ...shamanism took over a great deal from prehistoric epics, and much of it has been preserved in the wondertale [Propp's word for fairy tale]. If we collect shamans' tales of their trances – how the shaman went to seek a soul in the other world, who helped him in this endeavour, how he was conveyed, and so forth – and compare these with the wanderings and flight of the wondertale hero, the correspondence will be obvious. I have traced this correspondence for individual elements, but it also exists at the level of the whole. (Propp 1984: 122)

Other fairy tales, says Propp, are records of our ancestors' initiation and death rituals:

> If one envisions everything that happens to the initiate [as he/she travels through the Otherworld] and narrates it in sequence, the result will be the compositional basis of the wondertale. If one narrates in sequence everything thought to happen to the deceased, the story will produce the same core, with the addition of some elements absent from the rites. The compositional unity of the wondertale lies neither in the specific features of the human psyche nor in the peculiarities of artistic creation; rather it lies in the reality of the past. (1984: 117)

Although none of the above theories explain all the defining characteristics of fairy tales, the theory that does the worst job is the "fairy tales are only entertainment" theory. If fairy tales were only entertainment with no further meaning or purpose, why would they be so restrictive? Why, for example, would they refuse to tell us where, when, and to whom the action happens?

No other literature is so close-mouthed about these important internal elements. And why would fairy-tale action so often begin and end in the family sphere but take place mostly in a fantasy world? Why would characters never blink an eye when magic happens? Why do fairy-tale protagonists almost always need helpers – in most other European fiction, characters take great pride in overcoming the odds on their own, with no help from anyone else.

But the psychological theories don't do a much better job either of accounting for the defining characteristics of fairy tales. Yes, they do fairly well at explaining why characters might have fuzzy names like "the princess", "the poor man" and "a king" instead of "Princess Elizabeth", "Richard Woodman" or "King Henry" (fairy tale characters are not supposed to be real people but only symbols and archetypes), and why supernatural events are taken wholly for granted by fairy-tale characters (supernatural events are totally taken for granted in our dreams, which according to Jungian theory are also prime carriers of archetypes). But the psychological theories don't explain much of anything else. Why do fairy tales always take place in a world of enchantment?

Archetypes and symbols can be conveyed perfectly well outside "worlds of enchantment" – my dreams are full and ripe repositories of archetypes occurring in completely unenchanted worlds complying perfectly with the laws of physics: a lovable little boy hugs me, a friend rejects me, an elderly woman tries to cope with a group of rambunctious children.

Neither do the psychological theories explain why in so many fairy tales magical helpers suddenly appear out of nowhere to aid protagonists. And they don't explain why so many protagonists are forced to complete a set of tasks. Dreams don't typically include helpers or sets of tasks to complete. Also, in my dreams I never start out in a family setting, enter a world of enchantment, and then return to some kind of family setting at the end of the dream. So why do so many fairy tales follow these exact same streams of circumstances? What's more, although Jungians consider fairy tales pan-human carriers of archetypes – just as dreams are pan-human carriers of archetypes – they are wrong on this count. They're wrong because fairy tales are not found all over the world. Besides being missing in parts of Asia and Africa, before the arrival of Europeans they were also absent over all of the Americas (Davidson and Chaudhri 2003: 9).

Unlike those above, the theories of Heide Gottner-Abendroth and Vladimir Propp provide explanations for almost all fairy tales' defining characteristics:

1. **The World of Enchantment:** Fairy tales always take place in an enchanted realm, where animals talk, cats walk on two legs, and dragons appear because fairy tales take place in the pre-Christian Otherworld, a realm where spirits and deities reside, and where natural laws do not apply.
2. **The Supernatural is Taken for Granted:** Propp's shamans and puberty initiates, who are the characters in fairy tales, know they're taking trance journeys into a world crackling with magic (the spirit world). There's no reason they'd be surprised by finding magic there.
3. **The Family Sphere:** Although fairy tales take place in the enchanted realm, they begin and end in a family setting. Of course, says Propp. Shamans go into trance to journey to the "enchanted realm" (spirit world), but before they go they're in the world of ordinary, or home reality – as they are when they come out of trance.
4. **Helpers:** Fairy-tale characters have helpers because (says Propp) shamans always had spirit helpers, or spirit guides.
5. **Earthy Realism Missing:** While bodily functions are frequently mentioned in other kinds of folklore, in fairy tales they're not. The theories of both Propp and Gottner-Abendroth explain this too, and perfectly: the Otherworld,

where almost all fairy tale action takes place, is a world of the spirit, not the flesh. In other words, without bodies there can be no bodily functions.

6. **Nature is the Setting:** Fairy tales almost always take place outside cities or even villages. Propp maintains this is so because fairy tales ultimately stem from rituals carried out by migratory hunter-gatherer Europeans who lived outside human settlements (Propp 1984: 117-18). Gottner-Abendroth would say they take place in nature because they are oriented around pre-Christian religions, which were almost always nature religions.
7. **Tests for Protagonists:** In many fairy tales, protagonists must pass tests set by one or more other character. Of course, says Propp, again. Shamans don't enter the spirit world just for kicks. They enter to accomplish something – whether it's healing the sick, locating lost objects, completing their own initiation as magic practitioners, or to reach some other goal. In ancient Europe this often would have involved fighting and winning against evil spirits, or passing other kinds of tests. As a matter of fact, several relatively recent writers have described medieval and early-modern magic practitioners who believed their souls left their bodies to enter the spirit world and fight evil beings there; beings making people sick or making the community's crops die. More on this later.

8, 9. **Secrecy about When, Where and to Whom the Action Occurs:** If fairy tales take place in the spirit world, the secrecy about when and where the action occurs becomes completely logical, since time and place have no meaning in the spirit world. In fairy tales, the code words for this are "long, long ago", "once upon a time", "in a land far away" or other similarly vague and noncommittal phrases. Heide Gottner-Abendroth says fairy tales are simply the old pre-patriarchal religious myths which were, for the sake of safety, secretly coded as secular stories; the old pre-patriarchal worldview "thrived uninterrupted in the lower social classes and geographical fringe groups" of Europe. However, the people "... no longer referred to the Mother Goddess, but spoke of the 'mother'; [they] no longer call[ed] the daughter Goddess ... by name, they simply spoke of 'the princess'." (Gottner-Abendroth 1995: 135)

10, 11. Female Helpers and Antagonists: In fairy tales protagonists' helpers and thwarters both tend to be female: fairy godmothers, mothers who help from the grave, and "wise old women" are the helpers, and witches and stepmothers the thwarters. Rarely if ever in fairy tales does one encounter fairy godfathers, fathers who help from the grave, warlocks, wizards or evil stepfathers. Even wise old men are outnumbered by wise old women. While Gottner-Abendroth would explain this in terms of the pre-patriarchal nature of fairy tales, Propp offers no good explanation here.

12. Young and Old Contrasted: To some extent Propp's theory explains why many fairy tale characters are either very young or very old: according to Propp many of these tales are about the elders in the community initiating the young – in coming-of-age ceremonies, for example, or initiation into the status of shaman. It is doubtful, however, that all fairy tales are records of initiation ceremonies. Later in this chapter we'll discuss what might be a better explanation for this defining characteristic of fairy tales.

Although between them Propp and Gottner-Abendroth explain most of the distinguishing characteristics of fairy tales, they fail to clearly explain the final three: the preponderance of female helpers and antagonists, and the preponderance of very old and very young characters. What is needed is a theory that explains all aspects of fairy tales, and I believe tweaking and combining the theories of Propp and Gottner-Abendroth goes far in producing such a theory. I call this "the secret-code theory" of fairy tales. According to the secret-code theory, fairy tales were invented to serve as a secret repository of information about an outlawed goddess-centred religion, with the information in them hidden in code words, code characters and code images so it could be safely learned, shared and transmitted from one generation to the next. In short, the corpus of literature we call oral fairy tales is a secret goddess-centred "Bible". This body of oral literature was passed along secretly from one person to the next, when the Church was hell-bent on destroying any and all parts of Europe's pre-Christian past, i.e., during the medieval and early-modern eras. Unlike the Christian Bible, however, the "Fairy Tale Bible" was communicated not in writing, but orally, since anything non-Christians put in writing was soon destroyed.

Although the history of Europe's conversion to a patriarchal social order, and then to Christianity, is a long and complex one, from the beginning it seems to have involved the undermining, weakening and dilution of Europe's old religions. As we saw earlier, when the Indo-Europeans promenaded into Europe, beginning in the 4th millennium BC, their male gods gradually degraded and undermined many of Europe's more powerful goddesses. A few millennia later, all of Europe's indigenous religions were fair game. By the beginning of the 5th century AD, all non-Christians in the Roman Empire had been declared "outlaws" and emperors began ordering all traces of their religions smashed, burned, or otherwise destroyed (MacMullen 1984: 101). In 1184, Pope Innocent III made persecution of heretics the duty of Catholic kings (Roberts 1997: 188; Thurston 2001:37), the Inquisition began after 1227, and in 1252 Inquisitors acquired the right to torture non-Christians (Thurston 2001: 37).

Nevertheless, peasants in France still expressed their pagan beliefs openly (Cohn 1977: 214-15), and in 1520, Martin Luther was complaining that in Germany too, the people were still freely exhibiting their non-Christian practices in, for example, the form of "tree shrines and field crosses" (Porras 2011: 493). So the Church upped the ante. In 1486/87, with the publication of the infamous *Malleus Maleficarum*, or "Hammer of the Witches". It began what scholars used to think frightened non-Christians so badly that it finally eradicated all traces of them. As mentioned previously, however, today's scholars aren't so sure of this.

Estimates vary as to how many were murdered in the so-called witch persecutions of the early-modern era; while some say as few as 40,000, others say as many as 100,000 (Thurston 2001: 93-96). Interestingly, it was right around the time Mother Goose was first mentioned in print that the persecutions began to end. In England, the percentage of "witches" tried but acquitted increased "enormously" after 1620 (except for a flare-up in 1645-46). While the *Parlement* of Paris began rejecting witchcraft cases in the 1640s (Thurston 2001: 159, 180), Loret gives us one of the first mentions in print of Mother Goose in the year 1650, with, *"Mais le cher motif de leur joye, Comme un conte de la Mere Oye, Se trouvant fabuleux et faux, Ils deviendront tous bien penauts."* (Whitmore 1969: 2) As we learned earlier, this translates into something like, "Since the reason behind their happiness is as fabulous and false as a Mother Goose tale, they will eventually be very disappointed."

The point is, in many places in Europe, throughout the Middle Ages and beyond, if your religion wasn't Christianity you were taking your life in your hands by committing anything about it to paper. And even if you were brave enough to take a chance here, the authorities eventually destroyed your document anyway. A second reason it made no sense to have a written goddess-oriented Bible was that before the modern era few Europeans could read.

After a while, it became unsafe even to talk privately about pre-Christian religion – especially after the witch persecutions began. In fact, the witch persecutions got so bad that eventually a kind of mania settled over many parts of Europe. It seemed everyone suspected everyone else of being a witch ("witch" was defined by the Church as someone who had made a pact with the Christian Devil). Your neighbours were very likely to turn you in as a "Christian" witch and even stand up in court to testify against you. In the 20th century, scholars believed the concept "witch" was one wholly fabricated by the Church. Today, however, increasing numbers of academics are convinced that medieval and early-modern Europeans actually did believe that certain people used black magic to harm others – and that the "witches" themselves believed they possessed such powers (Gaskill 2010, Bever 2008, Wilby 2005, Behringer 1998).

Of course Europeans also believed in what are variously called white witches, cunning folk, healers, shamans, and several other terms designating people considered able to use magic in a positive way to satisfy a multitude of human needs (Bever 2008, Wilby 2005, Gaskill 2010). And it turns out they believed in such magic practitioners a lot longer and a lot more fervently than we used to think. In 2013, fairy-tale scholar Jack Zipes said scholars have recently done an about-face regarding early-modern beliefs in magic: "In the past twenty years, scholars ... have published a vast amount of essays and books ... demonstrating that most people believed in witches, fairies, wizards, and magic up through the Renaissance, if not through the nineteenth century." (2013: 59) And they believed in them with much more intensity than we used to think:

> Historians have long recognized that magical beliefs and practices of pre-Christian origin survived into the early-modern period; however, in recent decades there has been a growing acknowledgement that these beliefs were more pervasive and influential than previously thought. One

> (admittedly controversial) scholar has gone so far as to claim, for example, that "pre-Reformation European peasants were virtually pagan, that [their] beliefs were overlaid in varying degrees by Christian notions which were to a large extent adapted to animism". (Wilby 2005: 14, speaking about French historian Jean Delumeau)

The idea that fairy tales were born out of pre-Christian religion is not a new one. Over the years scholars often wrote about fairy tales being pre-Christian in origin. In fact, almost as soon as literate Europeans began to take an interest in fairy tales they admitted these stories contained secret, coded information about non-Christian religions:

> Scientific interest in [fairy tales] began in the 18th century with Einckelmann, Haman, and J.G. Herder... Herder said that such tales contained the remnants of an old long-buried faith expressed in symbols... Dissatisfaction with Christian teaching and the first longings for a more vital, earthy and instinctual wisdom began then; later we find it more explicitly among the Romanticists in Germany. It was this religious search for something which seemed lacking in official Christian teaching that first induced the famous brothers Jakob [sic] and Wilhelm Grimm to collect folk tales. (von Franz 1987: 3)

According to von Franz, fairy tales reside "in the realm of the gods" (1976: 4). Likewise, Gottner-Abendroth says fairy tales are ancient religious myths: "...the fairy tale, being a veiled myth, conveys the same religious message as the myth, and is equally complex." (1993: 136) And according to Jungian scholar Bettina Knapp, "With the onset of Christianity, fairies, along with other supernormal figures, were said to have descended from ancient gods and goddesses, or in other cases from nymphs, fallen angels, unbaptized souls." (2003: 6) Even Jacob Grimm himself assumed that many to most fairy tales were all about non-Christian religion.

But the evidence points to fairy tales being not just pre-Christian, but goddess-oriented as well. According to Jack Zipes, professor emeritus of comparative literature at the University of Minnesota and author of dozens of treatises on fairy tales:

> There is enough evidence to indicate that there were strongly held beliefs in pagan goddesses throughout western and eastern Europe that were transformed into [fairy] tales enabling peasants and also members of the elite classes in all regions to contend with their suffering while offering some hope for a better life. (2012: 76)

Zipes also believes that Holda-Perchta is related to Baba Yaga, the malevolent/benevolent witch-like woman who dominates more than one Russian fairy tale: "There is also good reason to believe that [Baba Yaga] is related to the ancient Germanic Perchta, who gave rise to the famous Frau Holle of the Brothers Grimm's and northern German tales."

Zipes makes a tantalising suggestion: Baba Yaga (and perhaps Mother Holle too?) was a powerful challenger to the new usurper religion – Christianity – that threatened her existence: "Her ambiguous quality of witch and fairy was actually a common trait by the late Middle Ages in Europe, for she had not only become a malevolent/benevolent figure that harked back to a great pagan mother goddess and initiation rites but a majestic, dangerous figure of resistance to Christianity that had demonized her virtues..." (2012: 70).

At one time, claims Zipes, the witches, fairies and other paranormal female characters in Western European fairy tales were probably goddesses. Gradually, however, they were demonized by the Church:

> Though there is no absolute proof that all the witches and fairies in eastern and western Europe stem from pagan beliefs and rituals, there is strong evidence that Baba Yaga is an amalgamation of various pagan deities that underwent gradual transformation in the Greco-Roman period and early Middle Ages. (2012: 70)

According to Zipes a main reason early books of fairy tales were banned in Russia is that Russians were aware these tales were about powerful goddesses – and the Russian power structure could have none of that:

> The tales told, collected, and published in Russia were like a breath of new life for the listeners and readers. This was one of the reasons they were frequently banned or censored. The tales were filled with Baba Yagas, who possessed just as many fairy virtues as witch powers… If the Baba Yagas … caused humans to be fearful, it was with good reason… [The tales they were in were] still paying tribute to notions of some kind of a great goddess. (2012: 73)

Although fairy tales are sometimes compared to myths, the only surviving ancient European myths are patriarchal Greek, Roman and Scandinavian ones. And fairy tales are nothing like these myths, which contain gallons of gods, many of whom use their magical powers to hurt goddesses, each other, and mortals too. Unlike fairy tales, many patriarchal myths revolve around war, armies and armed combat. Often even the good guys take things by force and hurt others — and this seems to be just fine and dandy with everyone involved. According to Greek myth, as soon as Zeus was born his father Cronus tried to eat him alive. And while Zeus grew up into a god who seemed to enjoy raping women, the Greek goddesses were not much better; Artemis turned Actaeon into a stag – and then turned his own dogs on him to tear him to pieces.

In contrast, the main message in fairy tales is that good magic always triumphs over bad – for any and everyone, whether meek and mild, or brave and ambitious (Tatar 2012: xxxiv). Could this be why we don't often think of fairy tales as religious mythology – because they're part of a religion diametrically opposed to the patriarchal foundation of Greek, Roman and Scandinavian myths? At any rate, it was after stumbling across the idea that fairy tales might be religious myth that it finally occurred to me that the whole corpus of such tales might have functioned as a secret pre-patriarchal Bible.

It seems clear that fairy tales describe a culture not only pre-Christian, but pre-patriarchal too. They contain more disguised goddesses than gods, and more disguised priestesses than priests. And their general tone and values are pre-patriarchal: up with the underdog; down with social ranking; use magic to control the universe instead of meekly begging for the goodwill of gods and goddesses who often seem uncaring and unfeeling.

In a later chapter we'll revisit this unusual fairy-tale value system. For now, however, here's a question for you: why do some animals appear in fairy tales in droves while others don't show up at all? For example, why does the word "hedgehog" appear over 70 times in the 200 fairy tales collected by the Brothers Grimm, whereas the mole, vole, mink and badger appear not once? Several other European animals don't figure in the Grimm tales either: the weasel, salamander, polecat, mongoose, martin, beaver and bat, for example. On the other hand, the Grimm tales include more than 200 mentions of canines (dogs, wolves and foxes), 133 mentions of the Mother-Goose-related *Anatidae* (geese, ducks and swans), and over 50 references to bears. Fish appear 35 times, stags/hinds/deer 31 times, frogs/toads 19 times, and snakes and goats more than 20 times each.

So why some animals and not others? A possible clue: the

animals in the Grimms' tales are those archaeologist Marija Gimbutas says were sacred to the pre-patriarchal "Old Europeans" of south-east Europe from roughly 6000 BC to 4000 BC. These sacred animals include water birds (geese, ducks and swans), hedgehogs, bears, fish, dogs, goats, snakes, doves, owls, frogs, toads, boars, hawks, pigs, bulls, sheep, cuckoos, deer and turtles. Gimbutas includes all of the above animals in chapter headings in two of her books on Old Europe (1982, 1989). Amazingly, of Gimbutas' 21 species, the only one not appearing at least once in the Grimm fairy tales is the turtle.

So the specific types of animals in fairy tales tie them to Old Europe. Another trait tying fairy tales to Old Europe is their elevation of very old and very young women, another fascinating and enormously mysterious aspect of Old Europe. If anyone was revered over others in Old Europe, it was young girls and old women. For us who live in patriarchal societies (and these days that's close to everyone in the world), this is an almost absurd statement; it feels like it's forever been true that the hierarchy goes the other way around: adult men at the top – like the star at the top of the Christmas tree – and baby girls and old women at the bottom near the floor, right above the tree skirt. But Marija Gimbutas gives piece after piece of cemetery evidence showing that those Old-Europeans with the largest and most elaborate graves, and containing the most elaborate and coveted grave goods, were almost always young girls, infant girls, and very old women (she's talking here, remember, about south-east and central Europe from about 6500 BC to 500 BC):

- "The graves of girls and female infants were consistently equipped with exceptional ritual objects not found in other graves."
- "In the cemetery of Cernica at Bucharest ... the richest grave out of 362 graves was of a girl about sixteen years old."

- In Old European cemeteries in western Hungary, "...in addition to the great numbers of vases in female graves, the most exceptional graves ... were those of girls and female infants. Boys' graves were poor and adult and mature male graves were equipped rarely with more than one or several tools."
- In western Poland, four older women aged 50 to 70, and a man 50-55 were buried near a house. While the man had nothing in his grave, the women's graves were filled with jewellery, beaded belts, vases, and other prized possessions.
- Also in western Poland: "huge long barrows were raised" to bury one, lone woman. An example: "At Sarnaowo in Kujavia ... a triangular barrow thirty meters long covered a central grave pit in which the bones of a woman about 70 years old were found. She was buried in a wooden coffin."
- "In the cemetery of Aszod, the most outstanding grave was that of a teen-age girl which contained a large temple model of clay with a bird's head on top, standing on a human foot."
- "The same pattern repeats in a number of [Old European] culture groups where cemeteries are known. Most frequently teen-age girls were either richly equipped with jewellery or included in their graves [were] items of exceptional ritual value." (Gimbutas 1991: 334-38).

Although we don't know why the ancient Old Europeans revered the very young and the very old, they apparently did; archaeologists have forever agreed that the contents of a grave indicate the occupant's social status. And in fairy tales it's these same two age groups that appear so consistently.

Now let's look at specific kinds of code and code words that scholars have identified in European fairy tales. The first kind of coding in fairy tales revolves around the royals. While Jack Zipes says the fairy-tale princess is code for female deity, others go even further, contending that all royals in fairy tales represent pre-Christian deities. If Sleeping Beauty was actually a goddess, what about the man she married? Although he was coded a "prince", Gottner-Abendroth thinks he was the *heros* of the goddess – her mortal lover. In some tales of course princes could also have been code for specific gods. In other words, when the Church began threatening them, non-Christian deities seem to have dropped undercover as fairy-tale princesses, kings, queens and princes.

A second kind of coding in fairy tales revolves around the non-royal characters. If the princesses and princes were actually goddesses, *heros* and gods, who were the ordinary characters like Jack in Jack and the Beanstalk, or the miller's daughter in Rumpelstiltskin? The answer: often they were the priestesses and priests of the goddess, or the community's shamans, cunning folk, and other magico-religious practitioners. And who were the fairy tale helpers? In almost every fairy tale the main character has a human, supernatural or animal helper without which the story would not roll on to its happy ending. I believe fairy-tale helpers – fairy godmothers, wise old men, wise old women, and friendly talking animals – are usually code for "supernatural aide", "spirit guide" or "familiar spirit".

In the pre-Christian belief system, spirit guides included among others the spirits of animals and deceased people who helped European shamans and other magico-religious practitioners practise their callings. Over the past several years a growing body of literature has focused on medieval and early-modern magic practitioners ("cunning folk", "folk healers", "wiccans" etc.) and their resemblance to the shamans anthropologists have studied in North American, Siberian and other indigenous societies around the world. By definition shamans are magic practitioners who use spirit guides to help them heal people, prognosticate, and perform other kinds of tasks for the members of their communities. At least one scholar – Vladimir

Propp – believes many fairy tales are actual historical records of journeys European shamans took through the spirit world while they were in trance; more on this in a later chapter.

So the helpers in fairy tales – the magic old people, the fairy godmothers, the helpful dwarfs and others – were code for the supernatural helpers European pre-Christians actually believed in – just as many Christians believe in angels. For the royal/deity characters in fairy tales, helpers were their supernatural aides – just like the "laminak" discussed in earlier chapters, were aides to the Basque goddess Mari. For non-royal fairy-tale characters on the other hand, helpers were their spirit guides – analogous to the spirit guides that helped Siberian shamans when they journeyed in trance through the spirit world.

In addition to royals, helpers and ordinary people, fairy tales also include supernatural bad guys: witches, stepmothers, evil dwarfs, dragons etc. These are often code for the supernatural adversaries that must be fought in order to cure or prevent illness, to ensure human, animal and plant fertility, to keep the earth's grand cycles going, and to satisfy a range of other human needs. All fairy-tale protagonists, whether they be deities, priests, priestesses, shamans or other magico-religious practitioners, fight these bad guys to help humanity in its struggle to keep the universe in balance.

A final kind of code in fairy tales revolves around geographical place names, and time dates. In how many fairy tales are we told exactly where the action takes place, and when? In very few. What we get instead is the classic fairy-tale beginning: "Once upon a time, in a land far, far away, there lived a beautiful princess..." As noted previously, this is due to the fact that fairy-tale narratives take place in the Otherworld, a sacred land located in no place and no time. And since talking about this Otherworld and the religious beings who inhabited it would get you burned at the stake, the place and the beings were never referred to by their real names but only by code phrases.

The Otherworld apparently existed in a time parallel to that on the ordinary plane, making "once upon a time" a very interesting phrase indeed. Could the phrase "upon a time" refer to a conception that time in the Otherworld rested on top of time in the world of ordinary reality?

- "Once upon a time there was a queen who went out driving." (From The Twelve Wild Ducks, Asbjornsen and Moe 1982.)
- "In old times when wishing still helped one, there lived a king whose daughters were all beautiful…" (From The Frog King, the Brothers Grimm.)
- "Once on [sic] a time a poor couple lived far, far away in a great wood." (From The Lassie and Her Godmother, Asbjornsen and Moe ND.)
- "In days gone by there was a land where the nights were always dark, and the sky spread over it like a black cloth…" (From The Moon, the Brothers Grimm.)
- "There was once a king and a queen who had no children…" (From The Three Princesses in the Mountain-in-the-Blue, Asbjornsen and Moe 1982.)
- "In a certain kingdom, beyond the thrice ninth land, in the thrice tenth realm, there lived a strong and mighty king." (From The Firebird and Princess Vasilisa, Afanas'ev 1973.)
- "There were once on [sic] a time a king and a queen who lived happily together and had twelve children, but they were all boys." (From The Twelve Brothers, the Brothers Grimm.)

Even well into adulthood many of us still adore fairy tales. In *The Irresistible Fairy Tale* Jack Zipes, one of America's foremost students of the genre, says we don't know why fairy tales are so captivating – and never will (Zipes 2013: 40). I disagree. To me it's very clear why these particular stories are so irresistible: they show us an old way of life we've lost and forgotten, one in which war, prejudice, ageism and sexism are replaced with love, laughter, adventure, creativity and magic. We love fairy tales because they show us a world we instinctively know was in many respects superior to the one we live in today.

In classical mythology some people are considered superior to others, but in fairy tales everyone's equal (as we've seen, royals aren't really royals). And although fairy tales suggest it's better to be wealthy than poor, they also suggest wealth must be shared equally among all – the giant is forced to share his wealth with Jack, and the witch with Hansel and Gretel; what's more, Two Eyes gladly shares her new-found wealth with her sisters One Eye and Three Eyes. The goal is for all to become wealthy – and equally so. In fairy tales helping others brings huge rewards. And unlike patriarchal teachings, fairy tales tell us that dreaming, wondering and being adventurous are good things, that singing, dancing and making merry are far superior to fasting and self-chastisement.

In fairy tales animals are almost always helpful to humans, and almost never the villains (Little Red Riding Hood is one of the few exceptions). In Puss in Boots it's a talking cat who saves the day, and in The Goose Girl, a Grimms tale, when the servant of a princess tricks the princess into trading places with her, it's a horse who rescues her – by telling the king who the real princess is. In The Queen Bee – also a tale collected by the Brothers Grimm – the protagonist is helped by ants, bees and ducks. And in Grimms version of Cinderella, it's doves (Aphrodite's birds) who help Cinderella out of her trouble. The snake in The White Snake teaches a man how to talk to animals, a skill that helps advance the story to its happy ending.

In patriarchal myth on the other hand, animals are often the enemy. Actaeon was torn apart by his hounds, and the three-headed dog Cerberus terrorised any mortal who crossed its path. Leda was raped by a swan (actually Zeus in disguise), and

Hercules wrangled with the man-eating mares of King Diomedes, King Minos' bull, and a venomous nine-headed snake called the Hydra (Hamilton 1969: 171-72). What's more, Greek and Roman mythology is fat with toxic animal-human hybrids: harpies (ugly bird-women), lecherous satyrs, "horse-demons" (Harrison 1955: 387), and Medusa with her hair of snakes, so hideous that any man who even glanced at her turned to stone.

Another part of fairy tales that attracts many of us is the magic. When it comes right down to it, magic is a matter of being in the driver's seat – in control of your destiny. Magic means not having to depend on the good will of a universe often seeming to have poor control over its own anger. Magic can be defined as referring to "the techniques used to manipulate various supernatural forces and sometimes supernatural beings. Individuals may use magical recipes or formulas, or they may call upon someone with special knowledge of these formulas to perform them." (Lenkeit 2004: 245)

In sum, at least part of the reason fairy tales are so popular is that they show us a healthy world we've lost. This is a world in which animus is balanced with anima. It is a world in which humans, through their belief in magic, are in control of at least a portion of the universal forces at work against them. In fairy tales we return to the time before we became totally and helplessly at the mercy of primarily unfeeling, uncaring, and self-centred male gods who have no female gods to – when necessary – hold their feet to the fire.

In this chapter we've looked at scholars from the early 19th century Brothers Grimm to the 21st century scholar Jack Zipes who have recognised fairy tales as pre-Christian in nature and filled with disguised deities and other pre-Christian lore, history and information. We've also talked about why goddesses and other religious elements in fairy tales had to be disguised – because of centuries of persecution by European authorities. We talked about the code permeating fairy-tale literature: royals are code for deities, non-royals for magico-religious practitioners, and magic helpers for spirit guides akin to those connected to Siberian and Native-American shamans. We also talked about the possibility that fairy tales are religious myth, akin to myths about Zeus, Hera, Dionysus and other ancient Mediterranean deities.

In fact, many European fairy tales might at one time have functioned as a kind of secret pre-Christian Bible, composed in code to protect its followers. And just as Jehovah presided over the Christian Bible, presiding over this fairy-tale corpus of literature, I believe, was a powerful goddess known by different names in different places, but hidden incognito in some parts of Europe in the shadowy figure of Mother Goose. In fact, I would suggest that fairy tales provide us with some of the same kinds of information found in the Christian Bible, including:

- Stories about creation, the first humans, and religious history.
- Stories about deities and supernatural beings akin to Christian angels and demons.
- Stories about how humans should interact with deities and other supernatural beings.
- Stories about right and wrong behaviour.
- Stories about the future.

In the next several chapters we'll look at specific European fairy tales and the information they provide about how our goddess-centred ancestors viewed religious history, the creation of the universe, the first humans, supernatural beings, human interaction with supernatural beings, right behaviour, and what the future holds for humanity.

Chapter 11

Fairy Tales about the History and Future of Europe's Old Religions

The "sacred text" through which the female divinity was revealed to her Russian worshippers is the folktale, told originally at ritual periods in the life of the community.
Hubbs 1988: 41

In part or in whole, some fairy tales seem to preserve a record of the colossal clash between ancient European goddess religions and the people who drove these religions underground. In this chapter we'll take a look at Cinderella and a few other fairy tales to see how they might be secret repositories of information about this bloody chapter in European history. As we saw previously, it could be that the tale Cinderella is a coded message recording the clash between Christians and pre-Christians in medieval and early-modern Europe. Cinderella's wicked stepmother would be code for the Church, and her ugly stepsisters code for the Church hierarchy (priests, bishops, archbishops etc.) and the European military aristocracy (Walker 1996). Cinderella herself is code for the goddess Hel/Hella/Ella, whose regenerative fires have been reduced to cinders by the onslaught of the Church.

In this theory, Cinderella's dead mother, who in Charles Perrault's version of the tale comes to Cinderella as a fairy godmother but in the Grimms version as a white bird, represents the Mother aspect of the triple goddess. From an earlier chapter you might remember that the triple goddess was the Virgin-Mother-Crone or Daughter-Mother-Grandmother, a triune deity often represented by the three phases of the moon. In the story of Cinderella, humanity is represented by the prince, who finally sees the light: it's not her stepsisters, but Cinderella herself he wants to spend his life with. The main message of the tale: although she's currently reduced to cinders, at some point in the future the goddess Ella/Hella/Holla/Holda will burst into the light of day again and resume her beloved place in the hearts and minds of humanity.

In his 1993 work *The Trials and Tribulations of Little Red Riding Hood,* Jack Zipes includes what he says is likely the real, honest-to-goodness peasant version of Little Red Riding Hood before Perrault fussed over it and turned it into his "high-society" version. Zipes calls this version of the tale "The Story of Grandmother":

> There was a woman who had made some bread. She said to her daughter:
>
> "Go carry this hot loaf and bottle of milk to your granny."
>
> So the little girl departed. At the crossway she met *bzou,* the werewolf, who said to her: "Where are you going?"
>
> "I'm taking this hot loaf and a bottle of milk to my granny."
>
> "What path are you taking," said the werewolf, "the path

of needles or the path of pins?"

"The path of needles," the little girl said.

"All right, then I'll take the path of pins."

The little girl entertained herself by gathering needles. Meanwhile the werewolf arrived at the grandmother's house, killed her, put some of her meat in the cupboard and a bottle of her blood on the shelf. The little girl arrived and knocked at the door.

"Push the door," said the werewolf, "it's barred by a piece of wet straw."

"Good day, Granny. I've brought you a hot loaf of bread and a bottle of milk."

"Put it in the cupboard, my child. Take some of the meat which is inside and the bottle of wine on the shelf."

After she had eaten, there was a little cat which said: "Phooey! ... A slut is she who eats the flesh and drinks the blood of her granny."

"Undress yourself, my child," the werewolf said, "and come lie down beside me."

"Where should I put my apron?"

"Throw it into the fire, my child, you won't be needing it anymore."

And each time she asked where she should put all her other clothes, the bodice, the dress, the petticoat, and the long stockings, the wolf responded: "Throw them into the fire, my child, you won't be needing them anymore."

When she laid herself down in the bed, the little girl said:

"Oh, Granny, how hairy you are!"

"The better to keep myself warm, my child."

"Oh, Granny what big nails you have!"

"The better to scratch me with, my child!"

"Oh, Granny, what big shoulders you have!"

"The better to carry the firewood, my child!"

"Oh, Granny, what big ears you have!"

"The better to hear you with, my child!"

"Oh, Granny, what big nostrils you have!"

"The better to snuff my tobacco with, my child!"

"Oh, Granny what a big mouth you have!"

"The better to eat you with, my child!"

"Oh, Granny, I've got to go badly. Let me go outside."

"Do it in bed, my child!"

"Oh, no, Granny, I want to go outside."

"All right, but make it quick."

The werewolf attached a woollen rope to her foot and let her go outside.

When the little girl was outside, she tied the end of the rope to a plum tree in the courtyard. The werewolf became impatient and said: "Are you making a load out there? Are you making a load?"

When he realized that nobody was answering him, he jumped out of bed and saw that the little girl had escaped. He followed her but arrived at her house just at the moment she entered. (Zipes 1993: 5-6)

To say the least, this version of Little Red Riding Hood is miles removed from those gracing the pages of 19th and 20th century fairy-tale books for children. One major departure from Charles Perrault's version is that Little Red escapes the wolf with her own quick wits. As the canine is about to crunch her for lunch, she claims she needs to relieve herself in the outdoor privy, and once outside ties the rope to a plum tree and races away. Although the ending is the most glaring difference between the tales, two other differences may provide clues to the true significance of this story. First, in The Story of Grandmother, Red takes the "path of needles" to Grandma's house, the wolf "the path of pins". Strangely enough, Red gathers not flowers on the way, but sewing needles. Zipes suggests this may attach the tale to a ritual connected to one of the major arts of medieval women: the production of flax, wool, thread, cloth, and then clothing, through the labour-intensive arts of planting, harvesting, spinning, weaving and sewing (Zipes 2006b: 35).

A second, and even more illuminating difference between the two tales is this: in The Story of Grandmother there's a galloping contrast between the food and drink of the females (Little Red, mother, grandmother), and that of the wolf. At the beginning of the story, Red's mother gives her a warm loaf of bread and bottle of milk to take to grandmother. But at Grandma's, the wolf offers her meat and wine (the body and blood of Grandma). So we have bread-milk versus meat-wine.

Considering these differences between The Story of Grandmother and Little Red Riding Hood, it's a good bet that the former was written in code by pre-patriarchal European rebels. If so, it was composed to look like an innocent story about a girl escaping a wild animal. Breaking the code of the story, however, reveals it as anything but innocent. A case could be made that it is instead a dangerously radical treatise that damns the medieval masters of Europe and extols the virtues of the old goddess religions and worldview. Underneath its benign exterior, I believe the tale communicates an historical event, a prediction for the future, a road map showing goddess-oriented Europeans how to respond to the onslaught of patriarchal authority, and maybe even a ritual meant eventually to push that authority over a cliff.

Just like North American Indians and other indigenous peoples, preliterate Europeans had no other way to record their history or theology except through oral "historians" and "theologians" – men and women gifted with the talent of memorising and remembering oral tracts for long periods of time, and of being able to repeat them verbatim each time they told them. It could be that many people dubbed by medieval writers as "storytellers" were actually oral historians and theologians in disguise. As mentioned earlier, even when non-Christians published information about their worldview, the authorities almost always found a way to destroy these written materials.

So what are the secrets encrypted in The Story of Grandmother? If we'd break the code, what would we discover? In order to find out we need to identify the code words and concepts contained in the tale, starting with Little Red, her grandmother, and her mother:

Code Words and Concepts in The Story of Grandmother

1. **Red Riding Hood, Mother and Grandmother:** Code for the triple goddess: Virgin-Mother-Crone.
2. **The Wolf:** Code for the Christian Church, which was, to European pre-patriarchals, a dangerous wild animal, threatening not only their lives, but also their entire way of life.
3. **The crossway where Red meets the Wolf:** Code among pre-Christians for a sacred place of high magic.
4. **Wolf devouring Grandmother:** Code for the Church crushing one part of the triple goddess, the Crone.
5. **Hot bread and milk:** Code for the love dispensed by ancient European goddesses. Baking bread is a prominent goddess symbol (in the Grimms' tale Mother Holle, loaves of bread baking in Holle's magic ovens beg to be removed). Milk is food that flows directly from the sacred body of the fertile, life-giving goddess.
6. **Meat and wine:** Code for the body and blood of sacrificed deities, in this case the crone aspect of the triple goddess, Red's murdered grandmother.
7. **Red ingesting her Grandmother's body and blood:** Code for gaining the sacred magic necessary to escape the wolf-church. It was Little Red's need to eliminate this meal that gave her a plausible excuse to exit the house, and therefore escape the wolf.

8. **Little Red's sewing-needle path:** Code for one of humanity's earliest and most powerful tools, the needle. Vital for the manufacture of clothing, shoes, boots, hats, coats, tents, saddles, stockings, gloves, shawls, scarves, and much more, the needle allowed humans to move into the colder parts of the globe, including Europe in the Ice Age (try making shoes sturdy enough to get you through a northern European winter without the aid of needles or awls).
9. **The Wolf's sewing-pin path:** Code for a tool similar to the needle but less helpful and less kind. Like needles, pins hold cloth, skins, and other kinds of material together, but less effectually. While a tent held together with needle and sinew will turn away rain, one secured by pins will not. Clothes held together with pins might prick your skin, let in rain, and expose more of you than you'd like.
10. **The Wolf-Church taking "the path of pins":** Code for the Church being a temporary institution, an inferior one with a flimsy, make-do foundation.
11. **Little Red Riding Hood taking "the path of needles":** Code for the idea that the goddess religion is safe, sound, and correct for humanity, a permanent, long-term solution to life's issues and problems.
12. **Little Red's clothing:** Code for civilisation, especially goddess-centred civilisation. A primary distinction between humans and animals is our felt need to wear clothing. In the Middle Ages and before, the manufacturing of clothing was primarily the province of women (who used, among other tools, pins and needles).
13. **The Wolf's destruction of clothing by fire:** Code for the Church/State's attempted wholesale destruction of goddess culture. One is reminded here of the burning of non-Christians at the stake in the early-modern era (16th-18th centuries).

14. **The Wolf's fur, the first thing Red notices that tells her he might not be her grandmother:** Code for human regression to an era before the manufacture of clothing, i.e., to the days when humans wore animal skins.
15. **The plum tree:** Code for agriculture; in contrast to the pastoralist Indo-Europeans, many of the early European goddess peoples were settled agriculturalists.
16. **The woollen rope:** Code for pastoralism (sheep), i.e., the Indo-Europeans.
17. **The Wolf pretending to be Grandma:** Code for the Church pretending it could give Europeans what the goddess could.
18. **Little Red returns safely home to her mother:** Code for the prediction that, in the future, the goddess will win out over the Church.

In summary, once decoded The Story of Grandmother reads as follows:

> Little Red Riding Hood's mother (the Mother Goddess) gave her natural sustenance, bread and milk, to Red (the Virgin Goddess) to take to Red's grandmother (the Crone Goddess). Little Red travels to the Crone along a path in the forest/Otherworld. In the forest, she comes to a crossway where the path forks into the high path of needles (security, warmth and longevity), and the low path of pins (insecurity, cold and pain). There she meets the wolf (the Church). At this point Little Red trusts the Church, revealing to it the residence of the Goddess (i.e. her Crone aspect). Since the Goddess offers humanity warmth, good health and security, Little Red Riding Hood takes the high path of needles. And because the Church is only a temporary, painful, unhealthy religion, the wolf/Church takes the low path of pins.
>
> Once at the Crone's home, the wolf/Church kills this Crone

aspect of the triple goddess. He drains the corpse of blood and carves its meat, storing both in the cupboard. When Little Red/the Virgin Goddess arrives, the wolf/Church feeds her the body and blood of the Crone, thus infusing Little Red with her grandmother's sacred power.

Next, the wolf/Church tries to devour Red. But as Red notices the wolf's ugly teeth, claws and mouth, she begins to realise she's been duped. At that precise moment, the Crone Goddess, "dead" but still viable, comes to Red's rescue by moving the meat and wine quickly through Red's digestive system. Red informs the wolf/Church that she needs a bit of privacy to eliminate the meat and wine. At first, the wolf/Church – symbol of danger to the health and safety of humanity – urges her to engage in the unsanitary act of eliminating in the bed they lie in: "Do it in bed, my child," says the wolf.

But Little Red Riding Hood refuses to obey. Goddess peoples were more hygienic than medieval Christians. The goddess-oriented Minoan and Indus Valley civilizations, for example, are renowned for the extent and sophistication of their bathing facilities, while medieval European Christian people were renowned for the opposite:

> …[T]he early Christian church frequently discouraged cleanliness. "To those that are well, and especially to the young," commanded Saint Benedict in the sixth century, "bathing shall seldom be permitted." Saint Francis of Assisi considered an unwashed body a … badge of piety. Queen Isabella of Castile boasted that she had had only two baths in her life – at birth and before her marriage. (Stuller 1991)

Although Red convinces the wolf/Church to allow her to exit the house for the courtyard, before she leaves he ties a rope around her foot to prevent her escape. She unties the rope, however, and fastens it to a plum tree, thus fooling the Church into thinking she's still in the courtyard when in fact she's flying home to her Mother Goddess.

Could it be that this tale was meant to teach younger pre-patriarchals that trickery and subterfuge were acceptable weapons against those attempting to destroy not only their religion but their entire way of life? As underground rebels battling a powerful political system in league with a vicious religious system, both backed by an armed military, non-Christian Europeans had few other options. Although Little Red grew up in a community in which people trusted each other, she had to learn that Church and civil authorities could not be trusted, and that one way to survive them was through deception and duplicity.

As a possible ritual or "passion play" designed to hasten the demise of the patriarchy, The Story of Grandmother would have been enacted with four actors: Mother, Little Red, the wolf and Grandmother. The characters would symbolise the battle between the triple goddess and the patriarchy. Props: a loaf of bread, a bottle of milk, a jug of wine, a plate of meat, a handful of needles, some pins, a rope, a symbolic plum tree. Although the wolf/Church kills the Crone, ingesting the body of the Crone gives Red the Virgin Goddess the magic she needs to outwit the Church and restore the triple goddess to her former power and glory.

Although it seems to be a fairy tale about the history of the clash between goddess religion and the Church, Little Red Riding Hood is not the only fairy tale addressing this clash. The Church – one in a string of patriarchal religions over the millennia to storm through Europe – shows up in few of the Brothers Grimm tales, but when Christian elements do enter the picture, they're often shown in a negative light. In Godfather Death, for example, the protagonist is looking for a godfather for his child. At the end of the tale he turns down Jehovah in favour of Death, explaining that "Death is fair to all," and Jehovah only to a favoured few. Death treats everyone equally, claiming the rich as well as the poor, but God gives only to the rich and lets the poor go hungry.

The Church is shown as the bad guy in other fairy tales as well. In the Grimm fairy tales, for example, Christian priests and parsons are an unsavoury lot. Old Hildebrand, for example, begins like this: "Once upon a time lived a peasant and his wife, and the parson of the village had a fancy for the wife, and had wished for a long while to spend a whole day happily with her." So one Sunday, when Hildebrand's wife was ill and couldn't travel to church, Hildebrand went alone and listened to the parson preaching that whoever had an ill family member should travel to Göckerli hill and bring back laurel as a cure. While Hildebrand was on his way to Göckerli hill, however, the parson waltzed over to Hildebrand's house and spent a happy day with his wife. Fortunately, Hildebrand met his cousin the egg merchant on the road, who alerted him about the tryst, and drove him back home in his cart, so that Hildebrand could send the parson packing.

In The Little Peasant too, the parson fancies someone else's wife, in this case the miller's spouse, and plots to spend private time with her. The hero of the story – the "little peasant" – saves the day. When the parson finally realises his dream of rendezvousing with the miller's wife, the miller returns home unexpectedly and the little peasant's magic raven points to the closet where the cleric is hiding.

* * *

In conclusion, some fairy tales seem designed to illustrate the differences between goddess religion and the Christian religion. They describe the present and forecast the future, or paint pictures of Christianity's weak points. In the following chapter we'll look at another set of fairy tales – ones about how goddesses created and cared for the world, and about pre-patriarchal religious belief and practice in general.

Chapter 12

Fairy Tales about Creation, Cosmology and Theology

> *It seems there is a psychological need for something that only the fairy tale can give...*
> Davidson and Chaudhri 2003: 12

According to the folklorist Vladimir Propp the Russian fairy tale The Frog Princess explains how a Great Goddess created the world. In this tale a king asks his sons to shoot arrows and marry the women who return the arrows. Unfortunately, the youngest son's arrow is returned by a frog (spoiler alert: she's really an enchanted princess). While dancing at her wedding, the frog princess creates forests, lakes and birds with a wave of her hand. Later, by using magic she wins all the contests and competitions set by the king.

One night the frog princess sheds her amphibian skin, and meets her husband at a dance – where she is revealed as a startlingly gorgeous woman. When he stumbles onto the frog skin, the prince burns it – to prevent his gorgeous wife from morphing into a frog again. But the moment her skin disappears, the princess disappears too. Only by completing a punishing task involving a spindle, gold thread, a locked box and a key, does the prince manage to win back his bride. But at this point their troubles begin in earnest: a man from the princess' past begins to hound and pursue them. In the end the prince and princess are saved by an old woman who gives them a magic carpet. On this "they took off and flew like birds" and soon "...began to live and prosper, for the glory of all the people." (Afanas'ev 1973: 123)

Propp thinks this princess is a very old, pre-agricultural goddess who created the world via her dancing: "She danced and danced, whirled and whirled, and everyone was amazed. She waved her right hand, and forests and lakes appeared; she waved her left hand, and all sorts of birds began to fly." This very ancient, totemic princess-goddess belonged to people still following the old hunting-gathering way of life, says Propp.

Although the princess is the giver of water, sometimes she's also water itself. "And he noticed that wherever the princess went, wherever her horses stepped, springs appeared, and he followed her by the trail of springs she had left". And even though it is the princess-goddess who chooses her husband – by returning his arrow – the chosen man nevertheless must pass a test before winning her. In the end, as we saw above, both the goddess and her consort "prosper for the glory of all the people." (Propp 1984: 143)

Some fairy tales seem designed to point out the clear and striking differences between the creation myths of the goddess religions and those of the Christian religion. For example, in the Grimm Brothers' The White Snake, you'll find everything that's present in the Biblical Adam and Eve myth: a snake, an apple, a garden, and a man and a woman who love each other. The White Snake is obviously a pre-patriarchal version of the Adam-and-Eve myth. In many respects the two tales are identical. For example, both involve a pair of lovers, the Tree of Life, the Apple of Life, and a garden. What's more, in both tales the snake and the eating of the apple lead to the outcome of the story.

Here's where the similarities end, however, and the giant differences begin. The most profound difference is that instead of being condemned to eternal damnation for eating the apple, the Grimms Adam and Eve, by eating that same apple, are consigned to eternal bliss.

And there are other differences as well. In The White Snake the woman doesn't hog the apple all to herself; she cuts it in half and shares it with the man. What's more, it's this sharing of Aphrodite's "apple of love" that triggers the woman's love for the man in the first place, and is partly responsible for the tale's happy ending: "They cut the Apple of Life in two and ate it together; and then her heart became full of love for him, and they lived in undisturbed happiness to a great age." As we all know, for eating that same apple Adam and Eve were consigned to the opposite fate: living in sorrow forever outside The Garden of Eden.

Another huge difference between the two tales revolves around the snake. In the Christian Bible, the snake deals only with Eve, never Adam. As a matter of fact, throughout the entire story Adam is a passive, do-nothing kind of dude. Not so with the hero in The White Snake. In this story, the snake teaches "Adam" how to talk to animals, and therefore allows him to play a large part in moving the story toward its happy ending. In short, the goddess-worldview tale is about men and women being strong, active – and equal. It is about the sexes working together with animals to ensure elegant-life outcomes. In contrast, the Christian story is the opposite on all counts: passive males are burned by demonic women who listen to "dumb" animals. The outcome? Pure misery.

While some fairy tales enlighten us about how goddesses created the world, others explain how goddesses care for the world and keep it safe. This is where Heide Gottner-Abendroth's (1995) theories come in. If they haven't been totally mangled by the patriarchy, says Gottner-Abendroth, fairy tales are stories about the pre-patriarchal goddess and her relationship to humans as well as the rest of life on earth. Gottner-Abendroth divides fairy tales into three groups: (1) "the abundance-giving women in the Other World", (2) "the gift-giving woman in a deathlike state", and (3) "fairy tales of the redeemer". In group one, a woman gives gifts to and initiates a younger woman. The gift giver is the goddess, and the initiate will become her earthly priestess. Examples of fairy tales in this first category include Mother Holle, Cinderella, and One Eye, Two Eyes and Three Eyes.

In Gottner-Abendroth's second group, "the gift-giving woman in a deathlike state", the heroines in some tales are swept into comatose states in which they either give birth or renew life in some other way; Sleeping Beauty and Snow White are examples (originally both women gave birth to babies). In these tales the heroine is the goddess herself. In other tales in this category the goddess, in order to lift a curse dropped onto her brothers, remains mute for years. Examples here include The Twelve Brothers, The Seven Ravens, The Six Swans, and Little Brother and Little Sister. In Gottner-Abendroth's third group, "fairy tales of the redeemer", the goddess marries her *heros* (her chosen mortal lover), and one of the main characters in the tale dies (symbolically) and is later brought back to life. Into this category fall such tales as The Frog King and The Four Ingenious Brothers.

As noted, Gottner-Abendroth's theory works for fairy tales largely unmangled by the Church or other male-centred religions. The problem is that most fairy tales have been so mangled. In some, large segments were dropped – segments vital to the tale's meaning. A glaring example is the Brothers Grimm's version of Sleeping Beauty, in which the entire second half of the story is hacked off – the part in which Sleeping Beauty bears twins, moves in with the prince, and is almost murdered by the prince's mother. Patriarchal tampering with fairy tales sometimes leads to female characters becoming male, or even getting kicked out of the story altogether. Hansel used to be Gretel's sister, for example, not her brother, and the princess in The Frog King was not an only child; like Cinderella, she too had sisters – but they were kicked out of the story. Patriarchals also trivialised the goddess and her priestesses, turning them into nothing more than "curious girls" (Cinderella and Sleeping Beauty, for example) who were "constantly doing housework" (Cinderella and Gold Marie) (Gottner-Abendroth 1995: 169-176).

Not only the goddess but her symbols too were stripped of their dignity. In the opening scene of the Grimms version of The Frog King, the princess-goddess is tossing around a childish golden ball. In other versions of the tale, however, we get the real story: it wasn't a ball at all, but Aphrodite's golden apple of love that the princess played with. So when she accidentally tossed the love-apple into the well, of course the frog eagerly followed her home and hopped into her bed. But was the frog really a frog? In the Scottish, Holstein and Slavic versions of this tale the "hoppity, though somewhat slippery little frog" was a far more powerful animal: a giant snake, i.e., a phallic symbol. Along these same lines, the dwarfs who took pity on Snow White were not "clever but helpless ... garden dwarves" but powerful supernatural figures who in Celtic mythology were "graced with charm and magical powers" (Gottner-Abendroth 1995: 174, 158, 149).

Finally, the male-centred religions fooled around extensively with the ancient sacred marriage, which in the Grimms tales especially is whittled down to "a kiss" or "'playing' in the bedroom". Good examples: Sleeping Beauty and Snow White. According to the Brothers Grimm in both these tales the princesses were wakened from their comatose states by a prince's kiss. In fact, however, it was their babies who wakened them – children born from the sacred marriage, consecrated while these two goddesses were in the same slumbering state plants enjoy before they germinate underground in early spring (Gottner-Abendroth 1995: 174).

Now let's take a closer look at each of Gottner-Abendroth's three fairy-tale groups, starting with the first, "the abundance-giving women in the Other World". In this type of tale, the goddess-heroine initiates young girls into priestesshood. The sequence of events goes like this: leaving her family, a girl enters the Otherworld, where the goddess initiates her, turning her into an ordained priestess, and then showers her with gifts to carry back to the earthly plane. An example is Mother Holla, in which the heroine Gold Marie tumbles down a well and into the Otherworld where she is initiated by the goddess Holda, who requires that she learn the pre-patriarchal arts of baking, horticulture and stock breeding (as symbolised by the baking bread Marie pulls from the oven, the apples she shakes from the tree, and – in versions other than the Grimms – by the cow she relieves of its milk). Before Marie leaves the Otherworld, Holda showers her with gold, symbol of abundance, and Marie totes this wealth with her back to the earthly plane.

In Gottner-Abendroth's second type of fairy tale, "the gift-giving woman in a deathlike state", in order to make certain that life on earth continues the goddess fades away into a kind of coma, from which she eventually emerges. The plot sequence in this case is as follows: first, the goddess falls into a coma-like state and, while there, either gives birth or renews life in some other way; next, her life is threatened, but eventually she escapes the threat. An example of this class of tale is Sleeping Beauty (Gottner-Abendroth 1995:145-48). After an irate fairy drops a curse on her, Beauty plunges into a 100-year deep sleep. While she slumbers, however, a prince finds her, and they consummate the sacred marriage, after which Beauty gives birth to twins, Sun and Moon. Sun and Moon suck the poisoned flax from her finger, wakening her from her sleep. In Charles Perrault's and other versions, Beauty and the twins move into the prince's castle where his mother tries to kill Sun, Moon and Beauty too, but the prince rushes onstage to rescue them all – in the nick of time, of course (Appelbaum 2002:130).

Snow White belongs in this second category too, but like Sleeping Beauty, in a sadly mangled state. After her stepmother (seething with envy over the girl's remarkable beauty) feeds her a poisoned apple, Snow White drops into a comatose state. Assuming she's dead, the desolate seven dwarfs place her in a glass coffin (in some versions a glass mountain or glass castle). Next, the tale becomes an almost exact duplicate of Sleeping Beauty: the sacred marriage in this tale too is consummated while the princess-goddess slumbers, after which she bears two children, who waken her – in this case "by sucking the ring of sleep from her finger". The ending of the tale, in which Snow White is threatened and saved, has been lopped off. Also, in this tale as in Sleeping Beauty, the prince was an add-on, since this tale-type originated in Europe's middle pre-patriarchal era – when the goddess could reproduce life by herself, with no help from males (Gottner-Abendroth 1995:148-150).

In Gottner-Abendroth's third group of fairy tales, "fairy tales of the redeemer", a type Gottner-Abendroth thinks dates to the late European pre-patriarchal era, the goddess depends upon the male principle to consummate the sacred marriage. Plot sequences here are based on earth's life cycle – plants die in winter, "mate" in spring, offspring pop up in summer and die in winter. Likewise, the plot sequence of this third group of fairy tales includes three repeating phases: initiation, sacred marriage, and death-and-return. First, either the goddess or her *heros* (or sometimes both) are initiated in some way. Next comes the sacred marriage: the goddess marries her *heros.* Third, the *heros* dies (often symbolically), but is later resurrected, and after that the cycle begins all over again – just as the cycle of earthly life begins again each spring.

Even though it's been badly butchered, one example of this third type of tale is The Frog King (Gottner-Abendroth 1995: 157-160). In the version handed us by the Brothers Grimm, a frog follows a princess home and tries to crawl into bed with her, whereupon she hurls it against the wall – turning it into the handsome prince it really had been all along. But this is a badly truncated tale, with both its beginning and ending lopped off. Ever wonder how the prince had the bad luck to become a frog in the first place? It was the mother of the daughter he refused to marry who did it – in raging fit of fury.

At any rate, once the princess-goddess frees the prince from his frog body, the two consummate the sacred marriage. Here, the Grimms' tale ends. In other versions, however, the ending serves up the death-and-resurrection part of Gottner-Abendroth's holy goddess cycle. In this alternative ending, the frog prince suddenly disappears. After the princess scours the cosmos – she goes to the moon, the sun, and the wind all three – and finally finds him, she discovers with a shock that he's engaged to another woman. The princess "buys three nights from the false bride", giving the prince a chance to recognise her, the princess, as his one true love. In another more poignant version of the tale the princess disguises herself as the driver of the prince's wedding coach, and it's when he hears the sound of her heart breaking that he finally recognises her (Gottner-Abendroth 1995:158).

Also illustrating this third type of tale is the story of The Four Ingenious Brothers. In this story a princess (a goddess, remember) promises to marry whichever one of four brothers brings her the most luscious gifts. But before the men finish their task, the princess falls sick, and the brothers' gifts must be sacrificed to save her life. These life-savers include a magic mirror, an apple and a carpet (symbolising the three ancient feminine arts of magic, healing and weaving). After she recovers, the princess is forced to formulate a new test: whoever can kill a dragon will inherit her hand in marriage. Although the youngest brother wins the contest, he's knocked out cold in the process, and another brother whisks the dragon's head off to the princess and claims her as his bride. To the youngest brother, this is the essence of death: he has lost "all he holds precious": the contest, his good name, his fame, his recognition and his honour. However, after lugging the dragon's tongue to the princess, she sees he's the true hero, marries him, and as a consequence his life is restored. He is "redeemed".

Some fairy tales recall the Greek myth of the goddess Demeter and her daughter Kore, which, like Gottner-Abendroth's second type of fairy tale deals with nature's annual cycle of birth, growth, death, birth, growth, and so forth. A major difference between the Demeter-Kore myth and these spin-off fairy tales, however, is that the myth is unafraid to designate goddesses as goddesses, whereas the fairy tales are forced to disguise them as royal figures. In the Demeter-Kore myth, Kore is forced by the god Hades to spend winters with him underground. Each spring, however, she's allowed to return above ground to be with her mother Demeter. When Kore is pulled underground Demeter becomes so miserable that she lets the earth's vegetation die, but when Kore returns in spring Demeter lets everything bloom and blossom again.

In the fairy tale The Flower Queen's Daughter, from Bukovina in Eastern Europe, the Demeter-Kore myth is switched backwards: during winters, the Flower Queen's daughter (the "princess") lives underground with her mother (the "queen"). But each spring she returns above ground to her prince, who won her hand in marriage by passing several arduous tests. In this tale it is the union between the goddess-princess and her *heros*-prince that leads to the rebirth of life in spring. But winter is the time when the seeds of life begin to germinate, and this is why the daughter must drop underground during that season. Unlike Kore, who despises Hades and her forced time underground, the Flower Queen's daughter doesn't seem to mind at all spending time underground with her mother. In other words, in contrast to the male-centred Greek myth, this goddess-centred fairy tale offers a win-win situation for all involved.

Tucked away in The Flower Queen's Daughter is an interesting element that makes the tale seem quite old: as he works to win the princess' hand, a dragon's mother gives the prince "a cloak made of copper". Before bronze became popular in Europe during or before the 2nd millennium BC, copper was Europe's metal of choice. It was also the only metal known in Old Europe, of which Bukovina used to be a part. Of course the presence of copper in this story doesn't prove it originated in Copper-Age Old Europe, but it is nevertheless one of the tale's more interesting aspects.

Keep in mind that any particular fairy tale might have served more than one purpose. For example, while it recalls the classical myth of Demeter and Kore, The Flower Queen's Daughter also seems to shed light on the concept of "evil" as it might have been viewed by some of Europe's goddess-oriented populations. One thing I forgot to mention about The Flower Queen's Daughter was that the prince needed to rescue the daughter from a dragon's mother, who was holding her captive. Now, this dragon's mother was no raving beauty. As a matter of fact, she was "the ugliest woman under the sun, and, added to it all, she had three heads. Her appearance was a great shock to the prince and so was her voice, which was like the croaking of many ravens. She asked him, 'Why have you come here?'" (Lang 1894) So it was this charming old woman who gave the prince the tests he had to pass before he could marry the princess-goddess.

> The Prince answered the dragon's mother at once, "I have heard so much of your beauty and kindness, that I would very much like to enter your service."
>
> "Very well," said the Mother Dragon, "but if you wish to enter my service, you must first lead my mare out to the meadow and look after her for three days; but if you don't bring her home safely every evening, we will eat you up."

So the prince risks his own life to save his beloved, and, with the help the kings of the fishes, foxes and eagles finds the mare each time she runs away. By passing Mother Dragon's tests, the prince saves his own life and that of his beloved princess too.

As you might have guessed, the "Mother Dragon" is not really a dragon at all, but code for something. What? According to Heide Gottner-Abendroth, in the old goddess religions the dragon was code for death and the death goddess, whereas slaying the dragon was code for conquering one's fear of death. In mangled fairy tales, however, dragons represent all aspects of the goddess, even the life-giving parts, since the patriarchy hated her and wanted to broadcast the message that proper men sliced and diced her whenever they got the chance (Gottner-Abendroth 1995: 163). In relatively untouched fairy tales like The Flower Queen's Daughter, however, dragons still represent death and the death goddess.

According to Heide Gottner-Abendroth, to goddess-oriented Europeans death was not a bad thing but only a gateway to the next life. "The horror of death," she says, "is a patriarchal concept." (1995: 97) The idea that death is only an avenue to the next life is often illuminated in fairy tales. In more than one fairy tale, for example, the protagonist dies only to be reborn. Both Snow White and Sleeping Beauty died and were reborn, as were both daughters in Mother Holle (no one can live long at the bottom of a well, and these women spent days if not weeks there). In the fairy tale The Juniper Tree it's a boy who dies and then resurrects. After being murdered and then morphing into a bird, the boy sings out:

My mother she killed me,
My father he ate me,
My sister, little Marlinchen
Gathered together all my bones,
Tied them in a silken handkerchief,
Laid them beneath the juniper-tree,
Kywitt, kywitt, what a beautiful bird am I!

It's fairly obvious that this boy is not all that bothered by his death. And why should he be? Before the tale ends he's magically born again.

So what for us is typically a bad and frightening thing – death – was not necessarily so for pre-patriarchal Europeans. Likewise, what for us is a dualistic world of "good" versus "evil", was probably a much more complex situation to these ancestors. In most European religions today a good god gives us good things, and a bad god (Satan) gives us bad things. In contrast, for goddess peoples all things came from different aspects of the same deity, who was triune – with Daughter in charge of new life, Mother in charge of fertility, and Crone in charge of old age, the death passage, and then rebirth into a new life.

So how did pre-patriarchal Europeans respond to cruelty – both in nature, and perhaps also in the occasional incidence among them of human cruelty? (I don't think people had much reason to be cruel in pre-patriarchal societies; one finds little if any human cruelty in modern peaceful societies such as the Semai of Malaysia, the Lepchas of northern India, and others, which suggests cruelty is a learned not innate human trait.) Marie-Louise von Franz thinks fairy tales give us a clue here. She comes to a surprising conclusion: they turned their heads away.

Von Franz is right when she says nature can be horribly cruel:

"...a fox will partially eat a swan frozen on the ice and leave it to struggle for hours and hours with a wing eaten away – unless a human being comes by and gives it the coup de grace..." She talks about seeing "...a roebuck trying to crawl over the ice with a cancerous growth hanging on it – the other roebucks kick it aside and it sinks, then struggles up and walks a few steps further, dragging itself along for weeks with the cancer, until one day, thank God, it does not get up anymore." (1976: 167) The idea that the correct response to cruelty in nature is to walk away from it, to turn your head, came to von Franz from fairy tales in which women are rewarded for lying, tales which had always "fascinated" her. In one:

> ...a girl pokes into the horrible secret of the mother-goddess, who says afterwards to her, "My child, did you see me in my suffering?" and the girl denies it, saying she had noticed nothing. She ... is rewarded for her lies. So not poking into Mother Nature's horrible secrets, or lying about it if one had done so, pretending one has not seen anything ... is the right thing to do, according to the story. If the mother-goddess were a human being, we could understand it; she does not want her deficiencies, her shadow, or her suffering to be seen. (1976: 173)

Von Franz also uses the Grimms' fairy tale Frau Trude to illustrate her point. In Frau Trude a little girl is:

> ...very obstinate and never obeyed her parents. One day her parents tell her never to go to Frau Trude's hut or that will be the end of her. The little girl runs immediately to Frau Trude's house, and Frau Trude turns her into a stick of wood which she immediately throws into her fire, saying, "That makes a good, bright light!" ... And this fairy tale says it shows a certain kind of healthy reaction, or wisdom, not to poke into these things too much, and not to ask too many questions. (1976: 167)

Of course since most of us now live in a patriarchal world, we are undoubtedly cursed with much more human-on-human violence than our pre-patriarchal ancestors were. Von Franz, however, thinks that even we could benefit sometimes from following their "don't look" rule:

> ...[I]f one looks at evil too closely and not in a mature way but naively, one gets cynical. If you walk through the museum [at] Auschwitz, what is your conclusion? Schopenhauer said that another man is to a human being just good enough to grease his boots... If you land with that philosophy the next consequence is that you say, "I am going to take a Luger, or a Colt, and I intend to survive and to hell with the others! They are murderers anyhow. They all want to kill me, so I am going to shoot first." ... If I cannot do the human thing of turning away, then by looking at it, I become the cruelty of nature. That's why in the reverence of the chthonic god in antiquity, people turned away and covered their faces, and when they prayed to Hecate they put on a black veil not to see her – in order not to become her. (1976: 175)

So if we could ask them, perhaps our pre-patriarchal ancestors would put it this way: "Don't look at the dark side too long or you yourself will turn dark." Of course this doesn't mean we shouldn't change things from dark to light when we can – we must – but in some cases there's nothing one can do. And in those cases, maybe it is indeed best to look away. As for human cruelty, looking the other way in a society in which human cruelty was rare might have worked wonders; I can imagine that almost nothing would be more demoralising than being shunned by your entire community, and with only a small dose of it a cruel person might straighten up and fly right in a hurry.

So far we've looked at several spiritual beliefs that have been coded into fairy tales, including those revolving around creation, nature's life cycles, the training and ordination of priestesses, and concepts of death and evil. Another set of spiritual beliefs that I think are secretly tucked away in fairy tales are about archaeological artefacts called "female figurines". Most Neolithic female figurines were sized to fit comfortably in the human hand. Many appear "otherworldly", their ancient makers having given them women's bodies but bird heads and beaks, for example, or coiled snakes for legs. Since they are typically accompanied by few if any male figurines, and are inscribed with many of the same symbols found on the walls of associated temples, the renowned Harvard/UCLA archaeologist Marija Gimbutas suggested that these female figurines represent goddesses, and that their makers belonged to societies oriented around female deity.

Among some indigenous peoples, sacred human figurines are still revered today. This is true for northern Siberian peoples like the Chukchee, Koryak and Evenki, and the Hopi of the American southwest. The Hopi make and revere figurines called kachinas (mistakenly labelled "dolls" by non-Native Americans), and out of 260-plus such figurines, "about 32 are epiphanies of deities, [and] the others are personifications of spirits of lower ranking." (Haarman 2009: 17, 123)

For quite some time I'd known that archaeologists have been digging up thousands of female figurines from ancient Neolithic archaeological sites, both in south-eastern Europe ("Old Europe") and elsewhere around the world. But recently I was surprised to find two Russian fairy tales that seem to contain the literary equivalents of these ancient statuettes: Vasilisa the Fair and Prince Danilla Govorilla. Both tales contain magical "dolls" that help young fairy-tale women through rough times. After reading these tales, I wondered: are their dolls code for "goddesses"? And if so, could these tales provide clues about how ancient Europeans interacted with their female figurines: about what they did with them – and when, and why, and how?

Vasilisa the Fair is about a beautiful young Russian girl whose mother is dying. From her death bed, the mother hands her daughter a magic doll, small enough to fit in a skirt pocket – in other words a size similar to Neolithic goddess figurines. Her mother instructs Vasilisa to keep the doll with her always – but to breathe not a word about it to anyone: "Together with my maternal blessing I leave you this doll… If you get into trouble, give the doll food and ask its advice. When it has eaten, it will tell you what to do in your trouble."

The doll does indeed help Vasilisa out of several bad scrapes. When her father remarries, for example, and Vasilisa's new stepmother seems extremely anxious to irritate and vex the girl, the doll intervenes – by briskly completing the impossible chores the stepmother demands of Vasilisa, or by advising Vasilisa when the stepmother sends her into the forest to borrow fire from the dreaded Baba Yaga (the Crone and death aspect of the goddess). The doll seems to be alive, and loved as a human being would be loved. For instance, Vasilisa feeds it the choicest portions of her meals, and tells it all her troubles. And at the end of the tale we learn that the girl "carried the doll in her pocket 'til the end of her life." (Afanas'ev 1973: 439-447)

Could this fairy tale tell us anything about how Neolithic Europeans might have behaved around the female figurines they produced so abundantly? Like Vasilisa, were they sometimes instructed to carry such figurines with them on a daily basis – but to let no one know it? Or is this part of the tale simply a reference to the medieval and early-modern church in Europe forbidding goddess worship and, so, forcing non-Christian Russians to carry their sacred objects on the sly? If so, this suggests the fascinating possibility that even after goddess worship was beaten back by the Church, some Europeans at least still carried three-dimensional, hand-held goddess images with them, but secretly, in their pockets, or maybe even sewn into hidden parts of their clothing.

It's important to point out that just because archaeologists haven't unearthed female figurines at any particular archaeological site doesn't mean such figurines weren't produced there. The inhabitants could have carved them out of wood, for example, sewn them out of cloth, or manufactured them out of straw. As a matter of fact, the clay and occasional metal figurines that survive well buried in soil would be far more of a pain to carry around in a pocket than a straw or wooden figurine. Clay breaks easily, and metal weighs more than straw by a long stretch. My guess is that Old-Europeans produced goddess figurines out of cloth, wood and/or straw as well as clay, but that the former disintegrated quickly in archaeological deposits. At some point too, making figurines out of clay could have lost favour, so that people began making them instead out of lighter, less fragile materials. This would explain why we find far fewer post-Neolithic goddess figurines – most of them might have quickly disintegrated through time.

In addition to Vasilisa the Fair I discovered a second fairy tale about dolls. In Prince Danilla Govorilla a witch casts a spell on a prince to make him want to marry his sister. Not surprisingly, the sister is mortified – until a group of wise old women pull her aside and tell her to make four "little dolls". "Tuck them into the corners of your bridal chamber," they advise. This solves the problem: the dolls help the princess drop into the Underworld long enough for the prince to come to his senses:

> And the dolls in the four corners cried like cuckoos… The earth began to open, the sister began to fall in. Her brother cried: "Sister Catherine, come to the featherbed!' … The dolls cuckooed... Only the sister's head was still above ground … The dolls cuckooed [again], and she vanished into the earth. (Afanas'ev 1973: 351-56)

What these dolls bring to my mind are the hundreds if not thousands of small clay female figurines archaeologists have dug out of niches in the walls of almost every house in the large, ancient Indus-Valley-Civilisation cities of Harappa, Mohenjodaro and Chanhudaro. In the first several millennia BC these three cities were part of a sophisticated and peaceful Bronze-Age civilisation in what is now India and Pakistan. According to archaeologist Jane McIntosh (2002: 7), the Indus Valley people lived "a lifestyle that would be the envy of most today." Like the Indus Valley people, the princess in Prince Danilla Govorilla placed her small human figures into protected spaces in her home. Were her figures, like theirs, actually goddesses?

Incredibly, as late as 980 AD public worship of goddesses was still allowed in Russia. In that year the Russian Great Goddess Mokosh still glowed brightly in the official Russian pantheon. What's more, according to Professor of Russian and European Cultural History Joanna Hubbs, an unnamed 16th century writer claimed that Mokosh continued "long after" 980 AD as one of Russia's three primary deities (Hubbs 1988: 17). Without a hint of doubt, Hubbs maintains that Russian fairy tales are secret repositories in which priestesses of Mokosh hid their theology for safekeeping in dangerous times. If true, the ancient Russian goddess religion still survives today in Russian fairy tales. But any goddess figurines in Russian tales would never be called goddesses. Too dangerous. Might they have been called "dolls" instead?

> The goddess and her priestesses could be eliminated neither by the pagan *volkhvy*, nor by the Varangian rulers, nor by the Christian priesthood… Instead [she] … was appropriated by the male ruling elite… Consequently, the religion of the mothers moved underground, into the home or as secret rites at rivers and in groves, fields, and gardens. The cult of the Mother Goddess in her various forms and functions was carried into the religious folk tradition of the peasantry. (Hubbs 1988: 22-23)

According to Hubbs, Vasilisa the Fair contains secret code describing ancient pre-patriarchal initiation rites for girls. When Vasilisa's evil stepmother forces the girl to beg for fire from the frightening Baba Yaga, Baba agrees to fork over the fire on two conditions: that Vasilisa work for her, and that the girl passes certain tests. With the help of her doll Vasilisa satisfies both conditions, and thus successfully completes the first stage of her initiation ordeal. Next, with the doll in her pocket she journeys over the countryside, and after an old woman gives her work as a spinner and weaver, she spins, weaves and sews a shirt for the king. As a result, the king falls for and marries her. "She is now fully ordained as a priestess of Baba Yaga, the maiden who would become a bride, a mother, and herself a witch in her old age." At the end of the tale, we learn that Vasilisa, the old woman, the king – and the "amuletic" doll – all live together, happily ever after (Hubbs 1988: 48-51). Could Old European women have carried goddess figurines throughout their initiation rites into the priesthood, to help them navigate these rites successfully? If so, might they, like Vasilisa with her doll, been careful to keep the same figurine throughout their lives?

Both Vasilisa the Fair and Prince Danilla Govorilla contain mothers who are either dead or dying. In fairy tales, dead mothers probably serve as code for the Mother Goddess (Gottner-Abendroth 1995: 142), and when fairy-tale "mothers" die they often leave their children magical helpers (Davidson 2003: 102-04). In various versions of Cinderella, for example, the bequeathed helper is a bird or fairy godmother while in the Grimms' tale The Juniper Tree the mother, from her grave, merges with her son as a bird to help him battle his evil stepmother. And in Vasilisa the Fair the bequeathed helper is what appears to be a tiny, three-dimensional image of the goddess herself. In Prince Danilla Govorilla too, the dolls who make the sound of the cuckoo might also be a gift sent to the prince and princess from their dead "mother", possibly a bird goddess. Tellingly, as Miriam Dexter points out, "In some Baltic folksongs, the cuckoo is an incarnation of the dead mother." (Dexter 2011 quoting Gimbutas 1989: 195)

Mythology and anthropology both show that European "dolls" sometimes represent goddesses. Speaking about the ancient Celtic goddess Brigid, Marija Gimbutas says "girls carried dolls in her image." Gimbutas says Brigid, like Holda-Perchta, descended from the Neolithic goddesses of Old Europe (the same civilisation that churned out female figurines by the cartload) (Gimbutas 2001: 185, 187). Anthropology shows the same. When in 1959 and 1960 anthropologist John Messenger did fieldwork on the island of Inis Beag off the west coast of Ireland, he found modern evidence of women and girls carrying "Brigid dolls", with at least one low-income owner of such dolls using them to obtain food from others in her community. From his informants Messenger learned that early in the 20th century an impoverished island resident habitually carried her immaculately dressed straw "Brigid's Doll" from door to door. After she showed them the figure and recited the following charm, islanders would give her food:

Here comes Brigid,
Dressed in white.
Give her something
For the night.
She is deaf and
She is dumb.
For God's sake,
Give her some.

After collecting the food, the woman used her miniature model of a human figure to bless each person in the house. In the 1960s Messenger found small groups of island girls going from house to house using the same kind of figure and method to extract candy money and alms for the Church from island adults (Messenger 1983: 103).

I wonder, did Old Europeans actually feed and talk to their goddess figurines as Vasilisa did? Did they use them to gain confidence to successfully pass through rigorous initiation rites? Did some use figurines to elicit needed or desired items from their neighbours – as the Inis Beag Islanders did? Did Old Europeans tote clay figurines around in their pockets and then lodge them at home in sacred wall niches at night, or in other secret, private places? Or did they use images made of lighter and less fragile materials to carry out into the world, and leave the clay ones at home? Did they place figurines in certain locations where they felt the potential for evil lay, as Prince Danilla's sister did, in order to prevent that evil from happening? While we may never know for certain how prehistoric peoples interacted with their anthropomorphic figurines, the suggestions above certainly constitute a few interesting possibilities to mull over.

Chapter 13

Fairy Tales as Magic Spells and Incantations

> *In 1604 Northumberland cunning women Katherine Thompson and Anne Nevelson were convicted for putting the bill of a white duck to a patient's mouth and then mumbling charms.*
> Wilby 2005: 35

The most startling result to come out of my research was evidence that many European fairy tales were medieval and early-modern magic spells designed to heal people, attract a lover, catch a thief, and so on. Many such tales seem to have originated as descriptions of shamans' journeys to the "spirit world". In fact, as we'll see later, fairy tales do share several basic features in common with the stories shamans told about their spirit-world journeys. Later, possibly in the Early Middle Ages, shaman's stories about their journeys would be sold, traded or otherwise disseminated as lengthy "magic spells" or incantations (Bever 2008: 277-78).

Still later, around 1000 AD, story-spells were replaced by short, formulaic magic spells in which pre-Christian characters were disguised by turning them into Christian figures (God, angels, demons, etc.). But this probably happened in some places only. In other places the old, lengthy story-spells would have soldiered on. In the early-modern era (16th-18th centuries), however, the pre-Christian characters in the story-spells too were rendered incognito – not by turning them into Christian figures this time, but into secular ones – princesses, wise old men, wicked stepmothers, and so on. As they do with shamans' journeys, fairy tales too share several basic features with medieval and early-modern magic spells.

To refresh your memory: a shaman is a religious specialist, either male or female, who travels to "the cosmic realm" to convince supernatural beings to act on behalf of individuals or groups in relation to health, healing, fertility, and protection. To contact supernatural beings shamans enter into the "trance séance", either privately with one individual or in a public ritual "rich in drama" (Schultz and Lavenda 2009: 211-12). Shamans have spirit helpers. Shamans are animists, i.e., they believe everything in the universe has a spirit, even inanimate objects like stones, straw and pieces of coal (Wilby 2005: 128).

If you think shamans never practiced in Europe, think again. Tacitus reported that shamans existed in ancient Germany in Brandenburg among the Semnones, and that they used trance and possession trance in their practices. And even after Europe was Christianised shamans just went right on practicing their craft: "Soon thereafter, Christianity was introduced ... but magical practices reminiscent of shamanism continued to be used widely, albeit with a heavily Christian symbolism..." (Bever 2008: 193) As a matter of fact, in recent decades, scholars have identified shamans practicing in several parts of Europe as late as the early modern era (1500-1800) (Wilby 2005: 125).

> From many parts of Europe and far beyond, we know of ecstatics who obtained special healing arts from their soul travels. The benandanti of Fruili ... the Hungarian taltos ... the healers of Romania ... (descantatore) ... It is the same in the traditions of Bulgaria and Dalmatia, and the Hungarian historian Gabor Klaniczay has argued that this whole complex of ideas is related to shamanism. (Behringer 1998 p. 87-88)

In 16th century north-eastern Italy, people called "benandanti" reluctantly admitted to the Inquisition that they sent their souls out at night to fight witches who were threatening their community's grain stores and livestock (Ginzburg 1992). Interestingly, the benandanti were linked to the goddess Holda-Perchta: "There was a connection, still of a rather general nature, between the popular divinity of the many names – Abundia-Satia-Diana-Perchta – and the complex of beliefs which revolved about the benandanti." (Ginzburg 1992: 42)

As we saw previously, Vladimir Propp says fairy tales (or "wondertales" as he calls them) sprang from this European shamanic tradition. Propp says fairy tales are historical records documenting what shamans experienced when they trance-journeyed into the Otherworld:

> If we collect shamans' tales of their trances – how the shaman went to seek a soul in the other world, who helped him in this endeavour, how he was conveyed, and so forth – and compare these with the wanderings and flight of the wondertale hero, the correspondence will be obvious. I have traced this correspondence for individual elements, but it also exists at the level of the whole. (Propp 1984: 122)

Propp gives us the following example of a shamanic journey into the spirit world. It explains how the founder of a Pawnee Indian clan first found the family's sacred medicine bundle. First the founder travelled into a forest, where he met a buffalo. The buffalo whisked him off to "the buffalo kingdom". There the founder received the medicine bundle, which he brought back to his clan. And from then on, the bundle protected the clan. According to Propp this kind of tale is "a sort of verbal amulet, a magic agent to affect the surrounding world." In other words, a magic spell. And a powerful spell at that: if the buffalo-medicine-bundle tale were not recited at the end of a certain ritual, the ritual would not work (Propp 1984: 119) (Propp got this tale from George Dorsey's 1904 *Traditions of the Skidi-Pawnee*). Often, North American shamans put themselves into trance and then sent their souls flying off to the spirit world to contact spirit helpers and collect magic power. After coming out of trance, these shamans would describe their journeys to others, and then use their spirit-world magic to "predict the future or prescribe behaviour for the people, which would be aimed at improving their plight." (Driver 1964: 514)

Many fairy tales mirror the stories shamans told about their spirit-world journeys. Like shamans, fairy tale protagonists too leave their families to travel to a spiritual plane (which in this book we've been calling the Otherworld). Just as fairy-tale protagonists do battle with supernatural beings in the Otherworld (witches, trolls, Baba Yagas, wicked stepmothers, etc.), so do shamans often battle supernatural beings in the spirit world (hostile souls of the dead, witches, other shamans, or just plain evil spirits) (Wilby 2005: 152). A third thing fairy tales and shamans' spirit-world stories have in common is that both often include supernatural helpers. Many times the fairy-tale hero or heroine gets a helping hand from a fairy godmother, a talking animal, or a "little old man" (who almost always has magic powers). Shamans too have supernatural helpers – usually called "spirit guides" (Wilby 2005: 130).

What follows is a description of a shamanic journey that sounds like a fairy tale, but which was really a trip taken into the spirit world by an actual Siberian shaman, in order to cure a sick person. This séance was reported in 1924 by the Russian writer A. V. Anokhin. Before starting out on his journey, Anokhin's shaman prayed to Erlik, the evil supernatural being who had caused the sick person's illness. Next the shaman called his helper spirits, and with them at his side "'set out' for the lower world".

Before he could meet Erlik, the shaman had to jump over seven sets of hurdles with 10 to 15 obstacles in each hurdle – obstacles like "black tongs, endlessly opening and closing … a place where … one can lose one's head … swarms of black frogs … swarms of black gluttons … roaring black bears … a boiling black lake, a boiling black hell" and many more. When he finally overcame all the obstacles and reached Erlik, the shaman struck a bargain with the supernatural creature: "another sacrifice will be sent (to you) ... Father Erlik, bestow your blessing!" After that the shaman returned to the ritual setting (i.e., came out of trance) and "answered questions on the outcome of the séance." (Balzer 1990: 63-64)

To reach their goals in the spirit world, early 20th century Eastern Siberian Yakut shamans were sometimes forced to use trickery or coercion. One shaman was described as "riding" into the spirit world with his supernatural helpers (a fish, a bull and a bear), his goal being to heal a sick client by finding and bringing back the client's *kut* (soul), which had been stolen by an evil supernatural being. To accomplish his task the shaman first had to catch the being and then offer it gifts in exchange for the stolen *kut*. Although this strategy worked at times, if it didn't, shamans resorted to subterfuge or force to capture the *kut*, bring it back to the patient, and "incorporate the soul in him". These shamans described their journeys as they happened, to spell-bound audiences (Balzer 1990: 54-58).

Generally the stories shamans told about their spirit-world journeys were not used by others to do their own magic. In

Europe, however – perhaps during the Early Middle Ages – this changed. Shamanic spirit-world stories began to be passed around and used by other magic practitioners, i.e., turned into "magic spells". Even though we typically think of magic spells as shorter than fairy tales there's no reason they need be. The Brothers Grimm and other fairy-tale collectors padded many of their tales, adding both dialogue and details about the characters and physical background of the story. This not only made tales longer, it often made them considerably longer.

At any rate, in some areas, shamans' spirit-world-journey stories began to be appropriated and used by other magic practitioners. Although these practitioners hadn't made a spirit-world journey themselves, they nevertheless felt they could use the journey stories of others to trigger their own magic. The historian Edward Bever calls these appropriated shamanic stories "charms", "spells", and – significantly – "narratives":

> … [A]t least some Germanic charms started as shamanic performances in which the shamans spontaneously described their experiences and combats in ecstatic trances that, by the time they were first recorded had long since become conventionalized narratives and formulaic spells … [These] at most, inspired and guided shaman healers' ecstatic experiences, and, at least, provided a string of rhythmic vocalizations and a series of imagined scenes that, when recited by a skilful practitioner, created an emotional engagement, hypnotic dissociation, and viscerally cathartic release in the patient, similar to those produced by a shaman in an actual trance. (Bever 2008: 278-79)

The earliest Germanic narrative-charms go back to the early Middle Ages. They are about deities facing a problem (a problem similar to the patient's problem), and then overcoming it. In the second half of the Middle Ages these charms/spells became "homogenized", i.e., the same spell would "circulate from region to region" so that eventually there existed a "European wide stock of [spell] motifs" (Bever 2008: 277-78). And of course the same is true of fairy tales: through time they circulated from region to region so that eventually there existed a European-wide stock of them. Most parts of Europe, for example, have their own versions of the story of Cinderella.

We don't know why shamans' stories morphed into magic spells that could be used by others. Did shamans give their stories away willingly? Or were they stolen? Were they bought, borrowed or traded? Among North American Indian shamans, some short magic incantations were "open to the public" and could be used by anyone. Other more secretive ones, however, were bought, sold, and willed from one shaman to another at the point of death, in a secret language known only to shamans (Driver 1964: 514).

What exactly is a magic spell? According to my copy of *Merriam-Webster Unabridged Dictionary* it is: "A word, phrase or form of words supposed to have magic power." Webster's goes on to say, however, that in Old and Middle English the word meant "discourse". I was amazed to find in the *2013 Merriam-Webster Unabridged Dictionary* that an obsolete meaning of the word "spell" is "story" or "tale". Checking an etymological dictionary produced the same results: in the past, the word "spell" meant "story" or "speech" (Barnhart 1995: 745).

As I mentioned earlier, over time story-spells in some parts of Europe evolved into simpler, shorter and more vivid incantations – incantations much less story-like. Around 1000 AD, pre-Christian deities in these spells were replaced by Christian figures: God, angels, demons and so forth (Bever 2008: 278). Although like European shamanic tales, the non-story, formulaic spells of the High and Late Middle Ages are as scarce as hen's teeth, Bever has nevertheless stumbled onto a few – in the witch-trial records of southwest Germany. Although the pagan figures in Bever's spells have all been replaced by Christian ones, the nature of these spells is anything but Christian. The first spell, from the 1590s in the town of Canstatt, belonged to the popular healer Jacob Schaffer (Jacob was also a "cow herder") and was meant to be used by a father to heal his son:

1. *God greet you beloved moonshine,*
What I stroke, that is mine,
I stroke my blood, and my flesh,
In the name of the Father, Son, and Holy Spirit.

The second spell is also from Jacob Schaffer, who used it "for a woman with a bad cold":

2. *Here I go over the sea,*
I spew therein all my woe,
In the name of the Father, Son, and Holy Spirit.

The third incantation, which was found in the accused's own handwriting, was presented at a witch trial in 1709. The accused, Leonard Weissinger, was a 50-year-old judge in the village of Weilheim, near Kirchheim. The paper with the incantation on it still rests in the judicial archives:

3. *Slander and complaint,*
Cares and anger,
All that restrain and compel be yielding,
Depart from me as the moon withdraws from the sun.

The fourth and fifth incantations were found with the first, also in Weissinger's handwriting. The fourth might have been meant for protection in battle; Weissinger had been tried previously for using magic while he was in the army:

4. *Bullets hold fire and flame*
As when Christ on the holy cross came,
His innocent blood forgotten,
So should he stand their shot.

5. *There flow two streams,*
The one is named the Daradra,
The other the wedge doesn't bite,
It is not God's will.
(Bever 2008: 276, 317)

Why at the beginning of the 11th century were some story-spells replaced by short formulaic charms, and also stripped of their gods, goddesses, fairies and witches? We don't know. What's interesting, however, is that at this same time the Church began expending energy in bruising and battering non-Christians again. They also battered non-Christian magic practitioners, and while some of these practitioners gave up, abandoning their practices, others combined their old pagan arts with Christian beliefs (Wilby 2005: 156-159).

Five hundred years later, in the 1500s, the Church began another crackdown on non-Christians – and story-spells morphed again. This crackdown actually began in 1486, with the publication of the *Malleus Maleficarum*, the "Hammer of the Witches". Soon after, the persecution of Europe's "witches" began in earnest, with a "general clustering of the [witch] trials" between 1550 and 1680 (Thurston 2001: 97). This time story-spells kept their story quality, but plugged queens, princesses and witches into the slots where the Mother Goddess and Death Goddess had been. It's worth noting that it's during this same time period, the 1500s and 1600s, that the first published fairy tales begin to appear: *The Facetious Nights of Straparola*, the first publication to include fairy tales, was published in Italy between 1550-53, Tom Thumbe, the earliest known printing of a fairy tale in Britain, was printed in pamphlet form as early as 1621 (Wilby 2005: 248), and the first book published with nothing in it but fairy tales – Basile's *The Pentamerone* – was published in Naples in 1634 and 1636.

But what did the historical witch persecutions of the 16th and 17th centuries have to do with magic spells, pre-Christian religions, or magico-religious practitioners? No one in the 1500s or 1600s still believed in magic, did they? As a matter of fact, they probably did. Over the past few decades, scholars have dug up very convincing evidence that as late as the early-modern era (1500s-1700s) Europeans of all stripes and stations did indeed still believe in magic and magic practitioners. Most early-modern Europeans either consulted magic practitioners, or used their own magic spells to solve their personal and family problems. Magic practitioners too – many of them labelled and prosecuted as witches – believed in their own magic powers, wholeheartedly (Wilby 2005, Gaskill 2010, Bever 2008).

Until recently, academia has vigorously insisted that Europeans accused of witchcraft were simply unlucky souls who found themselves caught up in the whirlwind of the witch persecutions. The problem is, during their trials many accused people admitted that, yes, they had indeed practiced magic to cure the man down the road, to help a woman find her lost gold ring, and so forth. Academia's answer to this was (1) some accused people were mentally ill, (2) others had poor judgment (saw things that weren't really there; what looked to them like a goblin was really an ordinary human being); and/or (3) still others were coerced by their judges into confessing (the judges threatened them with death by fire if they didn't confess).

But recent scholars have begun arguing that the above explanations don't hold water. The new idea is that most people tried as witches were actually practitioners of a religion rooted in shamanism:

> Historians such as Carlo Ginzburg, Gabor Klaniczay and Eva Pocs have argued that descriptions of Sabbath experiences and familiar-encounters found in early-modern European witch trials were expressions of popular experiential traditions rooted in pre-Christian shamanistic beliefs and practices. (Wilby 2005: 5)

Although most early-modern European housewives still knew healing spells and herbs, when these weren't enough to do the trick, the next step was to visit the local magico-religious practitioner. The most important service these practitioners had to offer was healing; trained and licensed doctors were not only scarce, even when they were easily found, the poor often couldn't afford them (Wilby 2005: 32-33).

It seems likely that magic spells were still being handed down in some European families as late as the 20th century. For example, in 1911 McCulloch wrote that in Brittany, Scotland and Ireland:

> [T]he survival of the belief in spells among modern Celtic peoples is a convincing proof of their use in pagan times, and throws light upon their nature. In Brittany they are handed down in certain families, and are carefully guarded from the knowledge of others… In the Highlands similar charms are found, and are often handed down from male to female, and from female to male. They are also in common use in Ireland… (1911: 326)

And in 1978 the American sociologist Hans Sebald too reported that in the area of Germany he grew up in, magic practitioners were still practicing their craft as late as the early 1900s. In fact, Sebald's own paternal grandmother had been a "folk healer" in Sachsendorf, a village situated in Bavarian Germany, in an isolated area called Franconian Switzerland (*Frankische Schweiz*).

According to Sebald although witch persecutions ended in Germany in the 18th century, the belief in witches did not – at least in many isolated German peasant communities. "Exorcism and an array of folk magic – with the figure of the folk healer playing a prominent role – resumed where the witch tribunals left off." (Sebald 1978: 7, 52) This "array of folk magic" used would have included heavy use of magic spells and incantations.

Considering the brutal and centuries-long persecution of Europe's pre-Christian religions it's hard to believe that any part of them survived. However, Emma Wilby believes they did, and largely because they were oral traditions and therefore easier to pass on in secret:

> The institution, the teachings, the sheer physical presence of medieval and post-Reformation Christianity in Britain was so ubiquitous that it is difficult to see how magical beliefs and practices of pre-Christian origin could have retained enough influence and coherence to inspire and inform a popular mysticism... This challenge becomes far more comprehensible, however, when we take into account the fact that magical beliefs and practices held an incredibly powerful ace up their collective sleeve. An oral legacy. A legacy as old as mankind... A complex inheritance of magical beliefs and practices worked together over millennia... (Wilby 2005: 254)

The evidence suggests that when it came to magic, many if not most British magico-religious practitioners had subjectively "real" experiences. First, in the witch trial records there's ample corroboration between the testimony of the accused and the accusers – not all of which can be blamed on trial judges' merciless interrogation techniques. Second, accused people often denied they'd done anything wrong, which puts the kibosh on the idea that they were simple-minded, impressionable or easily influenced. And third, still others actually agreed they were "guilty as charged" – even when trial managers were sympathetic and trying to get them off the hook (Wilby 2005: 30-31).

How exactly did early-modern (16th-18th centuries) magico-religious practitioners carry out their profession? What was involved? I've suggested that one of their techniques was reciting what we now call fairy tales, to produce a pleasurable outcome in the physical world – a boy's broken leg healing, a hunter getting good luck on the hunt, a woman conceiving a child. But magic practitioners also had other tricks up their sleeves. For example, in addition to magic spells early-modern British practitioners relied on medicinal herbs, the "laying on of hands", rituals, and a variety of ritual paraphernalia (candle wax, holy water, stones, pieces of lace tied to the patient's arm, amulets made of wheat, salt, pieces of rowan tree, live animals, etc.). Sometimes healers sucked their patients' illness out of their bodies, or transferred these illnesses to animals (Wilby 2005: 34-6).

Interestingly, objects used by British healers sometimes crop up in fairy tales. For example, among other things, British healers used ducks, frogs and clothing to heal people. In 1604, for example, "Northumberland cunning women Katherine Thompson and Anne Nevelson were convicted for putting the bill of a white duck to a patient's mouth and then mumbling charms." (Wilby 2005) As you know by now if you've read from the beginning of this book, ducks are one of only three species in the biological family *Anatidae*, along with swans and geese, and all three of these *Anatidae* birds are some of the most common animals found in fairy tales. As for frogs, they show up in several Grimm Brothers' tales: The Frog Prince, Briar-Rose, The Good Bargain, The Three Languages, The Griffin, and several more. And as we've seen, an important Russian tale is The Frog Princess. But frogs were also prized by British healers for their medicinal qualities: "Frogs and spiders could also be either ingested or put onto afflicted parts. Many such cures were based on ancient beliefs in the dynamic inter-relationship or 'sympathy' between different elements of nature or creation." (Wilby 2005: 35)

Also important both in fairy tales and in the bag of techniques used by early-modern British healers is clothing. For instance, it was the blinding beauty of their dresses that finally helped Cinderella and the Donkeyskin princess to win the heart of the prince. The same is true of the heroines in The True Bride and The Iron Stove. In the second tale, it is only when the heroine discovers three magic dresses hidden in nuts, and slips into these dresses, that the prince recognises her again and gives his false bride her marching orders.

But historical magic practitioners too thought clothing contained powerful magic. For example, in 1623, "Perthshire cunning woman Isobel Haldane claimed … to have cured a child by washing him in water and then discarding the water, along with the child's shirt, into a stream." And in 1591, when cunning woman Agnes Sampson wanted to ease the labour pains of Euphame MacCalzean, she used "enchanted molds and powders … wrapped in a piece of paper to roll up in her hair…" However, Sampson also told Euphame that when her labour began, she must fold up one of her husband's shirts and place it under her feet. In Russia too men's shirts held considerable magic: when babies were born into Russian Slavic families, for example, they were bundled in their fathers' shirts – in order to magically trigger the father's love (Hubbs 1988: 59).

Even archaeological finds support the notion that to early-modern Britons cloth contained magic power. Remember the 2002-2011 archaeological discovery near Saveock Water, Cornwall, in which pits lined with swan feathers were radio-carbon dated to the 1640s? Near these pits lay the remains of two spring-fed pools filled with, among other ritual objects, 350-year-old scraps of material, "the vivid blues, golden yellows, and vibrant greens … preserved by the moist environment." (Ravillious 2008)

As they did in Britain, early-modern magic practitioners in Germany too used techniques in addition to fairy-tale spells to practice their craft. The 17th century German healer Hans Rocklin, for example, used a "healing stone" to rid children of tumours, and to heal horses suffering from swelling or stiffness. Hans' stone was a red and gold crystal he used while he "recited a charm" (could Rocklin's "charm" have been what we now call a fairy tale?). Also, to cure a cow the German healer Jacob Kurzen used "a pair of soles" from a pair of shoes (Bever 2008: 281).

Even though herbal medicines were illegal in early-modern Germany, some German folk healers sneaked them into their medical bag of tricks anyway. Bietigheim's Barbara Maurer, for example, bought the forbidden herbal concoctions and gave them free to her patients "so the poor people can get them," she explained. Another healer immersed a boy in an herbal bath to cure him, and another administered a healing salve concocted from eggs, bark and sap. German magico-religious practitioners also used amulets. These might be a "bundle" of bread, salt, twigs, roots and hazel wood on a cord, or simply a bag with a root in it. One common type of amulet was words on paper – which the sick person might or might not ingest (Bever 2008: 279-84).

Not only do fairy tales resemble shamans' journeys, they also resemble magic spells. First, the fairy-tale's main character is analogous to the magic practitioner. Both leave ordinary reality, for example, to journey into the Otherworld. Both confront nasty supernatural characters there. Both get help from other, kinder, supernatural characters. And finally, both get hold of magic power in the Otherworld, bring it back to ordinary reality, and use it to change things. Second, fairy tales resemble magic spells too in that they both often contain rhyming verses.

Let's take a closer look now at how fairy tales resemble early-modern magic spells. First, both the fairy tale hero/ine and the historical magic practitioner abandon the "real world" for the

Otherworld. We've talked a great deal about how fairy-tale protagonists, at or near the beginning of the story, typically leave home and for most of the rest of the story roam around the Otherworld. Magic practitioners too, however, left "home" (ordinary reality) to enter the spirit world – the equivalent of the fairy-tale Otherworld.

To travel to the spirit world, magic practitioners first went into a trance produced by food or sleep deprivation, repetitive auditory stimuli (drumming, chanting and the like), hallucinogens or one of a variety of other techniques. In the early-modern era, magico-religious practitioners in Italy, Hungary, Romania, Bulgaria and Dalmatia engaged in "soul travel" – probably in trance – in order to heal people, protect their communities' harvests, and practice divination (Behringer 1998: 88). British cunning folk, on the other hand, often "travel[ed] into Fairy Land" to work their magic. Even the so-called witches' Sabbat was in all likelihood a trance-induced journey into the Otherworld:

> Over the past few decades, Continental historians have argued that descriptions of attendance at the witches' Sabbath, found in trial records in different parts of Europe throughout the early-modern period, were likely to have originated in folk beliefs about travel with the fairies, or into fairyland. (Wilby 2005: 85)

Once in the Otherworld, fairy-tale characters and magic practitioners alike came face to face with nasty supernatural beings. After Jack climbed the beanstalk into the Otherworld, he had to contend with the nasty giant ogre. And after entering the Otherworld through the forest, Hansel and Gretel had to wrestle with the witch. Cinderella, Snow White and many others entered the Otherworld after the death of their mothers, and had to do battle with the nasty entities masquerading as their stepmothers.

But historical magic practitioners too fought nasty characters in the spirit world. Over many parts of early-modern Europe, magico-religious practitioners left their bodies at night to fight supernatural beings that threatened their communities with disaster (Klaniczay 1990: 137). British cunning folk too sometimes did battle in the spirit world against deadly enemies – "hostile souls of the dead/spirits/shamans etc." – to keep their communities safe (Wilby 2005: 152).

While in the Otherworld, fairy-tale characters and magic practitioners alike hooked up with supernatural helpers. Cinderella and Sleeping Beauty had their fairy godmothers, Simpleton had a little old man in the forest who gave him a magic goose, and Jack had the giant's wife, who hid him in her oven. Likewise, Europe's magic practitioners also had their supernatural helpers. These were often known as "familiars" or spirit guides. Although most of us think we have no idea what the familiar of the British cunning man or woman was like, we actually do says researcher Emma Wilby – we know them from fairy tales.

> …[T]he basic dynamics of the relationship between a cunning woman or witch, and her spirit ally, is easily recognizable to all of us, being encapsulated in narrative themes running through traditional folk tales and myths… Rumpelstiltskin, Puss-in-Boots, the Frog Prince and so on, are representative. In these tales the protagonists usually find themselves alone and in some kind of trouble, when a supernatural being appears suddenly before them and offers to help in some way. (Wilby 2005: 59)

While in the Otherworld, both fairy tale characters and magic practitioners too acquired magic powers. Jack got magic beans, Simpleton got a magic goose, and Cinderella got magic dresses, coaches and footmen. Likewise, historical magic practitioners collected magic powers in the spirit world, powers that enabled them to foretell the future, to heal, to locate lost objects, and so forth.

> ...[F]airyland experiences were not only associated with festivity and merriment, they were also sacred events associated with the more serious business of magic. Under the supervision of the presiding supernatural figures, magical skills and magical objects could be acquired and/or communal magical activities performed. (Wilby 2005: 86)

But when the fairy-tale character or the magic practitioner grabbed magic in the Otherworld neither just left it there. Both brought it back to their home communities. Hansel and Gretel lugged the witch's jewels back home, for example, Jack lugged the loot he lifted from the ogre's castle back home, and Cinderella returned home with a prince. What's more, both fictional characters and actual practitioners too used their Otherworld magic to make changes in the world of ordinary reality: the loot lugged home by Hansel, Gretel and Jack lifted their respective parents out of grinding poverty, and Cinderella's good marriage promises her an awesome future. Likewise, historical magico-religious practitioners too brought back magic that healed their neighbours or improved the lives of those neighbours in countless other ways.

Finally, both fairy tales and magic spells included rhymes. Although you might have forgotten it, fairy tales often have a rhyming verse or two tucked into them somewhere:

To-day I bake, to-morrow brew,
The next I'll have the young Queen's child.
Ha! glad am I that no one knew
That Rumpelstiltskin I am styled.

Fee-fi-fo-fum,
I smell the blood of an Englishman,
Be he alive, or be he dead,
I'll have his bones to grind my bread.

Mirror, mirror on the wall,
Who's the fairest of them all?

In Lambkin and Little Fish we find the following three rhymes:

Ah, brother, in the pond so deep,
How sad is my poor heart!
Even now the cook he whets his knife
To take away my tender life.

Ah, little sister, up on high,
How sad is my poor heart,
While in this pond I lie.

Eneke Beneke, let me live,
And I to thee my bird will give.
The little bird, it straw shall seek,
The straw I'll give to the cow to eat.
The pretty cow shall give me milk,
The milk I'll to the baker take.
The baker he shall bake a cake,
The cake I'll give unto the cat.
The cat shall catch some mice for that,
The mice I'll hang up in the smoke,
And then you'll see the snow.

Hansel and Gretel, Snow White, The Goose Girl, The Juniper Tree, Little Brother Little Sister, Maid Maleen, Mother Holla, The Fisherman and His Wife, Jorinda and Joringel, The Hut in the

Forest, Lambkin and the Little Fish, and many more fairy tales all have rhymes tucked into them here and there.

European magic spells too, however, included rhymes. Our ancestors considered words – and especially rhymes – fat with potential power. For example, the ancient Celts believed that "... a poet's word in ancient Ireland ... could be so stinging that it could raise welts on a person's face," or "(connected with ritual) could bring about a person's death." (Monaghan 2008: 382-83) In fact, the earliest recorded spells were nothing but rhyming verses (Bever 2008: 277). Through time, however, as the old gods and goddesses in these spells were replaced by Christian and secular figures and trappings, the spells' rhyming patterns were weakened. Finally most of the rhyming crumbled away (Bever 2008: 277).

In conclusion, the great Russian folklorist Vladimir Propp equated fairy tales with shamanic journeys, while witchcraft expert Edward Bever connected shamanic journeys with magic spells. It seems logical, therefore, to suggest that fairy tales – at least some of them – might actually be old magic spells in disguise. This possibility is supported by the facts that fairy tales share almost all of the core characteristics of the old European magic spells and rituals, and that the Old-English meaning of the word "spell" is, in fact, "tale" or "story".

Below are a few fairy tales that might have begun as shamanic magic spells. You've seen alternate explanations given for some of these tales in earlier parts of this book, but remember: any particular fairy tale could have, and probably did have, multiple purposes.

- **Spell for child protection:** Rumpelstiltskin (Grimms)
- **Spell for finding lost children:** Hansel and Gretel (Grimms)
- **Spells for healing a sick child:** Lambkin and Fish (Grimms); The Juniper Tree (Grimms)

- **Spell for conceiving a child:** The Swan Maiden tales (various)
- **Spell for healing adults:** Kate Crackernuts (Scottish; Andrew Lang)
- **Spell for winning good luck or wealth:** Jack and the Beanstalk (English; Joseph Jacobs)
- **Love spell:** Spindle Shuttle Needle (Grimms)
- **Spell for winning back a lover:** The True Bride (Grimms)
- **Spells for protection against sexual predators:** Donkey-skin (Charles Perrault); The Nettle Spinner (Flemish and French; Andrew Lang)
- **Spell for retrieving stolen goods:** Mollie Whuppie (English; Joseph Jacobs)

What follows is a short synopsis of each of the hypothesised tale-spells above. For each fairy tale, I've also suggested possible ritual paraphernalia and behaviours early-modern magic practitioners might have used before, during or after reciting the tale-spell. Please remember that what I'm offering here are only possibilities, and based on scant evidence at that. The evidence is scant because in order to save their necks, magic practitioners put a lot of hard work into disguising and hiding their spells and rituals.

The ideas for ritual paraphernalia came from the objects in each fairy tale – bread crumbs, necklaces, rings, sewing needles, white stones, etc. However, as mentioned previously even as late as the 1800s the brothers Grimm were padding their fairy tales to make them longer and more descriptive. As a result, a "ring", "necklace" or "poisoned ribbon" might have been Grimm additions and not items in the tales as the Brothers originally collected them.

Rumpelstiltskin as a Spell for Child Protection

In this tale a "little man" spins straw into gold for a miller's daughter, who will die if he doesn't. In exchange for his help the dwarf demands the woman's necklace, then her ring, and finally her firstborn child. Of course the woman is devastated at the idea of giving up her child, so the little man agrees to return it – if she can guess his name. After several unsuccessful tries, the woman finally asks her servant to follow the dwarf. Deep in the forest the servant hears the little man singing a verse that includes his name: "Rumpelstiltskin".

Some of the names the miller's daughter guesses for Rumpelstiltskin might be code for ritual paraphernalia used with this fairy-tale-spell: "Shortribs", for example, "Sheepshanks", and "Laceleg". Could these be code referring to pigs, sheep and some third kind of animal? Rumpelstiltskin shouted his name in a rhyme while hopping around a fire; the rhyme (or spell within a spell) includes lines about baking bread and brewing beer:

To-day I bake, to-morrow brew,
The next I'll have the young Queen's child.
Ha! glad am I that no one knew
That Rumpelstiltskin I am styled.

Originally the tale "Rumpelstiltskin" might have been a spell used by magic practitioners or even mothers themselves for ensuring the protection of their infants. After reciting the Rumpelstiltskin tale-spell over the baby (a short form perhaps including only the basic structure of the tale), the magic practitioner might also have performed a ritual, using the following kinds of paraphernalia:

Possible ritual paraphernalia

Bread, beer, ground-up pig or sheep bones, a necklace and ring, and a baby rattle attached to a post (the original purpose of baby rattles was not to entertain babies but to frighten away evil spirits lurking around the cradle [Warner 1998]). A modified version of Rumpelstiltskin's four-line rhyme: "*To-day I bake, and then I brew,*

And then I'll have _______*'s* [insert mother's name] *child. Ha! glad am I that no one knew That Rumpelstiltskin I am styled."*

Possible ritual sequence

Mix a bit of the bread, beer and powdered bone into a paste, apply to baby's rattle, and attach rattle to the baby's cradle. Place necklace and ring on the child while singing Rumpelstiltskin's rhyme.

Remember: we learned earlier that lullabies sometimes included serious violence in order to prevent that violence from occurring – "a maneuver akin to a blessing in the form of a curse, the 'Break a leg' variety." (Warner 1998) An example: "Rock-a-bye Baby in the Tree Top."

Hansel and Gretel as a Spell for Finding Lost Children

Since Hansel and Gretel's parents are too poor to feed them, they abandon their children in the forest. Hansel, however, drops white stones along the path so he and Gretel can follow them home again. When the parents try to lose their children a second time Hansel drops bread crumbs, which are eaten by birds, leaving the children truly lost. Soon, however, they find their way to a little house made of sugar, bread and cake – the home of a witch who feeds them "milk and pancakes, with sugar, apples, and nuts".

Eventually the witch admits she is fattening Hansel to make him a tastier dinner dish. Whenever the half-blind old woman checks his finger for fat, however, Hansel holds out a bone for her to feel. Finally, her patience at an end, the witch heats up her oven for cooking the boy. But when she orders Gretel to climb in to check the oven's temperature, the girl cagily claims she doesn't know how to climb into an oven. When the witch tries to show her, the girl shoves the old woman in and slams the door. And so the two children make their way home with enough of the old witch's riches to feed their family for a long, long time.

Rhyming Verses in Hansel and Gretel (spell within a spell)

Nibble, nibble, gnaw,
Who is nibbling at my little house?
The wind, the wind,
The heaven-born wind.

(In the original German, this four-line verse might have rhymed. Also "the heaven-born wind" was likely changed from something like "the goddess-born wind".)

Originally the fairy-tale Hansel and Gretel might have been a secret magic spell used to find a lost child. After reciting the tale in its entirety, magic practitioners (or their clients) might also perform a ritual like the following:

Possible ritual paraphernalia
White stones, bread crumbs, sugar, milk, apples, nuts, an oven and the internal rhyming incantation above.

Possible ritual sequence
Bake a cake of bread crumbs, sugar, milk, apples and nuts and leave it on the kitchen table in the child's home. Then, while chanting the internal rhyming spell above, drop the white stones outside the child's house, in a line leading to the house (so the child can follow them home).

We know early-modern British magic practitioners used the following methods to locate lost objects and people: astrological divination, geomancy, techniques such as "sieve and shears" and "Bible and key", and "remote viewing through crystal balls, fingernails, bowls of water, polished mirrors and so on." (Wilby 2005: 38) These were not the only methods they used, however. Some techniques might have been so secretive they've never been recorded in print.

The Lambkin and the Little Fish as a Spell for Healing a Sick Child

In 1653, in Northumberland, England, Margaret Stothard "was alleged to have used her breath to literally suck a sickness out, putting her lips to a child's mouth and making such 'chirping' and 'sucking' noises 'that the mother of the said child thought that she had sucked the heart of it out, and was sore affrighted'." (Wilby 2005: 36)

In The Lambkin and the Little Fish, although a stepmother turns her two stepchildren into a lamb and a fish, a "wise woman" "pronounces a blessing over" the children and turns them back again. The primary rhyming sub-spell in this tale is as follows:

Eneke Beneke, let me live,
And I to thee my bird will give.
The little bird, it straw shall seek,
The straw I'll give to the cow to eat.
The pretty cow shall give me milk,
The milk I'll to the baker take.
The baker he shall bake a cake,
The cake I'll give unto the cat.
The cat shall catch some mice for that,
The mice I'll hang up in the smoke,
And then you'll see the snow.

In the fairy tale itself, children stood in a circle while they recited this rhyme, one line per child. The child reciting the last line ran until the others caught him or her. Originally The Lambkin and the Little Fish might have been a magic incantation to heal a child. After reciting the tale, a magic practitioner might perform a ritual like the following:

Possible ritual paraphernalia

A fish, a lamb, a bird, straw, cow's milk, a cake, a cat and smoke from a burning bundle of a spice such as sage.

Possible ritual sequence

The sick child's family might carry out the instructions in the sub-spell: give a bird to the magic practitioner, give straw to a cow, give milk from the cow to a cook as payment for baking a cake, feed the cake to a cat, arrange for the cat to kill a caged mouse, and hang the mouse outside the sick child's room over smoke from burning sage. "Stand in a circle" could be a ritual instruction for the sick child's family to gather around the child, perhaps laying hands on the child. Perhaps a lamb and a fish were sacrificed. The "wise woman" in the tale would be the magic practitioner, and her "pronouncing a blessing" would be code for casting her spell.

This fairy-tale spell contains two additional rhymes: The lamb says to the fish:

Ah, brother, in the pond so deep,
How sad is my poor heart!
Even now the cook he whets his knife
To take away my tender life.

The fish answers:

Ah, little sister, up on high,
How sad is my poor heart,
While in this pond I lie.

These rhymes suggest that a knife and a water pond might also have been part of the ritual.

The Juniper Tree as a Spell for Healing a Sick Child

After birthing him, a boy's mother dies and is buried under a juniper tree. His stepmother kills the boy, rendering him into a pudding she serves to his father. Wrapping his bones in a handkerchief, the boy's sister buries him under the juniper tree beside his mother, after which the boy emerges from the tree as a bird and flies off to collect a gold necklace and a pair of red shoes. After donning the red shoes the sister dances around the juniper tree. Next, after sitting in a "lime-tree" near a mill, the bird-boy collects a millstone and drops it on the stepmother, who disappears in a cloud of smoke and fire. At that, the boy suddenly appears again as a living child.

Rhyming Verse in The Juniper Tree (spell within a spell):

My mother she killed me,
My father he ate me,
My sister, little Marlinchen,
Gathered together all my bones,
Tied them in a silken handkerchief,
Laid them beneath the juniper-tree,
Kywitt, kywitt, what a beautiful bird am I!

In the original German this seven-line verse no doubt rhymed. Like The Lambkin and the Little Fish, The Juniper Tree too might have been a magic incantation for healing a child. After reciting the tale, a magic practitioner might also perform a ritual like the following:

Possible ritual paraphernalia

Extracts from juniper and lime (linden) trees, a game bird, a pair of red shoes, or shoes with something red attached.

Possible ritual sequence

The sick child is administered medicinal extracts from the juniper and linden trees. The child's mother cooks a game bird (pheasant, partridge, blackbird, etc.) and serves it to the child's family. A sibling wraps the bird bones in a piece of cloth and buries the bundle under a juniper tree, then dons the red shoes and dances three times widdershins (counterclockwise) around the tree.

Even today juniper-tree extracts are used medicinally – to treat seborrhea, eczema, psoriasis and neurasthenic neurosis. In folk medicine they're used to treat urinary infections, gout, arteriosclerosis, bronchitis and diabetes (*PDR for Herbal Medicines* 2004: 478-79). And the lime tree too (the lime tree is also known as the linden tree) has been harvested for medicine: linden extracts have been used as diaphoretics, antispasmodics, expectorants, diuretics, and sedatives, and modern scientists are testing them for their "sedative-anxiolytic" and anti-stress effects (*PDR for Herbal Medicines* 2004: 521-22).

The Swan Maiden Tales as Spells for Conceiving a Child

In the Swan Maiden tales a young man steals a magic robe of swan feathers from a swan maiden. Without her robe the woman can't fly away, and she marries the man. She bears his children. When they're older, the children tell their mother where her feather robe is, and she dons it immediately and flies away. Although leaving her children may sadden her, she leaves them nevertheless. If the husband locates her it's a gruelling task, and sometimes the impossibility of it is so clear he doesn't even try.

Remember the mysterious 350-year-old pits in Cornwall lined with swan skins and filled with stones, fertilised birds eggs, and birds claws? The excavator of believes these pits were connected to magic rituals meant to help women conceive:

> "My theory is that maybe if you got married and didn't become pregnant in the first year, you might make an offering to St. Bride in a feather pit," says Wood. Women who then became pregnant might have had to empty their pits and burn the contents, she postulates. (Ravillious 2008)

Although Wood thinks it was mothers who removed the swan skins from the pits, the swan-maiden tales suggest otherwise: in these tales, it's the children who give their mothers back their swan coats, so my guess is it would have been not the mother, but the conceived children who, in the secrecy of a dark, moonless night, dug up their mother's pit and removed the skin.

Possible ritual paraphernalia
The skin of a swan with feathers left intact, sacred magic stones, fertilised bird eggs and the claws of a sacred bird.

Possible ritual sequence
After listening to the swan-maiden tale, a woman wishing to conceive killed a swan, removed its "feather coat", and lined a secret pit with it, deep in the woods. Before closing the pit, the woman might drop magic stones, fertilised bird eggs, and/or the claws of sacred birds like the magpie on top of the swan coat. If the woman conceived, her child, upon reaching puberty, would secretly remove the skin from the pit. The idea: the swan skin held the essence of the swan goddess, who gave women children in exchange for getting her feather coat back.

Kate Crackernuts as a Spell for Healing a Sick Adult

In 1660, a magic practitioner in Owen, a town in the Duchy of Wurttemberg in south-west Germany, produced a healing amulet for a sick woman. It consisted of "'a bundle' containing 'bread and salt, many twigs and roots, and Hazelwood … on a cord.'" The magic practitioner hung this bundle "down [the patient's] back between her shoulder blades." (Bever 2008: 280)

In Kate Crackernuts, Kate's mother marries a king with a beautiful daughter, Anne. Jealous of Anne's beauty, the queen plots against her. She orders Anne to fast and then fetch eggs from the henwife, who is to switch Anne's head with a sheep's head. But instead of fasting, Anne eats a crust of bread. After receiving the same orders the next day she eats a handful of peas. To prevent her from eating on the third day, the queen accompanies Anne to the henwife's house, where Anne's head falls off and is replaced by a sheep's head.

At this point, Kate "took a fine linen cloth and wrapped it round her sister's head and took her by the hand and they both went out to seek their fortune." Soon they came to a castle. In it was a prince suffering from a wasting sickness caused by his nightly dancing with the fairies. To heal both Anne and the prince, Kate rolls nuts at a baby fairy, making it drop its magic wand. Kate uses the wand to cure her sister. By rolling the nuts again Kate captures the fairy's magic bird, and with it cures the prince.

Originally the fairy tale Kate Crackernuts might have been a secret healing incantation. A magic practitioner might perform a ritual like the following:

Possible ritual paraphernalia

A linen cloth, the crust from a piece of bread, dried peas, claws from a sacred bird, cracked hazelnuts, a magic wand made of hazel wood, hazel wood twigs and roots.

Possible ritual sequence

Mix a healing amulet from bread crusts, ground dried peas, ground-up bird claws, cracked nuts, and hazel wood twigs and roots. Pour the mixture into a small linen-cloth bag. Hang the bag on a cord down the patient's back between her shoulder blades. While reciting the magic tale-incantation Kate Crackernuts, tap the woman lightly with the wand on her shoulders.

In early-modern Britain (1500s through the 1700s), the most important thing magic practitioners offered were healing rituals. A few illnesses treated by actual German magic practitioners: stomach ache, sore leg, goitre, bleeding, jaundice, mental illness and burns (Bever 2008: 286). Bever discusses why spells might have actually worked: through the placebo effect, through auto suggestion, and because they involved social support (in folk healing the social group was often included in healing techniques, reducing patient stress levels and boosting their immune systems). In addition, modern studies show that touch has beneficial health effects, and touch was the most common "ritual action" performed by healers in the German witch-trial records studied by Bever (2008: 289-300).

Jack and the Beanstalk as a Spell for Winning Good Luck or Wealth

In the past, bones were sometimes used to do magic. In 17th century Germany, a magic practitioner dug up a bone that she said had been planted by a black witch to cause her client's illness (Bever 2008: 303-04).

Jack and his mother are poor, so Jack journeys to the Otherworld to remedy their situation. There he finds helpers: an old man who gives him magic beans, and an ogre's wife who feeds him bread and eggs and hides him in her oven (symbol of birth and transformation). With help from the goddess, Jack conquers the ogre (the evil spirit causing his poverty) and runs off with the ogre's bag of gold, gold-egg-laying hen (possibly a goose in older versions), and singing harp. As Jack clambers down the beanstalk for the final time, the ogre follows, but Jack's mother hands him an axe to fell the stalk, and the ogre falls to his death.

Rhyming Verses in Jack and the Beanstalk (spell within a spell)

Fee-fi-fo-fum,
I smell the blood of an Englishman,
Be he alive, or be he dead,
I'll have his bones to grind my bread.

Originally Jack and the Beanstalk might have been a magic incantation used to attract wealth or good luck. After reciting the tale, a magic practitioner might also perform a ritual like the following:

Possible ritual paraphernalia
Blood from pricking the client's finger, bones from a chicken or other animal, bread and dried beans.

Possible ritual sequence
Why would anyone want to "grind bread"? And with bones of all things? The ogre's "Fee-fi-fo-fum" incantation is easier to understand if it's seen as a set of secret ritual instructions. After the Jack and the Beanstalk spell was incanted, the remainder of the ritual might have gone something like this: a magic amulet would be concocted using a bone to grind dried bread and beans into fine powder. Into this three drops of the client's blood would be mixed. The resulting mixture would be deposited into a small cloth bag with a string attached, and as the amulet was hung around the client's neck the sub-spell would be recited three times.

The Spindle, the Shuttle and the Needle as a Love Spell

In this fairy tale, a girl's godmother (i.e., an Otherworld goddess or spirit) teaches her how to magically capture the love of a prince using three innocent looking tools: a spindle, a shuttle and a needle. The girl commands her spindle to spin out a golden thread to guide the prince to her hut, her shuttle to weave a carpet that also shepherds him toward her, and her needle to adorn her hut with awesome coverings for her tables, benches, chairs and windows. When the prince finally arrives, he falls madly in love, marries the girl, and they live happily ever after in his castle.

Interestingly, in this tale no secret is made of the fact that the rhyming couplets in the tale are magic spells. These couplets are part of what makes the prince fall in love:

Spindle, my spindle, haste, haste thee away,
And here to my house bring the wooer, I pray.

Shuttle, my shuttle, weave well this day,
And guide the wooer to me, I pray.

Needle, my needle, sharp-pointed and fine,
Prepare for the wooer this house of mine.

This tale could very well have been a disguised love spell designed to provoke one person into falling hopelessly in love with another. There's little doubt that early modern Europeans used love spells. In 1590, for example, in Canterbury, a cunning man admitted giving his male clients love spells and giving a woman a spell to make her husband fall in love with her:

> …a cunning man was taken before the Church authorities in Canterbury, confessing that he had given three men "magical writings" to "secure them the love of maids" and had also given a woman a charm "to make her husband love her, for which he was paid six and eightpence plus two half-kittles and a gold ring". (Wilby 2005: 40)

After reciting the Spindle, Shuttle and Needle love spell, a cunning man or woman might perform a ritual like the following:

Possible ritual paraphernalia
Needle, spindle, shuttle and the tale's three sub-spells.

Possible ritual sequence
The cunning woman would teach her client the above magic rhymes. At home, the client would spin, weave and sew a shirt for her desired lover. As she spun she would recite the first sub-spell, substituting her lover's name for the word "wooer" ("Spindle, my spindle, haste, haste thee away, And here to my house bring John Archer, I pray."). She would repeat the same process with the second and third verses while weaving and sewing the shirt. If she knew her desired lover well enough, she might actually give him the shirt.

The True Bride as a Spell for Winning Back a Lost Lover

In this tale a girl's stepmother gives her impossible tasks involving feathers and a spoon with holes in it, but an "old woman" steps in and magically finishes each task. Next the girl meets a handsome prince, and as the two of them sit under a lime tree, the prince tells the girl to wait for him under the tree while he rides home to get his father's permission to marry her. Although the girl waits, the prince fails to return. In her grief, she takes a job as a shepherdess. One day she recites the following sub-spell to a calf:

Little calf, little calf, kneel by my side,
And do not forget thy shepherd-maid,
As the prince forgot his betrothed bride,
Who waited for him 'neath the lime-tree's shade.

The girl wins the prince back, of course – by slipping into three magic dresses she gets from the magic old woman, one decorated with suns, another with moons, and a third with stars. On their way to their wedding, the girl and her prince ride past the lime tree, and see "countless glow-worms ... swarming about it. It shook its branches, and sent forth their fragrance."

As mentioned earlier, lime (linden) tree extracts are used to treat a whole host of modern ailments. Currently scientists are testing them as sedatives and stress relievers (*PDR for Herbal Medicines* 2004: 521-22). Any plant with powerful pharmaceutical properties was probably considered magic by early-modern and medieval folk healers. Glow-worms too, with their ability to produce light at night, must have been thought magic, and modern medicine uses them even today, for diagnostic purposes: "An immunoassay technique to measure proteins and hormones in blood using light-producing molecules obtained from glow-worms and luminescent fish instead of radioactive iodine, has been developed by biochemists..." ("Medical Diagnostics Glow Worms Used" 1985: 14).

Originally The True Bride might have been a magic incantation used to win back a straying lover. After reciting the tale a magic practitioner might also perform a ritual like the following:

Possible ritual paraphernalia

Linden-tree extracts, glow-worms or glow-worm extracts, the above rhyming sub-spell and articles of clothing belonging either to the client or to the lover.

Possible ritual sequence

The magic practitioner might give the client a linden-extract potion, with instructions to take it orally before any contact with the lost lover. This would have a calming and stress-relieving effect on clients, and would therefore help them interact successfully with the lover. Perhaps the glow-worm extract was used to draw magic neon suns, moons and stars on the clothing, which the client might wear while reciting the sub-spell.

Donkeyskin as a Spell for Protection Against Sexual Predators

In Charles Perrault's tale Donkeyskin, a fairy godmother helps a princess escape her incestuous father, the king. The girl's first challenge is to keep her father at bay. After failing this, her second is to muster the courage to leave home – which she finally does, disguised in the skin of her father's dead magic donkey. Her third and final challenge is to get a particular prince to marry her. She accomplishes this by working as a scullery maid in his kitchen and dropping her ring into his cake batter. The prince finds the ring, searches for the woman whose finger it fits, and finally finds and marries the princess.

The magic practitioner's recitation of this tale-spell might have been seen as a way of transmitting the protection the princess enjoyed in the tale to the practitioner's client. After reciting the tale a practitioner might also perform a ritual:

Possible ritual paraphernalia

Three different outfits: one representing the sun, one the moon, and one the stars; a ring, an herbal concoction ("bowl of soup") and a cape made from the pelt of a spiritually powerful animal.

Possible ritual sequence

On three consecutive nights the client wears a yellow outfit, next a white outfit and finally a silver outfit, and over them each an animal-skin cape. On each night, as the magic practitioner recites the tale the client dips the ring into the herbal brew, slides the ring onto her finger, and then drinks the brew.

The Nettle Spinner as a Spell for Protection against Sexual Predators

A woman refuses the advances of an evil count, so he refuses to give her permission to marry the man she loves. He punishes her further by ordering her to spin two "shifts" out of nettles. "One shall be your bridal shift, and the other shall be my shroud. For you shall be married the day that I am laid in my grave." As the woman weaves his shroud, however, the count begins to die. Although the count's wife has no trouble persuading the heroine to stop weaving, the count later becomes so sick that he actually wants to die – and cannot. He begs the woman to finish his shroud, and when she does, he dies.

The nettle is another plant so medicinally powerful that it's used in medicine even today, and early-modern folk healers no doubt considered it magic. Originally The Nettle Spinner might have been a magic incantation to protect a person from sexual predation. In addition a ritual similar to the following might have been performed along with the incantation:

Possible ritual paraphernalia
Nettles or nettle extract, hemp, flax, a spinning wheel and weaving equipment.

Possible ritual sequence
The healer prepares a magic nettle extract. The client weaves a shirt for the sexual predator out of hemp and flax. After soaking the shirt in the extract she buries it near the foundation of the predator's home.

Molly Whuppie as a Spell for Retrieving Stolen Goods

After healing, the second most important service rendered by the British magic practitioners studied by the researcher Emma Wilby was the recovery of lost goods. As in the rest of early-modern Europe, British commoners were not only poor, they had no insurance protection either. Even a shirt stolen off the line or a pilfered chicken could take weeks of work to replace (Wilby 2005: 37-38).

In the tale Molly Whuppie, Molly and her two sisters are abandoned in the forest by parents too poor to feed them. Soon the girls come to the home of a giant. At night, Mollie hangs the necklaces the giant's daughters wear, onto her own and her sister's necks. Thinking they are Molly and her sisters, the giant kills his own daughters. After the three sisters escape and tell the king their story, the king says if Molly can steal the giant's sword, he will let her oldest sister marry his son the prince. Molly steals the sword, and the king asks her to steal the giant's purse. Molly succeeds again and the king asks her to abscond with the giant's gold ring, which she does. Molly's reward: she and her sisters marry the king's three sons.

Originally Molly Whuppie might have been a magic incantation used to locate stolen items.

Possible ritual sequence

After someone steals your pig, purse and prize rooster, you ask a magic practitioner to identify the thief and help get the goods back. The practitioner recites the magic spell we call Mollie Whuppie. She might recite it silently to herself, or to you too. She might even go into trance and become Mollie, nosing out the thief and locating the items. Wilby reports that some British magic practitioners had excellent reputations for recovering stolen goods.

* * *

This completes our look at a few of the fairy tales that might have been spells used by magic practitioners in parts of medieval and early-modern Europe. In the next chapter, we'll look at what fairy tales might tell us about the moral codes of pre-patriarchal Europeans. As we'll see, "right behaviour" for pre-patriarchals is in many ways the opposite of what it is in our own patriarchal cultures.

Chapter 14

Fairy Tales about Right and Wrong

> *The threshold separating life from death is called the laughing threshold... That side of the threshold it is forbidden to laugh; this side it is necessary to laugh.*
> Propp 1984: 133

Like many Christian Biblical characters, fairy-tale characters too often model correct behaviour – but according to pre-patriarchal, not patriarchal values. Pre-patriarchal values are often the opposite of patriarchal ones, making fairy-tale "right behaviour" often the opposite of what most of us today consider right behaviour. Think about it: did you ever read a fairy tale that takes place on a battlefield? In a warrior's camp? No. In fairy tales there is no war. I think this is because most pre-patriarchal societies – just like several modern human societies – didn't engage in warfare (Studebaker 2008: 148-164). Also in fairy tales you find little of the fortuitous violence that saturates patriarchal religious texts and myths. What violence you do find was probably added by later male-centred revisionists like the Brothers Grimm.

The violent behaviour of black witches – take the one in Hansel and Gretel for example – might also be the result of patriarchal revisioning. The witch in the Brothers Grimm version of Hansel and Gretel is pure evil. Her entire *raison d'etre* seems to be trapping and eating little children. According to German culture historian Heide Gottner-Abendroth, Hansel and Gretel is a patriarchal rendering of tale of Mother Holla (See Appendix C for the full text of Mother Holla), in which the goddess Holda has been demonised. If you think about it, the two tales are indeed similar: in both, a girl finds her way to the home of an old woman who is at first very frightening, in both the girl works in the old woman's home, and finally, in both, when the girl leaves the old woman, she leaves with magic gifts. In Mother Holla, for example, Gold Marie leaves with loads of gold, while in some non-Grimm versions of Hansel and Gretel, Gretel leaves with a magic mirror, a magic scarf, and the water of life – symbols of her new-found skill in the arts of magic, weaving, and healing. Even in the Grimms version Gretel leaves with the witch's jewels. The big difference between the two tales is that while the old woman in Mother Holle is benign and lovable, in the Grimms' Hansel and Gretel she has morphed into the personification of evil (Gottner-Abendroth 1995: 140).

But yet another stark difference exists between fairy tales and patriarchal myths. While in the myths heavy-duty ranking systems shoot men to the top of the social ladder, drop adult women beneath them, children beneath women, and animals and plants beneath humans in general, in fairy tales you'll find none of this folderol. It's true that fairy tales are chock full of princesses and other royal figures, but these are deities, not actual royalty. In general, fairy-tale women, men, children, the elderly, and animals too all seem equally valued and valuable. In The Hut in the Forest the main character wins out in the end only because she is kind to animals. In Puss in Boots, Puss is as smart as, and as admirable as, any human in the tale (if not more so). And in many tales children outwit adults – take Hansel and Gretel, Molly Whuppie, Jack of Jack and the Beanstalk, and Charles Perrault's Little Thumb for example. And of course in a previous chapter we learned that fairy tales contain a great number of strong heroines. We just don't hear much about them – mainly because they've been passed over by patriarchal publishers and media moguls for relatively passive females like Sleeping Beauty, Cinderella and Snow White.

Also considered lesser-thans in male-centred societies: the elderly, the poor and the disabled. Not so in fairy tales. Old women and men appear often in these tales, and are highly valued for their wisdom. And more often than not, fairy-tale main characters are poor – but are obviously considered just as good as anyone else in the tale. Also equal to everyone else in fairy tales are those lying outside the physical norm: dwarves, the mentally challenged, and the physically unattractive. Charles Perrault's Little Thumb, for example, discussed in Chapter 1, is a wise and skilful protagonist who just happens to be a little person. Dummling, the mentally challenged protagonist in The Golden Goose wins, at the end of the tale, the hand of the princess. And in Charles Perrault's Riquet of the Tuft, in Beauty and the Beast, and in Kate Crackernuts too, the main characters all fall outside the norm of their society's standards for physical beauty.

In the Grimm Brothers' One Eye, Two Eyes and Three Eyes, this tendency of fairy tales to normalise those falling outside patriarchal norms takes an interesting twist. In this tale "normal" people have either one eye or three eyes, and it's having two eyes that drops a person into the "abnormal" category. So it's Two

Eyes who falls outside the norm and is mistreated by her family. When a wise woman gives Two Eyes a magic goat who rewards the girl with wonderful food whenever she wants, the girl's mother kills the goat. After a handsome knight marries Two Eyes, however, her sisters fall into poverty and come knocking at Two Eyes' door begging for food. Two Eyes is good to them "so that they both with all their hearts repented the evil that they had done their sister in their youth."

Fairy tales go out of their way to reward characters for being kind – not only to humans but to the earth too, and to everything that comes from it. In fairy tales, even inanimate objects are worthy of respect and kindness. In the tale of Mother Holla, for example, Mother's apples are in a state of panic – they are ripe and need to be shaken from the tree – and her loaves of bread too cry out for help. And the right behaviour involves helping all these inanimate objects out of their misery. While Gold Marie does so and is rewarded, Pitch Marie refuses – and so goes unrewarded.

To patriarchal people, the three characters in The Straw, the Coal, and the Bean would be as significant as … well, straw, coal and beans. And yet this fairy tale invites us to see these three inanimate objects as equal to ourselves – in their fear of death (using straw and coal, a woman builds a fire to cook beans), in their feelings for each other, in their complex thinking, in their mutual cooperation, in the coal's "impetuous disposition", and so forth. This tale undoubtedly goes back in time to ancient European beliefs in animism – the idea that everything, even inanimate objects, possesses spirit. To our ancestors, the entire earth was alive.

Fairy tales also put great stock in romance, physical beauty, and other sensual pleasures. Male-centred societies on the other hand often seem suspicious of pleasure, and tend to use not pleasure but pain as a way of achieving personal growth. The number of fairy tales about romantic love is staggering; in fact, almost all the best known fairy tales include at least one pair of lovers: Cinderella, Sleeping Beauty, Beauty and the Beast, Snow White, Rapunzel, Puss in Boots, The Frog King, East of the Sun and West of the Moon, the Golden Goose, The Goose Girl, The Goose Girl at the Well, and the list could go on. Lesser known tales circling around romance include Allerleirauh, Donkeytail, The Drummer, Fair Katrinelje and Pif-Paf-Poltrie, The Flower Queen's Daughter, The Iron Stove, Jorinde and Joringel, Maid Maleen, Snow-White-Fire-Red, Sweetheart Roland, The True Sweethearts, The Twelve Huntsmen, and many others.

According to German culture historian Heide Gottner-Abendroth most if not all of these pairs of lovers symbolise the romance between the goddess and her *"heros"*, a mortal man with whom the goddess chose to mate annually in order to make sure life on earth continued. Originally, all these tales would have included the entire story of the annual mating: the marriage, followed by the death of the *heros*, his return, and finally his competing again to become – for another year – the apple of the goddess' eye (Gottner-Abendroth 1995). In many of these fairy tales, however, large chunks of the story have been truncated over time, or just plain deleted.

Although fairy tales celebrate human physical beauty, their characters rarely notice the beauty of nature. This is because fairy-tale characters spend 95 percent of their time not in the natural world but in the Otherworld. Instead, the beauty appreciated most is the beauty of princesses and princes – who as we now know are actually disguised goddesses, gods, or the mortal lovers of goddesses. Perhaps a good 50 percent of all European fairy tales are populated by at least one drop-dead gorgeous princess:

- **From The Frog King (aka The Frog Prince):** "In old times when wishing still helped one, there lived a king whose daughters were all beautiful, but the youngest was so beautiful that the sun itself, which has seen so much, was astonished whenever it shone in her face."

- **From Cinderella:** "And when Cinderella appeared at the festival in this dress, everyone was astonished at her beauty."
- **From The Six Swans:** "As she was so beautiful, the King's heart was touched, and he was smitten with a great love for her… Then he caused her to be dressed in rich garments, and she shone in her beauty like bright daylight…"
- **From Sleeping Beauty:** "She was so beautiful, she looked like an angel... her cheeks were pink, and her lips like coral…" (Appelbaum 2002: 121)
- **From The Glass Coffin:** "… he saw therein a maiden of the greatest beauty! She lay as if asleep, and was wrapped in her long fair hair as in a precious mantle. Her eyes were closely shut, but the brightness of her complexion and a ribbon which her breathing moved to and fro, left no doubt that she was alive. The tailor was looking at the beauty with beating heart…"

More specifically, many fairy tales show a marked appreciation for the skin, lips and hair of their heroines:

- **From Snow White:** "Once upon a time in the middle of winter… a queen sat at a window sewing, and the frame of the window was made of black ebony. And whilst she was sewing and looking out of the window at the snow, she pricked her finger with the needle, and three drops of blood fell upon the snow. And the red looked pretty upon the white snow, and she thought to herself, 'Would that I had a child as white as snow, as red as blood, and as black as the wood of the window-frame.' Soon after that she had a little daughter, who was as white as snow, and as red as blood, and her hair was as black as ebony…"

- **From The Goose Girl at the Well:** "When the Queen was alone, she began to weep bitterly, and said, '... I had three daughters, the youngest of whom was so beautiful that the whole world looked on her as a wonder. She was as white as snow, as rosy as apple-blossom, and her hair as radiant as sun-beams..."

Another common theme throughout fairy-tale land is the power of beautiful clothing. Dazzlingly spectacular dresses play important roles in Cinderella, Allerleirauh and Donkeyskin. In The Iron Stove the heroine finds three gorgeous magic dresses inside three nuts, and in The True Sweethearts the heroine wins the prince by dressing in certain remarkable garments given to her by an "old woman". The Drummer is about a girl who uses a beautiful dress to jog the memory of her lover who has forgotten her.

Fairy tales also put great stock in the sensual pleasure of dancing. Quite a few fairy-tale characters enjoy dancing at balls and festivals (it's where they often meet their dream princes and princesses), but in The Frog Princess dancing becomes a magical, mystical, joyous thing, through which the natural world is created:

> The time came for dancing; the tsar called upon his elder daughters-in-law, but they deferred to the frog. She straightway took Prince Ivan's arm and came forward to dance. She danced and danced, and whirled and whirled, a marvel to behold! She waved her right hand, and lakes and woods appeared; she waved her left hand, and various birds began to fly about. Everyone was amazed... (Afanas'ev 1973: 121)

Laughter is another sensual pleasure dealt with in fairy tales – and one that seems to be good for our health as well (Martin 2001). The core meaning of more than one fairy tale, in fact, is related to laughter. In these tales, men who can make a princess laugh are handsomely rewarded – in big contrast to Christian religious texts, which use laughter mostly to express ridicule or contempt. "In Christianity it is death that laughs, the devil laughs, and mermaids laugh; the Christian God never laughs. 'Christ never laughed,' the artist A.A. Ivanov remarked to Turgenev, while painting his Christ…" (Propp 1984: 137) I don't know about "Christian" mermaids, but I've certainly have never heard anything about Christ or Jehovah breaking out in fits of laughter.

As a matter of fact, when it came to laughter, Christians and pagans were worlds apart. On the one hand, the Church was known to actually prohibit people from laughing (both in and outside church services), while for many pre-Christians laughter was a religious duty. They believed, for example, that it was not only okay to laugh at funerals but absolutely necessary. "Thou shalt laugh at the birth of a baby" might be an understandable commandment, but, "Thou shalt laugh during funerals" takes a bit of explaining. According to Vladimir Propp the key to understanding pre-Christian beliefs about laughter is this: although the living can laugh, the dead cannot. Therefore, if one is in the land of the dead (as Propp maintains shamans sometimes were, for example), one must not laugh.

But conversely, if one is in the land of the living – at a funeral, for example, when you're not the person in the casket – one is commanded to laugh:

> It has long since been observed that laughter had a special meaning in the religious life of the past… Usener compared laughter accompanying death and funerals with laments, and believed that laughter frees people from grief. Someone who is grieving must be made to laugh and, therefore, buffoons mix with mourners. (Propp 1984: 126-27)

And who knows? It could be that our ancestors were on to something, that laughter does indeed help us get over our grief, and that pitching the clowns out of funerals was a move backwards, not forwards.

It was, of course, the Church that tossed the clowns out of funerals. For centuries the Church has frowned upon any and all kinds of gaiety at services for the dead. Burchard of Worms (Bishop of Worms from 1000 AD to 1025 AD), for example, and Regino of Prum (Bishop at Prum from 892 AD to 899 AD) worked like the devil to wring all merriment out of funerals, insisting that merriment was disrespectful to the dead. They both lashed out at the following kinds of pre-Christian funeral activities:

> "Devilish" songs, eating and drinking, jesting, dancing and wild laughter... Unlike Irish monks, Regino and Burchard had no objection to lamentations and wailing but only to what Burchard called the "unsuitable gaiety" and "noxious singing" which gave the appearance of rejoicing rather than grieving at the death of one's fellow. (Filotas 2005: 320-21)

While pre-Christians considered it laudable to laugh at funerals, they considered it definitely uncool to laugh in the Land of the Dead. According to Propp, rites of passage in many ancient cultures involved the initiate cruising through the Land of the Dead (typically in trance). Vladimir Propp believes that certain fairy tales are about this pagan belief in the ability of the living to travel with the dead, with one example being the Brothers Grimm's tale The Twelve Brothers, in which twelve boys are bewitched and turned into ravens. Their sister saves them by refusing to talk or laugh for seven years:

> In myth and folktales, as well as in ritual, we can also observe the interdiction of sleep, yawning, speech, food, looking, etc. Consider just one example: in the Grimms' tale about twelve

> brothers, the girl is told, "For seven years you must be dumb, you must neither speak nor laugh..." All these interdictions point to the opposition of life and death... (Propp 1984: 130)

Other tales similar to The Twelve Brothers include The Six Swans, also from the Grimms, in which a girl's six brothers are turned into swans, and she must not speak or laugh until she has woven shirts for each of them; and The Twelve Wild Ducks, a Norwegian fairy tale collected by Peter Christen Asbjornsen and Jorgen Moe.

As we've seen, while laughing in the Land of the Dead was decidedly uncool, laughing in the land of the living was not only desirable but "commanded"; what's more, it was a tool so powerful it could create new life:

> If all laughter ceases and is forbidden upon entrance into the kingdom of death, then entrance into life is accompanied by laughter. Moreover, if there we saw the interdiction of laughter, here we observe the command to laugh, or laughter under compulsion. The thought goes still further: laughter is endowed not only with the power to accompany life but also with the power to call it forth. (Propp 1984: 131)

Propp names three different goddesses, from three widely separated ancient societies, who had to be coaxed into laughing in order to prevent catastrophic damage to their people: in Greece it was Demeter, in Japan, Amaterasu, and in Scandinavia, Skadi. In the first two cases, failure to make the goddess laugh would have been deadly. Demeter's laughter brought back the spring, and Amaterasu's the light (Propp 1984: 139-143), and without the warmth of spring and the sun, of course, plants and animals die, squeezing the life out of the human food supply. So getting the goddess to laugh actually puts food on the table at lunchtime, and failing to do so means human starvation. We're getting down to the nitty-gritty here when you talk about yanking away the world food supply!

Propp insists that this relationship between goddess laughter and the food supply is the meaning behind the The Princess Who Would Not Laugh fairy tales. In these tales, the princess (goddess) refuses to laugh – until someone provokes her into it by being funny, silly or doing something unexpected. In the Grimms' The Golden Goose the main character Dummling is kind to an old man in the forest, and the man rewards him with a magic goose dressed in golden feathers. However, whoever touches this goose (and who wouldn't want to?), is stuck fast, so Dummling is soon leading a long line of folk all stuck to the goose or to each other.

Meanwhile, the king of the land is worried sick about his daughter the princess, who refuses to laugh. To anyone who can get her to break out in a fit of the giggles he promises her hand in marriage. And when Dummling jogs by with his long line of stuck country folk, this does the trick. At the sight the princess "began to laugh quite loudly, and as if she would never leave off," and as a result Dummling won not only the princess, but the kingdom as well. In his *Green Fairy Book,* Andrew Lang includes a similar story, The Magic Swan, in which a wise old woman replaces the old man, and a swan takes the place of the goose. And from Russia Aleksandr Afanas'ev also collected a similar tale: The Princess Who Never Smiled or The Unsmiling Tsarevna.

In contrast to this pre-Christian view of laughter, the Church's views are grim: Ecclesiastes 2:2: "I said of laughter, 'It is madness,' and of pleasure, 'What does it accomplish?'" Ecclesiastes 7:3: "Sorrow is better than laughter, For when a face is sad a heart may be happy." Habakkuk 1:10: "They mock at kings, and rulers are a laughing matter to them. They laugh at every fortress and heap up rubble to capture it."

* * *

Although more could be said about the value system that shines through in fairy tales, it's time to move on. As I began my research for this book questions kept popping up, questions that puzzled me. While some have been answered in the preceding chapters, a few have not. How did we lose track of the true identity of Mother Goose? And Charles Perrault, the first man to use "Mother Goose" in a book title – was this the move of a secret revolutionary? Also, how did Mother Goose, in the late 19th century, become a witch? In the next chapter, we'll look at possible answers to these questions.

Chapter 15

Questions, Questions and More Questions

As I was beginning my research for this book several questions puzzled me. If Mother Goose was truly a goddess in disguise, how did we lose sight of her divinity? Was Charles Perrault – the first to publish a book with "Mother Goose" in the title – a secret revolutionary? And why did some late-19th and early-20th century artists begin to portray Mother Goose as a witch? It's time now to see if these questions are answerable.

First, how did Europeans lose sight of the real identity of Mother Goose? Was it due to a loss of interest on the part of a public increasingly forgetful of their pre-Christian roots? Or was Mother Goose's sacred identity a secret so tightly guarded that it didn't reach enough people in time to keep her memory alive? Or maybe parents finally feared the Church so much that they stopped telling their children about goddesses – even disguised ones like Mother Goose? It is true that before they ended, the early-modern witch persecutions got so fierce and horrific that most parents might have feared teaching their children about pre-Christian religions would be an automatic death sentence for their offspring.

Another part of the reason thousands of European children probably stopped hearing about non-Christian religions has to do with the state-run "foundling homes". Beginning in the 1300s, increasing numbers of children lived not in their home communities, but in new-fangled devices for unwanted or abandoned children. These foundling homes as they were called (orphanages is what we call them today) were unknown in the ancient world, or even during most of the Middle Ages. They didn't become widespread until the 14th century – the same century in which non-Christians were first tried for witchcraft.

Most Europeans thought these new homes for unwanted children were good things. By 1550, "nearly every major European city would have some public institution specifically for exposed children... The accessibility of municipal foundling hospitals and the general presumption that children were well cared for within them caught on with stunning rapidity in the urban centres of Europe..." (Boswell 1988: 49, 416-17) But 1550 is exactly when the witch burnings began to take off in a big way (Thurston 2001: 97). So one has to wonder: could the purpose of the foundling homes have been to suck in the thousands of children orphaned by parents being burned at the stake? And if so, what happened to these "witch" children once they were swallowed up by the innocent looking European foundling homes?

The problem is, the public was not allowed in the foundling homes, so that no one really knows what went on inside them. Even those handing over their children were allowed only so far inside the admitting buildings. What we now know for certain, however, is that the number of orphans who never escaped these institutions alive is staggering. In some cases over 90 percent of the children in foundling homes died – a statistic always hidden from the public. When referring to these astonishing statistics, Yale historian John Boswell uses words and phrases like "carnage", "horror" and "horrifying mortality rates" (1988: 424, 431-33).

> A majority of the children died within a few years of admission [into foundling homes] in most areas of Europe... [T]he mortality rate at the Innocenti [in Florence] in the fifteenth century ranged from 25 to 60 percent... Billot finds ... at Chartres in the fifteenth century ... a death rate of "nearly 100 percent" for infants in some years. The ... mortality figures for foundling homes of the eighteenth century are appalling.... Bardet finds a mortality rate of ... 86.4 percent ... in Rouen... In Paris, 77 percent of those in foundling hospices died before the age of 12... In ... St. Yves at Rennes, of 112 children admitted in 1747, only two survived for a year. (Boswell 1988: 432, 421-22, n. 83)

Why did up to 90 percent of children secretly die in these new child-eating machines? No one knows. Early-modern orphanages did not keep good records, and few gave explanations for the deaths of their charges. When explanation is given, the blame is often put on those who nursed the infants – in the homes of the nurses, of course, and never at the orphanage itself (Boswell 1988: 422). Some of the explanation behind these death rates could be communicable disease, but if so, why don't orphanage records cite disease as the cause of their strikingly high mortality rates?

Although it cannot be proven decisively, it's certainly possible that European foundling homes were designed in part to "train" children away from pre-Christian beliefs and behaviours. Those deemed untrainable might well have been left to die. Those "successfully trained" would have been inserted back into society – minus any links to their pre-Christian families, neighbourhoods or other social groups – and with a burning desire to follow and spread the State (Church) religion.

Is there evidence that European foundling homes were designed to serve as re-education and death camps for the offspring of non-Christians? I believe there is. First, the timing is suspect. Foundling homes began when the witch trials began – in the 1300s. They quickly swelled in size and almost immediately began showing incredible death rates. The Innocenti orphanage, for example, opened in Florence in 1445, and by 1500 was accepting nine hundred children a year – and it was opened only because the other foundling homes in Florence couldn't handle the rising influx of children (Boswell 1988: 417-18). As we saw previously, 15th century death rates at the Innocenti ranged from 25 to 60 percent. It wasn't until after the witch trials ended in the late 1700s that foundling home death rates in Europe dropped to normal levels.

Second, the heavily guarded secrecy maintained by foundling homes is highly suspect. If the public had known what was going on inside these institutions, would most have trusted their children to them? Almost certainly not, and this could explain the secrecy – if foundling homes relished a constant stream of incoming sacrificial children, they would not have wanted this stream to go dry. Foundling homes also kept few records about the parents of foundlings; in early-modern Europe "information about the parents [of foundling home children] is available only for a very small percentage of abandoned children" (Boswell 1988: 17 n. 34). This leaves wide open the possibility that the majority of these parents might well have been Inquisition casualties.

Third, when foundling homes began cropping up in the 1300s, the old ways of handling abandoned children were still working just fine, thank you very much. As a matter of fact, the old ways were superior to the foundling homes, since they preserved a place in the community for young men and women when they were old enough to leave their caregivers and strike out on their own. Before foundling homes cropped up, many orphans were taken in by godparents, while the orphaned children of the wealthy became servants in other wealthy households. The Church often took in children until their parents got on their feet again, and if all else failed, poor parents could sell their children into slavery. In all these cases, children retained their family names, family ties, and community ties. In other words, they had a support system when they left home, making it far easier for them to make their way in the world.

Not so with the new foundling-home system. Once devoured by these "homes", children's ties with their communities were totally severed. Often even their family names were stripped away, to be replaced with the surname "Orphan". In Italian the word for orphan is *esposito*, and if you look up the Espositos in your phone book my guess is you'll find a few if not several. Looking in my little phone book for Portland, Maine, I found 23, and in the 1988 phone book for New Haven, Connecticut, John Boswell found 328 (Boswell 1988: 432). And thus we have a fourth piece of circumstantial evidence that European foundling homes were designed as re-education camps for the offspring of pre-Christians. When these institutions released those few of their charges who survived into adulthood, it would have been next to impossible for these survivors to find their way back home again to their pre-Christian families, family friends, and communities – where, of course, they could have been "infected" again with pre-Christian ideas.

Fifth and finally, it was well known by all civil authorities in early-modern Europe that children of witches were sired by "devils". Issued by Pope Innocent VIII on or around 1486 in order to define witches, the *Malleus Maleficarum* insisted that children of a witch could and did result from her copulation with "Incubi and Succubi":

> ...the foulest venereal acts are performed by such devils, not for the sake of delectation, but for the pollution of the souls and bodies of those to whom they act as Succubi or Incubi.... [T]hrough such action complete conception and generation by women can take place, inasmuch as they can deposit human semen in the suitable place of a woman's womb... (Kramer and Sprenger 1971: 28)

The Hammer contained detailed and precise instructions on how officials must identify, interrogate, torture and punish "witches" and was therefore, for nearly three centuries, the casebook on every magistrate's desk – from the late 1400s through to the late 1700s when witch persecutions more or less ended. How likely is it, then, that children of women burned as witches would be greeted by authorities with anything but fear and loathing? Especially considering the growing realisation by modern scholars that most if not all early-modern Europeans actually believed in the "reality" of witchcraft and magic? At any rate, although thousands of children suffered and died in Europe's early-modern foundling homes, many did escape alive – thoroughly brainwashed no doubt into the state's preferred mode of thinking and behaving. In short, Europe's new-fangled device the "foundling home" might be a large part of the reason the world finally lost touch with the real Mother Goose.

* * *

In Chapter 1 I presented evidence that Charles Perrault might have been a secret revolutionary who published *Tales of Mother Goose* in 1697 in order to fire up a resurgence of the old pre-Christian religion. After digging a bit more into Perrault's life, I'm still not certain I was right or wrong about this. However, if Wilby (2005), Bever (2008) and others are right, Europe's pre-Christian religions lasted longer and were far more powerful and pervasive than previously thought – meaning Perrault could very well have known that what he was peddling in his fairy tales was an ancient – and forbidden – pre-Christian religion.

What's more, I discovered too that certain of Perrault's contemporaries were actually using fairy tales to communicate unorthodox political views. In the mid 1600s French aristocrats began exchanging fairy tales among themselves containing hidden political code, as a way of communicating "dangerous" ideas without getting caught by the crown. If communicated openly some of these ideas would have definitely landed these aristocrats in hot water with the French power structure:

> Sometime in the middle of the 17th century, a passion for the conversational parlour game based on the plots of old folk tales swept through the [French] salons. Each salonniere was called upon to retell an old tale or rework an old theme, spinning clever new stories that ... slyly commented on the conditions of aristocratic life... The decorative language of the fairy tales served an important function ... disguising the rebellious subtext of the stories and sliding them past the court censors. Critiques of court life (and even of the king) were embedded in extravagant tales and in dark, sharply dystopian ones. (Windling 2000)

Jack Zipes lays this subversive coding of fairy tales directly at the feet of French women writers, who transformed oral fairy tales into, "marvellous fairy tales that were serious commentaries on court life and cultural struggles at the end of the eighteenth century in Versailles and Paris." (2001b: 858)

So it would seem that Perrault – himself a French aristocrat closely connected with women writers of fairy tales – would have already had the notion in his head that fairy tales were useful vehicles for passing on subversive information. What's more, others in his social set knew it too. Could it be that by the late 17th century many in Europe saw fairy tales primarily as secret vehicles for passing on dangerous information? The difference between Perrault and these others is that he was the first French person to put fairy tales in writing and hand them over to a publisher who would disseminate them widely (although Marie-Jeanne Lheritier published her book of fairy tales, *Assorted Works*, in 1696 – a year ahead of Perrault's – it enjoyed nowhere near the success of Perrault's *Tales of Mother Goose* [Zipes 2001: xii]). The question remains, however: did Perrault mean for his subversive messages to be pre-Christian, to promote the old pagan religions? It's certain that long before Perrault or the French salonnieres fiddled with these tales in the 17th century, fairy tales had threatened Europe's ruling classes, both civil and religious. Long before, the Church had declared fairy tales "sacrilegious, heretical, dangerous, and untruthful" (Zipes 2001b: 847, 850).

For the first half of his life Perrault lived in a country in which witchcraft – a practice deeply connected in everyone's minds with pre-Christian religion – was still illegal. It wasn't until the 1670s that Louis XIV declared witchcraft no longer a crime in France (Thurston 2001: 162), and by that time Perrault was well into his 40s. As we've seen previously, Perrault behaved like a man a bit frightened to publish his *Tales of Mother Goose*. For starters, he didn't list himself as author of the book. Instead he used a confusing form of his 17-year-old son Pierre's name: "P. d'Armancour", Armancour being a piece of land Perrault had given Pierre in the past (Philip 1993: 125-27).

What's more, although it's crystal clear that the first edition of *Mother Goose Tales* was meant to be published under the title *Mother Goose Tales*, at the last minute Perrault dropped "Mother Goose" from the title, and published the book as *Stories of Times Past with Morals*. The phrase "Mother Goose Tales" was retained in the book's frontispiece, however – on a sign hanging on a door in the drawing (Appelbaum 2002; Stedman 2008). When the phrase "Mother Goose" was officially added to the title of Perrault's book I'm not certain, but in 1764 an English translation was published in London by J. Melvil under the title *Tales of Passed* [sic] *Times by Mother Goose with Morals,* with Charles Perrault this time listed on the title page as author. By this time, however, Perrault had been dead for over half a century. The Dutch too waited until Perrault had died before publishing *Tales of Mother Goose* under his name (Philip 1993: 127).

Also mysterious is that Perrault decided against publishing his Mother Goose book with his usual publisher. Before he published *Tales of Mother Goose,* Perrault had authored several books, but for some reason when it came to publishing *Tales of Mother Goose* he sought out a brand new publisher – one few (if any) would connect him with. Leach explains this odd behaviour as a matter of Perrault seeming "to be somewhat embarrassed about this charming little collection of tales." (Leach, Maria 1950: 751) But was it embarrassment – or nervousness? Or maybe even fear?

According to fairy-tale researcher par excellence Jack Zipes, Perrault "believed that France and Christianity could progress only if they incorporated pagan beliefs and folklore..." (2000: 379). Two of France's leading literati – Racine the dramatist, and Nicolas Boileau the literary critic – disagreed with Perrault. They felt France should stick with the old Classical Greek way of presenting literature and art. This widely publicised disagreement even had a name: the "Quarrel between the Ancients and the Moderns". While Racine and Boileau were the "Ancients" who wanted to stick with classical ways, Perrault was the "Modern" who wanted to shake things up a bit by re-introducing pre-Christian stuff into France's cultural mix.

And this is when Perrault published his story Donkeyskin (1694), a nakedly obvious story about The Great Mother Goddess, who wears the skin of a donkey to disguise her true and beautiful identity. More than any of the eight stories in

Perrault's subsequent *Tales of Mother Goose,* Donkeyskin is blatantly about female deity. And then in 1697 – three years after Donkeyskin appeared – Louis the XIV "ended the quarrel (or debate)" between the Ancients and Moderns by coming out on the side of Racine and Boileau, and against Perrault (Zipes 2000: 379). Was this a matter of Louis chastising Perrault for daring to push the old pre-Christian religion back again into the French limelight? Was he warning Perrault to be careful? It was in that same year – 1697 – that Perrault published *Tales of Mother Goose* – with a publisher no one would connect him with, under a false name, and after having dropped the title containing the phrase "Mother Goose". Although some say the reason Perrault behaved so stealthily was "to mask his own identity so that he would not be blamed for re-igniting the 'Quarrel of the Ancients and the Moderns'" (Zipes 2000: 380), I'm wondering if it might instead have been to avoid being punished for being a pagan.

Did Perrault know that Mother Goose was a disguised goddess? We'll probably never know. However, when at the end of the 1600s French women began publishing their fairy tales, they pictured the teller of their tales not as a "spinning peasant woman" as Perrault had, but as aristocratic women, or *as Greek goddesses* (Harries 1996; emphasis is Harries'). All of which makes it easier to imagine that Perrault too recognised his Mother Goose as a goddess.

When Perrault published *Tales of Mother Goose* it was undoubtedly still somewhat dangerous to publish fairy tales. Only two others before him had tried to publish fairy tales – and the evidence is that both published under pseudonyms. It was in 1550 that the first book with fairy tales in it was published in Christian Europe, and in 1624 the book was banned by the Catholic church (placed in its *Index of Prohibited Books*) (Haase 2008: 927). This was Straparola's *The Facetious Nights,* published in Italy. And since next to nothing is known about Straparola the man, and since the word "straparola" means "babbler", some think Straparola was merely a pseudonym. The second time a European tried to publish fairy tales she did so, like Perrault, under a pseudonym. This was Giambattista Basile's *Pentamerone*, published after Basile's death by his sister Adriana in Naples, Italy, in 1634 and 1636, under the pseudonym Gian Alesio Abbattutis ("Giambattista Basile" 2013).

In addition to his *Mother Goose Tales* Perrault was a prolific writer in other areas, including the Christian genre. Louis the XIV's revocation of the Edict of Nantes in 1685, which had granted religious freedom to French Protestants, "induced Perrault to write pious Catholic works for the rest of his life." (Appelbaum 2002: vi) This too smacks of a frightened, or at least extremely cautious man, of an attempt to cast suspicion away from himself and possibly his pre-Christian views. While all of the above does suggest that Perrault was sympathetic toward a return to certain kinds of pre-Christian viewpoints, none of it proves conclusively that he was trying surreptitiously to promote a resurgence of any of the pre-Christian religions.

On the other hand would it really be all that surprising if Charles Perrault, in 1697, were indeed a closet pre-Christian – one who wished that Europe could and would return to its ancient mother-goddess religions? As noted previously, 21st century scholars now believe that pre-Christianism in Europe lasted far longer, in every socioeconomic group, over a much wider area, and with much more vigour than earlier scholarship has allowed (Wilby 2005: 14; Zipes 2013: 59; Behringer 1998: 139). As late as 1977 the people of Sicily still believed in "ladies of the night" – women who before the witch persecutions began were openly described as travelling with the goddesses Diana, Habondia and Holda. These supernatural beings were "tall and beautiful damsels with long, shining hair". At night, they entered homes through keyholes or cracks in the doors. Those who respect them are rewarded with "every kind of blessing in return" (Cohn 1977: 216).

We've also seen that in 21st century Austria beliefs surrounding the goddess Holda-Perchta are even today still being openly observed. What other ancient pre-Christian beliefs and practices are being observed privately in Austrian homes? Outlawed religions can be practiced in secret. Christianity didn't reach parts of rural Lithuania until the end of the 17th century – exactly when Perrault published *Tales of Mother Goose* – and even today the Christian "layer of belief is very thin" among the Lithuanian Balts (Gimbutas 2001: 197). Lithuanians kept their pre-Christian religion alive in part by hiding it underground: "Pagan practices [in Lithuania] persisted, sometimes secretly, sometimes mixed into Christian rites, for many generations." (Urban 1987) In short, although it can't be proven conclusively, the idea that Charles Perrault was a secret revolutionary supporting a resurgence of Europe's ancient goddess religions, is not beyond the realm of possibility.

* * *

The third and fourth questions from Chapter 1 of this book are, if Mother Goose was a pre-Christian goddess in disguise, why would artists portray her as a witch? And since to the Church witches symbolised the absolute worst of the pre-Christian religions, wouldn't a witchy garb be like hanging a sign on Mother Goose's back, "I am pre-Christian, please persecute me"? When I asked the second question I didn't realise it was based on a faulty assumption: that Mother Goose was shown as a witch during the time the European witch persecutions still raged. On the contrary, Mother Goose didn't begin appearing as a witch until the late 18th century (Warner 1995: 156), when witches were no longer being actively persecuted by civil society.

It's the first question, then, that is still the mystery: why did late-18th century artists and writers suddenly begin painting Mother Goose with witch-like characteristics? Here's one possibility: it could be that even in the late 1700s certain artists were still aware of the connection between Mother Goose and the old European goddesses. And since the persecutions of pre-Christians had died down some by then, these artists now felt somewhat safe creating visual representations again of these goddesses. On the other hand, they were still too close in time to the persecutions to show goddesses completely openly. They were too frightened to do that. So as Charles Perrault did in 1697, they painted the goddess in disguise. Unlike Perrault, however, they showed her not as a young nursemaid, but as Holda-Perchta was usually said to appear: as a Crone.

But some artists showed Mother Goose as a sweet old woman while others showed her as an evil old hag. Why the difference? It might have to do with each particular artist's view of paganism. Those sympathetic to the pre-Christian worldview would show Mother Goose as a beneficent old Crone – as playwright Thomas Dibdin did in his 1806 production of *Harlequin and Mother Goose.* On the other hand, those unsympathetic to pre-Christianism would show Mother Goose not just as an old woman, but as a frightening, predatory old woman – as we saw Thomas Nast doing in the January 3, 1880, edition of *Harper's Weekly*, or Arthur Rackham doing in 1916 to illustrate the cover of the children's book *Mother Goose: The Old Nursery Rhymes*.

Dibdin's 1806 disguise was much thinner and more courageous than Perrault's in 1697. Perrault had connected his Mother Goose with the goddess Holda only by giving her Holda's interest in spinning and children. Unlike Dibdin's, Perrault's Mother Goose had none of Holda-Aphrodite's monumental supernatural abilities – to govern the weather, for example, to shapeshift, or to fly on the back of birds. Giving her such super capabilities would have been a dead giveaway that she was divine, and therefore a move too risky for Perrault.

A century later, however, artists and writers had apparently gotten brave enough to add a bundle of super powers to Mother Goose's disguise. They did so by making her into the most powerful female archetype known to Westerners at the time (and even today): the witch. For centuries Westerners have been stripped of the right to openly and safely act on their beliefs about powerful female deities. The only female archetype left to us with any personal or political power was and is the witch. Of all females in the West, it's the witch and the witch only who is totally free – to live life as she pleases, to go where she wants, when she wants and more or less without fear (she has her magic to back her up). Best of all, none of the male-centred gods possess enough power to squelch her, bridle her, or even tell her what to do. After all, they've tried for centuries, using every trick in the book – and here she still is, just as powerful and wonderful as ever.

* * *

In previous chapters I've alluded to several notions I think Mother Goose is trying to sift into our heads: social hierarchy is bad. Treat everyone and everything with kindness and respect. Love everyone the way a healthy mother loves her child. Laughter is some of the best medicine. Here's one more thing I think Mother is trying to tell us; get your anima and animus in balance. It's a fact; the modern industrialised world is blood-soaked in animus, leaving almost no room for a balancing dose of anima – vital feminine energy. There's just no denying that world governments are still run primarily by men, and men top heavy with animus. All of the industrialised world's major social institutions – medical, legal, religious, economic and industrial alike – are run by men crippled by an undersupply of anima.

In fairy tales we catch glimpses of the world as it used to be when our anima and animus were in balance. In this world both men and women are stronger and gutsier than they are today.

Walt Disney aside, the fairy tale world is teeming with active, quick-witted and assertive women – women who help make fairy-tale men into the kind of powerhouses modern men can't hope to be. But while fairy tales are chock-full of strong, courageous people, they are completely empty of war, warfare and warriors. War is a disease that strikes when a society's anima/animus equation is tragically out of balance. Likewise, left to itself, fairy-tale land contains no human-on-human violence – that by the end of the tale, at least, doesn't right itself.

In summary, the fairy-tale worldview is one that seems consistently kinder and gentler than the worldviews found in patriarchal societies – either today or in the past. While the holy books of the male-centred world religions bulge with passages about war, gratuitous violence, and social inequality, Mother Goose's "holy books" are clean of all three of these disturbing ills. In closing, one thing seems certain: if our pre-patriarchal ancestors did actually manage the secret, as many now suggest, of living without war, social violence or social hierarchy (Studebaker 2008), and if what we call "fairy tales" form the remaining corpus of their sacred literature, then fairy tales are some of the most vital and valuable literature ever produced. It might be to our great advantage, therefore, to study this literature with new eyes, and with hearts open to the lessons it might have to teach us.

Appendices

Appendix A: Frequently Used Terms and Time Periods

Magic: A term referring to the calling upon of supernatural beings to help one achieve one or more desired earthly outcomes.

Magic practitioner: A person who uses magic to bring about healing, divination, good fortune, fertility, the location of lost and stolen goods, and happy relationships between and among individuals. Other terms used in place of magic practitioner include shaman, priestess, priest, cunning man, cunning woman, witch, wiccan, warlock, wizard, medicine man, conjurer, medicine woman, etc.

Old Europe: An advanced pre-patriarchal culture area in south-eastern Europe. At its peak (around 4500 BC), Old Europe was one of the most sophisticated regions on earth. Over the millennia the inhabitants fashioned thousands of small female figurines (and very few male likenesses), many of them other-worldly in appearance. Because of this and other kinds of evidence, many believe this peaceful, non-hierarchical culture was organised around female deity. Old Europe extended over what is today all of Romania, Bulgaria, Moldova, Hungary and Slovakia as well as southern Poland, eastern Czech Republic, eastern Austria, south-western Ukraine, north-western Albania, most of Greece, and most of the former Yugoslavia.

The Otherworld: In Celtic and Slavic mythology a mysterious enchanted land literally "out of this world" (Leeming 2005: 303-04).

Patriarchal: A term referring to a social system in which a relatively small group of elite males monopolises power and authority. Many believe patriarchal systems did not arrive in Europe before around 4000 BC (See, for example, Clark 2005: 394).

Pre-patriarchal or **non-patriarchal**: A term referring to a social system in which maternal symbolism defines and guides almost everything in and about a community, including thought, behaviour, beliefs, institutions and so forth (Sanday 2005).

Pre-Christian: a term referring to the indigenous religions that existed in Europe before Christianity arrived in the first century AD. Although after about 400 AD most of these religions contained both patriarchal and pre-patriarchal elements, some were more pre-patriarchal than others. In the 4th century AD, the Church began outlawing all such religions and persecuting their followers.

Time Periods

Neolithic: The time period when people switched from hunting and gathering their food, to settling down and depending on agriculture, stock breeding, or both. In Europe the Neolithic lasted roughly from 7000 BC to 2000 BC.

Copper Age: The time period when people discovered how to smelt copper and so replaced their stone tools with copper ones. The Copper Age fell between the Neolithic and the Bronze Age.

Bronze Age: The time period when people began to use bronze, a much stronger metal than copper. In Greece the Bronze Age began before 3000 BC, but in Britain not until about 1900 BC.

Iron Age: The time period when bronze was replaced by an even harder metal: iron. In south-eastern Europe the Iron Age began about 1200 BC.

Middle Ages: About 400 AD to 1500 AD: The time period from the fall of the Roman Empire to the discovery of the New World in 1492. The Middle Ages are broken down into the following sub-periods:

Early Middle Ages: 400s, 500s, 600s, 700s, 800s, 900s
High Middle Ages: 1000s, 1100s, 1200s
Late Middle Ages: 1300s, 1400s

Early Modern Era: the 1500s, 1600s and 1700s: The time period beginning with the discovery of the New World and ending with the beginning of industrialisation.

Modern Era: 1800s to the present.

Appendix B: Mother Goose Timeline

1626: The term "Mother Goose" first appeared in print, in France.
1650: Loret's *La Muse Historique* was published, in France; it included the line *"comme un conte de la Mere Oye"* – "Like a Mother Goose story".
1685: By now, Parisian women were telling each other fairy stories, acting them out, and dressing up to play the parts.
1690s: Fairy tales began to appear in French.
1697: *Tales of Mother Goose* was published by Charles Perrault, in France.
1719: Son-in-law of Bostonian Elizabeth Foster Goose supposedly published *Songs for the Nursery, or Mother Goose's Melodies,* but no copies have ever been found.
1729: In England, the phrase "Mother Goose" – as a teller of tales – was probably first used in a book of fairy tales published by J. Pote of Charing Cross.
1764: An English translation of Perrault's *Tales of Mother Goose* was published by J. Melvil, with Perrault listed as author; title: *Tales of Passed* [sic] *Times by Mother Goose with Morals.*
1765: *Mother Goose's Melody* first published?
1781: *Mother Goose's Melody; or Sonnets for the Cradle* was published by John Newbery, in Britain.
1785: The first U.S. edition of *Mother Goose's Melody* was published by Isaiah Thomas (reprinted from the British Newbery edition).
1791: The oldest extant copy of *Mother Goose's Melody; or Sonnets for the Cradle* dates from 1791.

Appendix C: Grimms Fairy Tale #24, Mother Holle (From Grimm et al, 1972)

There was once a widow who had two daughters – one of whom was pretty and industrious, whilst the other was ugly and idle. But she was much fonder of the ugly and idle one, because she was her own daughter; and the other, who was a step-daughter, was obliged to do all the work, and be the Cinderella of the house. Every day the poor girl had to sit by a well, in the highway, and spin and spin till her fingers bled.

Now it happened that one day the shuttle was marked with her blood, so she dipped it in the well, to wash the mark off; but it dropped out of her hand and fell to the bottom. She began to weep, and ran to her step-mother and told her of the mishap. But she scolded her sharply, and was so merciless as to say, "Since you have let the shuttle fall in, you must fetch it out again."

So the girl went back to the well, and did not know what to do; and in the sorrow of her heart she jumped into the well to get the shuttle. She lost her senses; and when she awoke and came to herself again, she was in a lovely meadow where the sun was shining and many thousands of flowers were growing. Along this meadow she went, and at last came to a baker's oven full of bread, and the bread cried out, "Oh, take me out! take me out! Or I shall burn; I have been baked a long time!" So she went up to it, and took out all the loaves one after another with the bread-shovel. After that she went on till she came to a tree covered with apples, which called out to her, "Oh, shake me! Shake me! We apples are all ripe!" So she shook the tree till the apples fell like rain, and went on shaking till they were all down, and when she had gathered them into a heap, she went on her way.

At last she came to a little house, out of which an old woman peeped; but she had such large teeth that the girl was frightened, and was about to run away.

But the old woman called out to her, "What are you afraid of, dear child? Stay with me; if you will do all the work in the house properly, you shall be the better for it. Only you must take care to make my bed well, and shake it thoroughly till the feathers fly – for then there is snow on the earth. I am Mother Holle."

As the old woman spoke so kindly to her, the girl took courage and agreed to enter her service. She attended to everything to the satisfaction of her mistress, and always shook her bed so vigorously that the feathers flew about like snow-flakes. So she had a pleasant life with her; never an angry word; and boiled or roast meat every day.

She stayed some time with Mother Holle, and then she became sad. At first she did not know what was the matter with her, but found at length that it was home-sickness: although she was many thousand times better off here than at home, still she had a longing to be there. At last she said to the old woman, "I have a longing for home; and however well off I am down here, I cannot stay any longer; I must go up again to my own people."

Mother Holle said, "I am pleased that you long for your home again, and as you have served me so truly, I myself will take you up again." Thereupon she took her by the hand, and led her to a large door. The door was opened, and just as the maiden was standing beneath the doorway, a heavy shower of golden rain fell, and all the gold remained sticking to her, so that she was completely covered over with it.

"You shall have that because you have been so industrious," said Mother Holle, and at the same time she gave her back the shuttle which she had let fall into the well. Thereupon the door closed, and the maiden found herself up above upon the earth, not far from her mother's house.

And as she went into the yard the cock was standing by the well-side, and cried – "Cock-a-doodle-doo! Your golden girl's come back to you!"

So she went in to her mother, and as she arrived thus covered with gold, she was well received, both by her and her sister.

The girl told all that had happened to her; and as soon as the mother heard how she had come by so much wealth, she was very anxious to obtain the same good luck for the ugly and lazy daughter. She had to seat herself by the well and spin; and in order that her shuttle might be stained with blood, she stuck her hand into a thorn bush and pricked her finger. Then she threw her shuttle into the well, and jumped in after it.

She came, like the other, to the beautiful meadow and walked along the very same path. When she got to the oven the bread again cried, "Oh, take me out! Take me out! Or I shall burn; I have been baked a long time!"

But the lazy thing answered, "As if I had any wish to make myself dirty?" and on she went. Soon she came to the apple-tree, which cried, "Oh, shake me! Shake me! We apples are all ripe!"

But she answered, "I like that! One of you might fall on my head," and so went on.

When she came to Mother Holle's house she was not afraid, for she had already heard of her big teeth, and she hired herself to her immediately.

The first day she forced herself to work diligently, and obeyed Mother Holle when she told her to do anything, for she was thinking of all the gold that she would give her. But on the second day she began to be lazy, and on the third day still more so, and then she would not get up in the morning at all. Neither did she make Mother Holle's bed as she ought, and did not shake it so as to make the feathers fly up. Mother Holle was soon tired of this, and gave her notice to leave. The lazy girl was willing enough to go, and thought that now the golden rain would come. Mother Holle led her also to the great door; but while she was standing beneath it, instead of the gold a big kettleful of pitch was emptied over her. "That is the reward for your service," said Mother Holle, and shut the door.

So the lazy girl went home; but she was quite covered with pitch, and the cock by the well-side, as soon as he saw her, cried out – "Cock-a-doodle-doo! Your pitchy girl's come back to you!"

But the pitch stuck fast to her, and could not be got off as long as she lived.

Appendix D: Perrault's *Tales of Mother Goose:* A Synopsis of Each Tale

Cinderella, or the Little Glass Slipper

A mother dies, leaving behind her husband and a beautiful daughter: Cinderella. Soon the husband remarries a woman who mistreats Cinderella, after which a fairy godmother saves the girl from her stepmother, and also helps her marry a prince.

The Sleeping Beauty in the Wood

A mother bears a beautiful daughter who is cursed by an old fairy: the daughter will grow up, prick her hand on a spindle, and die. A young fairy modifies the curse: Beauty will not die, but only sleep until a prince kisses her. They marry, but the prince's mother, an ogre, tries to kill Sleeping Beauty and her children; the ogress fails and the prince kills his mother.

Blue Beard

A mother has two daughters, one of whom marries a blue-bearded man. After giving his new wife keys to all the rooms in his castle, Blue Beard tells her she may open any door but one. The wife opens the forbidden door, finds the dead bodies of Blue Beard's former wives, and is rescued from the castle by her sister and two brothers.

The Fairy

A mother has two daughters: one beautiful and industrious, the other ugly and lazy. After the beautiful daughter helps a poor woman at the well, the woman – who is really a fairy – gives the girl a gift: whenever she speaks, flowers or jewels will pour forth from her mouth. When the ugly daughter visits the well, she's rude to the fairy, and receives as her reward a mouth full of snakes and toads.

Little Red Riding-Hood

A mother sends her daughter to grandmother's house with goodies. On the way, the daughter meets a wolf. Before Little Red can get there, the wolf races to grandmother's house, eats the old woman, dons her nightclothes, and jumps into her bed. When Red arrives, she fails to recognise the wolf, and the wolf devours her too. Perrault neglects to include the part of the story about the huntsman coming to empty the wolf's stomach of Little Red and the grandmother.

Riquet of the Tuft

A queen mother gives birth to a prince so ugly that a fairy godmother gives him the gift of "uncommon good sense" to offset his bad looks. The godmother says he may give the same gift to the woman he loves. At the same time, a second queen mother gives birth to a princess who is destined to lack sense, so the fairy gives the girl the gift of great beauty, along with the ability to give beauty to the man she loves. After the prince and princess meet and fall in love, they exchange gifts, and live happily ever after.

Little Thumb

A mother bears seven sons. The youngest and smallest, Little Thumb is also the smartest. The brothers' parents are so poor they abandon the boys in the woods, thinking a quick death kinder than slow starvation. When the boys become trapped in the home of ogres – mother, father and seven girls – the mother ogress talks her husband out of eating the boys for dinner. After all 14 children are asleep, however, Little Thumb puts the girls' gold crowns on his brothers' heads and his brothers' sleeping bonnets on the girls' heads, the ogre eats his daughters – mistaking them for the seven boys.

The Master Cat, or Puss in Boots

A cat helps his master befriend the king and marry the king's daughter.

Appendix E: Fairy-Tale Code Words and Their Meanings (From Heide Gottner-Abendroth's *The Goddess and Her Heros*)

Apple: 1. The healing arts; 2. Aphrodite's fruit of love and death
Apple tree: The horticultural arts
Bread: The art of agriculture
Cloth, clothing: Spinning; the weaving arts
Dead mothers: Goddesses, in the Otherworld
Dove: Aphrodite's sacred bird
Dragon: Death; in patriarchal tales it is a symbol of the goddess herself, who is to be conquered
Dragon, slaying the: Conquering one's fear of death and of the death goddess. In patriarchal tales this symbolises conquering the feminine principal itself
Egg: The world egg from which, when it opens, all things emanate
Female rivals: A patriarchal add-on (Gottner-Abendroth believes women were not rivals in the "original" tales)
Glass coffin or glass mountain: The glass mountain or glass castle in which the goddess resides; she could be seen there but not touched, a situation that could spin her *heros* into a love trance.
Gold: Fertility in every sense; the richness of life
Gold star on forehead: 1. Astral symbol; 2. Supernatural powers
Golden ball: Aphrodite's golden apple of love
Men turned into animals and then back again: The death-return aspect of the initiation/sacred marriage/death-return structure of the ancient Great Goddess religion
Mirrors: Magic cultic knowledge
Oven: The agricultural arts
Poetic verses: Can be magic spells
Pomegranate: 1. Trance-like passion; 2. Death
Prince: The goddess's *heros* (sacred marriage partner)

Princess: 1. Priestess, earthly representative of the goddess; 2. The goddess herself

Princess, marriage to: The sacred marriage aspect of the initiation/sacred marriage/death-return structure of the ancient Great Goddess religion

Red, white and black: The three sacred colours, symbol of the triple goddess (could put the *heros* in a love trance)

Sister, youngest: In many parts of pre-patriarchal Europe the youngest sister, according to Gottner-Abendroth, was the one who received the family inheritance

Sleep, extended: Journey into the Otherworld

Snakes, serpents: 1. Death; 2. Death goddess; 3. The phallus. In tales altered by the patriarchy snakes become negative symbols of the goddess, who is to be conquered

Spindle, spinning: Fate; destiny

Well: A gateway to the Otherworld

Well, falling through: A journey to the Otherworld

Witch: Death goddess. Converted into a malevolent hag by the patriarchy

Appendix F: Discussion Questions

1. **Your Favourite Fairy Tale:** What is your favourite fairy tale? Try to decode it. What might our pre-patriarchal ancestors have been trying to tell us or each other through this tale?
2. **Fairy Tales as Magic Spells:** Do you think the author makes a good case for the idea that many fairy tales are coded magic spells? Why or why not?
3. **Nursery Rhymes:** Gather a few of your favourite Mother Goose rhymes and analyze them: are they patriarchal, or pre-patriarchal? What specifically makes you think so?
4. **Other Goddesses:** Can you think of goddesses (other than the ones mentioned in this book) who possess some of the characteristics of Mother Goose as she appears in Old Mother Goose When She Wanted to Wander, in 18th and 19th century pictures of Mother Goose, or in Thomas Dibdin's play Harlequin and Mother Goose?
5. **Men and Mother Goose:** What is the relationship between Mother Goose and men?
6. **Strong Fairy-Tale Heroines:** Can you name strong fairy-tale heroines other than those listed in Chapter 10? Which fairy tales do you think have the strongest female protagonists? Why?
7. **A Pre-Patriarchal Goddess?** It's fairly clear that Mother Goose at one time was a goddess. Do you think, however, she was a pre-patriarchal goddess?
8. **Mother Goose as Malevolent Hag:** Why do you think some artists in the late 19th and early 20th centuries portrayed Mother Goose as a malevolent hag?
9. **Cruelty:** What do you think of Marie-Louise von Franz's idea that the best response to cruelty is to turn your head? ("...if one looks at evil too closely and not in a mature way but naively, one gets cynical...")

10. **The Majority Response?** Do you think the idea that Mother Goose was a goddess will turn most people away from her – or might it, on the other hand, make them less sympathetic toward patriarchal systems?
11. **Is Mother Goose Important?** Why or why not?

Bibliography

Afanas'ev, Aleksandr. 1973. *Russian Fairy Tales*. New York: Pantheon Books.

Anderson, Graham. 2000. *Fairytale in the Ancient World*. London: Routledge.

_ 2003. "Old Tales for New: Finding the First Fairy Tales." In Davidson, Hilda Ellis and Anna Chaudhri, eds. 2003. *A Companion to the Fairy Tale*. Cambridge, UK: D.S. Brewer.

Ankarloo, Bengt, and Stuart Clark, eds. 2002. *Witchcraft and Magic in Europe: The Middle Ages*. Philadelphia: University of Pennsylvania Press.

"Aphrodite". *Encyclopædia Britannica Online Academic Edition*. Encyclopædia Britannica Inc., 2013. Web. 22 May. 2013. http://www.britannica.com.ursus-proxy-9.ursus.maine.edu/EBchecked/topic/29573/Aphrodite.

Appelbaum, Stanley. 2002. *The Complete Fairy Tales in Verse and Prose [of Charles Perrault]/L'integrale des contes en vers et en prose: A Dual Language Book*. Mineola, New York: Dover Publications.

The Apple Seed: A Discourse into Feminine Essentialist Science and Metaphysics. March 29, 2013. "The Symbolism of Fairy Tales." http://appleseedtreeoflife.wordpress.com/2013/03/29/fairy-tales/ Accessed April 15, 2013.

Asbjornsen, Peter Christen, and Jorgen Moe. 1982. *Norwegian Folktales*. The Pantheon Fairy Tale and Folklore Library. New York: Pantheon Books.

– ND. *East of the Sun and West of the Moon: Old Tales from the North*. Accessed 11/6/13 from Gutenburg.org. http://www.gutenberg.org/files/30973/30973-h/30973-h.htm

Balzer, Marjorie, ed. 1990. *Shamanism: Soviet Studies of Traditional Religion in Siberia and Central Asia*. Armonk, New York, London, England: M. E. Sharpe, Inc.

Baring, Anne, and Jules Cashford. 1991. *The Myth of the Goddess: Evolution of an Image.* London: Viking.

Baring-Gould, William, and Ceil Baring-Gould. 1962. *The Annotated Mother Goose.* New York: Bramhall House.

Barnhart, Robert. 1995. *The Barnhart Concise Dictionary of Etymology*. New York: HarperCollins Publishers.

Basile, Giovanni Batiste. 1943. *Il Pentamerone: Or the Tale of Tales.* Translator, Sir Richard Burton. New York: Liveright Publishing Corp.

Behringer, Wolfgang. 1998. *Shaman of Oberstdorf: Chonrad Stoeckhlin and the Phantoms of the Night.* Charlottesville and London: University Press of Virginia.

Benard, Elisabeth, and Beverly Moon. 2000. *Goddesses Who Rule.* Oxford and New York: Oxford University Press.

Berger, Pamela. 1985. *The Goddess Obscured: Transformation of the Grain Protectress from Goddess to Saint.* Boston: Beacon Press.

Bever, Edward. 2008. *The Realities of Witchcraft and Popular Magic in Early Modern Europe: Culture, Cognition, and Everyday Life.* Houndmills, Basingstoke, Hampshire, UK, and New York: Palgrave MacMillan.

Biaggi, Cristina, ed. 2005. *The Rule of Mars: Readings on the Origins, History and Impact of Patriarchy*. Manchester, CT: Knowledge, Ideas & Trends (KIT).

Billington, Sandra, and Miranda Green. 1999. *The Concept of the Goddess*. London & New York: Routledge.

Birnbaum, Lucia Chiavola. 2005. "Patriarchy and Its Toxicities, Matriarchy and Its Possibilities". In Biaggi, Cristina, ed. *The Rule of Mars: Readings on the Origins, History and Impact of Patriarchy*. Manchester, CT: Knowledge, Ideas & Trends (KIT).

Boswell, John. 1988. *The Kindness of Strangers: The Abandonment of Children in Western Europe from Late Antiquity to the Renaissance.* New York: Pantheon Books.

Bottigheimer, Ruth. 2003. "The Ultimate Fairy Tale: Oral Transmission in a Literate World". In Davidson, Hilda Ellis and Anna Chaudhri, eds. 2003. *A Companion to the Fairy Tale*. Cambridge, UK: D.S. Brewer.

Brewer, Derek. 2003. "The Interpretation of Fairy Tales". In Davidson, Hilda Ellis and Anna Chaudhri, eds. 2003. *A Companion to the Fairy Tale*. Cambridge, UK: D.S. Brewer.

Budge, E. A. Wallis. 1969. *The Gods of the Egyptians, or Studies in Egyptian Mythology*. New York: Dover.

Caldwell, Richard S. 1987. *Hesiod's Theogony*. Newburyport, MA: Focus Information Group, Inc.

Calvino, Italo. 2002. "Cybernetics and Ghosts". In *The Literature Machine: Essays*. New York: Vintage.

Campbell, Joseph. 1964. *The Masks of God: Occidental Mythology*. New York: Viking.

"Carnival". 2013. *Encyclopædia Britannica Online Academic Edition*. Encyclopædia Britannica Inc., 2013. Web. 17 Jul. 2013. http://www.britannica.com.ursus-proxy-9.ursus.maine.edu/EBchecked/topic/96363/Carnival. Accessed July 17, 2013.

Clark, Mary E. 2005. "Evolving Beyond Our Dependence on Evil". In Biaggi, Cristina, ed. *The Rule of Mars: Readings on the Origins, History and Impact of Patriarchy*. Manchester, CT: Knowledge, Ideas & Trends (KIT).

Clark, Rosalind. 1991. *The Great Queens: Irish Goddesses from the Morrigan to Cathleen ni Houlihan*. Irish Literary Study 34. Savage, MD: Barnes & Noble Books.

Cohn, Norman. 1977. *Europe's Inner Demons*. New York: Meridian/New American Library.

Collins, Andrew. 2006. *The Cygnus Mystery*. London: Watkins Publishing.

Condren, Mary. 1989. *The Serpent and the Goddess: Women, Religion, and Power in Celtic Ireland*. San Francisco: Harper & Row.

Darnton, Robert. 1984. "Peasants Tell Tales: The Meaning of Mother Goose". In *The Great Cat Massacre and Other Episodes in French Cultural History*. New York: Basic Books.

Darton, F. J. Harvey. 1982. *Children's Books in England: Five Centuries of Social Life*. Cambridge: Cambridge University Press.

Davidson, Hilda Ellis. 1993. *The Lost Beliefs of Northern Europe*. London and New York: Routledge.

_ 2003. "Helpers and Adversaries in Fairy Tales". *In* Davidson, Hilda Ellis and Anna Chaudhri, eds. 2003. *A Companion to the Fairy Tale*. Cambridge, UK: D.S. Brewer. Pp. 99-122.

Davidson, Hilda Ellis and Anna Chaudhri, eds. 2003. *A Companion to the Fairy Tale*. Cambridge, UK: D.S. Brewer.

_ 2003b. "Introduction". In Davidson, Hilda Ellis and Anna Chaudhri, eds. 2003. *A Companion to the Fairy Tale*. Cambridge, UK: D.S. Brewer.

Davies, Owen. 2003. *Cunning-Folk: Popular Magic in English History*. London: Hambledon and London.

De Angeli, Marguerite. 1954. *Book of Nursery and Mother Goose Rhymes*. Garden City, New York: Doubleday.

Delamar, Gloria T. 1987. *Mother Goose from Nursery to Literature*. Jefferson, NC, and London: McFarland and Company.

Dexter, Miriam. 2005. "The Roots of Indo-European Patriarchy: Indo-European Female Figures and the Principles of Energy". In *The Rule of Mars: Readings on the Origins, History and Impact of Patriarchy*. Cristina Biaggi, Ed. Manchester, CT: Knowledge, Ideas & Trends (KIT).

_ 2011. "The Monstrous Goddess: The Degeneration of Ancient Bird and Snake Goddesses into Historic Age Witches and Monsters". 2011. *The Journal of Archaeomythology* Vol. 7, pp. 181-202. Accessed November 21, 2013.

http://www.archaeomythology.org/wp-content/uploads/2012/11/Dexter-7.pdf.

"Dibdin, Thomas John". 1911. Encyclopedia Britannica, 1911 edition.

http://en.wikisource.org/wiki/1911_Encyclopædia_Britannica/Dibdin,_Thomas_John. Accessed 8-12-13.

Doniger, Wendy. 1998. *The Implied Spider: Politics and Theology in Myth*. New York: Columbia University Press.

Driver, Harold. 1964. *Indians of North America.* Chicago: The University of Chicago Press.

"Early Pantomime: Commedia dell'arte". The Victoria and Albert Museum, London, England, website. Available from: http://www.vam.ac.uk/content/articles/e/early-pantomime/. Accessed Sept. 8, 2013.

Emerson, Sally. 1988. *The Nursery Treasury: A Collection of Baby Games, Rhymes and Lullabies*. Delacorte Press: New York: NY.

Everson, Michael. 1989. "Tenacity in Religion, Myth, and Folklore: The Neolithic Goddess of Old Europe Preserved in a Non-Indo-European Setting". Paper given at the Second Conference on the Transformation of European and Anatolian Culture 4500-2500 B.C., Dublin, 15-19 September 1989, and published in the *Journal of Indo-European Studies* 17 Numbers 3 & 4, Fall/Winter 1989, pp. 277-95. Accessed 2/6/2013 at http://www.evertype.com/misc/basque-jies/basque-jies.html.

Fagan, Geraldine. 2010. "Soviet Anti-religion Has Returned, Claim Europe's Last Surviving Pagans". Od Russia: Post Soviet World. http://www.opendemocracy.net/od-russia/geraldine-fagan/russias-last-surviving-pagans-targeted-by-law-enforcement Accessed March 31, 2013.

Filotas, Bernadette. 2005. *Pagan Survivals, Superstitions and Popular Culture in Early Medieval Pastoral Literature*. Studies and Texts 151. Toronto: Pontifical Institute of Mediaeval Studies.

Gaskill, Malcolm. 2010. *Witchcraft: A Very Short Introduction*. Oxford: Oxford University Press.

"Giambattista Basile". *Encyclopedia Britannica Online Academic Edition*. Encyclopædia Britannica Inc., 2013. Web. 09 Dec. 2013. http://www.britannica.com.ursus-proxy-9.ursus.maine.edu/

EBchecked/topic/55102/Giambattista-Basile.

Gimbutas, Marija. 1989. *The Language of the Goddess*. San Francisco: Harper & Row.

_ 1991. *The Civilization of the Goddess: The World of Old Europe*. San Francisco: HarperSanFrancisco.

_ 2001. *The Living Goddesses*. Berkeley: University of California Press.

Ginzburg, Carlo. 1992. *The Night Battles: Witchcraft and Agrarian Cults in the Sixteenth and Seventeenth Centuries.* Baltimore: Johns Hopkins University Press.

Glass, Ira. 2012. "Send a Message". *National Public Radio.* Programme aired originally 9-28-12 on "This American Life". Transcript at http://www.thisamericanlife.org/radio-archives/episode/475/transcript. Accessed July 26, 2013.

Goldish, Matt, ed. 2003. *Spirit Possession in Judaism: Cases and Contexts from the Middle Ages to the Present.* Detroit: Wayne State University Press.

Gottner-Abendroth, Heide. 1995. *The Goddess and Her Heros.* Stow, Massachusetts: Anthony Publishing Co.

Goyau, G. 1912. "Troyes". In *The Catholic Encyclopedia.* New York: Robert Appleton Company. Retrieved October 13, 2013 from New Advent: http://www.newadvent.org/cathen/15067a.htm.

Green, Miranda. 1986. *The Gods of the Celts*. Totowa, NJ: Barnes & Noble.

Grimm, Jacob. 1835a. "Holda, Holle". In T*eutonic Mythology.* Transcribed by Aaron Myer, for http://www.northvegr.orgor http://www.northvegr.org/secondary%20sources/mythology/grimms%20teutonic%20mythology/01305.html, accessed 9/28/12.

_ 1835b. "Perahta, Berchte [Perchta]". In *Teutonic Mythology.* Transcribed by Aaron Myer, for

http://www.northvegr.orgor
http://www.northvegr.org/ secondary%20sources/mythology/grimms%20teutonic%20mythology/01306.html, accessed 9/28/12.

_ 1966a. *Teutonic Mythology* Vol. 1. New York: Dover.

_ 1966b. *Teutonic Mythology* Vol. 3. New York: Dover.

_ 1966c. *Teutonic Mythology* Vol. 4. New York: Dover.

_ 1966d. *Teutonic Mythology* Vol. 2. New York: Dover.

Grimm, Jacob, and Wilhelm Grimm. 2006. *The Project Gutenberg EBook of Household Tales by Brothers Grimm,* based on the book *Grimm's Household Tales,* 1884, Translator Margaret Hunt. http://www.gutenberg.org/cache/epub/5314/pg5314.html. Accessed 2012, 2013, 2014.

Grimm, Jacob, Wilhelm Grimm, Padraic Colum and Joseph Campbell. 1972. *The Complete Grimm's Fairy Tales.* New York: Pantheon Books.

Guerber, Hélène Adeline. 1993. *Myths of the Norsemen: From the Eddas and Sagas.* London: Studio Editions.

Haarman, Harald. 2009. *Interacting with Figurines: Seven Dimensions in the Study of Imagery.* W. Hartford, VT: Full Circle Press.

Haase, Donald. 2008. *The Greenwood Encyclopedia of Folktales and Fairy Tales.* Vol. 3. Westport, Connecticut, London: Greenwood Press.

Hale, Edward. 1905. *The Only True Mother Goose Melodies: An Exact Reproduction of the Text and Illustrations of the Original Edition Published and Copyrighted in Boston in the Year 1833 by Munroe & Francis.* Boston: Lothrop, Lee & Shepard.

Halliwell, James Orchard. 1886. *The Nursery Rhymes of England.* London and New York: Frederick Warne and Company. Project Gutenberg. http://www.gutenberg.org/files/32415/32415-h/32415-h.htm #page303. Accessed March 16, 2013. [First edition 1842.]

Hamilton, Edith. 1969. *Mythology: Timeless Tales of Gods and*

Heroes. New York: Warner Books.

Hammer, Jill. 2005. "Holle's Cry: Unearthing a Birth Goddess in a German Jewish Naming Ceremony". *Nasik: A Journal of Jewish Women's Studies & Gender Issues*. Jun 2005, Issue 9.

"Harlequinn". 1911. *Encyclopedia Britannica*. 1911 edition. http://en.wikisource.org/wiki/1911_Encyclopædia_Britannica. Accessed Sept. 16, 2012.

"Harlequin". 2012. *Encyclopedia Britannica Online*: Encyclopedia Britannica Inc. 01/2012. Accessed 9/16/12.

Harner, Michael. 1990. *The Way of the Shaman*. HarperSan Francisco.

Harries, Elizabeth W. 1996. "Simulating Oralities: French Fairy Tales of the 1690s". In *College Literature*, June 1996, Vol. 23, Issue 2.

Harris, Stephen and Gloria Platzner. 1995. *Classical Mythology: Images and Insights*. Mountainview, California: Mayfield Publishing Company.

Harrison, Jane. 1955. *Prolegomena to the Study of Greek Religion*. New York: Meridian Books.

Hendry, Margaret, and Jennifer Uglow. 2005. "Clotilda, [Clotilde]". *The Palgrave Macmillan Dictionary of Women's Biography*. Basingstoke: Macmillan Publishers Ltd, 2005. *Credo Reference*. Web. 15 October 2013.

Hennessy, Kathryn. 2012. *Fashion: The Definitive History of Costume and Style*. New York: DK Publishing.

The History of Old Mother Goose and Her Son Jack. Nd. (c 1874.) Little Folks Series. New York: McLoughlin Brothers.

The History of Old Mother Goose and Her Son Jack. Nd. Dame Trot Series. New York: McLoughlin Brothers.

Houlihan, Kathleen. 2012. "History of Mother Goose". Austin (TX) Public Library. http://library.austintexas.gov/blog-entry/history-mother-goose. Accessed May 22, 2013.

Hubbs, Joanna. 1988. *Mother Russia: The Feminine Myth in Russian*

Culture. Bloomington: Indiana University Press.

Jameson, Raymond Deloy. 1950. "Goose". In Leach, Maria. *Funk & Wagnalls Standard Dictionary of Folklore, Mythology and Legend*. 2 Vols. New York: Funk & Wagnalls.

Johnson, Buffie. 1988. *Lady of the Beasts: Ancient Images of the Goddess and Her Sacred Animals*. San Francisco: Harper & Row.

Jones, Prudence, and Nigel Pennick. 1995. *A History of Pagan Europe*. London: Routledge.

Joosen, Vanessa. 2010. "Back to Ölenberg: An Intertextual Dialogue between Fairy-Tale Retellings and the Sociohistorical Study of the Grimm Tales". *Marvels & Tales*. May 1, 2010: 99-115.

Jordan, Michael. 1993. *Encyclopedia of the Gods: Over 2,500 Deities of the World*. New York: Facts on File, Inc.

Kemmer, Suzanne. 2009. "Spelling and Standardization in English: Historical Overview". Rice University. Course Reading for Linguistics/English 395. http://www.ruf.rice.edu/~kemmer/Histengl/spelling.html. Accessed July 27, 2013.

Kissinger, Barbara Hallman. 2008. *Mother Goose of Yesteryear*. Gretna, Louisiana: Pelican Publishing Co.

Klaniczay, Gabor. 1990. *The Uses of Supernatural Power: The Transformation of Popular Religion in Medieval and Early-Modern Europe*. Princeton: Princeton University Press.

Knapp, Bettina. 2003. *French Fairy Tales: A Jungian Approach*. Albany: State University of New York Press.

Kramer, Heinrich, and James Sprenger. 1971. *The Malleus Maleficarum of Heinrich Kramer and James Sprenger*. New York: Dover.

Kremer, Jurgen W. 2006. "Dreams and Visions in Initiation and Healing". *ReVision*, Vol. 29, Issue 1.

Kurath, Gertrude Prokosch. 1950. "Perchten or Berchten". In Leach, Maria. 1950. *Funk & Wagnalls Standard Dictionary of Folklore, Mythology and Legend*. 2 Vols. New York: Funk &

Wagnalls.

Lang, Andrew. 1894. "The Flower Queen's Daughter". In *The Yellow Fairy Book.* http://www.gutenberg.org/files/640/640-h/640-h.htm#link2H_4_0017. Accessed June 11, 2013.

Leach, MacEdward. 1950. "Holda, Holle, Hulda, Hulle, or Holl". In Leach, Maria. 1950. *Funk & Wagnalls Standard Dictionary of Folklore, Mythology and Legend.* 2 Vols. New York: Funk & Wagnalls.

Leach, Maria. 1950. *Funk & Wagnalls Standard Dictionary of Folklore, Mythology and Legend.* 2 Vols. New York: Funk & Wagnalls.

Lecouteux, Claude. 2011. *Phantom Armies of the Night: The Wild Hunt and the Ghostly Processions of the Undead.* Rochester, VT: Inner Traditions.

Leeming, David. 2005. *The Oxford Companion to World Mythology.* Oxford: Oxford University Press.

Leeming, David, and Jake Page. 1994. *Myths of the Female Divine.* New York, Oxford: Oxford University Press.

Lenkeit, Roberta Edwards. 2004. *Introducing Cultural Anthropology.* Boston: McGraw-Hill.

Levinson, David. 1998. *Religion: A Cross Cultural Dictionary.* New York, Oxford. Oxford University Press.

Lewis, Philip. 1996. *Seeing Through the Mother Goose Tales: Visual Turns in the Writings of Charles Perrault.* Stanford, CA: Stanford University Press.

Lightfoot, Beryl Heflin. 1918. *Mother Goose and the Golden Eggs.* Racine, Wisconsin. Whitman Publishing Co.

MacCulloch, J.A. 1911. *The Religion of the Ancient Celts.* Edinburgh: T. & T. Clark. http://www.gutenberg.org/files/14672/14672-h/14672-h.htm#page333 Accessed 1/30/13.

_1911b. "Magic". In *The Religion of the Ancient Celts.* Edinburgh: T. & T. Clark.

http://www.gutenberg.org/files/14672/14672-h/14672-h.htm#page333 Accessed 1/30/13.

MacMullen, Ramsay. 1984. *Christianizing the Roman Empire*. New Haven and London: Yale University Press.

Martin, Rod. 2001. "Humor, Laughter, and Physical Health: Methodological Issues and Research Findings". *Psychological Bulletin* 127(4): 504-519.

Mayer, David III. 1969. *Harlequin in His Element: The English Pantomime, 1806-1836.* Cambridge, Massachusetts: Harvard University Press.

McIntosh, Jane. 2002. *A Peaceful Realm: The Rise and Fall of the Indus Civilization*. Boulder, Colorado and Oxford, UK: Westview Press.

"Medical Diagnostics Glow Worms Used". 1985. *The Globe and Mail*. Toronto, Ontario, Canada. 04 Jan. 1985.

Messenger, John. C. 1983. *Inis Beag: Isle of Ireland*. Prospect Heights, Illinois: Waveland Press.

Monaghan, Patricia. 2008. *The Encyclopedia of Celtic Mythology and Folklore*. New York: Checkmark Books.

"Morris dance" 2013. *Encyclopædia Britannica Online Academic Edition*. Encyclopædia Britannica Inc., 2013. Web. 10 Sep. 2013.
http://www.britannica.com.ursus-proxy-9.ursus.maine.edu/EBchecked/topic/392943/Morris-dance.

"Mother Goose". 2013. *Encyclopædia Britannica Online Academic Edition*. Encyclopædia Britannica Inc., 2013. Web. 22 May 2013.
http://www.britannica.com.ursus-proxy-9.ursus.maine.edu/EBchecked/topic/393992/Mother-Goose.

"Mother Shipton." 2013. *Columbia Electronic Encyclopedia*, 6th Edition. New York: Columbia University Press.

Motz, Lotte. 1984. "The Winter Goddess: Percht, Holda and Related Figures". *Folklore*, Vol. 95.

Neumann, Erich. 1991. *The Great Mother: An Analysis of the*

Archetype. Princeton: Princeton University Press.

Norman, Bruce. 1973. *Secret Warfare: The Battle of Codes & Ciphers*. New York: Dorset Press.

Opie, Iona, and Peter Opie. 1997. *The Oxford Dictionary of Nursery Rhymes*. Oxford, NY: Oxford University Press.

Opie, Iona, and Rosemary Wells. 1996. *My Very First Mother Goose*. Somerville, Massachusetts: Candlewick Press.

Paradiz, Valerie. 2005. *Clever Maids: The Secret History of the Grimm Fairy Tales*. New York: Basic Books.

PDR (Physician's Desk Reference) for Herbal Medicines. 2004. Montvale NJ: Thomson Healthcare, Inc.

Philip, Neil. 1993. *The Complete Fairy Tales of Charles Perrault* (translated by Neil Philip and Nicoletta Simborowski). New York: Clarion Books.

Porras, Stephanie. 2011. "Rural Memory, Pagan Idolatry: Pieter Brueghel's Peasant Shrines". *Art History*, Vol. 34, Issue 3, June 2011.

Potter, Stephen, and Laurens Sargent. 1974. *Pedigree: The Origins of Words from Nature*. New York: Taplinger.

Prideaux, William Francis. 1904. *Mother Goose's Melody*. London: A.H. Bullen. (facsimile of John Newbery edition of 1791) Accessed from the University of California Digital Library (CDL) Sept. 15, 2013. http://ia600305.us.archive.org/34/items/mothergoosesmelo00pridiala/mothergoosesmelo00pridiala.pdf.

Propp, Vladimir. 1972. *Morphologie des Marchens*.

_ 1984. *Theory and History of Folklore*. St. Paul: University of Minnesota Press.

_ 2012. *The Russian Folktale*. Detroit: Wayne State University Press.

Quaife, Geoffrey Robert. 1987. *Godly Zeal and Furious Rage: The Witch in Early Modern Europe*. New York: St. Martin's Press.

Ragan, Kathleen. 1998. *Fearless Girls, Wise Women & Beloved Sisters: Heroines in Folktales from Around the World*. New York:

Norton.

Ravillious, Kate. 2008. "Witches of Cornwall". *Archaeology* vol. 61, issue 6.

Robbins, Ruth. 1965. *Harlequin & Mother Goose*. Berkeley, California: Parnassus Press.

Roberts, J. M. 1997. *The Penguin History of Europe*. London: Penguin Books.

Ruck, Carl A.P., Blaise Daniel Staples, Jose Alfredo Gonzalez Deldran, and Mark Alwin Hoffman. 2007. *The Hidden World: Survival of Pagan Shamanic Themes in European Fairytales*. Durham, NC: Carolina Academic Press.

Samuel, K. O. 1944. *Mother Goose: A Pantomime in Six Scenes*. London: Samuel French.

Sand, Maurice. 1915. *The History of the Harlequinade*. Vol. One. New York/London: Benjamin Blom.

Sanday, Peggy Reeves. 2005. "Antigone in Sumatra: Matriarchal Values in a Patriarchal Context". In Biaggi, Cristina, ed. *The Rule of Mars: Readings on the Origins, History and Impact of Patriarchy*. Manchester, CT: Knowledge, Ideas & Trends (KIT).

Schacker, Jennifer. 2012. "Fairy Gold: The Economics and Erotics of Fairy-Tale Pantomime". In *Marvels & Tales*, Vol. 26, Issue 2.

Schmidt, Bettina and Lucy Huskinson. 2010. *Spirit Possession and Trance: New Interdisciplinary Perspectives*. London: Continuum International Publishing.

Schultz, Emily, and Robert Lavenda. 2009. *Cultural Anthropology*. New York, Oxford: Oxford University Press.

Sebald, Hans. 1978. *Witchcraft: The Heritage of a Heresy*. New York, Oxford: Elsevier.

Seligmann, Kurt. 1971. *Magic, Supernaturalism and Religion*. New York: Pantheon Books.

Shapiro, Ellen. 1987. "Foreword". In Betts, Ethel Franklin, 1987, *The Complete Mother Goose*. New York: Children's Classics.

Shaw, Philip. 2011. *Pagan Goddesses in the Early Germanic World: Eostre, Hreda and the Cult of Matrons*. London: Bristol Classical

Press.

"Mother Shipton". 2013. *Columbia Electronic Encyclopedia,* 6th Edition. New York: Columbia University Press.

"Spinning – [Cover art] from the cover of Perrault's Mother Goose Tales". http://pitt.edu/~jblyon/courses/Imagearchive.html Accessed 1/29/13.

Spretnak, Charlene. 1992. *Lost Goddesses of Early Greece: A Collection of Pre-Hellenic Myths*. Boston: Beacon Press.

Spufford, Margaret. 1982. *Small Books and Pleasant Histories: Popular Fiction and Its Readership in Seventeenth-century England*. Athens, Georgia: The University of Georgia Press.

Stedman, Allison. 2008. "Proleptic Subversion: Longing for the Middle Ages in the Late Seventeenth-Century French Fairy Tale". *Romantic Review,* May-Nov. 2008, Vol. 99, Issue 3.

Stone, Merlin. 1979. *Ancient Mirrors of Womanhood: A Treasury of Goddess and Heroine Lore from Around the World*. Boston: Beacon Press.

Studebaker, Jeri. 2008. *Switching to Goddess: Humanity's Ticket to the Future*. Hampshire, UK: O Books.

Stuller, Jay. 1991. "Cleanliness Has Only Recently Become a Virtue". *Smithsonian,* Vol. 21, Issue 11.

Summers, Montague. 1971. "Introduction". In *The Malleus Maleficarum of Heinrich Kramer and James Sprenger.* New York: Dover.

Tatar, Maria. 2002. *The Annotated Classic Fairy Tales*. New York, London: W. W. Norton & Company.

_ 2012. *The Annotated Brothers Grimm*. New York and London: W.W. Norton & Company.

Tate, Karen. 2006. *Sacred Places of Goddess: 108 Destinations*. San Francisco: The Consortium of Collective Consciousness.

Thurston, Robert W. 2001. *Witch, Wicce, Mother Goose: The Rise and Fall of the Witch Hunts in Europe and North America*. London: Pearson Education Limited.

Trachtenberg, Joshua. 2004. *Jewish Magic and Superstition: A Study in Folk Religion*. Philadelphia: University of Pennsylvania Press.

Tsurumi, Ryoji. 1990. "The Development of Mother Goose in Britain in the Nineteenth Century". *Folklore* Vol. 101: 1.

Updike, John. 1983. "Fiabe Italiane". In *Hugging the Shore: Essays and Criticism*. New York: Knopf.

Urban, William. 1987. "The Conversion of Lithuania 1387". *Lituanus: Lithuanian Quarterly Journal of Arts and Sciences*, Volume 33, No.4, Winter 1987.

Vandergrift, Kay E. nd. *Mother Goose: A Scholarly Exploration*. School of Communication, Information and Library Studies, Rutgers University.
http://eclipse.rutgers.edu/goose/ Accessed 1/5/13.

von Franz, Marie-Louise. 1976. *Problems of the Feminine in Fairy Tales*. New York: Spring Publications.

_ 1980. *The Psychological Meaning of Redemption Motifs in Fairy Tales*. Toronto, Canada: Inner City Books.

_ 1982. *Individuation in Fairy Tales*. Dallas, Texas: Spring Publications.

_ 1987. *An Introduction to the Interpretation of Fairy Tales*. Dallas, Texas: Spring Publications.

_ 1995. *Shadow and Evil in Fairy Tales*. Boston & London: Shambhala.

_ 1997. *Archetypal Patterns in Fairy Tales*. Toronto, Canada: Inner City Books.

Walker, Barbara. 1988. *The Woman's Dictionary of Symbols & Sacred Objects*. San Francisco: Harper & Row.

_ 1996. *The Women's Encyclopedia of Myths and Secrets*. Edison, NJ: Castle Books.

Ward, Tim. 2006. *Savage Breast: One Man's Search for the Goddess*. Winchester, UK: O Books.

Warner, Marina. 1995. *From the Beast to the Blonde: On Fairy Tales and Their Tellers*. New York: Farrar, Straus and Giroux.

_ 1998. "'Hush-a-Bye Baby': Death and Violence in the Lullaby". *Raritan*, Vol. 18, Issue 1.

Webster, Noah. 1944. *Webster's New International Dictionary of the English Language*. Springfield, Mass.: G. & C. Merriam Co.

Wheatley, Henry Benjamin. 1862. *Of Anagrams: A Monograph Treating of Their History*. http://archive.org/stream/ofanagramsmonogr00wheauoft/ofanagramsmonogr00wheauoft_djvu.txt.

Whitmore, William H. 1969. *The Original Mother Goose's Melody, as First Issued by John Newbery, of London, about A.D. 1760. Reproduced in fac-simile from the Edition as Reprinted by Isaiah Thomas, of Worcester, Mass about A.D. 1785, with Introduction Notes by William H. Whitmore. Albany: Joel Russell's Sons.* Detroit: Singing Tree Press, Book Tower.

Wilby, Emma. 2005. *Cunning Folk and Familiar spirits: Shamanistic Visionary Traditions in Early Modern British Witchcraft and Magic*. Brighton, UK: Sussex Academic Press.

Wilford, John Noble. 2009. "A Lost European Culture, Pulled From Obscurity". *The New York Times*, Nov. 30, 2009.

Wilson, A.E. 1974. *The Story of Pantomime*. Yorkshire, England: EP Publishing Limited.

Wilson, Edwin, and Alvin Goldfarb. 1994. *Living Theater: A History*. New York: McGraw-Hill, Inc.

Windling, Terri. 2000. "Les Contes des Fées: The Literary Fairy Tales of France". *Realms of Fantasy Magazine*. 2000.

Witt, R.E. 1997. *Isis in the Ancient World*. Baltimore & London: The Johns Hopkins University Press.

Wood, Jacqui. 2012. "Secret Bird Worshiping Cult at Saveock". *Saveock Water Archaeology*. Accessed 2/8/13. http://www.archaeologyonline.org/Site%20-%20Area%20Feather%20Pits.html.

Zarucchi, Jeanne Morgan. 1989. *Charles Perrault: Memoirs of My Life*. Columbia, Missouri: University of Missouri Press.

Zipes, Jack. 1993. *The Trials and Tribulations of Little Red Riding*

Hood. New York: Routledge.

_ 2000. *Oxford Companion to Fairy Tales*. Oxford, U.K.: Oxford University Press.

_ 2001. *The Great Fairy Tale Tradition from Straparola and Basile to the Brothers Grimm*. New York, London: W.W. Norton, pp 845-868.

_ 2001b. "Cross-Cultural Connections and the Contamination of the Classical Fairy Tale". In Zipes, Jack, 2001, *The Great Fairy Tale Tradition from Straparola and Basile to the Brothers Grimm*. New York, London: W.W. Norton.

_ 2006. *Fairy Tales and the Art of Subversion: The Classical Genre for Children and the Process of Civilization*. New York, London: Routledge.

_ 2006b. *Why Fairy Tales Stick: The Evolution and Relevance of a Genre*. New York, London: Routledge.

_ 2013. *The Irresistible Fairy Tale: The Cultural and Social History of a Genre*. Princeton and Oxford: Princeton University Press.

Index

MOON
BOOKS

Moon Books invites you to begin or deepen your encounter with Paganism, in all its rich, creative, flourishing forms.

9781782790228